GENTLE HANDS CUPPED SARA'S FACE. "I THINK you've bewitched me," he said. "What do you think? Tell me what you feel."

She felt as though she'd had too much to drink. She felt as though she had lost her bearings. She felt as though there was nothing in the world but this small room and the comforting presence of the man beside her.

It must be the darkness, the flickering lights, the rain that was now lashing against the windowpanes that wrapped them in this warm cocoon of intimacy. It couldn't last. It wouldn't stand the cold light of day.

She gazed up at him, straining to see him in that dim light. His hair was blond and his mouth was full and sensual—that much she knew, but the rest was left to her imagination. His eyes would be kind, she decided, and crinkling at the corners; kind eyes and a kind smile to match his voice.

"Do you want me to stay?" His lips brushed her cheek. "Tell me!"

This was madness. She mustn't say yes, but she couldn't seem to say no. . . .

Also by Elizabeth Thornton

WHISPER HIS NAME

YOU ONLY LOVE TWICE

THE BRIDE'S BODYGUARD

DANGEROUS TO HOLD

DANGEROUS TO KISS

DANGEROUS TO LOVE

Strangers at Dawn

Elizabeth Thornton

❧ Bantam Books

New York ❧ Toronto ❧ London
Sydney ❧ Auckland

Strangers at Dawn
A Bantam Book/November 1999

ISBN 0-553-58117-1
Published simultaneously in the United States and Canada

Bantam Books are published by Bantam Books, a division of Random
House, Inc. Its trademark, consisting of the words "Bantam Books" and
the portrayal of a rooster, is Registered in U.S. Patent and Trademark Office and in other countries. Marca Registrada. Bantam Books, 1540
Broadway, New York, New York 10036.

PRINTED IN THE UNITED STATES OF AMERICA

OPM 10 9 8 7 6 5 4 3

The Courier

❧

June 12, 1804

From our special correspondent.
Winchester County ❧ *Assizes* ❧ *June 11, 1804*

THE SENSATIONAL TRIAL OF SARA Carstairs, 21, for the murder of her brother-in-law, William Neville, opened today at Winchester County Assizes, Hampshire.

The Courier's special correspondent reports that never, in his memory, has a murder trial aroused such a degree of interest. Indeed, who would not be curious about this astonishing story? The accused is young, beautiful, and stands to inherit her late father's fortune when she turns twenty-five. Her background is respectable though not fashionable. The victim, whose body has never been found, is the son of Sir Ivor Neville, a prominent Tory supporter and personal friend of the Prime Minister.

The county town of Winchester is overwhelmed with visitors who are determined to take in the trial. Fops and dandies from London, as well as fashionable ladies, are very much in evidence. Outside the law courts, after the doors were opened this morning at eight o'clock, there was a near riot when people were turned away because the seats allotted to the public were all taken. Inside, spectators were sitting shoulder to shoulder. The heat was oppressive. Only the accused seemed unaffected by the heat or by the proceedings. Miss Carstairs, flanked in the dock by a prison matron and an officer of the court, appeared calm and detached throughout.

In his opening address, which took up the whole day, Sir Arthur Percy for the Crown outlined his case against the accused, as witnesses for the prosecution will present it to the court. To summarize: that while he was married to the accused's sister, Mr. Neville embarked on a licentious love affair with Miss Carstairs; that Miss Carstairs wished to end the affair when her engagement to Mr. Francis Blamires was on the point of being announced; that when Mr. Neville threatened her with exposure, the accused did murder him on the night of April 27th or the early hours of April 28th and concealed his body to avoid detection.

Sir Arthur dwelt on the speculation and rumors respecting the disappearance of Mr. Neville. He would establish, he said, that Mr. Neville had had every intention of remaining in the area. A man in his position did not disappear into thin air. He reminded the court that in West Hampshire there are many dwellings with secret passages and rooms—a result of the Civil War—and with the wilderness of the downs close by, there was no shortage of places to conceal a body. It was quite possible that Mr. Neville's body would never be found.

It would be, he said, a grave miscarriage of justice if murderers could escape the consequences of their crimes by disposing of their victims' remains. He was confident that the evidence he would present would lead the court to the inevitable conclusion that the accused was guilty as charged.

*There will be a special edition of **The Courier** on Thursday devoted entirely to the trial. Our parliamentary correspondent's report will appear, as usual, in Friday's edition of the paper.*

The Courier *wishes to announce that Sir Ivor is posting a reward of One Thousand Pounds for information leading to the discovery of his son's body.*

One

⁓

*M*AX WORTHE, OWNER AND PUBLISHER of the *Courier*, had been studying the woman in the dock for five days, and in that time, he'd gone from mild curiosity to something closely resembling fascination. She was young; she was beautiful; she was demurely dressed in a long-sleeved gray silk gown with a matching poke bonnet; the gloves on her hands were also gray; the whole effect was one of genteel respectability. And everyone in that courtroom knew that Sara Carstairs was a cold-blooded murderess.

All the same, no one wanted to see her pay the penalty for her crime. In the space of five days, the tide of public opinion had turned in her favor. Had she been an ugly old hag, he did not doubt that no one would have cared what happened to her.

She was, Max decided, studying her profile, a woman to attract men, not by beauty alone, but by something more subtle, an appealing blend of innocence and worldliness. Her complexion was fair; her features were finely sculpted. Her bottom lip was full and sensual. He did not know the color of her eyes or the color of her hair. She never looked out over the spectators, but kept her gaze averted, or fixed on her defense counsel and his attorneys, and every strand of hair was cunningly concealed by her bonnet. But if her complexion was anything to go by, then he would have to say that her hair would be fair, blond perhaps, and her eyes would be blue. A typical English rose, in fact, by all appearances. And how deceiving appearances could be.

His description of her in the *Courier* could not convey the oddness of her manner. The trial had been going on for five days, five grueling, suffocatingly hot summer days in that cramped courtroom, but Miss Carstairs seemed as unaffected by the heat as by the evidence that could send her to the gallows. It was as though she were indifferent to the outcome of her trial, as though what was going on had nothing to do with her.

Only once had he seen her falter, and that was when her sister, the victim's widow, had given evidence. Anne Neville had not been a good witness. She'd tried to give her sister an alibi, but she'd become nervous and confused. She could hardly remember what day it was, let alone what had happened two months ago. She'd left the courtroom, never to return, on the arm of one of the defense counsel's junior attorneys, and the spark of emotion on Sara Carstairs's face had vanished with her.

Her indifference nettled him. It made him wonder what it would take to unnerve her. It made him want to lay his hands on her and give her a good shaking. Would she flinch? Would she glare? Would she struggle or remain passive? And how could he, Max Worthe, scion of a great and noble house, where chivalry was bred in his bones, even contemplate laying his hands in anger on a member of the weaker sex?

Maybe she wasn't indifferent. Maybe she was confident of the verdict. Certainly, Sir Arthur's proud boast in his opening address had come to nothing. Her leading counsel, Mr. Cole, had a reasonable explanation for every point the prosecution had tried to make.

But it didn't wash, not with him. She was guilty of something. This wasn't a rational decision based on the evidence. It was based on instinct, intuition, the sense that nothing was as it seemed except one thing: she knew more about William Neville's fate than was contained in her written statement to the court.

There was a shuffling of feet as spectators shifted to ease their cramped muscles when the chief justice, Mr. Justice Stoner, began his summing up. Point by point, he sifted through the evidence, separating established fact from mere suspicion. There were no surprises here for Max. The most damning evidence was love letters written to the victim in Sara Carstairs's own hand, letters that proved she'd had an affair with William Neville when he was married to her sister. But Mr. Justice Stoner discounted the letters. A lack of sexual purity in a woman was one thing, he said, and murder was something else entirely.

Max thought it rank stupidity that, under English law, the accused could not be put in the witness box. It would have given him a great deal of satisfaction to cross-examine her, though the questions he wanted to ask would never be allowed in a court of law. Were the rumors about her true? How many lovers had she taken to her bed before William Neville? Is that why her family had deserted her, because they were afraid she would corrupt the morals of her youngest sister? And how could someone so lovely have given herself to someone like Neville?

Max was acquainted to some degree with the Neville family, and he'd never taken to Sir Ivor's heir. William Neville could be charming when he was sober, but when he was drunk, which was often, he became a different character. He became quarrelsome, cruel, foul-mouthed, and displayed a vicious temper. Except for his virility, he had nothing to recommend him to any female. The Carstairs women, in Max's opinion, had demonstrated a deplorable lack of taste.

Faint color tinted Miss Carstairs's cheeks, and Max gave his attention to the chief justice's closing remarks to the jury, remarks that had obviously distressed the accused. So Miss Carstairs was human after all.

"Sexual depravity in a woman," said Mr. Justice Stoner, scanning the rows of jurymen like an eagle among pigeons, "must disgust all decent people. But you must put your natural feelings of disgust aside as you consider your verdict. What is at issue here is the murder of Mr. William Neville. Whatever your suspicions against the accused, you must proceed on nothing you do not find established beyond doubt."

There was more in this vein, and Max felt the tension that gripped him gradually slip away. The chief justice was practically telling the jury that the case against Sara Carstairs had not been proved.

When the jurymen had retired to consider their verdict and the court was adjourned, the spectators erupted into speech.

"What do you think the verdict will be, Lord Maxwell?"

The question came from Peter Fallon, the youngest and brightest reporter on the *Courier*, and Max's employee. Fallon had made copious notes as the trial progressed, notes that he and Max used as a basis for the articles they composed and sent every other day by a relay of express riders to the *Courier*'s offices in London. As soon as the verdict was in, they would put the finishing touches to the piece they had already written for Monday's paper.

The *Courier* wasn't the only paper with reporters in attendance. Max had counted fifteen. Even Jameson of the prestigious *Times* was there. Murder, especially a murder such as this one, where the accused was young, beautiful, wealthy, and, above all, involved in a scandalous affair, could be counted on to double the circulation of any newspaper.

"You heard the judge," replied Max. "I've no doubt that Sara Carstairs will walk out of here a free woman."

He was searching the crowd for the tall, straight-backed

figure of Sir Ivor. When he caught sight of him under the gallery, he raised his hand in salute. Sir Ivor, he knew, would not lower himself to converse with ordinary members of the press. But Lord Maxwell Worthe was in a different class, literally, and that made all the difference. Sir Ivor was highly conscious of his dignity.

"I wouldn't be too sure of that," said Fallon.

"What?" Max frowned.

"That Miss Carstairs will walk out of here a free woman. The men on that jury are local people. They've heard all the rumors that have been circulating about her, and some of those rumors are really damaging."

"Such as?"

Fallon shrugged. "That she has had more lovers than we've had dinners."

"Even if that were true," said Max, his voice tipped with frost, "it has nothing to do with this case."

"I know. But juries are all too human."

Max brooded on that thought as he made his way to Sir Ivor.

$\mathcal{P}$ETER FALLON SMILED TO HIMSELF AS HE WATCHED Max in conversation with Sir Ivor. Sir Prig, as the reporters had named Sir Ivor, had allowed his stiff upper lip to soften into something like a smile. He'd aroused a good deal of sympathy at first. Not only had his son disappeared, but his only other child, a young daughter, had died of lung fever some years before. He'd seemed like a tragic figure, but his air of superiority, his pride and arrogance, had soon dispelled that impression. He was more of an avenging angel than a grieving father.

"Prince Charming does have a way with him, does he not?"

Fallon recognized the drawl and grinned at the gentleman who had joined him. Jameson of the *Times,* fortyish, portly, sweating and crumpled, had a caustic wit that Fallon rather enjoyed.

"Prince Charming?" said Fallon.

"Lord Maxwell. He has Sir Prig tamed to his hand."

"Well, you know how it is with the aristocracy. They talk the same language."

"Oh, yes. I know how it is. Bluebloods must stick together."

Fallon laughed. "You sound envious."

"You're mistaken, Fallon. I'm not envious. I just wish Prince Charming would do what he's supposed to do."

"Which is?"

"Marry a princess, carry her off to his castle, and live happily ever after. Then we lesser mortals might get the recognition we deserve."

Fallon laughed, but he was well aware that Jameson's remarks were prompted by pique. Though Lord Maxwell was too likable, too genuine a character to arouse real envy, it did seem unjust that a young man of thirty, a man who had everything to start with, should also possess more than his share of good luck.

Max Worthe was heir to his father, the Marquess of Lyndhurst. There really was a castle, only fifteen miles from Winchester. A castle, a house in town, a life of wealth and privilege—what more could a man want?

The fates had also blessed him with good looks. His fair hair was cropped short; his square jaw added a manly touch to a face that might have been considered too handsome. He was tall, an inch or so under six feet, and every trim inch was as solid as granite. It was no secret that Lord Maxwell's favorite pastime was boxing, and it showed.

Six months ago, he'd bought the *Courier* when it was on the brink of bankruptcy. Everyone thought it was a joke, the whim of a bored aristocrat, and predicted the *Courier's* demise within a matter of months. Fallon, himself, at four-and-twenty, and the youngest reporter on staff, was sure that his days on the *Courier* were numbered, and he began looking around for another position. He'd listened to those who should know. Lord Maxwell was a novice, they said. He didn't know the first thing about producing a newspaper. It was true that he published a periodical, the *London Review,* but that came out once a month and was devoted to literary works or essays by well-known wits. A newspaper was a different matter entirely. The competition was fierce. The *Times* was firmly established as London's leading paper, and most of its competitors had gone to the wall.

Lord Maxwell, however, had not taken the *Times* as his model. The first thing he did was take the parliamentary report off the front page and replace it with stories with a more popular appeal. Murders, tragedies, natural disasters, scandals—that's what sold papers. What the *Courier* had lost in prestige, it had made up in a dramatic increase in circulation.

Peter Fallon was not one of those who begrudged Lord Maxwell his success. As the *Courier*'s fortunes had risen, so had his. He admired Lord Maxwell; he studied his manners, his habits, his preferences, and tried, as far as was in his power, to emulate his mentor.

Jameson said consideringly, "I suppose he eats like a bird?"

"Actually, he eats like a horse."

Jameson sucked in his stomach. "You know, Fallon, if I really put my mind to it, I think I could muster a thorough dislike of your Prince Charming. But let's not quibble. Tell me your impressions of Miss Carstairs."

*H*ALF AN HOUR LATER, THE JURY ROOM BELL sounded, and there was a flurry of movement as spectators reclaimed their seats. Max could not ignore how tense he felt. His mouth was dry; his heart was pounding. He'd expected the jury to take longer to reach their verdict, and he didn't know whether their early return was a good or bad omen.

When the court had reassembled, Max turned to look at the dock. A moment later, Sara Carstairs emerged from the trapdoor and took her place. Nothing in her demeanor betrayed the least nervousness, yet, thought Max, she must know that if the verdict went against her, she would go to the gallows. If she didn't feel the gravity of her situation, he did.

Her gaze, once again, was fixed on one of the junior attorneys who assisted her leading counsel. A look passed between them, but it did not linger. The jurymen were filing in.

The next few minutes passed as though they were hours. The clerk of the court slowly called each juryman by name. When the foreman was asked to give the verdict, an expectant hush gripped the spectators.

"Not guilty."

An instantaneous burst of applause erupted throughout the courtroom. Sara Carstairs looked frozen, as though this was the last thing she expected. The prison matron took one of her hands and openly wept.

What in the name of Hades is the matter with the woman? thought Max irritably. The prison matron was weeping; spectators were cheering; he was shaking; and Sara Carstairs sat there like a cold, unfeeling block of marble.

The applause subsided only when the irate chief justice ordered two wildly enthusiastic young men to be taken into custody. When the court was adjourned, the reporters in the crush elbowed their way toward the exits. They would be chasing Miss Carstairs down, soliciting a comment for the next edition of their respective newspapers. Max was in no hurry. Peter Fallon had been one of the first out the door, and if Miss Carstairs was willing to give a statement, which Max doubted, Fallon would take care of it.

The verdict left him feeling less than satisfied. He'd

wanted her to be acquitted for only one reason: He believed that capital punishment was a barbarous practice, and he could not condone it under any circumstances. Now that she'd been acquitted, however, and could not be tried again for the murder of William Neville, he intended to use the considerable means at his disposal to get at the truth, no matter how many witnesses had to be interviewed or how long it took.

But only Sara Carstairs could lead him to William Neville's final resting place. That's what he wanted, of course. To be ahead of the pack. To be the first to print the whole story. He was a newspaperman now, and made no apology for it.

It had taken him by surprise, this fascination with the *Courier*. He'd taken it on because he liked a challenge, and people said it couldn't be done. In proving them wrong, he'd become caught up in the excitement of the thing. The newspapers of the day were deadly dull and were mostly read by an educated minority of men. His mother had pointed him in the right direction. She never picked up a newspaper, she said, because there was nothing in it to interest her. What she wanted were stories about real people, and that was only to be found in the tawdry broadsheets that his father would not permit in the house.

So, without sacrificing integrity, he'd changed the *Courier*'s direction to appeal to his mother, and in so doing, he'd turned the *Courier* around.

Now he had his eye on his next challenge, the *Manchester Post*.

When he came outside, he found that the crowds who had been waiting patiently to hear the verdict had gone wild with excitement. People were shouting, dancing, throwing their hats in the air. Only a week ago, they'd wanted to see Sara Carstairs hang. Her youth and beauty, thought Max cynically, had served her well.

Peter Fallon pushed his way through to Max. He was

short of breath. "No one knows where she is," he said. "They stopped her carriage, but the woman who was wearing her clothes was not Miss Carstairs. She could be anywhere."

Max chuckled. "I bet that junior attorney set things up for her. It's what I would do in his place. No need to look so glum, Peter. She'll turn up, and when she does, I have it in my mind to make the acquaintance of Miss Sara Carstairs. Now let's go back to the hotel and get that article in shape. We may not have a quote from Miss Carstairs, but Sir Ivor gave me an earful. That ought to keep our readers happy— 'The grieving father'—you know what I mean."

*I*N THE NEXT EDITION, THE *COURIER* DOUBLED Sir Ivor's reward, but no one came forward to claim it. Max had no luck with Sara Carstairs either. She had gone into hiding and, as he soon discovered, all the means at his disposal failed to find a trace of her.

Two

London, three years later.

SOMETIMES, WHEN SHE GAZED OUT OVER HYDE Park from her upstairs parlor window, Sara could almost believe that she was in the country. She didn't care for London. It was all paved streets and cobblestones, and great stone houses that stood shoulder-to-shoulder, as though the citizens were determined that no blade of grass or ray of sunlight should penetrate the fortress they had built for themselves. But the view from her window over the park was glorious.

It was June, and at this time of the morning, few people were about. There were nursemaids with infants, and the odd carriage and rider, but the smart set, the hordes of promenaders and fashionables in their open carriages, would not appear until five o'clock.

And that was the time of day she stayed indoors. She could never forget that at her trial three years before, the smart set from London had arrived in Winchester in droves. They'd packed the courtroom, shoulder-to-shoulder, just like their houses in town, and their eyes had fastened on her as though she were a freak in a country fair.

She'd never wanted to live in London for fear she'd be recognized, but circumstances had changed, and she felt safer here than she did in any of the small country towns where she'd resided since the trial. There were watchmen who patrolled the streets at night, and magistrates and constables close by. A fortress was exactly what she wanted at this point in time.

Her gaze chanced on a small boy who came racing out from under a stand of leafy plane trees. He was no more than four or five years old, and his whoop of delight as he pounced on the ball he was chasing carried to her open window. A gentleman she took to be his father strolled after his son. There was no sign of a nursemaid or a mother, and Sara thought how fortunate that small boy was to have a father who would take the time to play with him.

Her own father had never spent much time with his motley crew of children and stepchildren. He'd been too busy amassing his fortune, then too busy trying to climb the social ladder.

"A title for you, Sara," he'd told her jubilantly when she was just out of the schoolroom. "And why not? Money can buy anything. And you've had the education to make you a lady. Yes, a titled son-in-law would suit me very well."

He'd found his impoverished aristocrat for her to wed, but he could not buy her compliance. Samuel Carstairs was to discover that his eldest child was as stubborn as himself.

If her father could see her now, if he only knew how far she had fallen, he would turn in his grave.

She shivered, as though someone had just walked over *her* grave, and turned from the window. She began to wander aimlessly around the room, a slender girl of medium height whose calm, unhurried movements gave no hint of the inner turmoil of her thoughts. Her large dark eyes and chestnut tresses, scraped back from her face in a severe knot, added drama to finely sculpted bones and a surprisingly fair complexion. The drama was deliberately tempered, however, by Sara's mode of dress. In her scrupulously plain, high-waisted gown that buttoned all the way to her throat and at the wrist, and with a demure lace cap on her head, she could have passed for a governess, which was exactly the effect Sara wanted to create. She had, unjustly, earned a reputation for sexual depravity, and was determined that she would never be mistaken for a woman of easy virtue again.

A mirthless laugh escaped her. She had more to worry about than the false charge of sexual depravity. The charge of murder had made the greatest difference in her life. It had forced her to change her name, separated her from her family, and kept her moving from place to place whenever it seemed that her past was about to catch up to her.

And it had all been for nothing, *nothing,* for her past had caught up to her with a vengeance.

When the faint sound of the door knocker came to her, she turned to face the door. A few moments passed, then her companion-housekeeper, a stately woman in her late forties, entered.

"The boys are here," she said.

Sara smiled at Miss Beattie's choice of words. Her younger brothers, stepbrothers, in fact, were university men, but to Miss Beattie, who had been with the family since Sara's birth, Simon and Martin Streatham would always be "the boys," just as Sara and her sister, Anne, would always be "the girls," and Lucy, the youngest Streatham, would always be "the baby" of the family.

In years past, Miss Beattie had been nurse to all the children at Longfield, Samuel Carstairs's palatial home near the village of Stoneleigh, and when the children no longer needed her, Miss Beattie had retired to a small house in Salisbury. After the trial, when Sara had decided that it would be better for her family if she moved away, Miss Beattie had offered to go with her.

She was so glad now that Bea had overridden all her objections. Sara felt tears of affection stinging behind her eyes. It was a lonely life, much lonelier than she had imagined it would be, but Miss Beattie had never voiced any regrets for choosing to accompany her. Sara did not know what she had done to deserve such loyalty.

"Then show them in, Bea."

The two fashionable young gentlemen who entered the parlor practically pounced on Sara. She was hugged and kissed, first by one and then the other, as they exclaimed how well she looked, how tiny her new house was, how time passed, and how glad they were to see her again. Though Sara's greeting was more restrained, her pleasure was genuine. The Streatham side of the family was much more demonstrative than the Carstairs, but she and Anne were used to it. Their father had remarried when Sara was nine, and their new stepmother had brought into the family two rambunctious boys who were still in leading strings and their baby sister, a perfect child who'd since turned into a difficult adolescent.

"Sit down, both of you."

The first flush of pleasure dimmed when Sara remembered why she had sent for her brothers. As they were all aware, she had in her possession the numerous bills they'd run up in the last several months, bills they expected her to settle, and this was the day of reckoning. But worse by far in Sara's eyes was the fact that, because of their wild conduct at Oxford, they had been expelled for the rest of the term. "Rusticated" was the word her attorney in Stoneleigh had used in his letter, but that was just a polite way of saying "expelled."

Simon Steatham grinned disarmingly as he flopped into an armchair. At eighteen, he was a year older than his brother, Martin. "I see by the look on your face," he said, "that Prissy Primrose has got to you before we've had a chance to explain ourselves. Now don't get your bowels in an uproar, Sis. All the fellows get rusticated at one time or another. It doesn't mean anything. We'll be back at Oxford next term."

Once, Simon's charm would have softened her, but that

was a long time ago. Her experience of charming men, limited as it was, had taught her a harsh lesson. The devil, she was sure, would appear as Prince Charming himself.

Sara took a straight-backed chair. "Drew Primrose," she said coolly, "is a very fine advocate, Simon, and deserves your respect."

"He's an old woman! Oh, I know he's not much older than you, but really, Sara, he's as sanctimonious as an old maid. I cannot believe he was ever young. Some people are like that. They don't know how to enjoy themselves. I think he was born old."

Something in her expression made Simon lapse into silence.

"You could both learn a great deal from Drew," she said, "if you would only set aside your prejudice. He's honest, responsible, and has done well for himself given his lack of fortune and connections." She stopped when Simon smothered a yawn behind his hand. Inhaling a calming breath, she went on, "Do you think Drew enjoys acting as your trustee? He does it to oblige me, because your guardian, the man your own father appointed to handle your affairs, has washed his hands of you. Drew is under no obligation to you, and legally, neither am I. What we do, we do for your own good."

She didn't add, as she was tempted to, that their mother had given up her responsibility as well. It was guile with Constance, of course. As Samuel Carstairs's widow, she had the money to cover her sons' debts. But Sara was the heiress, and Constance could play the game of bluff much better than Sara could.

Martin spoke up, and voiced some of the thoughts that had frequently occurred to Sara. "It isn't fair that Father left everything to you to dispose of as you see fit. Actually, it's mortifying. He should have set up a trust fund for us so that we didn't have to come to you, begging for every penny. We're only the stepsons, of course, and you were always the favorite, but it does seem a shabby trick. After all, he was the only father we ever knew."

Martin worried her almost as much as Simon did. Like his brother, he was tall, loose-limbed, and darkly handsome, but he had none of his older brother's charm. When Martin was thwarted, he became as petulant as a child.

It would do no good to point out that her father had set aside money for their very expensive education, and that on Constance's death, they would inherit a substantial amount. They wanted their money *now* so that they could live like little lords.

But Martin had a point: the bulk of her father's estate had been left in trust to her until she turned twenty-five, when it became hers outright. Where Martin was wrong was in thinking that she'd been the favorite. She had been singled out because she was the only one her father trusted to do what was right.

Sometimes, she hated her father for putting her in this position. She'd been twenty when he'd died from the stroke that had felled him the year before, only twenty years old when control of the family purse-strings had virtually passed to her. Not only was it a terrible burden, but it had also made her into a tyrant in her family's eyes.

She wanted to be shot of the lot of them; she wanted to break the trust and give them their heart's desire, just to be rid of them. They were a passel of whiners and hangers-on. She couldn't stand it any longer: Constance's endless bleating in her letters about a Season in London now that Lucy had turned sixteen; her stepbrothers' assumption that they were fated to take their places among the idle rich and never do an honest day's work in their lives; and last but not least, Anne's dreamy references to the new vicar at Stoneleigh, and how kind and understanding he was.

She couldn't fault her father for worrying about his motley crew of dependents. She, herself, worried endlessly about them. But why had he thought she was strong enough and wise enough to manage their affairs when she couldn't manage her own? Of course, her father could not have foreseen the devastation William Neville would wreak on their family . . . when he was no longer there to protect them.

Simon had risen and was at the sideboard, pouring out a glass of sherry for each of them. "What you have to understand, Sis," he said reasonably, "is that it's devilishly expensive to keep up with the other undergraduates. And you wouldn't want us to be the odd men out, would you? Everyone at Oxford is under the hatches."

A confusion of thoughts was circling in her brain, and she automatically accepted the glass of sherry he offered her.

"As for being rusticated," Simon shrugged casually, "it was a matter of honor, a . . . a lady's honor. You know what I mean."

She looked at him sharply. "We're not talking about duels, I hope?"

"No, no! Fisticuffs is all I meant."

Martin interjected gleefully, "A *brawl* is what I'd call it, a regular melee. It was just bad luck that Simon's fist landed on the master's nose, else no one would have made a fuss, and we would not be rusticated. Tell her, Simon."

"I didn't know it was old Lewis behind me." Simon grinned at the recollection. "I felt this hand on my shoulder and swung at him before . . ." His voice trailed to a halt when Sara rose to her feet.

She eyed her brothers coldly. "You became involved in a brawl over an insult to a . . . a common strumpet? Is this what they teach you at Oxford?"

Simon's face flushed scarlet.

Martin's bottom lip stuck out. "Now look here, Sara, it wasn't like that at all. In fact—"

"Shut your mouth, Martin," Simon gritted through his teeth. He glared balefully at Sara. "There are some things a gentleman doesn't mention in polite company, especially not to his sister, and strumpets is one of them."

Bosom heaving, she walked to the table, picked up a large square packet and emptied out the contents. "One can tell a great deal about a man's character by the bills he runs up. Do you know what these bills tell me about you, Simon?"

"Lord have mercy, another lecture," he replied indifferently.

She ignored the taunt. "Gaming, wenching, drinking— I think that about sums up your character. You're a drone, Simon. Some might even call you a parasite." When Martin snickered, Sara rounded on him. "And you're no better. Wherever Simon leads, you follow. Don't you realize how lucky you are? You're the first men in our family ever to go to university, and not just any university, but Oxford. Father tried to give you all the advantages he never had. He wanted you to become gentlemen, real gentlemen, not . . ." Her eyes made an insulting appraisal of their buff-colored pantaloons and equally tight cut-away jackets, and boots that had ridiculous gold tassels hanging from them. ". . . not tailors' dummies. Your tailor's bills could dress me for the next ten years."

Martin said, "All Corinthians dress as we do. And at Oxford, if your tailor isn't Weston, you might as well cut your throat."

"Corinthians!" said Sara scathingly. "In my day, we called them 'dandies.' "

Simon interjected, "Now hold on, Sara. There's a lot more to it than that. Corinthians are athletes. They are the finest sportsmen in England."

"They're idlers," exclaimed Sara. "Bored aristocrats. Maybe you should remember that we come from humble stock. We're not blue bloods. Everything we have came to us through someone else's sacrifice, and hard work."

"I never wanted to go to Oxford, anyway," muttered Martin. "The fellows there are all—"

"Oh, stow it, Martin! Sara has no more love for whiners than I do."

Simon's scathing rebuke got Martin's temper going. "Don't patronize me! I wasn't the one who started that fight and got us rusticated. I wasn't the one who ran up those bills. I told you Sara would take a dim view of it, but did you listen to me? Oh, no. My opinion doesn't count. If she washes her hands of us, what's to become of us? If we don't make good on those gambling vowels, we'll have our legs broken, that's what. And it's all your fault."

Simon looked as though he might spring at his brother. "Why, you—"

"Be quiet!" Sara was as surprised at the shrillness of her command as her brothers were. She pressed a hand to her aching temples. "Be quiet," she repeated in a more controlled tone, "and I'll tell you what's to become of you."

She let her hand drop away, then said with precision, "I'll instruct Drew to pay off your debts, but this is the very last time. You see, I'm going to be married." She took a moment to savor the shock that registered on their young faces before she went on. "I'm sure you're as aware as I am that when a woman marries, control of her fortune passes to her husband. So you see, things are going to be very different from now on."

*A*FTER THE LAST CRESCENDO OF SCARLATTI'S sonata had died away, Sara flexed her fingers, then abruptly rose from the piano. Miss Beattie was watching her. She was thinking that Sara could hide her feelings from most people, but not from her. When she was upset, she invariably reached for Scarlatti.

"Scarlatti?" she said. "Now what brought that on?"

Sara smiled sheepishly, like a child caught out in a prank. "Simon said I was just like Father."

Miss Beattie went back to counting the stitches on her knitting needle. "And why did he say that?"

"Because I did what I said I wouldn't do. I lectured them. It was worse than that, Bea. I threatened them. I told them that my husband would have control of my fortune."

"And they believed you?"

Sara took the candle from the piano and began to light several other candles around the room. "They think I've fallen violently in love with someone and that I'm so blinded by love that I'm willing to jeopardize their share of father's fortune. As though I would be such a fool! Didn't you hear the racket they made when they left?" Sara's lips twitched. "They're going to seek legal advice to see if there's some way they can stop me."

Miss Beattie said carefully, "Whom did you say you were going to marry?"

Sara laughed. "I didn't. I told them they'd find out when it suited me, and not before. Now don't look at me like that, Bea. Simon and Martin are incorrigible. They take too much for granted. I've given them the fright of their lives, but they'll soon get over it. They always do."

"Well," said Miss Beattie hopefully, "it may come to nothing. Perhaps you won't find a man who is willing to take you on your terms."

"I have it on my father's authority," said Sara, "that money can buy anything." She was opening drawers and lifting cushions, obviously looking for something.

Miss Beattie hastened into speech. "But why burden yourself with a husband at all? You have only a year to wait, less than a year, then you can do as you like with your inheritance."

"You know why."

They'd had this conversation before, and Miss Beattie swallowed the long litany of arguments she'd marshaled to demolish Sara's harebrained scheme. Sara wanted her inheritance *now*, not next month or next year, and the only way she could get it, under the terms of her father's will, was by marrying before her twenty-fifth birthday. But

Sara didn't want a real husband. This was to be a business arrangement. Once the wedding ceremony was over and she'd paid off her husband-in-name-only, she never wanted to see him again.

The reasons she'd put forward for this rash enterprise were unconvincing in Miss Beattie's opinion. She'd come to the end of her tether, Sara said. She wanted to get on with her own life. Moreover, if anything happened to her, Anne would inherit everything, and if William Neville ever turned up, then where would the family be? As Anne's husband, William would have control of everything. Whereas, when *she* married, she'd make sure that her prospective husband signed an ironclad marriage settlement that would divide her father's fortune equally among his five children *before* she had the ring on her finger.

Had Sara put forward these arguments three years ago, right after the trial, Miss Beattie might have been more inclined to accept them. *But why now?* That's what she kept asking herself. Something had happened recently, something to upset Sara, and she had no idea what it was.

She chanced a quick look up, dropped a stitch, and muttered something under her breath. She'd been looking after Sara ever since the first Mrs. Carstairs had hired her as a nurse for her newborn baby. If Sara were to confide in anyone, it would be her. But that was Sara's greatest failing. She was an intensely private person and kept things to herself. She rarely allowed her emotions to show. Most people thought Sara was cold, and most people couldn't have been more wrong. It hadn't been easy to be Samuel Carstairs's eldest child. Only Sara had had the gumption to stand up to him. And if the younger children had fared better, it was only because they'd always turned to Sara to be their champion.

But where was Sara's champion? A husband-in-name-only did not fit the bill at all.

"Bea, where is it?"

Miss Beattie dropped another stitch and glared furiously at the work in progress, a lacy bedjacket for a married sister who lived in Folkstone. Without looking up, she said innocently, "Where is what, dear?"

"Today's edition of the *Courier*," replied Sara gently.

Miss Beattie was on the point of pleading ignorance, but one look at the determined set of Sara's chin made her stifle the impulse. "I don't know why you would want to read that trash," she said crossly.

"Yes, you do. Where is it, Bea?"

Miss Beattie sighed. Of course she knew. This was the third anniversary of Sara's acquittal for the murder of William Neville, and on each anniversary, the *Courier* carried a summary of the story. It had become a tradition with the *Courier* now, as had the increase for the reward offered by Sir Ivor Neville for information leading to the discovery of William Neville's whereabouts or final resting place.

With another resigned sigh, she dug in the knitting bag at her feet, withdrew the tightly folded newspaper, and handed it to Sara.

"What does the reward stand at now?" asked Sara.

"Five thousand pounds."

Sara's brows shot up. "I see."

She took the paper to the candle on the table, smoothed it out, and began to read. Her expression remained neutral, but that didn't fool Miss Beattie. Sara would have had to be made of stone not to be upset. The whole story had been gone through in lurid detail. Sara's name appeared on every other line. The innuendo—that Sara had been a selfish, calculating jade who was acquitted only because William Neville's body had never been found—was sickening. But what was truly frightening was the *Courier*'s declared intention of pursuing the story until justice was done. In her opinion, it wasn't justice the paper was pursuing, but a vendetta against Sara.

Sara said softly, as though to herself, "Whoever wrote

this article must really hate me. He's never going to let the world forget my name. But who is he? 'Special correspondent' . . . that doesn't tell me anything."

When she paused, Miss Beattie said, "What difference does it make who he is? He's a nasty piece of work, and I hope he rots in hell."

Sara folded the newspaper and said crisply, "He'd stop hounding me if he could find William's body."

"Of if William turned up," added Miss Beattie.

Sara looked up with an arrested expression on her face. She visibly shuddered. "I don't know which frightens me more, the thought of the *Courier's* special correspondent hounding me from pillar to post or the prospect of William turning up. Now do you see why I'm determined to break the trust? I want to get back my life and start over somewhere else. We've been wavering long enough, Bea. As soon as it can be arranged, we set off for Bath."

"Bath," repeated Miss Beattie.

This was something else Sara had carefully explained to her. In the summer months, the smart set followed the Prince of Wales to Brighton. There was little chance that Sara would be recognized in Bath. And if there were no likely candidates for the position of husband-in-name-only in Bath, they'd move on to Cheltenham.

An hour later, as Miss Beattie composed herself for sleep, she tried to comfort herself with the thought that it wasn't all black. This trip to Bath could well be a step in the right direction. For the first time since the trial, Sara would be open to meeting new people. As a devoutly religious person, Miss Beattie did not see why her Maker could not turn Sara's harebrained scheme around and make things come out right. A little nudge was all it would take and that husband-in-name-only could well turn out to be the champion Sara sorely needed and so richly deserved.

As she dwelt on that happy thought, she had a picture of Sara as she would like her to be. Her dreary wardrobe would be donated to the parish poorhouse, to be replaced by a new wardrobe of elegant silks and muslins in jewellike colors to set off Sara's dramatic good looks. There would be parties and balls, and jaunts to the theater and pleasure gardens. Sara would smile a lot.

And there would be no more Scarlatti. Definitely, no more Scarlatti.

And no more lace caps.

A champion for Sara, she decided, would figure prominently in her prayers from now on, just as she'd pray for confusion on all Sara's enemies, particularly on that no-good, low-down, despicable special correspondent who wrote for the *Courier*. Not that she wanted anything catastrophic to happen to him. She just wished someone would beat him to a pulp.

Three

~

THEY WERE TAKING HIM TO A BAWDY HOUSE.

This was to be his reward, Max supposed, for taking the beating of his life. It was a generous gesture, considering his friends had lost a packet when they'd bet heavily on him against Mighty Jack Cleaver, the prize pugilist of five counties around. They should have known better. And so should he.

He must have been out of his mind to let his friends talk him into it. Who in Hades did he think he was? He wasn't a professional fighter. He was an amateur. So, he trained with Gentleman Jackson when he was in town, but that was only as a form of exercise. From now on, he would stick to cricket.

He groaned when the coach hit a pothole. It didn't surprise him now that no one had ever claimed the thousand pounds' reward Mighty Jack Cleaver offered to anyone who could knock him down. The man was built like a mountain. Cleaver by name and Cleaver by nature.

He shouldn't be complaining. He should be thanking his lucky stars that he was still breathing. He hadn't broken any ribs or his nose this time around. He just felt as though a carriage had run over him.

"Ah, Reading," intoned a voice from one corner of the carriage.

Max opened his bleary eyes and looked out the window. There wasn't much to see at this time of night. The only light came from lanterns that were hanging outside every other building. It seemed that the good citizens of Reading were snug in their beds, and in his condition, that's exactly where he wanted to be.

There was no way he was going to a bawdy house tonight, or any night in the foreseeable future. In any event, his mistress would be waiting for him at the Black Swan, and Deirdre had a temper. If he didn't turn up, there would be hell to pay. He might even lose her, and that would be a pity, because Deirdre was definitely his kind of woman. Ripe and always ready for the plucking, with a wild mane of wavy dark hair and eyes as black as sin. Sinful eyes, sinful hands, and a sinfully ripe mouth. The thought made Max attempt a grin in spite of his sore jaw.

"A toast to Max," John Mitford cried out, and a chorus of masculine voices bellowed their approval. John's voice turned maudlin. "To a gallant sport; to the best friend a man ever had; to a champion fighter, even though he lost tonight; to the finest Corinthian of them all!"

"To Max," the highly inebriated voices bellowed, "the finest Corinthian of them all," and the open bottles of brandy were passed around yet again.

Corinthian. At twenty-one, he'd taken pride in his membership in that select group. All his friends had been Corinthians. They considered themselves gentlemen athletes, jockeys, pugilists, sportsmen.

But that was years ago. These days, they shook off their cares and responsibilities once a year, donned the fashionable garments they'd sported as youngsters, and tried to convince themselves they were still Corinthians. That's why he'd accepted Jack Cleaver's challenge tonight. More fool he.

His friends were as aware as he that things were changing. They were drifting apart as their interests diversified. And they simply did not have the time to keep up with each other. In an effort to stem the tide, they'd hit upon the idea of spending part of every July in Brighton. "The Bachelors' Last Stand," they called it. They'd been firm friends since their undergraduate days at Oxford and nothing, they vowed, would ever come between them.

Oxford. Those were the days, those golden, halcyon days of their youth.

"I wish to propose a toast," Max said, and was appalled at the crack in his voice. Maybe he'd had too much to drink as well.

"Lud, save us," drawled Ash Meynell, the dandy of the group. He gazed at Max through his quizzing glass. "I think the man is still alive."

This remark set everyone off, and they began to harangue Max for his dismal performance against Mighty Jack. Max took it in good part. In fact, these friends were so comfortable with each other that trading insults had become an art with them.

"To Oxford," he said, raising his brandy bottle.

"Oxford," they chorused, then guzzled down great, healthy swigs from the bottles that were passed around.

From the floor of the coach, a voice said musingly, "Refresh my memory. Did any of us ever graduate from that august establishment?"

A chorus of no's answered the question.

"Were we supposed to?" asked Ash, training his quizzing glass on the body on the floor.

Tony Palmer hoisted himself into a sitting position. "I was," he said. "Don't ask me why. My father didn't graduate either, but he expected better from his son. There was an awful scene when I was sent down."

This brought on a series of reminiscences about their years at Oxford, then led, in a convoluted way, to a round of toasts to the king, fox hunting, actresses and opera dancers in general, and finally, and more soberly, to "absent friends."

Three of them were now, sadly, married and obliged to accommodate their wives' wishes instead of their friends' wishes. There could be no bachelor parties in Brighton for married men. It was a great joke among them that the only thing married men were good for was gout, and no one wanted to contract gout before his time, if ever.

Max caught sight of the landmark he'd been looking for, the old church of Saint Laurence, and he roared, "Driver, stop the coach."

His friends were so stupefied by this sudden turn of events that Max had clambered out of the coach before they had come to themselves. When they protested, he held up his hand to silence them.

"Gentlemen," he said, "the carnal delights of Madame Capet's establishment are not for me. You may have noticed that during our bout, Jack Cleaver practically unmanned me. Frankly, I'm still in agony, and if I attempt the acrobatics you so graphically described, I may never rise from my bed again."

"What he means," said John, "is he can't get it up."

When the laughter had died away, Max said, "I can't argue with that. I'll meet up with you in Brighton, then."

"That's what you said last year," drawled Ash, "but you did not show. Do you know what I think, Max? I think you're becoming a prime candidate for gout. My mother tells me it happens to all Corinthians sooner or later."

This provoked a howl of protests. When there was a momentary silence, Max said, "Ash, you should know me better than that. I'm too careful to come down with gout. I'll make it to Brighton, though I can't spare more than a few days. My business is taking me to Exeter for the next month or two, and I can't get away for longer than that."

"What business?" a slurred voice demanded.

"Didn't you know? Max has made an offer for the *Exeter Chronicle,*" replied another. "He's on his way there now."

This brought to mind a bawdy drinking song on Exeter's accomplished equestrians, and before the coach moved off, five lusty voices were braying the lewd rendition at the top of their lungs.

Max winced as he turned in the direction of the High Street where the Black Swan was situated, and he delayed for a moment to take stock of his injuries. He ached all over, his nose throbbed, and his jaw felt as though it had been hit by a brick. The important question was, however—could he still perform? It was one thing to put his friends off, and quite another to put Deirdre off. She might fly into one of her famous rages if he were so boorish as to plead a headache or that he was feeling under the weather.

Bloody hell! He hadn't invited her to accompany him to Exeter, knowing she would only get in the way. But her doddering old husband, Sir William Honeyman, had gone off to his estate in Kent, and Deirdre had surprised him by turning up at the Black Swan. She'd known by the look on his face that he wasn't pleased to see her, and when he'd gone off to meet his friends, there had been a ferocious argument. If he put her off now, there would be a scene, and he wasn't in the mood for scenes.

Put her off? He was beginning to sound like an octogenarian. Of course he wasn't going to put her off. A man would have to have two feet in the grave if Deirdre couldn't revive him. He would perform if he died in the attempt.

At least he would die with a smile on his face.

The Black Swan was in darkness except for the lantern hanging at the front porch. Max made his way through the arch that led to the courtyard. There were more lanterns lit here. He didn't expect to meet anyone at two o'clock of the morning, nor did he. Reading was a country town, early to bed and early to rise. All the inns locked their doors shortly after sunset. But he'd taken that into consideration before he'd gone off with his friends.

In one corner of the courtyard was a deformed old apple tree, and obscured by its leafy branches was the window of his chamber. He'd left the window open so that he could return without rousing the whole house. There was no need for a bachelor to be so discreet, but every need in Deirdre's case. Though she and Sir William had an understanding, and went their separate ways, they kept up appearances. Not to do so could easily jeopardize Deirdre's position in society. That was the way of their world. Appearances were far more important than reality, especially for a woman.

There was a light at the window. So Deirdre had waited up for him after all. Sighing in resignation, he gritted his teeth and reached for the gnarled branch just above his head.

THE BOOK ON HER LAP FELL WITH A SOFT THUD to the carpeted floor, shocking her into wakefulness. Sara curled her hands around the armrests of her chair and made to rise. When she saw the book on the floor and realized that that was what had awakened her, sanity returned and she inhaled a slow, calming breath. There was nothing to fear here. She was in her bedchamber in the Black Swan, on the first stop of their journey to Bath, and she'd fallen asleep while reading *Cecilia*. No one knew where she was. *No one.*

Reaching down with one hand, she picked up the leatherbound volume and set it on the table beside her chair. She'd read Fanny Burney's novel so often, she could just about recite it by heart. It had done the trick, though. It had cleared her mind of all her troubles and given her a few hours' respite. But now that she was awake, she was wide awake, and wished that she'd read the cursed book in bed.

Thunder sounded off in the distance. There would be a storm before morning. She stretched to ease her cramped muscles, then lifted the weight of her unbound hair from her neck in an effort to cool herself. In spite of the window she'd opened earlier, it was hot and airless in that small room, so hot that even her flimsy nightgown seemed too heavy against her skin. She undid the tiny pearl buttons from throat to waist and pulled back the edges of the bodice to expose her breasts. She was still too hot, and she picked up the carafe of water on the table by her chair. It was empty. Sighing, she set it down again.

The candle on the mantel was well down and beginning to sputter. She rose, reached for it, then hesitated. There wasn't much chance that she would get back to sleep now. Maybe she should light another candle and—and do what? Torture her mind with visions of her loathsome brother-in-law as she'd last seen him? Debate endlessly whether William was alive or dead? Speculate on what he would do to her if he ever caught up to her?

She knew what he would do. He would kill her, of course. Then Anne would come into their father's money, and William would finally get his greedy paws on it. That's all he had ever wanted—money.

She would never let him hurt any member of her family again.

A harebrained scheme, Bea called this trip to Bath. In her saner moments, she agreed. But desperate straits called for desperate measures, and she was desperate. She'd wracked her brains endlessly for a better way, and there wasn't one. Once she was married and the marriage settlement was signed, William would no longer be a threat.

This was nonsense. She knew William was dead. She *knew*. Didn't she?

If only there was someone she could confide in . . . but there was no one. And some secrets simply could not be shared.

She smoothed her fingers over her brow. Her brain was befuddled by so much thinking. And really, there was nothing to think about. She'd made her decision. *Let it go,* she told herself sternly. *Put all your troubles out of mind and go to bed.*

She went on tiptoe, positioned her hand behind the sputtering candle and blew it out, and in the very act of blowing it out, from the corner of her eye, she caught the reflection in the mirror above the mantel of a man climbing over the windowsill.

In that blinding moment of darkness, her throat closed in panic. He'd found her! *William had found her!*

"William?" she whispered hoarsely.

There was no response.

Trembling violently, heart thudding against her ribs, she edged herself round to face the intruder. It took a moment for her eyes to adjust to the darkness. It wasn't pitch black. The light from the lanterns in the courtyard cast flickering shadows, but there was nothing to be seen, no man at the window now. But her hearing had never been more acute, and she could hear someone breathing. She sucked in a breath when his voice broke the silence.

"I had no idea," he said, "that there were red highlights in your hair. But I suppose ladies can change their appearance to suit themselves. Give me a moment. I feel as though I've just climbed the Matterhorn."

It wasn't William's voice! The thought brought a measure of calm. Not William, then, but one of his friends, someone who obviously knew her by sight. She supposed William had sent him as a forerunner of what was to come, when the real terror would begin. Or maybe he wanted to demonstrate that, in spite of all her stratagems, he could still get to her.

She was deathly afraid, but her fear was tempered by anger. She could imagine the lies William had told his friend about her: that she was a slut; that she was any man's for the taking. Well, this was one man who was going to find out that William had lied.

She had to be calm; she had to think what to do. If she screamed, he would be on her in a flash. Bea was in the room across the hall, but it would take an earthquake to waken Bea. Some of the other guests might hear her, but if they came to her rescue, she had no doubt that her assailant would plead they'd interrupted a lovers' tiff, and turn them away. And who would believe Sara Carstairs when her true identity became known? With the realization that there was no one to help her but herself, her mind became crystal clear. She couldn't make a dash for the door because she didn't know where he was. There was no pistol or knife concealed among her things, and if there had been she wouldn't have used them. A woman who had stood trial for murder would have a hard time explaining away a corpse in her bedchamber.

Other things gradually came to her. He smelled of strong spirits. If he had been drinking, that could work in her favor. The poker was on the hearth beside her feet, and as she well knew, a poker could be a lethal weapon.

Not the poker, she thought with a shudder. She couldn't bear to take a swing at him with the poker, except as a last resort. The water carafe, then. It was only a few steps away, on the table beside her chair. Then, when she'd disabled him, she would lock him in this room and hide in Bea's room.

If only it could be that simple.

She began to inch her way to the table, and was shocked into immobility when he spoke again. "I apologize for being so late," he said. "I didn't expect you to wait up for me. I thought I'd find you in bed."

Though his voice was pleasant, his words chilled her. He seemed to think that William had set this up with her and that she would welcome him with open arms. The sooner she disabused him of that notion the better.

"I want you to leave. *Now.*" She stopped when she heard the quaver in her voice, cleared her throat then went on. "If you lay a hand on me, I'll scratch your eyes out."

Silence. She had the distinct impression that he was weighing her up in much the same way as she was weighing him. Maybe he thought she had a gun. Maybe that's why he was holding off. And maybe she'd better do something before it was too late.

He said, "This isn't like you. You don't even sound like yourself. I must have had more to drink than I thought."

When his shadow suddenly loomed up in front of her, she moved like lightning. She snatched up the water carafe and backed away from him.

"Don't come any closer," she cried out.

He disregarded her warning. "Look—"

She brought the glass carafe down with all her might, but it shattered uselessly against the bedpost, and in the next instant, her assailant caught her in a flying tackle and carried her across the bed.

Sara stifled a whimper. Her legs were splayed wide and the press of his weight crushed her into the feather mattress; her wrists were held in an iron grip above her head, and the metal buttons on his coat bit into the soft flesh of her breasts. She flinched when his head descended.

His voice was husky. "You seem different tonight. I can't explain it." He laughed softly. "I think I may have underestimated your appeal. Ah, Deirdre, don't fight me."

When his mouth took hers, she braced herself for violence, but he was gentle, and that amazed her. And as that brandy-flavored kiss lingered and the thought of Deirdre circled in her mind, it came to her that she'd taken a wrong turn. She'd been thinking of William when the stranger climbed in through her window, and her imagination had done the rest.

She went limp with relief and tried, weakly, to push him

off. When that didn't work, she offered a passive resistance, neither participating in his embrace nor fighting it.

He went very still, then his head lifted. His features were indistinct, but she saw sculpted bones and the flash of white teeth as he smiled. "You're not Deirdre," he said.

"No."

"I think I knew it from the first. I climbed in the wrong window, didn't I?"

It was madness, but she found herself returning his smile. Her mind had already worked everything out. He wasn't William's emissary; he wasn't a thief; he wasn't going to rape her. He'd simply entered the wrong room, the room where he'd expected to find Deirdre, and instead he'd found her.

She should be ranting and raving at him for all the needless terror he'd put her through. She should be demanding that he get off her and leave her room at once. But the release of all the tension she'd been bottling inside her for weeks past left a curious void in its wake. She was far more inclined to weep into his shoulder than push him away.

"It seems we both made a mistake," she said.

There was a smile in his voice. "I'm not so sure that coming to your room was a mistake. Deirdre can be a virago when she's in a temper. She wouldn't have missed with that bottle you tried to brain me with. I think that's when I realized you weren't Deirdre."

"Is Deirdre your wife?"

"No, thank God!"

Once again she found herself returning his smile.

She liked him, she really liked him. He hadn't threatened her or lost his temper when she'd attacked him. He was a powerful male animal, but he seemed as tame as a lamb. She hoped Deirdre knew how lucky she was. Such men were few and far between.

But they were becoming too cozy, too intimate. Or maybe it was the flickering darkness that held her in thrall.

Now that she wasn't afraid of him, she was taking his impression through her senses, and all her senses were humming. But maybe, if she could see him clearly, she wouldn't like him at all.

It was time to put a stop to this. She pushed against his shoulders with both hands and he complied at once. He relieved her of his weight, but he made no move to get off the bed.

She rose on her elbows and said, as graciously as she could manage, "Let's forget this every happened, shall we? It was an honest mistake, and no one need ever know about it."

"Except us."

"Yes."

She could feel it again, the weighing and assessing of every breath she took, every word she uttered, and she said quickly, "I think you'd better go."

There was the oddest silence, then he said softly, "I don't want to leave, and I don't think it's what you want either."

A shiver passed over her, then another. She tried to muster a retort and failed miserably. He was right. She didn't want him to leave. But that was insane. He was a stranger. A few minutes ago she'd been terrified of him. Then what had brought about this change in her?

She didn't want to lie to him, so she asked a question instead. "What makes you think I don't want you to leave?"

"Nothing. Everything. Put it down to intuition, but I sense . . ."

"What do you sense?"

He stroked her face with the pads of his fingers, a fleeting gesture that—she really must be insane—she wished he would prolong. "I sense," he said gently, "that the lady is in need of a friend."

Unexpected tears stung her eyes. She rarely cried, and especially not in front of anyone. She was too levelheaded.

The last time she'd cried was after her father's funeral, and that was in the privacy of her own room.

This man really did possess an uncanny insight into how her mind worked. Even those who were close to her thought she was completely self-sufficient. She tried to be. No. She had to be.

She swallowed before she spoke, but her voice held a betraying quiver all the same. "That's a strange thing to say when you don't even know me."

He edged closer and she inhaled the heady flavor of brandy. "Do I seem like a stranger to you? Truthfully, mind."

"I . . . no."

"How do I seem?"

She had to think about it before she put her thoughts into words. "You seem familiar." In truth, he felt like a long-lost friend and that was absurd. "But that's nonsense, of course. I'm sure we've never met."

"So am I." Gentle hands cupped her face. "I think you've bewitched me. What do you think? Tell me what you feel."

She felt as though she'd had too much to drink. She felt as though she had lost her bearings. She felt as though there was nothing in the world but this small room and the comforting presence of the man beside her.

It must be the darkness, the flickering lights, the rain that was now lashing against the windowpanes that wrapped them in this warm cocoon of intimacy. It couldn't last. It wouldn't stand the cold light of day.

She gazed up at him, straining to see him in that dim light. His hair was blond and his mouth was full and sensual—that much she knew, but the rest was left to her imagination. His eyes would be kind, she decided, and crinkling at the corners; kind eyes and a kind smile to match his voice.

"Do you want me to stay?" His lips brushed her cheek. "Tell me!"

This was madness. She mustn't say yes, but she couldn't seem to say no.

When she didn't respond, he took her lips again. She wasn't afraid. Now that she'd taken his measure, she knew that she could stop him any time she wanted to. She sank back on the pillows and he followed her down, covering her with the upper part of his body. Even that didn't frighten her. His mouth on hers was warm and gentle; she felt safe and sheltered in his arms.

He raised his lips an inch from hers. "Don't be frightened," he whispered. "I won't hurt you. I won't let it go too far. I just want to touch you. Just a little."

One hand went up and brushed his face. "I'm not afraid of you," she said.

"I know." He gave a throaty chuckle. "I think I'm the one who should be afraid."

She was puzzling over his words when his lips settled on hers once more. This time his kiss was hot and tasted of passion. Her lips parted at the gentle urging of his. The hands that brushed over her from breast to waist to thigh were sweetly erotic. She felt as though she'd stepped into a gentle current that was taking her she knew not where.

He was going to make love to her.

It flashed into her mind that she wanted him to. She, Sara Carstairs, wanted this stranger to make love to her. She'd never felt this way before in her life, and doubted that she ever would again. But it would be a mistake to give into her feelings. She wasn't herself. She was overwrought, weighed down by all her worries. And he was kind. That's all it was. She would savor the strength of those sheltering arms for one moment more, then she would push him away.

Abruptly, the current she was floating in wasn't so gentle. His kisses grew hotter, deeper, wetter. He was no longer coaxing her; he was devouring her. Heat spread along her skin, making it unbearably sensitive to every brush of his hands. And those hands! There was magic in them. He knew just where to touch her to make her ache with wanting. She took one quick breath, then another, and suddenly she was fighting for every breath.

And she was drowning in pleasure.

She clutched at his shoulders to push him away and found herself clinging to him. As though she'd given him a signal, he covered her body with his, then adjusted his position so that she could feel the intimate press of his arousal through the fabric of his trousers. Her whole body contracted in shock.

His voice was hoarse and oddly bemused. "I must be out of my mind to put myself through this torture. But you have no idea what I'm talking about, do you?"

She was dimly aware of his words, but the feel of that powerfully aroused body grinding into hers was unbearably erotic. She tried to fight off the sensations that were beginning to overwhelm her, but she'd left it too late. A frantic little cry tore from her throat, then she convulsed against him as her body exploded with pleasure.

When it was over and she was floating back to a more rational frame of mind, he kissed her throat, her eyes, her lips, her breasts. Still fully aroused, he pulled himself off her and rose from the bed.

The amusement had returned to his voice. "I think," he said, "it's about time we introduced ourselves. But first, let's get a candle lit."

His words instantly dispelled the pleasant languor that had settled over her. "No!" She hauled herself up. "Let's not spoil things. This was . . . an enchantment. Yes, that's what it was. Let's not examine it in the cold light of day." Then more softly, because she didn't want to hurt his feelings, "Let's say our good-byes now. Really, I think it's better this way."

She hardly recognized the voice that came to her out of

the darkness. The velvet had been replaced by steel. "Midsummer madness? I hardly think so. You want to run away. I can understand that. But I'm afraid I can't permit it."

This wasn't the voice of her long-lost friend. Where was the charm? The gentleness? Sara sank back on her elbows as she heard flint strike on iron. Her tame lamb didn't sound so tame any more.

And suddenly, she was very afraid.

Four

⌒

MAX LIT TWO OF THE CANDLES ON THE mantelpiece, then slowly turned to look at the woman who had streaked into his orbit with the velocity of a comet. Once, as a boy, he'd taken shelter under a tree that was struck by lightning, and he'd had a miraculous escape. He was hoping against hope that he would have a miraculous escape this time around as well.

She was picking up the pieces of broken glass that littered the floor. When she'd disposed of them in the wash basin, she turned to face him.

Her fiery dark hair fell about her shoulders in a torrent of tight waves; she had the kind of bones that were to be found on the sculptures of Greek deities. But it was her eyes that held him, dark and huge against the pallor of her skin.

Those dark eyes were wary, but they gazed at him directly all the same. He liked her directness. She wasn't going to cry rape or try to evade her share of responsibility for what had happened between them. The question was—what exactly had happened between them?

He couldn't put a name to it. All he would allow at this point was that he had no more intention of allowing this woman to walk out of his life than he had of giving up ownership of the *Courier*.

She'd noticed that her breasts were bared. No blushes or hysterics, Max noted with approval. Her eyes still on his, she began to do up the buttons on her bodice. It was just as well. Unsated desire was still a threat to his control, and they had a great deal to talk over.

He gave her a smile that was calculated to reassure her and melt her heart at the same time. "I'm really quite harmless," he said.

The wariness in her eyes slowly dissipated. "Are you? You don't look harmless to me. In fact, you look as though you've just come from the wars."

God, he loved her voice—husky, prim, sinfully seductive— a study in contradictions, just like the lady herself. Her words registered, and he looked down at his clothes, saw that his shirt and neckcloth were spattered with blood, then looked up and grinned. "I was in a fight," he said. "I lost." He touched a hand to his face. "I've been told that I'll have a black eye by morning." He worked his jaw, and felt his nose. "It could have been worse."

"Are you a Corinthian?"

He could tell by her tone that she didn't think much of Corinthians. "I suppose I am. Why?"

"I have two brothers who are Corinthians, or aspiring Corinthians, and they're always getting into fights."

"This was a contest. There is a difference."

She was weighing him up, taking in the cut of his garments, the tight fit of his trousers, her eyes lingering on his Hessian boots with their gold tassels.

He said humorously, "In case you're too shy to ask, Weston of Bond Street is my tailor, and Schulz is my bootmaker."

"So I gathered," she answered coolly.

She'd summed him up as a fribble, a member of the dandy set. Max didn't know whether to laugh out loud or get on his high horse and tell her that in the newspaper world he was known as a force to be reckoned with.

She'd learn that he was a force to be reckoned with soon enough.

Trying to make the movement as unthreatening as possible, he took a step toward her. She didn't flinch or bolt; she simply reached for her robe and slipped into it.

"Please," he said, "sit down. We have a lot to talk about."

"I prefer to stand."

He regretted that it had come to a tussle of wills so soon. "I really must insist."

It looked as though she might argue with him, but one glance at his unsmiling face was all the persuasion required to make her do as he wished. She chose a straight-backed chair at a small mahogany table. He took the chair opposite.

When he was silent, she said impatiently, "Well? What is it you wish to say to me?"

"First," he said, "let's get something out of the way."

He reached for her left hand. One glance told him all he needed to know. He allowed her to tug her hand free. "You're not married," he said. "Neither am I."

"So?"

"So that makes things simpler. My name is Max Worthe. And no, I don't usually climb in through the windows of ladies who are strangers to me. I'm not a disreputable character in spite of appearances or," he grinned wickedly, "what transpired in this room only moments ago."

No blushes, but those long lashes lowered to veil her expression. "Mr. Worthe," she began.

"Please, call me Max."

She sighed. "I presume this is an apology. It isn't necessary, you know." Her eyes lifted to meet his in one of her direct stares. "I don't see why you're making such a fuss. After all, nothing of any significance happened. We're both adults, both responsible for our actions. But it's over now.

It was a . . ." She swallowed hard, and that made Max smile. ". . . a pleasant interlude. But, as I said, it's over, and it's time to call it quits."

His bark of laughter startled her, and she frowned. Shaking his head, Max said, "I can't tell you how often I've used those words myself at the end of an affair, but in this case, they won't do. In the first place, this is not an apology, and in the second, nothing of any significance happened, as you say, only because I didn't want it to."

He gave her a moment to absorb his words, noted the quick rise and fall of her breasts, and, at last, the faint blush that ran under her skin, and he went on, not without a certain degree of satisfaction, "I say this only to convince you that I'm a man of honor. I promised I wouldn't go too far and I didn't."

She made to rise, saw something in his expression that warned her against the attempt, and sank back in her chair. "If you want my gratitude," she said, "you have it. But where is this conversation leading? What is it you want from me?" She breathed deeply. "I warn you that my gratitude extends only so far. If you think you can persuade me to go to bed with you, you have vastly mistaken my character."

This little speech delighted Max. The lady was no missish prude. There was no false modesty or counterfeit outrage. Her speech was as direct as the looks she kept giving him.

"I don't know where this is leading," he said, bending the truth a little. He knew where he wanted it to lead. He wanted her with an intensity that both shocked and delighted him. He'd never met her like before. But he was a civilized man. He could defer what he wanted until the circumstances were right.

"That is, I want to get to know you better, as though we'd been introduced properly in my mother's drawing room." He gave her one of his disarming smiles. "Then we'll go on from there."

She leaned toward him. "It's almost three o'clock in the morning."

"I've never felt more awake in my life. You can begin by telling me your name."

"Then will you leave?"

"Perhaps."

"It's Sara," she said at once.

"Go on."

"Sara Childe."

"Sara," he said, savoring the sound of her name. "And who is William?"

She sat back in her chair. "William?"

"You said his name as I climbed in the window."

She bristled. "I might well ask you who Deirdre is."

"Deirdre," he said seriously, "has just become ancient history. You need not trouble yourself about her."

She studied him as though he were an odious weed she had just discovered in her flower garden. "That sounds heartless."

"I'm not heartless," Max protested. "Deirdre and I have an arrangement. It can be terminated by either of us at any time of our choosing. You don't approve?"

"I don't care one way or the other, just as long as you don't terminate your arrangement with your mistress because of me."

So, she didn't approve of such arrangements. Pity.

"Did I say something to amuse you?"

Max erased his smile. "It just occurred to me that I might be coming down with a bad case of gout, and I was wondering how I could avoid it. Go on, you were about to tell me about William."

Her look of perplexity gradually faded. "William," she said, "is ancient history as well."

"A former lover."

"Not in the way you mean."

When she took refuge in silence again, Max let out a

long, impatient sigh. "Look," he said, "we'll be here all night if you don't tell me what I want to know. You said William's name when I climbed in the window, then you tried to brain me. That leads me to believe that you're afraid of this man. I want to know why."

She stiffened as a thought occurred to her. "If you heard me say William's name, you must have known I wasn't your Deirdre."

Max made a face. "She's not *my* Deirdre. She's married, and her husband's name is William. Now don't go pursing your lips like that. It doesn't suit you. Deirdre and her husband have an understanding. They're free to go their separate ways."

She stopped pouting, but all she said was, "I see."

Max stifled a sigh. He was beginning to suspect it would be gout or nothing with this woman, and that did not sit well with him at all. Maybe once he got to know her better, her appeal would fade. It happened all the time. More than one mistress had called him a fickle lover, and it was the truth.

"You were telling me about William," he said. "Why are you afraid of him?"

"I'm not afraid of him."

"That's not how it appeared to me."

"William is dead. And I said his name because . . . because I'd been thinking about him. That's all there is to it."

"Nevertheless, I'd like to hear more about him. It's not just idle curiosity. If you're in some kind of trouble, I'd like to help you."

"You're . . ."

"Tenacious?"

She shook her head, and smiled. "I was going to say 'very kind.' "

Her smile dazzled him. It did more. He was struck by the uncanny feeling that he'd been waiting for that smile for a long, long time. But this was ludicrous. He'd never met Sara before. With her dramatic coloring, she wasn't the kind of woman a man would easily forget. Something hovered at the periphery of his mind, but he could not bring it into focus.

She said, "There's not much to tell. I thought I was in love with him once. I discovered that he was a brutal man." She paused, then answered the question in his eyes. "There was a local girl. She was with child, William's child. He deserted her. I found out about it, and that was that."

"And what happened to him?"

"He married someone else and met with a terrible accident."

He smiled. "And good riddance to the world."

"My feelings precisely." She looked pointedly at the clock. "I would offer you refreshments, but time is moving on."

"It's inclined to do that, isn't it? Did you say 'refreshments'? Thank you, I'll take you up on that offer."

Her lips tightened fractionally, but she rose without protest, went to a large battered trunk at the foot of the bed and after a moment or two, produced a silver flask and a small silver cup. She set them on the table in front of Max.

"Medicinal brandy," she said. "It's not the best quality, but it's all there is."

"This will do very nicely, thank you."

Since she didn't offer, he poured himself out a scant measure and cradled the cup in one hand. He wasn't interested in the brandy, but in prolonging the conversation that she so obviously wanted to terminate. He thought he understood her eagerness to be rid of him. She was reluctant to accept what had happened between them. Well, so was he. Maybe there was nothing to it. Maybe it was all in his mind, a trick of his imagination that had imbued this woman with vulnerabilities she seemed to take such pains to conceal. He hoped to God it was a trick of his imagination. Then he could return to his comfortable bachelor existence and forget all about her.

But he did not think so.

When he'd first caught sight of her, before he'd climbed over the windowsill, he'd been struck by the notion that maybe Deirdre cared for him after all. She'd been on tiptoe, about to blow out the candle, when she'd sunk back on her heels and rested her brow against the mantelpiece. She'd looked so helpless, so forlorn, and he'd been overcome with remorse for the callous way he'd rejected her to go off with his friends. He'd been so sure, until that moment, that Deirdre had never experienced a genuine emotion in her life, unless it was anger. Then she'd squared her shoulders, as though assuming burdens she knew she couldn't throw off, and in the next moment they were plunged into darkness.

And Deirdre's appeal had never seemed more potent. He hadn't been thinking of taking her to bed when he reached for her. All he'd wanted was to take her in his arms and comfort her.

And after he'd discovered that the woman in his arms wasn't Deirdre, her appeal had staggered him, all the more so because his relations with women were always tempered by a healthy dose of cynicism.

In this encounter, however, it was the lady who was cynical. She had herself well in hand now and, he was sure, regretted that she'd allowed him to get too close to her. Hell, they'd almost become intimate. She couldn't brush that aside as though they'd just shaken hands.

He took a minuscule swallow from his cup, then said softly, "Tell me about yourself, Sara. Where do you live? Where are you going?"

"Max . . ." She gave him a pleading look. "None of this matters. I should have told you at the outset. I'm going to be married. That's where I'm going right now, to meet my betrothed's family. It's all arranged." She touched his sleeve, then quickly withdrew her hand. "I'm sorry if I gave you the wrong idea about me." She glanced at the bed and visibly trembled. "I can't explain what happened between us and I won't even try. But—"

"You're going to be married!" His voice registered his shock.

She bobbed her head. "That's where I'm going now."

The crack of the silver cup as Max set it down on the table made her jump. "You're not wearing a ring."

"It's in my trunk for safekeeping."

"You can't love this man!"

She glanced at the bed again, then looked down at her clasped hands. "Perhaps not, but I'm very fond of him."

"Put him off. Delay the wedding. At least give yourself a chance to know your own mind."

"I do know my own mind."

The eyes that lifted to meet his betrayed no emotion, no regret. He'd seen eyes like hers in astute men of business as they haggled over the sum of money that would change hands. It made him want to reach out and shake her, if only to crack that emotionless mask she was hiding behind.

She went on quickly. "The marriage settlements have been signed. My betrothed has been very generous. When I marry, my brothers and sisters will be financially secure. I can't let them down."

He said through his teeth, "Not to mention your own financial security."

Her eyes clashed with his. "I'd rather be a wife than a mistress." She paused, and a fleeting smile came and went. "Or perhaps I've misjudged you? Perhaps you're a man of substance? Perhaps you're offering to marry me? Can you afford me, Max? Speak now, or forever hold your peace."

At these words, Max's cynicism rose in his throat like bile. He couldn't believe how completely she had taken him in. He'd thought she was different, and she was just like every woman he had ever known. They didn't see men as people, but as bank ledgers, and the larger the balance, the more a man rose in their esteem.

When her stare faltered and her eyes slid away from his, a niggling doubt began to demolish his anger. If she wanted to get rid of him, she was going the right way about it. Maybe he was being too hard on her. She was a female, and she had far more to lose than he did if she followed her heart.

"Sara," he chided, "forget these mercenary ambitions. Take a chance on me. Give us both time to get to know each other. That's all I ask."

She sighed. "It's just as I thought. You can't afford me, can you? And you're not offering marriage either, are you, Max?"

"No to both questions," he snapped. He got to his feet and stared down at her bent head with undisguised contempt. "Then all that remains to be said is to offer you my felicitations on your forthcoming marriage."

Her eyes did not meet his. "Thank you."

Max had hardly quit the room when that niggling doubt blossomed into a full-blown suspicion and finally a conviction. She'd deliberately picked a quarrel with him just to get rid of him. There was no betrothed. If there had been, she would have told him when he'd examined her left hand and found it ringless.

She was a coward, that's what she was, and that's *all* she was. Something extraordinary had happened between them in that room, but the lady was too craven to admit it.

He was tempted to return and have it out with her, but he heard the key turn in the lock and knew that no words of his could persuade her to open the door to him.

Coward, he said under his breath. Fortunately for the lady, he had enough courage for both of them. It wasn't over yet.

His next thought erased his smile. *Deirdre.* He had an unpleasant duty to perform, and the sooner it was over, the sooner he could direct all his energies to solving his problems with Sara.

SARA WAITED TILL SHE HEARD MAX'S STEPS RE-
ceding along the corridor before she moved away from the door. The window was her next object. Only when it was closed and secured did her heart begin to slow. She retreated to her straight-backed chair and wrapped her arms around her shivering body. She felt weak and shaken. She couldn't believe how close she'd come to throwing everything away.

Sara, take a chance on me.

No! No! No! That could only lead to disaster.

When he'd lit the candle and she'd seen at once that he was a Corinthian, she'd thought she'd had a lucky escape. She despised fops, whatever they called themselves. But she'd had to admit that, fop or not, he was a princely creature, princely and gracious and kind. Her imagination hadn't done him justice, but she'd been right about the laughter lines around his eyes and the kind smile.

And she'd been right about the steel in him as well.

Tenacious, he'd called himself, and he hadn't exaggerated. He wouldn't have been satisfied until he had dragged all her secrets out of her. Max Worthe was a dangerous man, and she hoped to God she never saw him again.

Sara, take a chance on me.

She looked at the bed and a shiver passed over her. She couldn't begin to explain what had happened in that bed, but it clearly demonstrated a glaring lack in her character. It was demeaning; it was degrading; it was . . . the most beautiful experience she'd ever had in her life.

That was one of her failings. She'd never been able to lie to herself. And the truth was, she was in mortal danger of losing everything, *everything* she'd staked her life on.

She stared at that bed for a long, long time, then suddenly rising, she moved quickly around the room, collecting her belongings to pack in her trunk. She would not be easy until she'd put herself well beyond Max Worthe's reach.

*T*HE FOLLOWING MORNING, MAX AWOKE WITH the birds. It was ever thus when he stayed in the country. Most people thought the country was idyllically peaceful compared to town, but he'd never found it so. The racket of crows and pigeons, not to mention pesky songbirds, never failed to awaken him, though he could sleep through a military parade that passed right under his bedroom window in Whitehall.

Town life was much more to his taste.

But this was one morning when he didn't mind getting up with the birds. Dawn was no more than a pale glow on the horizon. Inside the inn, nothing was stirring. It wasn't that he didn't trust Sara, but he wasn't taking any chances. She might be embarrassed to face him after what had happened last night. She might decide to make a bolt for it, and he had other ideas. Until he had met her betrothed in person, he was going to keep Sara Childe in his sights.

The thought that Deirdre was no longer a problem had him humming tunelessly. He smiled at his reflection in the mirror above the washstand as he lathered his face. When he'd entered his room last night, he'd found it empty, but Deirdre had left him an eloquent message, far more eloquent than anything that could be written on paper. She'd unpacked his clothes and cut off the arms of all his coats at the elbow and done much the same thing with his trousers. Only his shirts and underclothes had been spared. So he was reduced to wearing the same coat and trousers he'd worn yesterday.

He didn't know why he was laughing. He couldn't have

slept for much more than a couple of hours; his expensive Weston garments were strewn around the floor like a pile of old rags; he was aching all over; and last, but not least, the *Exeter Chronicle* might well go to someone else because he didn't have the time to pursue it right now.

Peter Fallon was waiting for him in Exeter. Peter would be the one to face the wrath of the irate proprietors when he, Max, didn't turn up to sign the documents. It couldn't be helped. Something that he didn't want to put a name to had touched him on the shoulder, and if he turned away now, he would always wonder . . .

Sara.

What was it about her that made her so different? He dwelt on that thought as he began to shave. He'd known more beautiful women, but none that fascinated him half as much. The only other woman who had come close to obsessing him was Sara Carstairs, but that was only because she'd got away with murder.

He was sitting on the bed, pulling on his boots, when thoughts of Sara Carstairs intruded again. He was remembering the trial and how nothing seemed to affect her. He remembered how he'd wanted to shake her, if only to put a crack in the mask she hid behind.

Just as he'd wanted to shake Sara last night.

He shook his head. Sara Carstairs was a typical English rose. She had fair hair and blue eyes. Her resemblance to Sara Childe was . . .

He sat there, staring blindly at his boots as impressions flashed like lightning inside his head. He'd been waiting for her to smile at him for a long, long time. She seemed familiar to him. He wanted to shake her, if only to put a crack in the mask she hid behind. William had married someone else and met with a terrible accident.

William Neville had married her sister and then she'd murdered him.

William. William Neville.

It couldn't be true. Sara Carstairs had fair hair and blue eyes. It was true that at the trial, her hair had been concealed by her bonnet and she'd never looked out at the spectators, but her complexion was so fair that he'd simply assumed she was a typical English rose.

And that's how he always remembered her.

He remembered something else about Sara Carstairs. She was a woman to attract men, not by beauty alone, but by an appealing blend of innocence and worldliness. And isn't that what had bewitched him last night? He hadn't known whether to ask Sara to become his mistress or whether she was the kind of woman who would settle for nothing less than marriage.

Sara Childe and Sara Carstairs were one and the same person. He tested his theory gingerly, then, after a long period of reflection, uttered an obscene profanity and flung one boot against the wall. *Sara Childe and Sara Carstairs were one and the same person!* He didn't know why he hadn't seen it before. Three years had passed since he'd seen her, but her impression had been branded on his mind. He thought he would recognize her again, the moment he set eyes on her, but he'd been fooled by that dark, exotic coloring.

He didn't know why he was so angry. He'd hoped for a miraculous escape, and the gods had just handed it to him. There could never be anything between him and Sara Carstairs. She'd had more lovers than he'd had dinners. He knew this for a fact because he'd amassed a file on the Carstairs woman with enough information to make a book. She wasn't fussy about who she took to her bed, as last night clearly demonstrated. He could have had her if only he'd persevered.

The very things that had enchanted him last night now filled him with disgust. He'd thought there was something special between them, but all that Sara Carstairs had wanted was a man, not him in particular. Any man would have done. And he had held off because he'd been taken in by her air of innocence.

He would never make that mistake again.

She'd lied between her teeth. There was no betrothed. She was an heiress in her own right. There was no necessity for Sara Carstairs to marry for financial security. She'd wanted to get rid of him and had hit on that story to throw him off the scent.

She would have flown the coop by now. Last night, he'd been tenacious in his curiosity, and that's what had frightened her. Well, it would be no great labor to follow her trail. There wouldn't be too many carriages on the road at this ungodly hour. He'd pursue her all right, but now his object was anything but loverlike. He wanted a story for his newspaper, and one way or another, he would get it.

Never in his life had he experienced such an icy rage. He waited until he had himself under control before he quit the room.

Five

M ISS BEATTIE OPENED THE NEWSPAPER AT
the personal columns and began to search for Sara's advertisement. It was hard to believe that so many gentlemen and
ladies could not find a mate in the ordinary way. But Sara
was right. There were more entries in the personal columns
than there were houses for sale.

She found Sara's advertisement and read:

> *Lady of substance, personable, reserved, wishes to meet
> gentleman of good character (age and fortune immaterial)
> with the object of contracting a Marriage of Convenience.
> Apply to Box 41, The Chronicle.*

"You'll never guess," said Sara, "how many replies I received."

"How many?"

"Twenty-five."

Miss Beattie's jaw sagged. *"How many?"*

"Twenty-five." Sara laughed. "I can hardly believe it
either. I thought I'd be lucky if I got one or two." She held
up a brown paper package. "But here they are. Maggie
brought them while you were dressing."

Maggie was the serving girl who came with the suite of furnished rooms Sara had rented for her stay in Bath, the ground floor of a solid, though modest house in Queen's Square. Their landlady, Mrs. Hastings, a widow who had fallen on hard times, lived in the floor above.

Sara had rented the rooms and placed the advertisement before she left London. She and Miss Beattie had arrived in Bath the night before, and the first thing Sara did on waking that morning was send the maid to the offices of the *Bath Chronicle* to collect her replies. She and Miss Beattie were now in the small morning room at the back of the house, enjoying a late breakfast of tea and toast.

Miss Beattie read the advertisement again. "I must be stupid, but what is there in this advertisement to attract such interest? It says very little."

Sara picked up the silver teapot and refilled Miss Beattie's cup, then her own. A small, cynical smile touched her lips. "That's where you're wrong, Bea. It says plenty if you read between the lines. Shall I translate for you?"

Miss Beattie nodded. "Please do."

"A young woman with a fat bank balance, who doesn't want anyone asking awkward questions about her past, is willing to pay handsomely for the privilege of marrying some impoverished, trustworthy gentleman who will have the grace to make himself scarce as soon as the marriage certificate is signed."

"What!" Miss Beattie choked on a mouthful of tea. She cleared her throat. "You're making that up."

"Oh, no, I'm not. Read it again, Bea. It's all there, though, of course, I've used pretty words to dress it up. We mustn't shock the finer feelings of the gentlemen, must we?"

Miss Beattie read the advertisement again and groaned. "You see what this means? You'll have an army of fortune-hunters and . . . and shady, disreputable characters beating a path to your door."

"A shady lady cannot be too fussy," declared Sara.

"Sara! Don't talk like that. This is serious."

The smile in Sara's eyes faded a little. "I was only joking, Bea." She didn't add what she was thinking, that many a jest was spoken in earnest. Bea was prejudiced in her favor and wouldn't hear a word against her, not even when it came from her own mouth.

Sara said, "Anyway, no one will beat a path to my door. I'm not that stupid. I'm not going to reveal who I am, not yet. What we're going to do, Bea, is go through all these letters and choose three or four suitable candidates. Then I'll find a way to meet each gentleman casually. When I'm sure I have the right man for me, then and only then will I tell him that I'm the lady who placed the advertisement in the *Chronicle*."

Miss Beattie thought about this for a moment or two. She looked at Sara. "You make it sound so easy, but have you considered that this could be dangerous?"

"Nonsense. It's done all the time. If it was dangerous, no one would advertise for a husband or wife in the newspapers, would they?"

"But . . ." Miss Beattie stopped, knowing that she'd already put forward every argument to persuade Sara to give up the scheme.

"What?" asked Sara.

Though she knew her words would fall on deaf ears and she'd said it all before, Miss Beattie couldn't hold back the words. "This is a drastic step you're taking. What if you change your mind next year, or the year after that, or ten years from now? What if you meet the perfect man for you?"

"The perfect man for me," said Sara dryly, "is the one who will make himself scarce right after he has signed the marriage register. Now, let's clear the table and get down to business."

They divided the letters into two piles and began to go through them. Miss Beattie took her time. Sara scanned each one quickly and more often than not tore it to shreds and tossed it aside.

Miss Beattie made a hissing sound.

"What?" asked Sara.

"The nerve of the man! He wants to know how much you're willing to pay for the privilege of acquiring his name." She was about to tear up the letter, but Sara plucked it out of her hand.

"Bea! This is just the kind of man I'm looking for." She quickly read the letter and set it to one side. "I know, I know. Major Haig sounds mercenary, and not very gentlemanly. But that's all to the good, don't you see?"

"No, I don't see," replied Miss Beattie crossly. "If you're determined to marry and break the trust, why not find a man who can make you happy?"

"Because the man who could make me happy would be too intelligent to marry a suspected murderess."

"But you were cleared at the trial."

"Was I? Then why are we living like this?"

Miss Beattie's gaze faltered. They were living like this because whenever Sara's identity became known, fingers started pointing, and friends and acquaintances melted away. No one was ever going to forget that Sara was once accused of murder, especially not with the *Courier's* special correspondent keeping the story alive. Sara was right. An intelligent man would want nothing to do with her, because fingers would start pointing at him too, and eventually at their children. It was all so hopeless.

Sara let out a long, quiet breath. "Bea," she said softly, "this is all going to work out for the best, you'll see. I've been thinking that once I'm free of all my obligations to my family, I could start afresh somewhere else. Oh, not in England. But what's to stop us going to America?"

"America," said Miss Beattie faintly.

"No one knows me there and best of all, there would be no *Courier* to hound me."

"But . . . but it's so far away."

"Yes. That's the whole point. But let's not think about it right now. Let's take things one step at a time, and the first step is to find some unsuspecting male who can give me my heart's desire."

Miss Beattie looked up quickly, saw the laughter in Sara's eyes and smiled in spite of herself.

*A*T THE END OF HALF AN HOUR, SARA HAD RE-duced the list of applicants to three likely candidates, with two to be held in reserve. The ones she had discarded were from men who were either too young—and might yet meet a woman they could love—or too sure of their ability to make her forget about a marriage of convenience and live happily ever after on her money and their skill as lovers.

Lucky her!

"What now?" asked Miss Beattie glumly.

"Now," said Sara, "we do a little sleuthing. Oh, nothing too obvious. All very discreet. We introduce ourselves to Bath society and find out as much as we can about"—she looked at her list of three likely candidates"—Mr. Townsend, Mr. Bloor, and Major Haig.

"We're going to the Pump Room, Bea. According to our landlady, that's where everyone in Bath congregates. I believe it's a daily ritual, not only for visitors, but for residents as well. And Mrs. Hastings will be there to introduce us around."

Miss Beattie made a short, sharp derisory sound. "Mrs. Hastings," she said, "is a silly, vulgar woman. Do you know what she said to me last night when your back was turned? She winked and said that she had quite a reputation as a matchmaker, and if she couldn't fix me up, no one could. What exactly did you say to that woman in your correspondence?"

Sara put her cup to her mouth to conceal her smile. After taking a sip of tea, she said, "What we agreed upon, of course, that you are my employer and I am your companion."

"I think you must have said a lot more than that."

Sara shrugged. "I may have given the impression that you were lonely."

In fact, Sara had been delighted with the tone of Mrs. Hasting's letters. She'd realized that the woman was a busybody. Normally she would have avoided such a person, but for her present purposes, Mrs. Hastings was a godsend. Sara had hinted that her "employer" was husband-hunting. That way, she'd reasoned, it would be easy to quiz their landlady on all the gentlemen who replied to her advertisement.

Miss Beattie drained her cup and set it down carefully. "So I'm your employer and you're my paid companion. Is this charade really necessary, Sara?"

"Absolutely, and you know why. I don't want to draw attention to myself. I don't want to be recognized. No one will spare a paid companion a second glance."

This was something that irritated Miss Beattie. She'd had visions of Sara buying new clothes, prettying herself up, enjoying herself. But she was still dressed in the mode of a governess.

"Bea, don't be difficult. Please?"

Miss Beattie could not resist that appeal. "Who's being difficult? Well, come along. Don't dawdle. Let's set Bath on fire."

S ARA WAS IN HER ROOM TYING THE RIBBONS of her bonnet under her chin when her thoughts strayed from her three likely prospects to Max. She'd thought about him constantly in the last few days, but it was only now, when she'd put some distance between them and was confident that they were not likely to meet again, that she could look back on their encounter with a calm and critical eye.

It seemed strange, almost laughable, that he, a Corinthian and a fop, should be the one to overcome her deep distrust of men. He'd done a lot more than that. He'd aroused sensations she hadn't known existed.

Passion. How was it possible for a man she did not know to have such an effect on her?

Maybe she shouldn't be surprised. He was the kind of man a mother would warn her daughter against—handsome, charming, experienced, and with the morals of . . .

No. She couldn't fault his morals. He wasn't like William. He was gentle and kind, and that's why she'd been susceptible to him. He could have seduced her easily, but he had let her go.

She wished now that he hadn't been so chivalrous. It would have been a beautiful memory to warm her in the cold nights ahead. She wasn't sorry that he'd climbed through her window. Every woman should have a Max Worthe in her past, if only to remind her that once, some man had found her beautiful and desirable. And this man had meant it.

She gazed wistfully into space as she remembered that night, and by small degrees, before she was aware of it, all her senses came alive. She remembered his powerful body pinning her to the mattress, the brush of his hands from her breast to waist to thigh; he was no longer coaxing her, he was devouring her. The memories were so vivid, so erotic, that she felt as though he were actually touching her now.

"Sara!" Miss Beattie poked her head around the door. "What is it? What's keeping you?"

Sara stared, stuttered, then came to herself with a start. "Nothing," she said breathlessly, "nothing at all." She picked up her reticule and hurried from the room.

· · ·

THIS WAS SARA'S FIRST VISIT TO BATH. THOUGH she liked what she saw on the short walk from Queen's Square to the Pump Room—a city of gleaming Bath stone built in the neoclassical style—her pleasure was dulled by the constant fear that someone might recognize her.

She had to go through with it. She couldn't do what she usually did when she was recognized. In the past, she'd solved her problems by starting over somewhere else. But now she was cornered. She had no choice but to fight back. All she had to do was keep out of William's reach a little while longer . . .

And marry a man who would take her on her terms.

It had started to rain. Miss Beattie, always prepared, unfurled a black umbrella. "Maybe we should have taken a chair," she said, indicating one of the many sedan chairs that had passed them on the way to the center of town.

"I've never seen so many sedans at one time," said Sara. "I suppose it's because the hills are too steep for carriages to navigate."

"Or," said Miss Beattie tartly, "it could be that the clocks in Bath stopped in the last century. At least, that's my impression." To Sara's questioning look she elaborated, "Sedans? Gentlemen in breeches and powdered hair? I feel as though I've taken a step back in time."

Sara laughed. Miss Beattie was right. The majority of people coming and going were, if not elderly, past their prime. The ladies had adopted the current fashions of high-waisted gowns, but the gentlemen's garments were out of date. Few wore the knit trousers and tight-fitting coats of the smart set in London.

That thought eased her fears. Bath was famous for the curative powers of its mineral waters. That's why there were so many old people here, to cure their ailments. That's why it was no longer a fashionable resort. It was too staid, too dull for the kind of people who had flocked to her trial at Winchester.

It took them less than fifteen minutes to reach the Pump Room, and when they entered, they found it thronged with people. Some were strolling around, some were sitting on benches, and some were at the famous pump set in a rounded bay, waiting their turn for a glass of Bath's beneficial mineral water. Above the hum of conversation, the stately strains of Handel's *Water Music,* courtesy of a small group of musicians at one end of the room, rose and echoed back from the coved ceiling high above the room's gilded Greek columns.

It was, without doubt, thought Sara, one of the loveliest rooms she had ever entered.

"Now what?" asked Miss Beattie, not for the first time.

Sara was scanning the crush of people. "Mrs. Hastings said that she would be here to show us around."

"And if she's not?"

"We take the waters and wait for someone to notice us."

They were almost at the pump when a lady swooped down on them. "My dear Miss Beattie! Miss Childe. I've been watching for you. And here you are!"

The speaker was their landlady, Mrs. Hastings, a plump, matronly woman in her early fifties with a formidable bosom and a mop of suspiciously brassy gold curls peeping from under a frothy bonnet. Her blue silk gown was smothered in bows and frills. She looked like a woman who was trying hard to look younger than her years. The unfortunate effect was just the opposite.

Miss Beattie, by contrast, was a model of simplicity. Her dark blue crepe gown with its matching shawl, completely unadorned, made her the more elegant of the two ladies.

Miss Beattie assumed her role without awkwardness or hesitation. "Mrs. Hastings," she said cordially, "how kind of you to notice us. My companion and I were just saying how lost we felt among so many strangers. Isn't that so, Sara?"

Mrs. Hastings beamed at them and her voice dropped to a stage whisper. "Then let's remedy that at once. I know everyone in Bath, and before much longer, so will you."

The next half hour sped by in a confusion of introductions as Mrs. Hastings proved that she did not make empty boasts. Sara's interest perked up when she heard two names she recognized, two of her likely prospects, Mr. Bloor and Mr. Townsend. They were both in their late forties, the former ruddy-complexioned, hearty, built like a bull; the latter lean, soft-spoken and far more gentlemanly than his companion. But that did not sway Sara. The qualities she wanted in a husband would send any sane woman into a swoon.

But it had to be a man she could trust. She'd survived one William. She did not think she could survive another.

To Sara's great disappointment, Mrs. Hastings cut their conversation short before they'd had time to do more than exchange a few pleasantries, and she led them toward a bench.

Mrs. Hastings shot Miss Beattie a shrewd look and shook her head. "They won't do, Miss Beattie, so you can take that hopeful look out of your eyes."

"I beg your pardon?"

The intimidating tone was lost on Mrs. Hastings. "Mr. Bloor and Mr. Townsend? They're both as poor as church mice."

"My dear Mrs. Hastings—" Miss Beattie stopped short when she caught Sara's warning glance. She cleared her throat and said in a different tone, "Well, I can't say I like the look of Mr. Bloor. Too much the country squire for my taste. And he smells of the stables."

"That," said Mrs. Hastings, "would be the least of your worries. Bloor is desperate for an heir, a legitimate heir, I mean, and I didn't think . . ." She left the question hanging.

"Certainly not!" exclaimed Miss Beattie when enlightenment dawned.

Sara mentally struck Mr. Bloor's name from her list of prospects.

"I thought as much." Mrs. Hastings was beginning to hobble. "Would you mind if we sat down? My bunions are acting up and I must take my weight off my feet."

As Mrs. Hastings lowered herself to the bench, Miss Beattie rolled her eyes and mouthed the words, "The woman is impossible." Sara's reply was a fierce frown.

As soon as they were all seated, Miss Beattie said, "Mr. Townsend seemed like a gentlemanly sort of man."

"Oh, he is, but if he marries again, and I suppose he must, it will have to be for money."

"He's a widower, then?"

Mrs. Hastings nodded. "His wife died a year ago. In fact, he's just out of mourning. I don't understand all the details, but she had a private income that died with her. Poor Mr. Townsend was left with five motherless children to raise and his house mortgaged to the hilt."

"Mmm," said Miss Beattie. "Perhaps he'll be lucky. Perhaps some wealthy lady will be happy to marry him."

"Indeed?" Mrs. Hastings looked curiously at Miss Beattie.

"But it won't be me," said Miss Beattie emphatically. "I've more sense than to take on five motherless children at my age, and besides, I'm not wealthy."

Mrs. Hastings laughed. "Oh, I know that! If you were wealthy, you wouldn't have taken lodgings in my humble home. No, you would have taken a house on the Crescent."

Sara took advantage of a pause in the conversation to mention something that had been puzzling her. "He looks like a sad little man. Mr. Townsend, I mean."

"Well, he is," agreed Mrs. Hastings. "Heartbroken, in fact. I can tell you this: If there was no shortage of money, he wouldn't dream of marrying again. He and his wife,

Mary, well, they chose each other when they were children, and they've always been together, until Mary died. He's the kind of man who should never marry again, like swans, you know? Sad state of affairs, isn't it?"

"Very," said Sara.

As Sara watched the sad figure of Mr. Townsend leave the Pump Room, she realized it wasn't pity she felt, but envy. He was one of those fortunate few who had found the kind of love others could only dream about.

She gazed reflectively at the open door for a long time, then, sighing, she dragged her thoughts back to the unpleasant reality of a woman who had to marry for convenience.

There was only one name on her list of likely prospects that she had yet to meet, the man whom Miss Beattie thoroughly detested, Major Haig. Sara hadn't cared for the tone of his letter either. It was too arrogant, too condescending, and betrayed a colossal ego. But none of that meant that the major was not ideal for her purposes.

He was a fine figure of a man, he'd written, and though his hair was silver (prematurely, of course), it lent him a distinguished air.

Her gaze came to rest on a gentleman who was in conversation with a lady in the bay where the pump was set up. He was well-dressed in the conservative manner of his generation—beige breeches, blue cutaway coat—and his hair was silver. His cheekbones and chin were ruggedly sculpted. "A fine figure of a man" was an apt description.

"Mrs. Hastings," said Sara, "who is that gentleman with the silver hair?"

Mrs. Hastings looked around and when she found the man with the silver hair, a transformation came over her. Her smile slipped and her eyes went blank. "That," she said, "is Major Haig."

There was a telling silence, then Miss Beattie murmured, "Major Haig? Now where have I heard that name before?"

Mrs. Hastings shook her head. "Anyone but him, Miss

Beattie. He's dangerous. I know of a lady . . . a friend . . . who was sorry she ever listened to him. She . . . she invested in one of his business enterprises, thinking they were to be married. She lost her money and there was no marriage."

There was no doubt in Sara's mind that Mrs. Hastings was speaking about herself, and what she'd said revealed far more than she knew. She'd had to rent out half her house, she'd said in one of her letters, because she'd lost a large sum of money on an investment that had failed. By the look of the rooms they rented, Mrs. Hastings had also been forced to sell furniture and paintings to cover her debts.

Miss Beattie tactfully changed the subject, and she and Mrs. Hastings embarked on a discussion of Bath in its heyday, leaving Sara free to study the major.

He was doing all the talking, and his companion, a lady whose blond beauty had long since faded, gazed adoringly up at him. But the major hardly spared her a glance. He was scanning the room, his restless gaze jumping from person to person.

He must have sensed her scrutiny, for he suddenly turned and their eyes met briefly before Sara looked away.

Maybe he was looking for the lady who had placed the advertisement in the *Chronicle,* trying to discover her identity. It was, thought Sara, a reasonable thing to do. All the same, his inattention was an insult to the lady by his side.

Trying to look casual, she carefully looked in his direction again, and saw that the major was openly staring at a lady in a green turban. He suddenly snapped his fingers, cutting himself off in midsentence, abruptly bowed, and strolled away, making a beeline for the lady in the green turban.

He was stalking his prey.

Sara shuddered. She'd been eighteen years old when William's restless glance had fallen on her, eighteen and incredibly flattered when he'd left the side of the young woman he'd been dancing with and made a beeline for her.

Though their father's estates adjoined, she and William were practically strangers. He'd been away at school, then at university, and the Nevilles did not mix with their Stoneleigh neighbors.

They'd met at an assembly in Winchester.

She hadn't been impressed by the fact that he was Sir Ivor Neville's heir. William was a romantic figure and glamorous beyond anything she'd ever known, a far cry from the middle-aged viscount her father had tried to buy for her.

William was wild, so the stories went. But William told her that now he'd met her, that was all in his past. And she'd believed him. He'd wanted to marry her, and she was the happiest girl in the world.

The one person who stood in their way was Sir Ivor. His father was a proud man, William said. When the time was right, he would tell him about Sara. So she'd met William in secret, and when it was impossible to meet, she'd poured out her heart in long, passionate letters.

And those letters had nearly got her hanged.

The major was giving his undivided attention to the lady in the green turban, and she was obviously flattered. Her eyes sparkled and she smiled up at him.

Prey, Sara thought again and shuddered. She couldn't go against her instincts. She'd never feel safe with someone who reminded her of William.

The major was no longer of any interest.

Having achieved her object in coming to the Pump Room, she would have been happy to leave. But Miss Beattie had other ideas. It would be criminal, she declared, to come to Bath and not partake of its famous water. So Sara was sent to the pump to fetch a glass of water for her "mistress."

Sara was well aware that what Miss Beattie wanted was a cozy, private chat with their landlady. Bea had got this absurd idea in her head that the perfect man could turn up at any moment, like manna from heaven. Sara was sure that Bea would be quizzing Mrs. Hastings on where all the young men in Bath were hanging out, supposing there were any.

Poor Bea just couldn't face facts.

Sara kept her eyes averted both coming and going from the pump when she passed Major Haig. As she approached the bench where she'd left her companions, she saw that she'd been right. Mrs. Hastings hadn't lost any time. She'd managed to scare up a gentleman who wasn't in his dotage.

His back was to her, but his garments spoke volumes: tight beige trousers molded like a second skin to the hard muscles of leg and thigh; broad shoulders hugged by a dark blue coat that wouldn't dare show a wrinkle; and Hessian boots with those absurd tassels on them.

The man was a dandy!

Her smile died the moment before he turned to face her, the moment an uneasy suspicion took root in her mind.

Brilliant blue eyes with laugh lines at the corners smiled down at her. He doffed his hat, and his fair hair caught and trapped an odd ray of sunshine that spilled in from one of the long windows. His grin was jaunty.

It was Max Worthe.

"Miss Childe," he said, "what a pleasant surprise. I was just telling your friends that you and I met in Reading when I performed a small . . . ah . . . service for you."

Sara acted without thinking. She put the glass to her lips and took a long, long swallow.

Six

IT HAD FINALLY HAPPENED, THOUGHT MAX. AT
long last, Sara Carstairs's mask of composure was beginning
to crack. It was more than a crack. A yawning ravine. She was
gulping down Bath's foul-tasting mineral water as though
she'd just walked out of the desert.

He liked her better this way: flustered, flushed, and afraid
of what he might say or do next.

The companion, Miss Beattie, who, he'd learned, had
been promoted to the status of Sara's employer, broke what
was becoming an awkward silence. "You met Sara in Reading, Mr. Worthe?"

"At the Black Swan."

"But that's where we were staying."

"I know."

There was a small pause as Miss Beattie digested this.
"And you performed a service for her?" Her eyes darted to
Sara. "Sara said nothing to me."

I'll just bet she didn't.

"It was a small service," said Max. "I shouldn't have
mentioned it. No. I'd rather you heard it from Miss Childe."

He knew he was being unfair, but he thought that maybe
Sara deserved it. She'd lied to him. She'd run from him. His

fury had long since cooled, but she'd touched his pride, and he didn't see why she shouldn't pay for it, up to a point.

Besides, he was enjoying himself enormously.

She'd drunk every drop of water in the glass. She wished, now, that she hadn't. Then she could pour it into Max Worthe's ridiculous boots.

Miss Beattie and Mrs. Hastings were looking up at her as though she'd suddenly taken off all her clothes. She had to fight the urge to turn and run.

Shrugging helplessly, she said, "I didn't want to worry you. That's why I didn't mention it. You see, I . . . fell down a flight of stairs, a *small* flight of stairs, and Mr. Worthe was kind enough to . . . to . . ." she looked down at the empty glass in her hand, ". . . to get me a glass of water."

Max spoke to Miss Beattie. "She was very shaken by the experience."

"True," said Sara in a tight little voice, "but fortunately, I'm quite recovered. I beg your pardon for drinking your glass of water, Miss Beattie, but I was overcome with the heat. Stay right where you are and I'll get you another. Mr. Worthe, would you mind giving me your arm?"

Max regretted that the delightful hesitation in her voice had vanished. She was in control again. She could not guess how that control both fascinated him and egged him on to try and shatter it.

They were hardly out of earshot of the two gawking ladies when Sara dropped Max's arm. "What are you doing here?"

"That must be obvious."

She darted him a fierce glance, then looked away. "Nothing is obvious to me."

"What else could have drawn me to this dreary place but you, Sara?"

"So you followed me here!"

"Well, I didn't come for the good of my health—and

I just about choked when you gulped down that glass of water—and if there are fleshpots in Bath, it's the best kept secret in England. Of course I followed you."

Her voice was cool and controlled. Her words were like darts. "Well, of course I know there is nothing in Bath to attract a man like you, a Corinthian and a fop. I suppose you have nothing better to do with your time than pursue innocent young women."

"Innocent?"

This time, her stare did not falter. "You're wasting your time, Mr. Worthe. So why don't you just go away?"

He smiled lazily. "You know us Corinthians. Time hangs heavily on our hands, and we'd do anything to relieve the boredom."

Though he concealed it well, he was annoyed because she'd summed him up as an idler with nothing more serious on his mind than the cut of his clothes and chasing women. Coming from her, a woman with a murky past, it was hypocrisy on a grand scale.

There was nothing he would have liked better than to tell her, straight out, that he knew who she was. But on that tedious, two-day drive from Reading, after his anger had cooled, he'd reflected on what approach he should take when they finally reached their destination. The last thing he wanted was for Sara to become frightened and go into hiding again.

His best bet, he'd decided, was to play this out as though he had not recognized her. That was something else that annoyed him; even if he hadn't recognized her, he would still be here, would still have come after her. His one encounter with this woman had rocked him back on his heels. In her own way, Sara Carstairs packed a wallop that would do credit to Mighty Jack Cleaver.

And look what had happened to him when he'd tangled with Mighty Jack!

She didn't like the sudden flare of laughter in his eyes; she didn't like the stupid smile on his face; and she particularly didn't like the way he was making her nerves jump.

She edged her way to the far side of the pump where they could no longer be seen by Miss Beattie and Mrs. Hastings. Her nervous fingers were clutching the empty glass in a death grip, and she carefully set it down on the pump's rim, then hid her hands in the folds of her gown.

"Mr. Worthe—"

"Max. Call me Max. It's friendlier."

"We're not friends."

"No. We've gone beyond that."

She waited till her heartbeat had slowed, waited till her brain was functioning before she put her thoughts in order. Finally, she said, "I want to know what you said to my companions before I arrived."

He quelled the impulse to say that her secret was safe with him. He wanted to shake her, not shatter her, and she was beginning to look frail. "I introduced myself," he said quietly, "and asked after you. That's all, Sara."

"But how did you know that Miss Beattie was my employer?"

"Sara, I've already admitted that I followed you from Reading. It wasn't difficult to find out who your traveling companion was. Last night, I saw you safely to your front door—your lodgings in Queen's Square, I mean—then I found lodgings for myself."

"How did you know we would come to the Pump Room this morning?"

"I called at your lodgings. Your serving girl—Maggie?—told me where I could find you."

She shouldn't be surprised, she told herself. It wasn't the first time she'd sensed the steel in him. On the surface, he was all casual charm and easy smiles, but there was more to Max Worthe than that. He was a dangerous male animal, and she'd be a fool to forget it.

"Sara? What did I say?"

She ignored the hand he held out to her. "You've been following me for two days and two nights. You've been sneaking around behind my back, asking questions about me. Why are you doing this? Why?"

"You know why."

Their eyes met and held. She trembled. He frowned. Heat and passion flared between them like a flash fire. Max was shaken. Sara was appalled.

She dragged her eyes away. "I'm going to be married, Max. I told you that already."

"I don't believe you. Where is this suitor?"

"There's been a delay. But he'll be here soon. Please, Max, don't spoil this for me."

He shrugged carelessly, but she could still sense the banked fires beneath the control. "He's a fool to leave you unprotected." When her eyes went wide, he said impatiently, "Don't let your imagination make something of that last remark. I won't hurt you, Sara. But I'm not going to stay away either."

She'd learned the value of keeping her emotions under a tight rein. A woman who was at the mercy of her feelings was vulnerable, and that was something she could not afford to be. Slowly and deliberately, she gathered her dignity. "You're way off the mark if you think you can make me do what I don't want to do, Max."

His smile dazzled her. "I don't know, Sara. You've been calling me 'Max' for the last little while. The trick is in knowing how to manage a woman."

"And you've had plenty of practice, I suppose?"

He laughed, reached past her and accepted a fresh glass of water from the pump attendant. "Just watch me, Sara, just watch me."

Not a word passed between them as they returned to the bench where they'd left the ladies. Sara inwardly fumed, but as much as she wanted to send Max Worthe about his business, she was afraid of a scene. She sensed a recklessness in him that alarmed her. If she didn't watch out, she'd find her name on the lips of all the gossip mongers in Bath.

She tried to nurse her temper to keep it hot, but her annoyance was soon overtaken by a grudging amusement. Max Worthe really did know how to manage women. The trick, she decided as she studied him, was to give them his full attention. His eyes didn't shift restlessly around the room as though his mind were elsewhere. He seemed to be enjoying himself as much as the two ladies who were the object of his attentions.

Her amusement dimmed when she realized that Miss Beattie, straitlaced, and a confirmed spinster, was flirting outrageously. She'd never seen Bea like this before—pink cheeks, fluttering eyelashes, and a vacuous smile. Bea was also talking too much, telling him about all the places they hoped to visit, practically inviting him along.

They were all becoming too friendly for Sara's peace of mind.

She tried to catch her companion's eye, to warn her off, but Miss Beattie was proving to be obstinate, and Sara knew why. Max Worthe was just the kind of man Bea had hoped would miraculously appear on the horizon and ride to their rescue. He was handsome, personable, and could have given Prince Charming a run for his money.

And that's precisely why he was the wrong man.

"And what brings you to Bath, Mr. Worthe?" asked Miss Beattie at one point.

"A friend," said Max. "He lives nearby, on the other side of Claverton. Marston Manor. Do you know it?"

Mrs. Hastings nodded. "Lady Meynell lives there. Then Ash Meynell must be your friend?"

"He is," said Max.

"Oh dear," said Mrs. Hastings. "I believe Mr. Meynell has gone to Brighton. He goes there every year at this time."

Max scratched his chin and glanced at Sara.

She said sweetly, "It seems that you've come a long way for nothing, Mr. Worthe."

"Oh, I don't know," he replied easily. "I'm at a loose end. I might as well stay on and take in all that Bath has to offer."

"I'm glad to hear you say that." Miss Beattie's sharp eyes flew from Max's face to Sara's. "In my opinion, Bath is vastly underrated. If you do decide to stay, Mr. Worthe, I'm sure you'll find the experience worthwhile."

He smiled. "I hope so."

Max did not stay long after that, and as he made his way out of the Pump Room, the older ladies began to compare notes.

"He seems like a nice young man," observed Miss Beattie.

Mrs. Hastings chuckled. "I've no doubt that he is, but if he is anything like his friend—Ash Meynell, I mean—the mothers in Bath had better start locking up their daughters, yes, and themselves as well. The stories I could tell you!" Her eyes twinkled and she shook her head. "You'll think I'm speaking ill of young Mr. Meynell, but really, I'm not. We all like him, in spite of his reputation. But when he's in town, he is inclined to shake us up a bit."

Miss Beattie looked wistfully at Max's retreating back and Mrs. Hastings gave another chuckle. "I'd wager that every lady's heart beats just a little faster when Mr. Worthe walks into a room. Well, just look around and tell me if I'm wrong."

Sara and Miss Beattie obediently looked around the Pump Room. There was no doubt about it. Max Worthe had caught the surreptitious glances of many ladies, irrespective of age.

Mrs. Hastings suddenly exclaimed. "Maxwell Worthe! I remember him! He's Ash Meynell's best friend. Lord Maxwell, that's who he is. He's a charmer, all right. Don't say you haven't been warned. And you, too, Miss Childe."

The warning was unnecessary. Sara had already made up her mind that Max Worthe was nothing but trouble.

OVER THE NEXT FEW DAYS, MAX MADE SURE he just happened to be at all the functions Sara attended. It wasn't difficult to do. Miss Beattie had taken a liking to him, and, when Sara wasn't within earshot, she would casually mention where they were going to be that afternoon, or evening, and Max would be there too.

On this occasion, he'd just returned from the Pump Room to his lodgings in the Christopher Hotel. There were no personal servants waiting for him when he entered his chamber, no valet to brush out his clothes or help him choose what to wear. He'd given up all the trappings of his rank and wealth when he'd become a newspaperman. An aristocrat who traveled with a retinue of servants was not taken seriously in his business, and Max was determined to be taken seriously.

He'd sent to Castle Lyndhurst, the family seat, for the garments he kept there, and one of the hotel's footmen was just finishing unpacking them and putting them away. When the footman left, Max opened the large mahogany wardrobe and made an inventory of what was there.

At last he had something decent to wear.

He wondered if Sara would notice the difference. Probably not. She was convinced that he was an idle dandy with nothing more serious on his mind than the cut of his garments and chasing women. She hadn't asked him any questions about his family or connections. She'd made up her mind that he was trouble, and the only way she could cope was to keep him at arm's length.

She'd practically handed him a script to keep her in his orbit.

With a muffled oath, he flung himself down on the bed. Sara. The only thing he was sure of was that the feelings she had aroused at the Black Swan were still there. In fact, they had only grown stronger, and that appalled him. He should know better. There was a file on her an inch thick in the *Courier*'s offices in London, and it wasn't pleasant reading.

Sara Carstairs was a woman of loose morals. She'd started an affair with William Neville right under her sister's nose, which wasn't hard to do, considering that the Nevilles lived in the dower house in the grounds of Longfield, the show home Samuel Carstairs had restored to its original Elizabethan splendor.

She'd never denied that she'd had an affair with her brother-in-law, and if she had denied it, the letters she had written to him would have proved her a liar. Moreover, William's friends had testified that he was inflamed when he heard that Sara was going to be married. He'd left them drinking at the King's Head tavern in Stoneleigh, swearing that he would make her pay, and he'd never been seen again.

It was William's father who had raised the alarm. The following morning, he'd found William's horse wandering the downs. And then had begun the massive search for William's body.

The constable had come to Sara first.

Her alibi was unconvincing. She wasn't at Longfield, but at the dower house, where she'd spent the whole night nursing her sister, so she said. Of course, it just happened that Anne Neville's only servant was conveniently visiting relatives in Winchester at the time.

And Sara swore under oath, in the statement that was read to the court, that William hadn't come home that night. Her sister had corroborated her story, but since Anne Neville had been dosed with laudanum, no one believed her.

Max threw himself off the bed and went to stand by the open window. His room overlooked the side of the abbey and beyond that, the gardens that sloped down to the river

Avon. What in Hades was a woman like Sara Carstairs doing in a place like Bath?

When he'd started out from Reading and realized she was traveling west, he'd guessed that she'd make the turn at Thatcham to take the road to Stoneleigh. He'd been so sure in his own mind that he'd sent an express to Peter Fallon telling him to drop everything and meet him in Stoneleigh. And that's where Peter was right now. But when they reached Thatcham, her coach did not make the turn to Stoneleigh but continued to drive west.

She was going to be married, she said.

He might have believed her if she had ordered him out of her room before things went too far.

William, she'd whispered when he'd climbed through her open window, and she'd sounded deathly afraid. But later she'd told him that William was ancient history because he was dead.

I thought I was in love with him once. There was a local girl. She was with child. William's child. He deserted her.

Was William alive or dead? That was the question that had obsessed Max on the long drive from Reading. If William was alive, then they'd all misjudged Sara, himself most of all. And if William was dead, it was entirely possible that at her trial, Sara Carstairs had had them all believing exactly what she wanted them to believe.

Her eyes were dark, but they weren't brown, as they'd seemed to him in the dimly lit interior of the Black Swan. They were gray, and as dark and fathomless as the waters of the cold North Sea.

What secrets was she keeping from him?

He would be going contrary to everything he stood for as a newspaperman if he didn't go after the story.

His mouth curved in a smile that revealed recklessness as well as humor. He couldn't lie to himself. There was more to his pursuit of Sara than getting his story. He had a vested interest in discovering the truth. He had to know whether she was the woman he'd met in the Black Swan or the Sara Carstairs who had been painted as a heartless murderess at her trial.

He turned from the window and began to pull off his clothes. He had things to do, plans to make. Sara and Bath could wait for a little while longer. He was going back to where it all started.

Seven

THE MANOR HOUSE, SIR IVOR'S ANCIENT FAMILY seat, was nestled in a lush valley about five miles out of Stoneleigh, on the road to Winchester. With its honey-colored stone walls and mullioned bay windows, it was a picturesque English gem. But that was only a facade. The manor, as Max remembered, had been built on a medieval fortress and was a warren of rooms and long passages that went nowhere.

Max was waiting in an anteroom while Sir Ivor's butler carried his card to his master. He'd hoped to have a few words with Lady Neville also, but the butler had told him that her ladyship was not receiving visitors. Max remembered the woman as a pathetic case of arrested development, a giddy schoolgirl entrapped in an aging shell. His mother, who was much more charitable than he, said it was a wonder poor Lady Neville had not ended up in an insane asylum, considering who her husband was.

His mother did not like Sir Ivor Neville. Though they could hardly be called neighbors, they were among the leading families in Hampshire, and inevitably their paths crossed. He wondered about Sara's family. In their own way, they would have been considered among the leading families in and around Stoneleigh. They were Sir Ivor's nearest neighbors, their house, Longfield, only a mile or two along the road. But Max doubted that Sir Ivor had made friends with Samuel Carstairs. He was too full of his own importance to make a friend of a man who made his money in trade. It must have stuck in his craw when his son and heir married Anne Carstairs.

The butler returned at that moment and indicated that Sir Ivor would see him now. When Max entered the library, Sir Ivor rose from his desk and offered Max his hand, then waved him to an oversized wing armchair that flanked a massive stone fireplace that could have heated a castle. Sir Ivor was dressed formally in blue cutaway coat and breeches. His silver hair was immaculate. Everything about Sir Ivor was immaculate. It was the first time Max had ever thought of William Neville with a twinge of sympathy.

The reporters at Sara's trial had dubbed this man "Sir Prig," and it was an apt description. Tradition and bloodlines were the yardsticks by which Sir Ivor measured the world. He was a proud man. It must have been hard for William Neville to meet his father's standards. Maybe that's why he had married Anne Carstairs—to spite his father.

"This is a pleasure," Sir Ivor said, "and a surprise. I understood from your father that you were spending the summer in Exeter, setting up a newspaper or something."

"Well I was, but the negotiations fell through."

"Ah, so you're taking a well-earned rest from your labors, are you?"

"Not exactly. Nothing for me," Max added when Sir Ivor held up a decanter of brandy and jiggled it invitingly. "I like to keep a clear head when I'm working. But I wouldn't say no to coffee."

Sir Ivor replaced the decanter, snapped his fingers and addressed the footman who stood just inside the door. "See to it, man." As soon as he and Max were alone, he took the chair behind the desk. "All goes well at Castle Lyndhurst, I hope?"

Sir Ivor always spoke as though he and Max's family were intimate friends, and that irritated Max. Keeping his expression bland, he said, "My parents aren't there. They always spend the summer in Derbyshire."

Sir Ivor snapped his fingers. "Of course. They are great hill walkers, are they not?"

Again, Max was annoyed, because he detected a thread of amusement in Sir Ivor's voice, as though hill walking were beneath his dignity. "They like to keep fit," he said, "and keep up with our Derbyshire relations."

Sir Ivor linked his long, thin fingers and rested them on the flat of his desk. "But you did not come into Hampshire just to pass the time of day with me."

"No," said Max. "I came to ask you about your son."

"Has someone claimed the reward?" Sir Ivor asked quickly.

"No."

"What then?"

There was no way of putting this gently. Sara had given him some clues the night he'd climbed in her window, and he had to follow them up. "What can you tell me," he said, "about a young woman, a local girl, who had a child to your son?"

Max had expected shock or anger, but Sir Ivor looked as though he'd turned to stone. All the color washed from his face, and he began to stutter. In the next instant, however, the color surged back in a fiery red, and he said furiously, "What has this to do with William's death?"

"You don't deny it?"

"William did not confide in me."

Sir Ivor rose abruptly, went to the sideboard and poured himself a drink. He bolted the first shot, then poured himself another. When he returned to his chair, he had himself well in hand.

He smiled faintly. "Forgive me. No one likes to hear ill of his son. If William had a child to some local girl, I know nothing about it. I trust you will be discreet. It would break his mother's heart if it got back to her. Who is the girl?"

"I don't know."

"But you'd like to know, wouldn't you? Personally, I don't think it's relevant. I'm not excusing my son's behavior if what you say is true, but many young men sow their wild oats. Regrettable, but not unnatural."

Max said, "I mention the girl only because it's possible that her father or brother may have killed William in revenge."

Sir Ivor shook his head. "You're on the wrong track. Sara Carstairs murdered my son." He sat back in his chair and his shrewd eyes narrowed on Max. "Who told you about this girl?"

"A reliable source. That's all I can tell you."

"Oh, no. It was her, wasn't it? It was Sara Carstairs!"

Max shifted restlessly.

"You had that from her, didn't you?" Then incredulously. "You've found her, questioned her, and she's trying to shift the blame onto someone else."

Max didn't confirm or deny it. "All I'm trying to do," he said, "is tie up a few loose ends."

"But why now? The case has been inactive for three years. Oh, no, you've found Sara Carstairs. Nothing else makes sense."

So much, Max thought, *for trying to keep Sara's name out of it.* Peter Fallon would have handled this much better. "Yes, I found her," he admitted reluctantly.

"She's here in Stoneleigh? My God, she'll be stoned when the local people get to hear of it."

"No. She's not here. She's still in hiding. And that's all I'm going to tell you."

"I see." Sir Ivor's face twisted in a sneer. "You're a fool if you believe anything that jade tells you."

Max kept his voice and expression neutral. "I'm only trying to get at the truth."

"I'm surprised she would confide in you. Your paper has hardly shown her much sympathy in the past."

"She doesn't know I'm connected to the *Courier*."

There was a silence, then Sir Ivor began to laugh. "Ah, now I begin to understand. I doubt if your father would approve of your methods, but I most certainly do. I know she cannot be tried again for William's murder . . ." His voice turned husky. "But if she can lead you to his remains, his mother and I will be forever in your debt."

He cleared his throat. "What else can I tell you?"

*L*ADY NEVILLE WAS WAITING IN THE LIBRARY when her husband returned after seeing Max out. He frowned when he saw that she was in her invalid chair. More and more of late, she'd taken to using the chair when the doctor said there was no necessity for it. It was all in her mind, Dr. Laurie said, a kind of hysteria, the result of losing first a daughter, then a son, under tragic circumstances.

Sir Ivor kissed her on the cheek and nodded a dismissal to the burly footman who was his wife's personal servant.

"You're looking well today, Jessica."

"Beckett wheeled me around the gardens. I think the fresh air did me some good."

She gave Sir Ivor a brilliant smile when he handed her a glass of sherry. "Thank you, dear."

Her figure was slight, almost frail; her features were as regular and as dainty as those of a china doll. There were lines on her face, but they hardly showed. As the years passed, her ladyship had become more adept in her use of powder and paint to preserve her youthful complexion. If there was silver in her pale blond hair, no one would have known it. She was dressed in primrose muslin, the color that Sir Ivor had told her, thirty years before, made her skin glow like warm honey.

"You would do better," Sir Ivor said, "to walk around the gardens. Jessica, you really must try not to give in to these foolish fancies. Dr. Laurie says—"

He stopped when her face fell and she looked at him with the hurt of a child. Once, he'd found her childlike innocence attractive. It was many years since it had begun to grate on him.

Berating her didn't do any good. "I'm sorry," he said. "I know you do your best. What is it you wished to say to me?"

The careless compliment did the trick, and the radiant smile appeared again. "I saw Lord Maxwell Worthe arriving when I was in the rose garden. What did he want, Ivor? Is it something to do with William?"

He could easily have put her off, but knew that if he did, she would only start questioning the servants, and servants' hall gossip was something he would not tolerate.

"He has found Sara Carstairs," he said. "She's still in hiding, but he's found her. I don't know what good it will do. She hasn't confessed, and even if she did, she can't be tried again. And it won't bring William back to us."

Her thin lips formed a round O.

"Jessica, did you hear me?"

Her eyes focused on his face. "Maybe she'll tell Lord Maxwell where she hid William's body."

He shook his head. "Not the Sara Carstairs I know, not the woman I saw at the trial. She's as hard as nails. Accept it, Jessica. We're never going to find out what happened to William."

She nodded, but her lips trembled, and her faded blue eyes filled with tears. He knew better than to try and comfort her. The tears would turn into a deluge.

But tears or not, he had something of importance to say to her. "The vicar was here earlier."

Her tears dried. "Oh?"

"He tells me that you and the Carstairs women have become quite friendly."

"The Carstairs women?" she asked innocently. "Do you mean Mrs. Carstairs and Anne?"

"Don't prevaricate with me," he snapped. "You know I do."

The childlike innocence was replaced by childish petulance. "We're in the ladies' guild. We are making plans for the Stoneleigh Fair. What would you have me do? Ignore them? Is that Christian? Besides, I don't go to Longfield, and I don't invite them here. We meet only in church. You told me I should go out and about more, and that's what I did. Have you changed your mind?"

"I thought you had more sense than to take up with any of that vipers' brood."

She looked down at her glass of sherry. "What should I do, then? Shall I resign from the guild?"

"No. That would only start gossip, and there has been enough of that already. Be careful, Jessica. Be very careful. Don't tell them anything, least of all that Lord Maxwell was here today. If you do, they'll only warn Sara Carstairs, and Lord Maxwell will get nothing more out of her."

She pounced on this. "Do you think Lord Maxwell will succeed where everyone else has failed?"

"It's highly unlikely." Her tears wore him down. "Maybe."

She put her index finger to her mouth. "My lips are sealed."

*H*ER LIPS WERE SEALED EXCEPT WITH THE PERson she considered her most trusted confidant, her footman, Beckett, the young man who carried her up and down stairs and saw to her comfort.

"Sara Carstairs," she said, "has come out of hiding. That

nice newspaperman, Lord Maxwell, has found her. She won't tell him anything, of course. But still, it's a step in the right direction."

She saw the gleam of satisfaction in his dark eyes and her own eyes sparkled. "Do you know what I think, Beckett? I think Sara Carstairs will be back in Stoneleigh before long. We have only to be patient, then we'll both get what we want."

"Yes, m'lady."

"How much does the reward in the *Courier* stand at now?"

"Five thousand pounds," he replied.

"And it will be yours, if we play our cards right. Now run along. I want to rest before dinner. I'll ring for you when I need you."

In the privacy of her own parlor, she did not use her invalid chair. Sir Ivor rarely entered this wing of the house. If she were to die tonight and Beckett was not around, it would be days before anyone noticed her absence, and longer than that before her husband noticed.

Tears formed at the ends of her lashes and she dashed them away. She did everything in her power to make herself pleasing to her husband, but what used to appeal to him was now tiresome. He'd told her that she could always depend on him, but it wasn't true. She'd learned that the older men got, the younger the females they lusted after.

She never made a scene, because Sir Ivor hated scenes. But she also knew what her husband wanted more than anything, and she was going to give it to him. Then she would be his pet again.

The tears vanished as she thought of how grateful he would be. He would lavish her with attention, and she would give up using her invalid chair.

She couldn't do it without Beckett, and she blessed the day that fate had sent him to her door seeking a position as a footman. She'd known at once that he was all wrong. He was too good-looking, too bold, too ambitious, and he did not have a character reference. She'd made enquiries and found that he'd been dismissed from his last post for making love to his master's daughter.

He was all wrong, and that made him just right for her purposes.

She unlocked a door and entered a tiny chapel. The windows were high up on the stone walls and the light did not penetrate to the floor. At the altar, she halted. There were two miniature portraits on stands, one of her daughter, Caroline, and the other of her son.

She picked up Caroline's portrait first. A solemn young girl stared back at her. Poor Caroline. She'd always been sickly. They'd taken her to the best physicians, as far afield as London, but they could do nothing for her. She'd died in London of a lung fever when she was sixteen years old. But at least Caroline had a grave in Stoneleigh's churchyard. There was comfort in that. William had nothing.

She replaced Caroline's portrait and looked at her son. "Soon," she told him, "we'll find you. I promise you, William. And you know that Mama never breaks her promises."

𝓟ETER FALLON WATCHED HIS EMPLOYER PACE back and forth in front of the empty grate. They were in a private parlor in the Cat and Fiddle in Stoneleigh, having just opened a bottle of burgundy while waiting for their dinner to arrive. Max had asked a few perfunctory questions about how things had gone in Exeter, but it was evident that the *Exeter Chronicle* was of little interest to Max now. Peter wasn't surprised. Sara Carstairs had always been something of an obsession with Max.

Peter was a lean man with light brown hair that was already beginning to recede at the temples, making him look older than his years. His face was far from handsome, but it was a pleasant face, warm, friendly, the kind of face that, as Peter freely admitted, served him well in his profession. His clothes were costly and well-tailored, and chosen to be neither in nor out of fashion. He wasn't the kind of man who stood out in a crowd, and that, too, had served him well in his profession.

On Max's instructions, he'd spent the day interviewing a lot of tiresome people who didn't want to be interviewed. He'd been tired when Max had walked in, but now he was wide awake. They'd finally got her. Sara Carstairs had crawled out of her hiding place, and the *Courier* had got to her first.

He was jubilant.

It was an act of God, Max said. He'd climbed through the wrong window, and there she was.

"Sara Carstairs."

"She's calling herself Sara Childe," Max said, "but I recognized her."

"And she doesn't know who you are?"

"She knows I'm Max Worthe, but not that I'm connected to the *Courier*. Not yet, anyway."

Peter let out a low whistle. "This could be tricky."

Max smiled. "Peter, you don't know just how tricky this is."

Peter looked at Max closely. "You don't look too happy."

Max shrugged. "I haven't figured out how I'm going to handle this. There's more at stake here than you realize."

"I don't see why you're worried. She can't be tried again for the same crime."

"That's what I keep telling myself."

Max then went on to tell Peter about his interview with Sir Ivor. "When I put it to him that William had fathered a child on a local girl, his face went purple. I was astounded at his reaction. After all, no one ever claimed William was lily white."

"Perhaps not, but parents always think their children are

blameless. Frankly, Max, I don't think it's relevant either. But I'll check it out if it makes you feel better."

"Thank you. Now what have you found out?"

The serving maid entered with the first course, and as they tucked into lamb stew and dumplings, Peter made his report. Stoneleigh, he said, was shut up tighter than a clam.

"The locals," he went on, "don't want to talk about Sara Carstairs or to anyone who had anything to do with the trial. You see, Max, last time around, they were famous. People and reporters from all over England converged on this little market town and interviewed the residents. It went to their heads. Everyone had a story to tell about Sara Carstairs and William Neville, and if you didn't have a story, you made one up, just to be the same as everyone else. Are you with me, so far?"

Max said slowly, "I think so. You're saying that the stories circulating about Sara were exaggerated?"

"Exactly. And some of those stories may have been out-and-out lies. A damn shame, I know, but remember, these juicy tidbits of gossip had no bearing on the trial. The circumstantial evidence against Sara Carstairs was, and still is, substantial. I still think she's guilty, Max."

"Go on. What else have you learned?"

"Well, take that story about her fiancé, for instance, Francis Blamires. The rumor was that he broke the engagement when she was arrested. In fact, it was the other way round."

"Whatever happened to Blamires?"

"Oh, he married and moved away. He's farming in Kent or someplace."

After a moment, Max said, "What about William's friends, the ones who testified at the trial?"

"There weren't locals. They'd come down from London at William's invitation. You know the sort, hangers-on. William put them up at the King's Head, no expense spared. No one knows where they are now."

Max said, "If Stoneleigh is as tight as a clam, where did you get all your information?"

"If I told you my methods, you could dispense with my services. Then where would I be? Now don't look like that, Max. I didn't do anything illegal."

"Peter—"

Peter laughed. "The local constable told me most of it. We shared a jug of ale in this very inn, and I told him I'd been looking for somewhere to settle, but the local people were so unfriendly that I didn't think I could be happy here. So, he proceeded to tell me why Stoneleighers—that's what they're called, by the way—are so tight-lipped around strangers."

"No one remembered you from before?"

"Hardly. That was three years ago, and I know how to melt into the background. If I didn't, I wouldn't be any good at my job."

"So what else did you learn?"

"Well, after the trial, the good people of Stoneleigh thought that things would go back to normal. By this time, Miss Carstairs was home and living with her family. But things didn't return to normal, largely because William Neville's father had posted a reward for information leading to his son's whereabouts. Hordes of people descended on the village. The residents couldn't turn around but they were falling over strangers who were poking around cellars and disused farm buildings or digging up gardens and farmers' fields. And when the *Courier* doubled the reward, that's when things turned ugly."

Peter stopped speaking when Max abruptly reached for the burgundy and refilled their glasses. "You couldn't have known that this would be the result," Peter said.

Max looked up briefly. "No. I couldn't have known. Finish what you were saying, something about things turning ugly."

Peter was beginning to wish he hadn't opened his

mouth. He knew Max well enough to recognize that he was stone cold angry, and that anger was turned against himself.

"Well?" said Max.

"Well," said Peter, belatedly choosing his words with care, "a party of young bucks, thugs, really, descended on the Carstairs's house. They'd been drinking. They had guns and demanded that Sara Carstairs show them where she'd hidden William's body. They fired shots through the windows. Luckily, no one was hurt, and when someone inside the house returned their fire, they backed off. But they weren't done yet. They found the dower house in the grounds, the house where Anne and William Neville once lived, and set fire to it. The next day, Sara Carstairs left Stoneleigh and went into hiding."

Peter took a long swallow of wine. He was tempted now, to kick his own backside. What had started off as a joke had turned flatter than stale ale, and he didn't know why. It was time to veer off in another direction.

"Do you know what I think, Max? I think she's making for Stoneleigh."

"That doesn't seem likely after what you've just told me."

"But that happened years ago, right after the trial. Things are different now. The locals are ashamed of the way they behaved then. They'll accept her, or they'll tolerate her, at least as long as the curiosity seekers stay away."

"That's not what Sir Ivor says. He says the locals will stone her."

"Oh, no. That's wishful thinking on his part."

"Why would she go home?"

"Maybe she's tired of living under an assumed name."

"Then why is she traveling as Miss Childe?"

Peter let out a long sigh. "I have no idea. All I know is what my nose is telling me: she's coming home. Look, she came all the way from London to Bath, where she's staying for a few weeks. Maybe she's waiting to make sure that no one is following her. Or maybe she's waiting for someone—a husband, a lover—who knows what she's been up to during the last three years? But my nose tells me she's coming home. Bath is only a day's drive from Stoneleigh. She's coming in, slowly and carefully, but believe me, she's coming in."

Max stared at the amber liquid in his glass. "You're convinced she's guilty?"

"Nothing has made me change my mind on that point. What happened to her at Stoneleigh after the trial was reprehensible. I truly regret it. And maybe William Neville was a swine. But that doesn't change anything. Sara Carstairs was involved with him. She's never denied it. And—"

Max held up a hand. "Stow it, Peter. I'm not a fool. I'm not swayed by feminine wiles. I want to know only one thing—is William Neville alive or dead?"

"And if she leads us to his body?"

Max brushed his hand over his sleeve. "Then we'll know she's guilty, and we'll publish the full story in the *Courier*." He looked at his watch. "I'd better get going while it's still light. I may make it as far as Salisbury before dusk."

"You're returning to Bath straight away?"

"Of course."

"What do you want me to do?"

"Stay here and wait for Miss Carstairs. What cover are you using?"

"Mmm? Oh, that I'm just getting over a respiratory infection and my doctors have advised me to convalesce in the fresh country air. But what about you? Where will you be?"

Max drained his glass. After a moment, he said, "If you see a shadow with Sara Carstairs, Peter, you'll know it's me."

Eight

SARA STUDIED HER REFLECTION IN THE LONG cheval mirror. As befitted a lady's companion, her high-waisted gown was of gray crepe and had long sleeves. Her hair was swept up and demurely covered in a lace cap. She'd achieved her object. She looked much older than her years, a staid, sensible lady who knew exactly what she was doing.

She was nervous, very nervous, because tonight she was going to reveal to her best prospect, Mr. Townsend, that she was the lady who had placed the advertisement in the *Chronicle*. He would ask questions that she didn't want to answer, but one thing she couldn't get around. She had to tell him who she really was. The name on her marriage certificate had to be her own. It had to stand up in a court of law if ever it were put to the test.

Just as the marriage settlement had to stand up in a court of law if ever it were put to the test. She had it rolled up in her reticule, a document that her London attorneys had assured her was as binding as any business contract. She wondered what Mr. Townsend would make of it all.

He'd answered her advertisement, she reminded herself. Only a man in desperate circumstances would go that far. There was every chance that he would accept her offer.

Over the last two days, they'd had several conversations, and with each conversation, she'd come to like him more. He spoke mostly about his children, occasionally about his wife. He was a nice man, and if only he could have been her uncle or her father, she would have been the happiest girl in the world.

The other applicants to her advertisement hadn't impressed her one bit. They'd practically ignored her because she was only a lady's companion, a paid servant, and not worth bothering about. She knew that she should be grateful that her little deception had worked. As a mere companion, she faded into the background while Miss Beattie held center stage. Even the conversations with Mr. Townsend had included Miss Beattie. No one had sought her out for herself. No one seemed to see her as a person in her own right.

Except Max Worthe. Lord Maxwell, she corrected. He'd been gone for two days, and she never expected to see him again. He'd finally accepted that there could never be anything between them, and he'd graciously left the field.

Now that she didn't have to worry about him, it was safe to admit that she missed him. Corinthian or no, she liked him, really liked him. She even liked his tasseled boots and his foppish neckcloth with its pretty bow. He said the most outrageous things that no lady should permit. He teased her, and that was a new experience for her. Perhaps, if things had been different, he could have taught her how to tease, too.

If things had been different. It happened all the time. Penniless aristocrats married heiresses whose fathers had made their money in trade. It had nearly happened to her. But Sara Carstairs, whom everyone believed was a murderess, was no one's idea of a bargain. Then again, neither was Max. He'd told her that his title was a courtesy title. She was curious, of course, but she'd stifled her questions because she feared that if she and Max became too involved, their parting would be that much harder to bear, at least on her part.

The less they both knew about each other, the better it would be in the long run. She was going to lock Max away in the deepest, darkest corner of her heart and remember him fondly from time to time. And that's all he could ever be, a distant, pleasant memory.

And there would be no regrets.

Miss Beattie was waiting for her in the front hall. She looked very smart in a dark blue gown and matching bonnet. Poor Bea had been quite cast down since Max had deserted them. She couldn't be made to see that he was a dangerous complication.

"Ready?" Miss Beattie asked quietly.

"Quite ready. Where is Mrs. Hastings?"

"She went on ahead with Miss Perry and Mrs. Harman."

"Then let's get started."

They were on their way to Sydney Gardens, to take in a concert and afterwards, when the sun had set, a fireworks display.

And that's when she would slip away to the Sydney Hotel and seal her bargain with Mr. Townsend.

$\mathcal{M}$AX DID THE RETURN TRIP TO BATH IN record time, and he gave the postilions of his hired chaise a handsome gratuity for living up to their promise. His first order of business when he entered his hotel was to ask the landlord to arrange for one of the hotel's footmen to be assigned personally to him. He was tired of haring back and forth across England in wretched hired carriages with broken springs, and tired of waiting his turn with servants who did not belong to him. And if that made him undemocratic, he could live with it.

The landlord noted the arrogant cast of his lordship's profile, the cold blue eyes and the smile that wasn't quite a smile, and he touched his forelock before he was aware of what he was doing.

That was the trouble with the quality, he told his wife as he personally saw to the drawing of his lordship's bath. They could be nice to you one minute and turn on you the next. And there was no redress, because they held all the cards. If you answered them back, they would tell all their friends, and after that, no one of any consequence would darken your doors. Then where would they be?

The footman he assigned to Max was his son and heir, and because Rollo had a vested interest in keeping his lordship satisfied, Max found himself, less than an hour later, bathed, changed and fortified with one of the best beefsteak sandwiches he had ever tasted.

The service improved his temper. It also tweaked his conscience. He hadn't been raised to lord it over his subordinates. He salved his conscience by leaving another large gratuity in his wake, then went to find the landlord and his wife, to compliment the astonished couple on their excellent establishment.

He left the hotel with a smile on his face, but as he struck out along the High Street and made the turn to the Pulteney Bridge, his smile soon faded. He was thinking about his meeting with Peter Fallon, and Peter had given him much to think about.

Maybe she's waiting for someone—a husband, a lover—who knows what she's been up to in the last three years?

I'm going to be married, Max.

He hadn't believed her, but after his conversation with Peter, he was seeing things in a different light. She hadn't come to Bath for the good of her health. If she was going home to Stoneleigh, then why was she hanging around here?

I'm going to be married, Max.

The more he thought about it, the more his suspicions bubbled over like a pot of burning stew.

Ahead of him, lights blazing from every window, was

the Sydney Hotel, and beyond that, Sydney Gardens, with lanterns strung from tree to tree. Before he'd left Bath, Miss Beattie had informed him that she and Sara would be here tonight to see the fireworks display. In fact, she'd practically invited him along.

After paying his subscription, he halted just inside the gates. It was after ten o'clock and almost dark enough for the fireworks to begin. The orchestra was still playing, however, and the strains of a country air carried to him above the laughter and singing. People were strolling about, admiring the elaborate illuminations that adorned the fountains and shrubbery.

This was Bath at its wildest, Max thought, and grinned.

He found his quarry, sans Sara, on the sweep of lawns where the orchestra was playing. Miss Beattie and Mrs. Hastings had availed themselves of one of the many benches that had been set out for spectators.

Mrs. Hastings saw him first, and letting out a squeal of delight, waved him over. Miss Beattie's face registered nothing but shock.

"I thought you had left Bath for good," Miss Beattie said as he bowed over her hand.

"Didn't I mention that I'd be back in a day or two?"

"Yes, but—" She shrugged helplessly. "Young people sometimes say one thing and do another."

Max searched Miss Beattie's face. She seemed tense, and, at the same time, now that her shock was beginning to wear off, genuinely glad to see him.

Mrs. Hastings drew his eyes to her. "If only we'd known you were returning in time for this gala evening, Lord Maxwell, we would have invited you to our little party after the fireworks." She smiled coyly. "I don't suppose you'd care to join four or five ladies for a bite of supper in the Sydney Hotel?" Her hand flew to her mouth. "I beg your pardon, Miss Beattie. I quite forgot that this is your treat."

Miss Beattie's smile was strained around the edges. "Of course you're invited, Lord Maxwell, but you won't hurt our feelings if you turn us down. I'm sure a young man can find better things to do than entertain a gaggle of elderly ladies."

"A hen party?" said Max. "Oh, no, I'd only be in the way." Then he added innocently, "But won't Miss Childe be there?"

His question seemed to throw Miss Beattie into some confusion. "Sara?" She looked around her as though she expected Sara to suddenly emerge from the crowds.

Her sigh, to Max's ears, sounded resigned, but when she looked up at him, it wasn't resignation he saw in her eyes, but something akin to hope.

"Of course Sara will be there," she said. "In fact, she's there now, in the private parlor I reserved in the hotel, making sure that everything will go off perfectly for our little supper. She doesn't care for fireworks, you see, so she offered to take care of things."

Having discovered what he wished to know, as he was sure Miss Beattie had already deduced, he made some idle remarks on the orchestra and gardens, then strolled away.

When he'd turned his steps toward the Sydney Hotel, he had a shrewd idea that Miss Beattie's blessing went with him.

At the front desk, he asked for the private parlor reserved in Miss Beattie's name. Five minutes later, he pushed through the door, and the sight that met his eyes made his temper explode.

Sara was in some man's arms, and that man was kissing her on the brow. Max sent the door back on its hinges with an almighty crash. The couple broke apart with a guilty start.

"Max!" Sara breathed out.

Max sauntered into the room, the glitter in his eyes at

odds with the smile on his face. "Mr. Townsend, is it not?" He made an elegant bow, which Mr. Townsend acknowledged with a slight inclination of his head. "I was sent by Miss Beattie," Max drawled, "to chaperon the chaperon, and that puts me in an awkward position. As a rule, I wouldn't interfere, but you see how it is."

Mr. Townsend said stiffly, "Sir, I hope you recognize an innocent kiss when you see it."

"Of course," replied Max in the same grating drawl. "I knew it was innocent, you being, Mr. Townsend, old enough to be this lady's father." He paused. "You were on the point of leaving, I believe?"

Mr. Townsend flushed scarlet, and that got Sara's dander up. She deliberately turned her back on Max and offered Mr. Townsend her hand. Smiling up at him, she said warmly, "Good night, Mr. Townsend, and I do thank you for . . . for everything." She turned to Max. "And now, gentlemen, if you'll both excuse me, I have work to do."

"Max said, "May I help?"

"No, you may not!"

"Then I'll wait quietly for Miss Beattie to arrive. It's what she expects of me. Good night, Mr. Townsend."

Mr. Townsend looked at Max, opened his mouth as if to say something, then, thinking better of it, bowed curtly and quit the room.

Ignoring Max, Sara began to fuss with the cutlery and napkins on the table. Max strolled to the sideboard, lifted the cover from a silver server and began to munch on a chunk of cucumber that was filled with chopped apple and dates. When he was finished, he started on another.

When Sara could bear the silence no longer, she stopped fussing and looked directly into Max's eyes. "I don't believe Miss Beattie sent you here to chaperon me."

"Well," acknowledged Max, "she didn't use those exact words, but I could see that she was worried about you. So when she told me where you were, I took it upon myself to offer my protection."

"I'm in more need of protection from you than from Mr. Townsend."

The glitter in Max's eyes had long since faded. Now they were brilliant with laughter. "If that means I wouldn't kiss you as Mr. Townsend kissed you, you're right."

She gave him a cool stare, then went back to fussing.

Max came away from the sideboard. "What did Townsend want?"

"Nothing. He saw me come in here, and came in to exchange a few words. He was only being polite."

"And what did you thank him for?"

"We got talking about books and he offered to lend me some. All right?"

"And why did he kiss you?"

There was a challenge in the way she lifted her chin. "I had just told him that I was to be married soon, and he was wishing me well. Not that it's any of your business."

"Ah, the phantom suitor again. At least, I hope he's a phantom, for your sake as well as his."

"I don't know what you mean."

"Don't you? You know, you're far too young to wear those lace caps. Is that supposed to put me off?"

Before she could evade him, he plucked the cap from her head, dislodging pins, and her hair tumbled down in a cascade of waves.

He grasped her shoulders. "Why is Miss Beattie worried about you, Sara?"

"You're talking nonsense, Max."

His hands brushed along her arms and slid around her waist. "There's only one language you seem to understand."

He brought his lips to hers in a kiss as chaste as the one Mr. Townsend had given her, only Max's kiss made her come alive. She'd known he was going to kiss her, and this time she was prepared. She fought the onslaught on her senses—the heaviness behind her eyes, the need to cling to him, the weakness that made her bones turn to water—she fought his power with the only weapon she possessed, her formidable self-control.

It was an effective weapon. When Max lifted his head, she was sure she had won, and she let out a relieved breath.

Laughter filled his eyes. "Sara," he said softly, "that won't work either."

The arms at her waist tightened, pulling her flush against his body, and his mouth came down hard on hers. This time he wasn't wooing her, he was taking possession, and her formidable self-control began to crack.

His fingers plowed into her hair and held her fast. Her mouth was soft, pliable; her body flowed over his. He could feel the current of passion sucking them both under. He wanted to take her here, right now, on the floor.

Thunder and lightning seemed to explode overhead. His power awed her. But at the next explosion of thunder and lightning, rational thought returned. Desire gradually receded, and her shoulders began to shake.

When Max released her lips, she choked out between gurgles of laughter, "I thought it was you! I thought it was you!"

She pushed out of his arms and waved toward the window.

"I thought it was you. And it was only a few fireworks going off."

Max's frown gradually melted, and he began to laugh, too.

Max was captivated by the sprite she had turned into. There were more facets to this woman than in a priceless diamond, and each one intrigued him. Now he understood the connoisseur's passion to possess. He would give just about anything to have her.

When he stepped toward her, her laughter died, but she held her ground. He cupped her cheek. "That's how it will be when we finally come together," he said. "I promise you fireworks."

Her eyes flashed then darkened. "My no is final, Max."

"Then make me believe it, Sara. Make me believe it."

When she stared at him doggedly, he patted her cheek as Mr. Townsend might, and strolled from the room.

He wasn't interested in the fireworks display, and when he reached the ground floor, he entered the taproom. The room swarmed with gentlemen who, Max gathered from the jokes that were flying around, had stolen away from their womenfolk while their eyes were on the sky, gentlemen who hoped to steal back again before their absence was noticed.

He ordered a neat brandy and, with one elbow on the bar counter, surveyed the room. He knew next to nobody in Bath, but the one face he did recognize, a gentleman he'd been introduced to in the Pump Room, rose from a table and began to weave his way toward the bar.

Bloor was the name, Max remembered, and he smelled of horses. On this occasion, Mr. Bloor smelled only of strong spirits.

"The same again," he told the barmaid in a belligerent tone of voice.

Max moved over to give Mr. Bloor room.

"Damned impertinence," muttered Mr. Bloor. When the barmaid handed him a half tumbler of whiskey, he drank lustily. His next few utterances were unintelligible, but when his eyes focused on Max, he said clearly, "It's Mr. Maxwell, is it not?"

"Close enough," replied Max.

"That's what I thought. We met . . . I forget where we met."

"In the Pump Room," said Max.

Mr. Bloor took another healthy swig of whiskey. "Blast and damn them all," he declared and wiped his mouth on his sleeve.

"Who?" asked Max without much interest. He was scanning the patrons to see if Mr. Townsend was among them. He'd been rude to the man, and he wanted to make it up to him by buying him a drink. Jealous of an old fogy like Townsend! His friends would laugh themselves silly if they knew how low he had sunk.

"Who?" demanded Bloor, glowering at Max. "Who? The whole regiment of women! Damn and blast them all, that's what I say. If I were not a gentleman, I would have laid her across my knee and walloped her backside."

"I know the feeling," commiserated Max.

It was time to go. Townsend was not here, Bloor was becoming a nuisance, and the taproom was beginning to empty now that the fireworks display was over.

"Lady Hoity Toity!" simpered Bloor, then roughly, "How was I to know she wasn't the one? Haig thought so too. And hasn't she been flirting with every man in breeches? I did no more than the major did, and she damn near broke my nose, just because I kissed her."

A slow, reminiscent smile curled Max's mouth. "She told *me*," he said, "that my kisses were like fireworks."

Bloor stared at him with open suspicion. "Who is she? That's what I'd like to know. At first, I thought it was Miss Beattie, but she's not well-lined in the pocket, or she wouldn't be staying with Mrs. Hastings. Then I thought it was Dame Hoity Toity, you know, Mrs. Penwarren. She spends money like water. But she said she didn't know anything about an advertisement. That was after she hit me on the nose. What in hell's name do women keep in their reticules—slabs of granite?"

It was Miss Beattie's name that sharpened Max's interest. Detecting an air of hostility in the other man, he said carefully, "The advertisement? I see. You must have misunderstood."

"Well, she didn't sign her name, if that's what you mean, but there aren't too many ladies in Bath with the wherewithal to buy themselves a husband. I wonder who she chose."

"Not me," said Max. He sipped his drink and waited.

Mr. Bloor stared at him, then smiled. "Well, I know that. You're just a stripling, and she wanted someone older."

"How do you know?"

"I know how to read between the lines. A gentleman of character, she wanted, didn't she? Age and fortune immaterial. And here I am ready to oblige." He drained his glass. "The trouble is, she has half the men in Bath only too willing to oblige, marriage of convenience or no." He dug Max in the ribs with his elbow and winked slyly. "Marriage of convenience be damned. She'd soon change her mind once I gave her a taste of it." A thought suddenly occurring to him, he exclaimed. "And you kissed her, you say?"

"No," said Max. "That was a different lady."

He stood there quietly, fitting together the fragments of Bloor's conversation: she wanted a man with character, age and fortune immaterial; her pockets were well-lined; she'd placed an advertisement in the paper; a marriage of convenience.

He was thinking of Miss Beattie, and it didn't add up. But it didn't add up with Sara, either. He couldn't figure out why she would go to such lengths.

All the same, it made him uneasy, and he made up his mind to do a little investigating.

The following morning, he started with the *Chronicle,* since, in his experience, newspapermen knew far more than they dared print in their newspapers, and Tom Kent, the *Chronicle*'s publisher, did not disappoint him. At the *Chronicle,* they were betting that the mystery woman who had placed the advertisement was Miss Beattie for the simple reason that it was her serving girl who had picked up the replies. But it wasn't Miss Beattie whom Max had surprised in a tête-à-tête with Townsend at the Sydney Hotel, and he reached his own conclusion.

Kent was as equally candid about Townsend, but only because he was talking to another newspaperman and knew he could count on Max's discretion. And what he told Max made his hair stand on end.

But Max did not let it rest there. He used his considerable charm to dig even deeper, and when his charm failed, he used bribery and corruption. At the end of three days, he had gathered enough evidence to convince himself that the prospect of Sara's marrying Townsend was anything but fantastic.

She was going to marry a man twice her age! Did she know about his debts? His character? Did she care?

What in hell's name was she up to?

Nine

SARA DID NOT BEGIN TO RELAX UNTIL HER chaise was well clear of Bath. Her destination was the small cathedral town of Wells. Mr. Townsend had left that morning, but she had decided to wait for cover of darkness. She didn't want anyone to see her. If anyone called at their lodgings, Bea would say that she'd already retired for the night. And in the morning, it wouldn't matter what Bea said. She'd be married to Mr. Townsend.

He was already in Wells, setting things up. He had the special license; he'd found a minister to marry them, and he'd arranged accommodations at the Angel in the High Street. Tonight, he would sign the marriage contract, and tomorrow she would become Mrs. Townsend.

It was too easy. Everything was going too smoothly.

Mr. Townsend had capitulated almost at once. The sum of money he'd asked for was well below what she was willing to offer. When she'd told him her real name, he'd been shocked, of course, but he was far more anxious about *her* future prospects than his own. It hadn't been easy to make him believe that this was no sacrifice on her part. She would never want to marry.

Max, her heart seemed to cry out.

Dear God, what was the matter with her? Everything was working out exactly as she'd planned. She should be glad; she shouldn't be plagued by all these uncertainties. Max Worthe was a dangerous complication, and that's all he was.

End of story.

End of something that should never have started.

She was so cold that she was shivering. Just a half hour before, she'd removed her coat because she was too hot. She shrugged into it and did up all the buttons, then she stared out the window.

There was nothing to see but the hedgerows that were picked out by the light from the chaises's box lamps. It couldn't be much longer now. Wells was only a two-hour drive from Bath, three hours at the most in these conditions. And in the morning, after the clergyman married them, Mr. Townsend would return to Bath, and she would set out for Salisbury, where Bea would catch up to her.

She wasn't running away anymore. She was going home to face all her demons.

IT WAS RAINING WHEN THEY ARRIVED AT THE Angel. The doorman, who seemed to be watching for her, came forward with an umbrella as she paid off her postboys. She had only one box and a leather bag that she insisted on carrying herself.

The hotel was much like the Christopher where Max was staying. It was of Tudor origin, with small rooms and long narrow corridors. Her chamber looked down on the courtyard. She was on the point of opening the window when she remembered another courtyard and another hotel.

She shut her mind to thoughts of Max, latched the window, and threw her bag on the nearest chair. It did not take her long to tidy herself. Then she picked up her bag and made her way downstairs to the front desk. The private parlor that Mr. Townsend had reserved was, the clerk told her, on the ground floor at the back of the hotel. She would find Mr. Townsend there.

She took a deep breath and pinned a smile on her face before entering the parlor. The sight that met her eyes froze her on the spot. A chair was overturned, and Mr. Townsend was slumped in a chair holding a blood-soaked handkerchief to his nose. Her gaze shifted to the figure who was negligently propped with one arm along the mantelpiece while he sipped from a glass of amber liquid.

Max.

She felt the blood drain from her face; her pulse slowed and she reached for the back of a chair. Any last, lingering doubts slipped away. She'd been right to be afraid. Max Worthe was unpredictable and more dangerous than a jungle cat.

As though oblivious to the carnage around him, Max raised his glass in salute. "Miss Childe," he said, "at long last. Townsend and I were beginning to wonder what was keeping you."

Miss Childe. Her fear abated a little. Mr. Townsend had not told Max that she was Sara Carstairs.

When Mr. Townsend made an inarticulate sound, she dropped her bag and hurried to his side. "What's going on? What is Lord Maxwell doing here? Here, let me help you."

Townsend threw off her hand. "I can manage."

Max ground his teeth together. "Don't waste your sympathy on him. He deserved what he got."

"How could you do this?" she cried, then to Townsend, "Shall I fetch a doctor? Are you all right? Speak to me, Mr. Townsend."

Max sounded thoroughly bored. "It's only a bloody nose, for mercy's sake."

She rounded on Max. "I'd like to hear what Mr. Townsend has to say."

"He attacked me," said Townsend. "For no good reason, he attacked me."

"All I did was stop him running away."

Her eyes met Max's. It was so hard to read him sometimes. He always looked easygoing and relaxed. But she'd learned that that was only one facet of his character. Beneath the charming veneer, there was cold, hard steel. His eyes never wavered from hers, intelligent eyes, alert and, right this minute, brilliant with emotion.

Well, if he was angry, so was she, blazingly angry. She said, "What are you doing here, Max? How did you find out about Mr. Townsend and me?"

"I put two and two together," said Max. "It wasn't hard to do, once I grasped the fact that you were the woman who had placed the advertisement in the *Chronicle*. I couldn't believe you would go through with it. But when Townsend left town this morning, I followed him. And here we are. Isn't it cozy?"

She ignored the sarcasm. "That doesn't explain why you're here or why you attacked Mr. Townsend."

"Attacked? Now that is going too far. I . . . ah . . . restrained him. You see, Sara, when the doorman came to tell us that you were in the hotel, your intended here tried to make a bolt for it. I stopped him. I don't think he wants to marry you, Sara, not now."

Though her heart was pounding so hard it seemed to echo in her head, she managed to keep her voice calm and her expression neutral. "Whether Mr. Townsend wishes to marry me or not is none of your business."

"I've made it my business. Listen to me, Sara. The man is in debt up to his neck. He can't marry you for less than forty thousand pounds. *Forty thousand!* Can you afford that? How much did you promise to pay him?"

She shivered, staring at him. "Eight thousand," she said. "That's the sum we agreed on."

Max said quietly, "He won't marry you for a mere eight thousand, Sara. Ask him."

Mr. Townsend's face turned a fiery red. "An allowance of eight thousand pounds a year," he said stiffly. "That's what I meant. But, now that I've had time to think about it, I've had a change of heart."

He rose slowly, carefully, but at Max's approach, he quickly sank back in his chair.

Max bent over Townsend until they were practically nose to nose. "You mean that now I'm here to see that you can't swindle Sara out of her money, you won't go through with it. Tell me, Mr. Townsend, did you ever have any intention of marrying her? How was this swindle going to work?"

Sara cried, "Stop it! Stop threatening him! Why are you keeping him here against his will?"

Max spoke through his teeth. "Because I knew you wouldn't believe anything I told you. Well, Townsend is here. Let him deny if he can that he's drowning in debt. Let's see if he's still willing to marry you for a paltry eight thousand."

Mr. Townsend was beginning to bluster his way out of Max's accusations, and she couldn't take any more. Turning her back on both men, she went to the window that overlooked the courtyard and stared out. She couldn't face what was behind her, the ugliness, the betrayal, so she concentrated on watching the ostlers who where unhitching a pair of bays from a flashy curricle. The ostlers cursed the rain, they cursed the horses, they cursed the driver who had brought them away from their game of dice when all decent people should have been snug in their homes at this ungodly hour.

She was shivering in earnest now, and she wrapped her arms around herself to conceal how shaken she really was.

Max said, "Sara, what do you want me to do with this sniveling coward?"

"Let him go," she said tonelessly. "You've made your point."

There was a hard edge in Max's voice. "I hope you know how lucky you are."

She didn't know whether Max's words were meant for Townsend or herself, so she didn't reply.

Max moved aside, his gaze still on Sara. Mr. Townsend got up, adjusted his rumpled coat and walked to the door. After opening it, he turned to look at Sara. He spoke with dignity. "My motives were pure," he said, "but you might ask yourself about Lord Maxwell's motives. He knows who you are. No, I didn't tell him. He's not the only one who can put two and two together. I think he wants your fortune for himself."

Sara whirled around, and her eyes collided with Max's. He was watching her intently, warily. She shook her head. He shrugged.

"I was going to tell you later," he said, "when we were alone."

"Tell me what?"

He hesitated, then said gently, "I was present at your trial."

"At my trial?" Her voice was barely audible. "You were at my trial?"

"Yes. I know you are Sara Carstairs."

She felt numb with shock; even her tongue seemed frozen and she had trouble articulating her words. "You were one of those dandies who came to gawk at me?"

A muscle tensed in his jaw. "I was there to cover the story for my newspaper. I would have told you even if Townsend hadn't forced my hand. Listen to me, Sara. I couldn't tell you who I was right away because I was afraid you would go into hiding again. There's more to us than the fact that you're Sara Carstairs and I'm a newspaperman. Can't you see that? And I want to help you."

"What paper?" she asked hoarsely.

"We'll talk later."

"What paper?"

There was a silence, then Max said softly, "The *Courier*. I own it, Sara. And publish it."

She had the curious feeling that her mind had exploded, leaving a vacuum inside her head. One hand went out to the window frame as she steadied herself. "The *Courier*," she said weakly.

Mr. Townsend, who had been following this interesting byplay with a smug smile, chose that moment to get off a parting shot. "Watch him, Miss Carstairs. I only wanted money. He'll try to put a noose around your neck."

With a furious oath, Max crossed the room in two strides. Townsend turned and fled along the corridor. Max shut the door, breathed deeply and turned to face Sara. "That's a lie," he said. "And anyway, you were acquitted. You can't be tried again."

Her numbness was beginning to wear off. She felt the blood rushing into her face, and as her mind slowly came together, everything became crystal clear.

Her words were punctuated by the harsh sound of her breathing. "In Reading . . . when you climbed through my window . . . you knew who I was."

"No. It was only in the morning it came to me that I'd seen you before." When he took a step toward her and she flinched, he halted. "What happened in your room that night, I mean what happened between us, was real. It was genuine, Sara, sincere."

Her head jerked back and she stared at him with unconcealed contempt. "There's nothing sincere or genuine about you. You played the role of the bored aristocrat with consummate skill, pretending that you were attracted to me, when all you wanted was a story for your newspaper."

He spoke tersely. "God help me, I *am* attracted to you,

whether I want to be or not. And yes, I wanted the story for the *Courier*. I'm a newspaperman, and I can't change my stripes, not even for you. But I want to help you, Sara."

She crouched as though she would spring at him. "You're the one who's been stalking me all these months. You're the one who's been sending me these terrifying notes."

"What notes? What are you talking about?"

"William!" she burst out. "Don't pretend you don't know." Tears stung her eyes. "From the very beginning, the *Courier* was against me. *You* set yourself up as judge and jury. And having found me guilty, you hounded me. You're still hounding me."

He came toward her with one hand held out in a gesture of appeal, but when she recoiled, he halted again. "Will you calm down and listen to me? I didn't know how difficult I'd made things for you. I swear I didn't know until recently, when I went to see . . ." He stopped in midsentence.

"Whom did you see?"

"One of my reporters, Peter Fallon. I sent him to Stoneleigh to gather information."

"You've been *spying* on me!" she cried out.

"I was trying to help you! You wouldn't tell me anything, so I decided to find out for myself. That's when I heard about the fire at one of your properties and that the reward I'd posted in the *Courier* had—well, had stirred things up. I didn't know, never imagined how much harm it would do. I'm sorry, bitterly sorry, and that's the truth."

"Well, that's just dandy, but if you're looking for absolution, you've come to the wrong person. I shall never forgive you."

"Fine. That's not important now. I want to hear about those notes."

"Why? So you can put a noose around my neck?"

"So I can protect you."

She started to laugh, then cut herself off abruptly.

"Sara," he said softly, placatingly, "let's sit down and talk this through like rational people."

No response.

He tried again. "Tell me about these notes. Did they come from William? Is it William who is stalking you? Is that what you think?"

"Do you really belive I would trust you after all you've done to me?"

"Don't you understand? I'm trying to make amends. Now, where are these notes? I'm warning you, Sara, I'm not giving you a choice. It's gone beyond that. If you're in some kind of danger, I want to know about it."

Alarm raced through her, making her stomach churn. This was the man she feared, relentless, coldly determined to have his own way. He would keep at her and keep at her till he got the truth. Then he really would put a noose around her neck, not in a court of law, but on the front page of the *Courier*.

She knew how to hate, but in that moment, there was no one she had ever hated as much as she hated Max Worthe.

Her shoulders heaved once, twice, then she let out a long shuddering breath. "They're upstairs," she said quietly, "in my room."

He held out his hand. "Give me the key and I'll get them."

She hesitated, then felt in her pocket and produced a key. "They're in my reticule, inside the top drawer of my dresser."

She ignored his outstretched hand and put the key on the table.

Max's lips flattened when she retreated, keeping well out of his reach as he moved to the table to pick up the key. "Sara—"

She turned her back on him.

Wordlessly, Max left the room.

When the door closed and she was alone, she put her fist

to her mouth. Thoughts chased through her head in heedless abandon. Max Worthe had witnessed her trial, had heard all the sordid details about her depraved love affair with William. He'd ruined her life, separated her from her family, and all for a story for his tawdry paper.

The *Courier*.

He would never give up until her got his story.

Without consciously making a decision, she opened the door and stepped into the corridor. The back door leading to the courtyard was on her right. She moved toward it. Outside, the rain was driving down. The only light came from lanterns on the wall. She saw nothing, heard nothing. Her mind was numb.

She didn't stop to take her bearings or take the time to return for her coat. She didn't know or care where she was going. All she wanted was to get away from Max Worthe.

As HE MOUNTED THE STAIRS, MAX CONSIDered how he was going to make things right with Sara. Her anger he could handle, but it was the stricken, haunted look that had come into her eyes when he'd told her he was the *Courier*'s owner that had shattered him. He didn't want to hurt her. The last thing he wanted was to hurt her. He'd had every intention of telling her about his connection to the *Courier* after he'd dealt with Townsend. But Townsend had taken his revenge before he'd had a chance to explain, and now the damage was done.

But it wasn't irreparable. He knew, hoped, he could make her see reason, because he wasn't the only one at fault here. She'd kept secrets from him as well. He would apologize. He was even prepared to grovel, up to a point. But what he would not tolerate were these appalling risks she ran.

She'd received notes from William Neville. Was that what had prompted this insane scheme to marry Townsend? She still had a lot of explaining to do.

He was sick and tired of playing games with Sara and equally sick and tired of all the lies she'd told him in return. But what really made him burn was how far she was prepared to go in this misbegotten scheme that only she understood. He hadn't believed she would go through with it. He'd been confident when it came down to it, her nerve would crack and she wouldn't show up.

And how wrong he'd been!

He found her reticule where she'd told him it would be, and though he was tempted to go through it and read the notes at once, he decided it would be better if Sara gave them to him in person. Then she couldn't accuse him of being underhanded.

When he returned to the parlor, he saw that it was empty. He wasn't alarmed. He had her reticule, and her leather bag was still on the floor where she'd dropped it. If she'd left her bag and reticule, he reasoned, she couldn't be far away. She'd be back for them.

He straightened the chair that had been overturned, poured himself another glass of brandy, a generous one this time, and sat down to wait for her. When ten minutes had passed and she had not appeared, he felt the first stirrings of alarm.

He left the room at once, but halted in the corridor when he saw the back door was ajar. He pushed it open and stepped outside.

There had been no letup in the rain for the last hour, and he turned up his collar for the little protection it gave him. When his eyes became accustomed to the shadows, he saw the ostler on duty standing under the stable eaves.

Max crossed the yard at a run, cursing fluently as the rain dripped down his neck and under his collar, cursing even more furiously when he stepped into one puddle after dodging another.

She couldn't have left the hotel on a wild night like this.

The ostler straightened at Max's approach.

"Did you see anyone leaving the hotel in the last fifteen minutes?" asked Max.

"A gentleman left for Bath in his chaise, but that were near half an hour ago. Mr. Townsend, yes, that was his name."

"Was anyone with him?"

"No. He was alone."

"What about in the last fifteen minutes? Someone on foot?"

The ostler nodded. "A lady, would it be, guv'nor?"

Max's alarm increased tenfold. "Yes, a lady."

"I tried to turn her back, but she paid no mind to me."

"Which way did she go?"

"She went through that there arch and turned right."

Without waiting to hear more, Max dashed through the entrance arch and into the High Street. It was completely deserted, no carriages, no riders, no pedestrians. It didn't surprise him. It was after midnight, and Wells was a small country town. There were few lights shining from windows. The town was shut up for the night.

Then where in Hades was she?

His face was grim when he returned to the hotel.

The first thing he did was go through her reticule. There were no notes. He got his coat and told the desk clerk in his most daunting manner not to lock up the hotel for the night until he returned.

He spent the next hour going from one hostelry to another, but Sara had not registered at any of them, and no one had seen a lady of her description.

$\mathcal{M}$AX WAS RAPIDLY DEPLETING WHAT MUST have been his third or fourth pot of coffee of the night when the knocker on the hotel's front door sounded.

He set down his cup. "I'll go," he told the droopy-eyed clerk whom he'd pressed into staying up with him.

The door was unlocked, but only because he'd insisted. If and when Sara returned, he hadn't wanted any obstacles to stand in the way of her entering the hotel.

When he opened the door, to his great disappointment, it wasn't Sara who stared into his face, but a great beefy man, fiftyish, with dark bushy eyebrows and an even bushier mustache.

"Constable O'Hanalon, here," said the stranger abruptly. "And who might you be?"

"That's Lord Maxwell." Sara came from behind the constable's huge bulk and entered the hotel. "I told you he would vouch for me. This has all been a ghastly mistake."

For one of the few times in his life, Max was speechless. He'd been imagining all sorts of hair-raising scenarios— Sara attacked by ruffians or footpads, her broken body thrown into the river, or worse. And here she was, whole and hearty, while he was a nervous wreck.

"Oh, do shut the door, Max," she said from the lobby. "Constable O'Hanalon wants to talk to you."

"What?"

"Shut the door," she repeated.

Max looked at the door. "Right." He shut the door and joined Sara and the constable in the lobby.

Now that his worst fears were relieved, and Sara seemed none the worse for her rash behavior, he gave free rein to his temper. "Do you know what I've been through these last three hours? Can you imagine what I've suffered not knowing where you were or what had happened to you?"

"I'm sorry, Max. It was only a case of bridal nerves." Her gray eyes beseeched him with unspoken messages, then she went on, "Constable O'Hanalon, this is my betrothed, Lord Maxwell."

"Is that right, sir?" asked the constable. "Are you this lady's betrothed?"

Max's eyes narrowed on Sara. "That remains to be seen," he said. "What scrape has she got herself into now?"

The constable chuckled. "The night watchman found her trying to break into the cathedral."

Sara said, "I thought the door was stuck. It never occurred to me that the cathedral would be locked up for the night. I thought churches were always open, you know, for people in distress."

The constable clicked his tongue. "That may be, ma'am, but you refused to give the watchman your name, or any explanation at all."

"I was"—she looked at Max, then looked away—"upset."

"If you'd told him straight away, you wouldn't have had to spend half the night in the city jail. We would have taken you home at once."

"The city jail?" Max stared at Sara. His voice rose alarmingly. "The city jail? Why didn't you send someone to get me? You must have known how worried I'd be."

Sara's face was pale. "I wasn't thinking."

"Then what *were* you doing?"

"I . . . I fell asleep."

"You *what*?"

Max broke off when the hotel clerk, whom he'd forgotten about, slammed from behind the counter and got between him and Sara.

"Miss Childe," said the clerk, "can I get you something? Coffee? Tea? A sandwich?"

For the first time in a long while, Sara smiled. "Thank you, George. It is George, isn't it? A cup of tea would be very nice."

George flashed Sara a shy smile. "I'll see to it right away, miss. Why don't you make yourself comfortable in the parlor and I'll bring it to you there."

Sara looked at the constable. "Do I have your permission?"

"I suppose it's all right, now that this gentleman is here to look after you. But mind what I told you." He took her hand, enfolding it in both of his. "You were lucky that it was the watchman who found you. A woman alone at night is asking for trouble."

"I'll remember. And I *do* thank you for your kindness to me." Then to Max. "I'll see you in the parlor, then, when you've finished with the constable."

Sara left with the clerk, and in the wake of silence that followed their departure, Max reflected wryly that as far as the constable and the clerk were concerned, he was the guilty party here. He looked at O'Hanalon and knew by the set of the constable's bushy eyebrows that he was in for a scold.

Ten

⁓

TEN MINUTES LATER, WHEN MAX ENTERED THE little parlor, he saw at once that George had not only brought the pot of tea he'd promised Sara, but also a plate of bite-sized sandwiches. And if Max was in any doubt about whose side George was on, the fact that there was only one cup and saucer to go with the tea was an eloquent pointer.

Her leather bag, which he'd left on a chair, was now on the floor by her feet. He'd been tempted to go through it, but to do that, he would have had to break its silver lock, and he had enough black marks against him without adding to them.

He sat beside her at the table and helped himself to one of the tiny sandwiches. Cheese and cucumber stuck to the roof of his mouth, but he managed to swallow it. If George had wanted to punish him, he couldn't have chosen better than cheese and cucumber sandwiches.

"Constable O'Hanalon," he said, "did not mince words. In fact, he tore me to shreds."

She glanced up at him, and quickly looked down at the plate of sandwiches. "I had to tell him you were my be-trothed. He wanted to take me home to my father or my brother. He wouldn't have let me go if he'd known that we weren't related."

"He said I should take better care of you."

"I told him we'd had a lovers' tiff." She put her cup to her lips and sipped cautiously. "It was easier than going into long explanations."

"He also said that you were in shock when you were first brought in. They were worried about you."

Her eyes met his in a long, unfaltering stare. "It brought back memories of another prison, when I was waiting for my trial."

Max's voice took on a rough edge. "If they frightened you, if they threatened you—"

"No! They were very kind. They dried my clothes. They fed me. The matron put me to bed. I wouldn't tell them who I was or answer their questions. That's why they kept me there."

He shook his head. "Sara, why did you run away?"

Another unfaltering stare from her. "You were badgering me, Max. I wanted to be alone. I wanted peace and quiet. I thought the cathedral would be open."

He didn't believe her, but he let it go. "And instead, you slept away the next few hours in the city jail."

"Yes."

She hadn't slept for long, and when she came to herself, she'd lain quietly in her cot, trying to come to grips with what had brought her to this awful state. The knife had turned once in her heart, but she wouldn't allow it to turn again.

So she'd lain there, thinking, thinking, thinking, gradually gathering her strength, subduing all her emotions. Her thoughts had drifted to Stoneleigh and what awaited her there. There was no turning back now. But first, she had to find a way to disarm Max Worthe.

She couldn't allow herself to think of him as "Max"

anymore, the foppish Corinthian who had charmed his way through her defenses. He was the *Courier's* special correspondent, the man who had practically crucified her in his paper and vowed that the *Courier* would never give up the search to find William Neville's body.

With the wisdom of hindsight, she'd examined every encounter she'd ever had with Max, going back to the night he'd climbed through her window. He'd made her believe that he was a bored fop with time hanging on his hands. He'd wanted only one thing: to get close to her so that he could get a story for his paper. Such a man wouldn't give up easily.

But neither would she.

Her head was bent as she refilled her empty cup, and Max made a leisurely study of her profile. This was the face of the woman he'd seen at her trial, calm and unaffected. But she wasn't calm and unaffected. She'd retreated behind a wall of ice to protect herself. He didn't want to smash the ice. He wanted to melt it.

"Why did you come back, Sara?" he asked quietly.

"I had left everything here, my money, my clothes. I had to come back for them."

"I think not. You're a resourceful young woman. You could have found a way to return to Bath without coming back here. So why are we in this parlor? Why are you talking to me? I would have expected you to storm from the room when I entered and lock yourself in your own chamber."

No fool, Max Worthe, and that was something she'd better remember. "What good would that do? You've been hounding me for years. It's true that I'd like nothing better than to forget I ever met you. Yes, I'd like to go on with my life. But it's not going to be that simple, is it, Max? You want your story, and nothing is going to stand in your way."

She let out a long, sighing breath. "I've decided, on thinking it over, that the only way to get rid of you is to answer your questions. That will be something for the *Courier*, won't it, to be the only newspaper ever to publish an interview with Sara Carstairs? Just think about it, Max. You may triple the *Courier's* circulation. That's all you were ever interested in anyway, increasing the circulation of your paper."

During this long monologue, Max's feelings had progressed from guilt to irritation, then finally to full-blown annoyance. He knew he'd made mistakes with her, but he wasn't a cold-blooded villain.

"Now, just a minute, Sara—"

But Sara wasn't in the mood to be interrupted. "I want something in return. I want your promise that if I answer all your questions, you'll hold off publishing the story until I've left England."

"You're . . . leaving England?"

"Just as soon as it can be arranged. It may take a little longer, now that you've chased Mr. Townsend away, but yes, that's what I intend to do. What I *must* do."

She was trying to slam the door again on anything that might be between them. And maybe he shouldn't blame her. Even a week ago, he hadn't been sure of where he stood. But now that he was sure, it was mortifying to see that she had a long way to go to catch up with him.

And she was still in trouble up to her pretty little ears.

He would play the game her way, but if she thought she could get rid of him that easily, she was way off the mark.

"Promise me," she said, "that you'll hold off publishing the interview until I've left England."

He nodded.

"I want to hear you say the words."

"I promise," he said harshly.

She took a long, leisurely swallow of tea and gazed at him over the rim of her cup. "So," she said, "what is it you wish to know?"

"You can begin by telling—" He stopped when she took

another sip of tea. "Bloody hell!" He got up, went to the door and opened it. "George!" he roared.

George arrived so quickly that it was apparent he'd been hanging around in the corridor. "Don't worry, George," said Max laconically as the young clerk tried to get a peek at Sara over Max's broad shoulders, "I haven't eaten your pet lamb yet, but if you don't bring me a pot of fresh coffee and a plate of fresh sandwiches, on the double, mind, I'll start by sharpening my fangs on you. Do you take my meaning?"

George did. He threw Max a look of reproach, squared his shoulders, and stalked off.

"And," roared Max after him, "remember I'm a carnivore. So don't bring me any of that cheese and cucumber pap."

He shut the door with a snap and returned to his chair. He glared at Sara. "What are you laughing at?"

She didn't know. She didn't feel like laughing, but laughter swept through her anyway. "I don't know. You. George. I doubt if he knows what 'carnivore' means. I wonder what kind of sandwiches he will bring."

He smiled too. "I like it when you smile. Your eyes get lighter, clearer. I could drown in them."

Her smile instantly vanished. "That," she said, "is the kind of twaddle I'd expect to hear from an adolescent."

"I can do better."

"Don't bother. You wanted to ask me some questions."

"Ah, yes, the interview." He looked down at his clasped hands then looked up with a rueful grin. "There's something I'd like to get out of the way first. I want to apologize, Sara. When I caught up to you in Bath, I should have told you straight out about my connection to the *Courier*. As I said, I was afraid that you'd take off and I'd never see you again. And, I'll be honest, I wanted the story."

He paused, then went on, "And I'm sorry about Stoneleigh. I'm sorry that my newspaper made life miserable for you. I know it sounds inadequate, but I don't know what else to say."

Her brows rose slowly. "Does this approach usually work for you, Max?"

"I'm sincere," he protested.

"No, what you are is transparent. You want to win my trust so that I'll tell you everything you want to know." She gave him a bland smile. "I don't trust you, Max, but I've made a bargain with you, and I always keep my word."

"The trouble with you, Sara, is that you have a suspicious mind."

"Yes, I know. Now can we get on with it?"

There were times, thought Max, when Sara's cool stare made him want to shake her, as now. But she'd had enough shocks tonight, and she deserved to be treated with kid gloves.

The devil, she did! Not after what she'd put him through! "You can begin," he said, "by telling me what in hell's name possessed you to place that stupid advertisement in the *Chronicle*. Where were your brains, woman?"

When her eyes flashed with sudden fire, Max sat back in his chair and enjoyed the spectacle. Her calm gray eyes had taken on the turbulence of a choppy sea.

"If you take that tone with me," she said, "I won't say another word."

"In that case," said Max pleasantly, "let me rephrase the question: Why was it necessary for you to marry Mr. Townsend?"

"It was the only way to break my father's trust fund. I want that money now, not in a year when I turn twenty-five. I want to protect my family, especially my sister. And that's the only way I know how to do it."

Max's brows were knit in a frown. "Protect them from what?"

"From William Neville," she said starkly.

"You think William is alive? Then he did send you notes?"

"Yes."

"They're not in your reticule."

"No. That was just an excuse to get away from you. I'm afraid I burned them, so I can't show them to you."

"You told me in Reading that William was dead."

"I don't know what to believe. Sometimes I wish he was dead. He was a brute, an animal. I know it's wrong to feel this way, but I can't help it. William Neville has caused enough grief to my family. I won't let him hurt them again."

This was something he would return to later, thought Max, after he'd learned the more salient facts. "Tell me about the notes."

"They started arriving about six months ago." She paused as she cast her mind back. "No, less than six months."

"Were they hand delivered?"

She hesitated, then said, "No. They came from the post office in Winchester. It doesn't matter who wrote them. The point is, someone is stalking me. And if it's William . . ." She shuddered. "If anything happens to me, Anne inherits practically everything. William is her husband. He'll finally get what he's always wanted—the Carstairs fortune."

Max said, "Why should William want the Carstairs fortune? He is . . . was Sir Ivor's heir."

"William quarreled with his father long before he married Anne. All I know is that he was always short of money."

Sir Ivor had not mentioned a quarrel to Max. After a moment, he went on, "But you were in hiding. How could William or anyone else know where to find you?"

She shrugged. "I write to my family. They write to me. I suppose one of them became careless. I really don't how he found me."

Sara stood up, and Max saw that she was trembling. "I'm going to stop him. I'm not going to let him win this time." She looked at Max. "And the only way I can do that is to break my father's trust fund and distribute the moneys as he always intended me to, equally among all his children. As soon as that's done, I'll start a new life in America with Anne."

Max said slowly, "You were going to marry Townsend just to inherit your father's fortune, a fortune that would come to you in another year anyway? That sounds extreme."

She sat down as suddenly as she'd risen. "Didn't you hear what I said? He's stalking me. I was in hiding yet he found me. I can't shake him off. Sooner or later, he'll catch up to me. If he kills me, Anne will become his next victim. The only way to stop him is to break the trust fund now."

Max thought for a moment. "You said Anne inherits everything if anything happens to you?"

"Most of it. There would be a small legacy for Simon and Martin and Lucy."

"And you've never considered that your sister, Anne, may be behind the notes? It seems to me that William isn't the only one with a motive for doing away with you. Your brothers and sisters—"

"You're wrong!" she said fiercely. "My family is incapable of such a thing."

He could see that he'd hit a raw nerve. She'd thought about it, all right, but she just couldn't face it. But now he understood why she'd wanted to marry Townsend *before* she returned to Stoneleigh. With her father's fortune equally divided, no one would have a motive for killing her, not William or anyone else.

He said finally, "Then could it be someone else? Someone who bears a grudge against you? Who are your enemies, Sara?"

"William and his father. And his friends perhaps. And

the only other I can think of is you, Max, or rather, the *Courier*."

"The *Courier* does not hold grudges. We try to get to the truth."

"No matter who gets hurt in the process!"

His jaw clenched and he said abruptly, "Tell me about the notes. What did they say?"

"Very little. I remember one said, 'Time to pay the piper,' and another, 'Absence makes the heart grow fonder.' They were all in that vein. It doesn't seem so frightening now, talking to you, but when I received them, I was terrified."

"And you're sure they were in William's hand."

"I know William's writing. He wrote letters to me before."

"Of course. I was forgetting that you and he were lovers."

That careless remark catapulted their conversation onto a different plane entirely. She stiffened. He squared his jaw.

Sara said, "You're the last one to preach morality to me, Max."

"I didn't sleep with my brother's wife."

"You slept with Deirdre. She's someone's wife, or so you told me."

"That's different. She has an understanding with her husband."

She eyed him coolly. "Maybe I was doing Anne a favor. Maybe she and William had an understanding as well. Why are you so angry?"

"I'm not angry." He raked her with angry eyes. "What I am is amazed. You said yourself that William was an animal. How could you have given yourself to such a man?"

Her fingers curled into claws. "You don't care about William." Then, because she was torn between anger and hurt, she added for good measure, "Or the others. Is that what is making you angry, Max? You've heard about my legion of lovers and you're sorry now that you didn't take me when you had the chance? Well, what's stopping you? You must know that I'm not fussy."

With lightning swiftness, he reached across the table, and his long fingers bit into the soft flesh of her arms. "If I thought for a moment that you meant that—"

"What?" she taunted, angry past caring.

"Don't test me, Sara, or you may not like the result."

She stared at him, wide-eyed, her breathing labored and audible. Every harsh line on his face warned her that his control was ready to snap. She'd heedlessly provoked him, but she'd never imagined he would react with such violence.

Max let her go and abruptly stood up. He, too, was appalled at his reaction to her taunts. Never would he have believed that he was capable of threatening a woman in such a base manner. How could he, Max Worthe, who'd been raised to treat all women with courtesy if not chivalry, have threatened her? And what was it about this woman that could arouse him to such anger?

He took a long, calming breath. "It was an empty threat. I hope you will believe that."

She was silent.

He should say more, but he didn't know how to apologize for something he didn't understand himself. "All this," he said, "is a long way from an exclusive interview for the *Courier*. Shall we return to neutral ground?"

She spoke quietly and without hesitation. "Yes, I think that would be best."

He moved to the fireplace, preserving as much space as possible between them in that small room. He didn't want to remind her of his superior strength.

"So where do we go from here, Sara?"

She gave a tiny shrug. "I'm to meet up with Miss Beattie in Salisbury. Of course, I thought I'd be married to Mr. Townsend by then and could produce a marriage certificate for my attorneys. Now . . ." She shook her head, "I suppose we'll return to Bath and I'll choose one of my other prospects."

He kept his voice unthreatening, when what he really wanted was to roar at her. "You're determined to go through with this marriage of convenience?"

"It's the only way."

"You're going to divide your father's fortune equally among his children, even his stepchildren? You expect me to believe that?"

She smiled faintly, and reaching under her collar, extracted a chain with a key attached to it. She undid the chain and offered him the key. "Maybe this will convince you. It's the key to my bag."

He took the key from her, then reached for the leather bag. Inside, there was nothing but legal documents. They were drawn up by a firm of solicitors in London, and were obviously the marriage contract Townsend would have signed. It was extremely complex and on his first reading, Max merely scanned each page. Sara had not lied to him. She'd divided everything equally amongst all her siblings.

He looked at her thoughtfully.

"What?" she demanded.

"Why didn't your father make a will like this? Why leave it all to you?"

"He trusted my judgement, and he didn't trust William. He wanted to protect Anne, I suppose. I don't really know."

He was missing something important here, but he couldn't figure out what it was. Maybe he hadn't been asking the right questions.

The trouble was, his mind was blunted with fatigue. He'd been up half the night worrying about her while she, by the sound of it, had been treated like royalty in the city jail.

He cast a baleful eye upon her.

"Satisfied?"

"I've only glanced at it."

"Take all the time you need."

She stretched, got up and began to wander around the room, eventually settling herself on a settee on one side of the fireplace. Max went back to studying the legal papers, reading every word slowly and carefully.

Sara STRETCHED HER CRAMPED MUSCLES AND slowly opened her eyes. The room was flooded with sunlight. Sounds ran together in her mind: the *clip-clop* of horses' hooves over cobblestones; muted masculine laughter outside her window; songbirds. She thought she smelled coffee.

When her blanket began to slip, she reached for it and her hand closed around something small and hard. A silver button, she remembered. It wasn't a blanket that covered her, but Max's coat. She wasn't in her bed, but curled up on the settee in the little parlor. It hadn't been a dream, then. Max had covered her with his coat and kissed her on the brow.

"Max."

"I'm here."

His voice acted on her like the report of a pistol shot. She gasped and hauled herself up.

He was towering above her, with the light behind him. "We're too late for breakfast," he said, "but I ordered coffee. They'll bring us something to eat shortly."

"What time is it?"

"It's past noon. We've both overslept."

She took the cup he offered her. "What are those?" she asked.

Max looked at the table. "Those," he said, "are the sandwiches George brought me last night while you were sleeping. And you were wrong, Sara. He knows well enough what 'carnivore' means." To the question in her eyes, he replied, "They're chopped liver, rare, chopped liver. Almost raw, in fact."

She smiled in spite of herself. "Is George still alive?"

"He was too quick for me. By the time I'd taken my first bite, he had vanished into thin air."

He was different this morning, she thought, more like his charming self. And that's when Max Worthe was most dangerous.

Max slumped into a chair and rested his booted feet on the seat of another chair. He'd removed his neckcloth and opened the top buttons of his shirt. He looked casual and unthreatening. But she was wiser now.

"It's amazing what a few hours' sleep will do for you, isn't it?" he said. "My head is as clear as a bell."

"Really?" she murmured.

"Yes, really. I've done a lot of thinking in the last hour or so, and I've found a solution to your problem."

She said slowly, "What are you talking about, Max?"

"William Neville. You think he's stalking you. I, on the other hand, am convinced William is dead. Therefore, it must be someone else. Just think about it, Sara. Why would William disappear like that? What did he hope to gain?"

"Maybe he wanted me to hang for his murder."

"Why send you notes? If he's alive and wants the Carstairs fortune, why is he holding off?"

"For revenge! That's how his mind works. He wants to see me suffer."

"Revenge for what?"

She cursed herself silently for being caught out, and she frantically searched her mind for a reason he would accept. "For breaking off our affair. For telling him that I was going to marry Francis Blamires."

His lips thinned in a disapproving line. "All the more reason, then, to flush this stalker into the open."

"Get to the point, Max."

"The point is, we can't be sure who this stalker is, and we can't know what his motives are. Maybe it has nothing to do with your father's will; maybe it's more personal than that.

So, marrying Townsend or any of your so-called 'prospects' wouldn't do you a bit of good."

Stalker. The word made her shiver, but it was the right word. Stalkers tracked their prey till they finally cornered them, then the hunters finished them off.

"It has to be William," she said. "No one else has a motive for wishing to harm me."

Max had his own ideas about that. He said mildly, "If he wants revenge, Sara, he won't care whether you're married or not."

"I wasn't going to hang around and wait for him to show up. I'm not stupid. I would have handed my proof of marriage to my solicitors and run off to America with Anne."

His charm swiftly evaporated. "And you'd go on running for the rest of your life. Or do you plan to change your name again and go into hiding? You'd always be looking over your shoulder, you know that, don't you?"

She shivered. "I hadn't really thought that far ahead."

"Well, think about it now."

Her eyes narrowed on his face. "Where is all this leading, Max?"

He folded his arms across his chest and leaned back, balancing his chair precariously on two legs. He said quietly, "I told you. We should be trying to flush this thug into the open. Once we know who he is, we can deal with him."

We. This was what she had feared. The *Courier*'s special correspondent wouldn't give up easily. "You want to come to Stoneleigh with me?"

"Who else is going to take you on? You can forget about your prospects in Bath. You don't imagine Townsend is going to keep his mouth shut? He'll make hay of what happened here in Wells. He'll exaggerate my involvement, make out, I suppose, that there is something between us."

"That wasn't my doing, it was yours!"

"It doesn't matter whose doing it was; the damage is done. Don't you understand? I'm trying to help you."

She briefly closed her eyes and thought of all the obscenities she'd heard on her brothers' lips but could never say herself.

"How?"

He smiled. "Simple. We more or less follow your plan."

He had managed to confuse her. They couldn't follow her plan unless she married, and she couldn't believe he would go that far just for a story. She said carefully, "I won't marry you, Max."

"God forbid!" He seemed genuinely shocked. "You don't imagine I want to marry every pretty girl I've ever . . . kissed?"

She was incredibly hurt. "I was thinking of my fortune," she snapped.

"Yes," he said thoughtfully, "you do think about money a great deal of the time, don't you? Don't marry a poor man, Sara. You'd only make his life miserable."

He brought his chair down with a thud to ret squarely on the floor. "Now about my plan. I'll play the part of your betrothed. We'll be the happy couple with stars in our eyes and a wedding to plan—not that it will ever come to that. There'll be no talk of having your husband sign away his rights to your fortune. As far as anyone will know, once the wedding takes place, control of your fortune will pass to me." He grinned. "That ought to stir up a hornets' nest. But more to the point, I'm convinced that William or whoever he is will show his hand, and I'll be ready for him."

Her worst fears had come to pass. It was on the tip of her tongue to tell him to go to hell, but she had too much to lose to be swayed by anger. She didn't want to see her name blazed on the front page of his newspaper; she didn't want the *Courier* to stir things up at this point. All she needed was a little time.

Then she would tell him to go to hell.

"Have a care, Max," she said and smiled. "For all you

know, you may be tangling with a woman who has already done murder. What's to stop me from murdering again?"

His brows rose slowly. He stared at her long and hard, and finally, he grinned. "Then kill me now, Sara, because that's the only way you're going to get rid of me."

He was impossible! He was unbearable! But what really rattled her was that he was as immovable as a brick wall.

Eleven

CONSTANCE STREATHAM–CARSTAIRS, AS SHE now styled herself, twitched the drawing-room curtains aside and looked out. The long avenue of old oaks drooped miserably under the weight of their sodden foliage, like mourners at the graveside of some departed friend. The melancholy vista did nothing to lighten her melancholy frame of mind. She could have wept in frustration. It was true, then. Sara really was going to be married. It was all in the letter she'd received yesterday by express. Sara would be arriving today with her betrothed. And once the wedding took place, once Sara's husband took control of the purse strings, Constance did not doubt that the Streathams would be out in the cold.

Then she'd be stuck in this dreary prison for the rest of her life. Tears of self-pity filled her eyes. It was so unfair. She was only thirty-six years old. She'd married a rich man with every expectation that her life would be glamorous beyond anything she had ever known, and she'd ended up in this godforsaken backwater, friendless and unappreciated, all her hopes in ruin now that the letter from Sara had arrived. She might as well be locked up in Newgate.

She hated this house. Longfield had not been refurbished to please her, but to gratify her husband's conception of how a country squire would live out his days. While other rich men were building stately marble homes in the neo-classical style, Samuel Carstairs had purchased a dilapidated Elizabethan manor with dark oak paneling, smoking chimneys, and depressingly small windows that barely let in the light. The stags' heads and antlers that adorned the Great Hall, as well as the gloomy portraits of no one knew whose ancestors, had all been bought at auction. Only this drawing room and her bedchamber had been refurbished to her taste. The wall paneling had been lightened to a pale gold, and the great beamed ceilings replaced with intricate plaster work in a classical design.

She might as well have saved herself the bother and her husband the expense. No one of any note ever came to Longfield. Their circle of friends had been drawn from the limited society in which they'd found themselves: the local doctor, the vicar, retired army types, and others of that class. But that was before Sara's trial. In the last three years, their friends and acquaintances had dwindled to almost no one.

It could all have been so different if Sara had only married the Viscount Hale. Such opportunities did not come a young girl's way too often. She, Constance Carstairs, had been the driving force behind that match. Her burning ambition had been to climb the social ladder. With a title in the family, with the right connections, they would have moved in far superior circles than Stoneleigh had to offer. But Sara could not be persuaded, and Samuel Carstairs had not insisted. Sara always got her own way.

If she was bitter, thought Constance, she had good cause. Her husband had never really got over the death of his first wife. He'd put Maria Carstairs on a pedestal, just as he'd done with Sara. They did not lack for common sense, he was fond of saying; they knew the value of money; they did not pine for the bright lights of the city. The list of their virtues went on and on. All that might have been forgiven if Samuel had rewarded her for her years of devotion, but all she'd got was her widow's portion, and it wasn't nearly enough to support her and her three children in style.

And now Sara was going to be married.

She needed a drink. Badly.

She turned from the window and looked at the other occupants of the room. Her sons, Simon and Martin, were hotly debating the merits of two prize pugilists who were to meet that week in nearby Romsey, and her daughter, Lucy, was curled up in the sofa with, it went without saying, her head in a book.

They wouldn't notice if she slipped upstairs to the secret bottle of brandy that was hidden in her clothes press. On the other hand, Sara and her betrothed could arrive any moment, and Sara would know. Sara always knew.

Sara was going to be married.

She hadn't believed Simon and Martin when they'd told her. But there was no getting around the letter from Sara. Well, she had herself to think about now. There was one virtue she possessed that put all the Carstairs in the shade: She had more ambition than all of them put together. Sara and Anne had let their opportunities slip through their fingers. She wasn't going to make the same mistake. And if no opportunities presented themselves, she'd make her own.

She'd made a beginning. She'd acquired a powerful ally who could open the right doors for her if only Sara would agree to sponsor a Season in London for Lucy. And if Lucy went to London, her mother, quite rightly, would accompany her. And why not? She was far too young to bury herself in this depressing tomb of a place. And when they reached london, she would shed the name Carstairs. It was a millstone around her neck, just like this house, this monument to her late husband. No one would connect Lucy Streatham and her youthful mother with the scandalous events at Stoneleigh. And if things worked out the way she wanted, she need never come back.

But it was all in Sara's hands.

Sara, on her own, wouldn't be too hard to persuade, because she had a soft spot for Lucy. But Sara's betrothed was a different matter. Until she'd sized him up, she wouldn't know how to play her cards.

No. She'd better not have that drink until after she'd met the mystery man.

She spoke abruptly to her sons. "Sara must have given you some hint about this man she means to marry."

"She didn't," said Martin glumly. "All she said was that when she was married, her husband would have control of her fortune."

Constance twitched her skirts and sat beside Lucy on the sofa. "Sit up, Lucy," she commanded. "You're not a child now. When I was your age, I was already married." She stopped when Lucy obediently sat up and laid aside her book. Her daughter, thought Constance, did not lack for beauty or intelligence, but the girl had no style. She was too unworldly for her own good.

Simon yawned and looked at the clock on the mantelpiece. "We'll know soon enough what he's like," he said. "They can't be much longer now."

Constance frowned at her elder son. "You're taking this much too lightly, in my opinion, Simon. You do realize what this can mean to our family? The man is probably a fortune hunter. I mean, what kind of man would marry a woman who had stood trial for murder?"

"She was acquitted," he pointed out quietly.

"That's not the point!"

Constance drew in a long, angry breath. She was surrounded by idiots, it seemed. She was the only one who took the threat of this marriage seriously. Even with Simon, she had to watch her step. After all the sacrifices she'd made for him, she had a right to more loyalty than this.

She went on, "All I'm saying is that he may be an unprincipled fortune hunter."

"You mean," said Simon dryly, "like us?" When it looked as though his mother might explode, he grinned disarmingly. "Mother," he said, "Sara is many things, but she is not stupid. If he's an unprincipled fortune hunter, she'll show him the door."

Constance glared at the son who had once been the apple of her eye. She said coolly, "Don't let Oxford go to your head, Simon. We're the poor relations here, and you'd do well to remember it."

"How could I forget when you keep reminding us?"

"Just be sure you do or say nothing to upset Sara. No snide remarks. No temper tantrums. And that goes for you too, Martin."

"Now just a minute," began Martin querulously, "I haven't—"

His mother's voice drowned out his words. "Lucy, do try to show a bit of spirit. Remember, our future rests with you."

"Oh, for God's sake," interjected Simon, "she's just a child."

Constance's eyes narrowed unpleasantly. "You had your chance, Simon, you and Martin both, and you made a mull of it. Now it's Lucy's turn, and I won't have you spoiling things for her." When no one contradicted her, she went on, "There will be no sneaking off to the local taverns, no cockfights, no gambling, and no prizefights while Sara is here. Understood?"

"We'll just be one big happy family, same as always," murmured Simon.

His mother chose to ignore the sarcastic remark. Her eyes strayed to the clock, and she wondered for the tenth time in as many minutes what on earth was keeping Sara.

• • •

THEY WERE STUCK, A MILE FROM HOME, IN ruts in a road that the rain had turned into a bog. Sara had pleaded helplessness and stayed warm and dry inside the coach, while Max stepped down to give their coachmen a hand. It was the first time she'd smiled in a long while, the first time she'd felt that things weren't all going Max's way. And when he fell in the mud and came up swearing, she laughed out loud.

She hadn't felt much like laughing when they'd met up with Miss Beattie in Salisbury. Bea was delighted with the way things had turned out. But Bea didn't know the whole story. All they'd told her was that Max had persuaded Sara to let him take Mr. Townsend's place. It wasn't hard to interpret the twinkle in Bea's eyes. She was hoping that this marriage of convenience would turn into the real thing.

Sara had wanted to tell Bea who Max was, but he had scotched that idea. It was essential, he said, that everyone believe his only interest in Sara was to make her his wife. That was the bait to lure William into the open. If it became known that he published the *Courier,* his credibility might be called into question. Yes, he knew Miss Beattie wouldn't say anything deliberately, but a careless word in the wrong ear could ruin everything.

Sighing, Sara huddled into the warm folds of her cloak as thoughts drifted in and out of her mind. Max had invited Bea to come with them, but she'd refused. She'd told Sara privately that she felt she would only get in the way, and Sara had not tried to change her mind.

And that's how it was left.

So, here she was, stuck in a bog with Max Worthe, the man who had hounded her for the last three years. Was she mad? What on earth had possessed her to make him her accomplice? Certainly not his charm. William had positively oozed charm when she'd first met him, and look where that had got her.

Max couldn't browbeat her either, though he'd made a fair attempt, because bullying only made her hackles rise. Then why had she given in?

She hadn't given in. The truth was, she hadn't had a choice. A fiancé might not be as good as a husband, but he was better than nothing. And maybe whoever was sending her those notes would be frightened off. At the very least, it would buy her some time so that she could do what she'd come home to do.

Her thoughts drifted to the dower house and the last time she had seen William.

She shivered and looked up as the coach began to move. It didn't go far, and when it stopped, Max entered.

"Don't say a word!" he said sternly.

She didn't, but the laugh that she tried to suppress turned into a giggle.

Max's lips flattened, then he, too, began to smile. "I must look like a warthog."

She nodded, eyes dancing.

"So much for the good impression I hoped to make on your family."

"Why should you care what they think?"

Max stripped out of his muddy cloak and used it to wipe off his boots and trousers. "I'm supposed to be the eager bridegroom, aren't I? It's only natural that I'd want to make a good impression on your family."

"You mean you want them to like you so you can take them unawares? They can't help you, and I don't want you badgering them with questions. They've suffered enough as it is."

He looked at her curiously. "I understood you didn't get along with your family."

She shrugged. "They think I'm a miser. They think I'm

standing guard on a well of money that will never dry up. But apart from that, we get along reasonably well."

"Then why weren't they at your trial?"

"What?"

"Why didn't they come to your trial to support you?"

"Because I didn't want them there. They would have been mobbed. Simon, the eldest, was only fifteen. What could he do? What could any of them do? I told Constance that the best way to help me was to stay at home. Besides, I didn't want them to see me like that . . . in the dock. I didn't want them to hear . . ." Her voice cracked and she shook her head, then she breathed deeply and went on, "Anne shouldn't have been there either. I was shocked when she went into the witness box. That was my attorney's doing. He thought the trial was going badly and that Anne's testimony would help clear me. I knew she wouldn't stand up well to an interrogation. She gets hopelessly confused when people try to intimidate her. Why are you looking at me like that? What are you thinking?"

"What I think," he said, "is that your family means a great deal to you. There's not much you wouldn't do to protect them, is there, Sara?"

"Don't start that. My brothers were far too young to have anything to do with William's disappearance. Lucy was only a child. Anne is too . . . she's just above reproach, that's all. You'll see what I mean when you meet her. And Constance had absolutely no motive for doing away with William. So, you see, I'm not trying to protect anyone, Max."

He studied her set expression. "I've never heard you refer to your brothers as stepbrothers."

"Why should that surprise you? We grew up together. We lived in the same house. I don't know what you're getting at."

"But you never refer to Constance as your mother."

"She prefers 'Constance.' Where is all this leading?"

"Nowhere. I'm just trying to take an impression of your family. When did you last see them?"

"I haven't seen Constance or Lucy or Anne for three years, but we've kept in touch with letters. As for the boys, they've visited me from time to time. Not that I wanted them to. I felt it was better to make a clean break. They had their own lives to lead and so did I. But as they got older, and got into scrapes . . . well, my letters didn't seem to make any difference, so I decided to talk to them face-to-face."

"Lecture them, you mean?"

Her lips thinned.

Max went on as though she'd answered in the affirmative. "Don't be too hard on yourself. It never does any good, not with boys of that age."

"And you could do better?"

"I hope so. After all, I was once a boy myself. What are they like?"

"Who?"

"Your brothers. Your family. You haven't told me much about them, really."

"You haven't told me anything about your family!"

"I asked first."

"There isn't much time. We're almost there."

"Give me a thumbnail sketch. There's time enough for that, isn't there?"

She looked at him as though she did not like him at all, but she complied just the same. "I've told you that Simon and Martin are Corinthians. We sent them to Oxford to get an education, and so far, being Corinthians is all they've picked up. But they're quite unalike in other ways. Simon, the elder, is really quite worldly, I suppose you'd say. And Martin . . . well . . . he's only seventeen. I believe it's quite a trying age in boys."

This was said so wistfully that Max couldn't help smiling. "What about Lucy?" he asked gently.

Sara sighed. "I don't know, I just don't know. When I

left Longfield, she was a charming child. But now all she can think about is having a Season in London. Constance must be putting these ideas into her head. But it won't do." She looked up with a wry smile. "Constance thinks I won't sponsor Lucy because of the cost. But it isn't only that. No one in our family has ever had a Season in London. We don't have that kind of connections. Who would call on Lucy if she went up to town? Who would invite her to parties? Who would come to a ball in her honor? No one I know. And even if all doors were miraculously opened for her, what would happen when someone remembered that Lucy's sister had stood trial for murder? They would cut her dead. Constance says she is willing to take that chance. But I'm not."

"And that makes you the wicked ogre?"

"That about sums it up."

"And Anne? What's she like?"

"Quiet. Thoughtful. Her burning ambition when she was a young girl was to be a nun. I don't think she's ever got over it." She didn't like talking about Anne, so she quickly changed the subject. "Now it's your turn. Who are your parents, Max? Where do they live?"

He folded his arms across his chest. "My father is Lord Lyndhurst," he said, "and he and my mother live on the other side of Winchester."

Her brow puckered. "I've heard of Castle Lyndhurst, though I've never seen it."

"It belongs to my father. That's where I was born."

"It must take a great deal of money to keep a castle in good repair, and keep it going, too."

"What are you getting at, Sara?"

Her eyes narrowed on him. "Mmm. You're not looking for an heiress to marry, by any chance, are you, Max? You know, your title for my fortune?"

He sat up straighter. "Certainly not!"

"Good. Because this heiress is not for sale. Besides, I don't think my share of my father's fortune would be enough to keep a castle going." She smirked when he glared. "Ah, here we are."

Max closed his mouth on a blistering reply and looked out the window as the coach made a turn and passed between two stone pillars with a gatehouse on one side. "What happened to the village of Stoneleigh?"

"It's a mile further on. Why do you ask?"

"No particular reason. I'm just trying to get my bearings, that's all."

The trees and shrubbery on either side of the drive were so dense that it was impossible to get any idea of the lay of the land. He wanted to ask where the dower house was in relation to the house, but decided that this wasn't the right moment. He was aware that Sara had suddenly gone as tense as a bowstring.

"Nervous?" he asked.

For a few seconds, her eyes held his, eyes that had a startled, fearful look about them, then the look was gone, and she said in a natural tone, "Does that surprise you?"

No. The nervousness didn't surprise him, but the fear did.

"You've got that look on your face again, Max. What are you thinking this time?"

"Nothing. Nothing at all."

What he was thinking was that it was about time that someone shouldered some of Sara's burdens; he was wishing that he'd known her before the trial, before he was prejudiced against her; he was wishing he could kick himself. But the idea that possessed his mind was that this lovely, willful, yet vulnerable girl was in sore need of a champion, whether she knew it or not, and he did not see why he should not fill that slot.

WHEN MAX CAUGHT SIGHT OF THE HOUSE, HE let out a low whistle. It was an Elizabethan gem that had been spared the sorry fate of so many centuries-old houses. It was intact, with no neoclassical facade to disfigure its stolid beauty and no spurious wings running off from the main building. With its ivy-clad stone walls and a stalwart tower at each corner, it resembled a miniature Hampton Court, the palatial home of Cardinal Wolsey, before later generations had tarted up the grand old dame and ruined her forever.

"When was it built?" he asked reverently.

"In the last years of the sixteenth century. It was originally owned by a wealthy wine merchant, who eventually held some minor position at court, so you can see why it appealed to my father."

"It's beautiful."

"Yes, isn't it? But before you get carried away with admiration, Max, let me warn you that my father restored the interior to its original state as well."

"Meaning?"

"Some people find Longfield too austere, too primitive."

"And you love it?"

"I was happy here," she replied simply.

No more was said as their hired coach swept through the great arch into the interior courtyard. Before the coach came to a halt, the front doors opened and footmen hurried down the steps.

As they reached for the baggage, Sara smiled and greeted each one by name. Max stood a little to one side, taking everything in. Sara was in no hurry to get out of the rain, and he wasn't sure if it was because she was genuinely interested in catching up on her servants' doings in the last little while or because she was afraid to enter the house.

Then, when everything was said, she squared her shoulders and turned to face the house. For some reason, Max found the gesture oddly touching. It was a moment he wanted to share with her.

"Take my arm," he said.

"I'm not afraid to face my family, if that's what you think."

"No, but I am. Please?"

The unfaltering stare faltered, then gradually melted. She took the arm he offered and returned his smile. "If I know you, you'll have them all eating out of your hand before the day is through."

They passed through a small vestibule and entered the Great Hall. Four people were waiting for them, stiff, lifeless figures that seemed frozen in place. They were all dark-haired and strikingly handsome in their different ways. When Sara dropped his arm and took a few paces toward them, they let out a collective breath.

"Sara!"

It was the youngest who broke the silence, Lucy, Max supposed, pretty, with delicate features, and clothed all in white muslin.

Lucy's voice quavered. "I thought you would *never* come home." She took a few mincing, ladylike steps toward Sara, then suddenly, childlike, catapulted herself into her sister's arms. "Oh, I've missed you, Sara!"

Here was real affection, thought Max, as he watched Sara embrace the younger girl, then all was confusion as the others came to life, all talking across each other. Simon and Martin, the aspiring Corinthians, received only a cursory glance. It was the woman whom Sara addressed as Constance who received Max's full attention.

The stepmother! thought Max, and was dumbfounded.

Constance Carstairs looked far too young to be the mother of the three grown children by her side. In fact, she looked no older than Sara. Her skin was unlined; her features were as delicate as her daughter's, and her dark, glossy hair framed a heart-shaped face.

Her figure was as youthful as her face. Her gown, a pale amber silk, made her skin glow. Here was a woman who knew how to make the most of herself.

Then Sara was making the introductions. "And this is the man who has made me the happiest woman in the world, Lord Maxwell Worthe, my betrothed."

Constance's finely chiseled eyebrows winged up, and her green eyes sparkled with interest. "Lord Worthe," she said, a delicate emphasis on the title.

"Actually it's Lord Maxwell," replied Max. "It's a courtesy title, you see."

"I'm very happy to meet you at last," said Constance in a low musical tone.

Max knew that she meant it. He'd had looks like this from women before, women who found him attractive and wanted him to know it. Any man's vanity would be flattered, and he was no exception. She was, he thought, the kind of woman who would show to best effect in the company of men, but who would, if he was not mistaken, possess few female friends.

"Charmed," he murmured, and lightly pressed a kiss to the hand she offered him.

He did the same with Lucy, who blushed rosily and turned away with a giggle. Martin bowed and mumbled something inarticulate under his breath; Simon surveyed him with a look that was faintly hostile.

"You must be Simon," Max said. "How do you do?"

Simon's reply was a curt bow that was barely civil.

Sara, who was oblivious to this exchange, said lightly, "Where is Anne?"

Constance dragged her withering gaze from her elder son. "Where else but out doing good? She's with Mr. Thornley, our new vicar. I told her when you were due to arrive, but you know Anne. Sometimes I wonder if that girl ever learned to tell the time."

"No doubt," said Sara in the same light tone, "she'll be here for dinner."

"I wouldn't count on it. She spends more time in the vicarage than she does here at Longfield. There's a prayer meeting she attends. Well, that shouldn't surprise you. Sometimes it runs late." Constance shrugged. "She is over twenty-one and has answered to no one since you abandoned . . . well . . . since you went away."

In the silence that followed these words, Max looked at Sara. It was as if all the life had been driven out of her. She looked frozen and very fragile.

"Sara," he said quietly, "shall I send a servant to fetch her?"

His voice brought her back to life. "A servant?"

"To fetch Anne."

"Good heavens, no! He'd only lose track of the time as well. Anne has that effect on people. Come along, Max, and I'll show you to your room."

They mounted the stairs in silence, but at the foot of the stairs, it sounded as though a quarrel had erupted. The words were inaudible, but Constance's voice eventually held sway. It wasn't low and musical now. A hard edge had crept into it, hard and domineering.

The woman was flawed, thank God, thought Max, for her appeal really was quite staggering, but not nearly as staggering as the appeal of the slight figure with the squared shoulders ahead of him on the stairs, who was leading him only the Lord knew where.

Twelve

$\sim$

SARA ENTERED HER BEDCHAMBER AND QUI-
etly shut the door. She'd told the maid that the unpacking
could wait till later. Just for a few minutes, she wanted to be
alone.

Hardly aware of what she was doing, she slipped out of
her coat, draped it over the foot of the big four-poster bed,
and walked slowly across the room to look out the window.
Below her, beautifully manicured lawns gave way to a vir-
tual forest, and beyond that, over the treetops, she could see
the spires of Stoneleigh.

The people of Stoneleigh had not been kind to her after
the trial. The prospect of walking along the High Street or
attending church services was quite frightening. It didn't
matter. If all went well, she would be gone before the locals
had any inkling that she'd returned.

She was home at last, the place she loved best in the
world, and already she was wishing she were anywhere
but here.

There had been many homecomings over the years, but
none as hollow as this one. When she'd come home from
school, her brothers and sisters would go wild with delight,

but of course, she'd always remembered to bring them a little present. And her father would be there, beaming his pride in her; and Constance, fussing, occasionally tart, but never sullen. And Anne . . .

She couldn't think of Anne without wanting to weep. Once, they'd been so close, but now Anne kept her thoughts to herself. Her letters said very little. Since William's disappearance, she'd devoted all her time and energies to the church, and that's all she wrote about.

Was she suffering from a guilty conscience? Is that why she devoted all her time to doing good? How much did Anne remember about that night?

She turned from the window and stared at the small portrait above her escritoire. Her father stared back at her. She was supposed to be very like him, not only in looks, but also in nature. The looks she couldn't deny. They had the same gray eyes, squared jaw, and fiery dark hair. But she could never be the person her father was. He was shrewd; he understood human nature; he'd kept the family together. She was completely unequal to the task, as events had proved. She would give anything if only her father could step down from the portrait, take her in his arms, and tell her that everything was going to be all right.

He'd never been an affectionate father, doting on his children, but she missed him. She'd always known she could count on him. And now there was only herself.

Defeat settled on her shoulders, and she sank down on the edge of her bed. But her eyes strayed to her father's portrait, and she was held. He'd had so much faith in her. She couldn't let him down.

She thought about Max. When she looked at him, she saw two men: the *Courier's* pitiless correspondent who had hounded her for three years and of whom she was mortally afraid, and the charming fop who had bewitched her one never-to-be-forgotten night in Reading.

Special correspondent. Those words were burned into her

brain and could never be erased. He'd kept her name alive long after it should have been forgotten. She feared and hated that man.

The man she thought she'd lost her heart to didn't exist. It was pointless to wish, to hope, to dream. She didn't know Max Worthe at all. Reading seemed like a mirage now, a foolish fantasy. What was real was that the *Courier's* special correspondent was here in Longfield.

And the game wasn't over yet.

Reading. She stared into space as the memory came back to her. When tears burned her eyes, she dashed them away. Suddenly rising, she went to the bell rope and pulled on it.

She was going through her clothes closet when the maid arrived. All her gowns were at least three or four years old, but they were far superior to anything she'd brought with her.

She shook out a sheer gray satin that was appliquéd on the bodice and along the hem with tiny vines.

"This will do," she told the maid. "It's Martha, isn't it? You're Cook's girl, aren't you?"

"Yes, mu'um. I never thought you would remember me. I was only a scullery maid when you went away."

"Yes, but I remember your mother. How is she?"

Martha's face fell. "She says that either that newfangled stove goes or she does. Not," Martha hastened to add, "that she means it. Longfield is the only home she's ever known."

"Oh."

Sara was momentarily nonplussed. She'd think about it later when she had more time. "Martha," she said, "I want you to press this dress straight away, and send a footman with water for my bath. And tell your mother to delay dinner by an hour. That should give me time to make myself presentable."

When Martha left, Sara began to disrobe. The clothes she was wearing and those she'd brought with her would be cleaned and sent to the parish poor. For three years, she'd dressed so as not to attract notice to herself, but now that she was no longer in hiding, she could please herself. She wanted to wear pretty things; she wanted to look her best. This had nothing to do with Max Worthe. She wanted to live like an ordinary girl.

Just for a little while, she wanted to live like an ordinary girl.

*I*T TOOK MAX ALL OF THIRTY MINUTES TO RE-vise his opinion on the Elizabethan gem that Samuel Carstairs had restored to its former glory. The sanitation was primitive, no more than a small closet concealing an elaborately carved throne with a chipped chamber pot under its lid; the bellpull in his room did not work, forcing him to troop down to the nether regions of the house to summon a servant. And when his bathwater arrived, it was tepid. By the time he was halfway through dinner, he'd come to the conclusion that it was a godawful house, a godawful dinner, and a godawful family.

They were curious about him, of course, but that didn't excuse the way they'd pounded him with a volley of blunt questions. It was almost like going up against Mighty Jack Cleaver. Who were his parents? Where did they live? How had he met Sara? Why wasn't she wearing a betrothal ring? When would the marriage take place? What was his profession? His prospects? How had he come by his courtesy title?

For his purposes, it was essential for everyone to think that he was marrying Sara for her money, so he told them only as much as he wanted them to know. His parents, he said, lived on the other side of Winchester in a decrepit ruin of a place that they were rebuilding piece by piece. He'd met Sara in a coaching house in Reading, and had been instantly taken with her. There was no betrothal ring because there hadn't been time to choose one. The wedding would take place as soon as he had obtained a special license. His courtesy title was passed on from father to son, and one day his own sons, should he be fortunate enough to have any, would have courtesy titles also. It was obvious that Sara and her family had no idea how the peerage worked, and he didn't enlighten them.

"You haven't mentioned your profession, Max."

At the sound of Sara's voice, he looked up. Their eyes met and held, hers enigmatic, his wary. This was the first time she'd addressed him personally.

When he'd first caught sight of her as she'd descended the stairs, he'd felt as though someone had knocked the wind out of them. "Lovely" didn't do her justice. She was stunning. Ethereal. Elegant. And oh-so-ladylike. And he was tempted to prove what a lie that was.

He'd guessed that the transformation was for his benefit, assuming that Sara had noticed his reaction to Constance when they'd first met. But now he wasn't so sure. Her face was as smooth and blank as a marble sculpture. But he knew her better now, and he knew that she was anything but calm.

"I might as well tell you," said Sara, resting her chin on her linked fingers, "Max doesn't do much of anything. He's a Corinthian, you see."

"You mean," said Lucy innocently, "like Simon and Martin?"

"That depends," said Max. "You see, Lucy, the test of a true Corinthian is in his skill in sports."

"Max," Sara continued, "is a pugilist, you know, a boxer."

Martin's mouth gaped, then he rolled his eyes.

Simon, in a perfect imitation of a world-weary sophisticate, appraised Max's physique in one leisurely stare, and dismissed him with a flick of his lashes. "How interesting," he said. "I wouldn't mind seeing you in action."

Martin snickered.

"Oh, you will," said Max easily. "You may depend on it."

Simon and Martin exchanged a quick look, then Simon said casually, "The Stoneleigh Fair takes place soon. There is a boxing contest. Maybe you'd like to enter it?"

It was a matter of honor (and saving face) to reply in the affirmative. But besides this, Max was confident of his ability to take on any of the country yokels, especially someone like Simon.

After this exchange, Sara's family settled down to what was obviously its forte—bickering amongst themselves. Simon wanted the fire lit to take the chill off the air; Martin did not. Lucy wanted to go with her friend to her grandparents' place in Romsey for the weekend; Constance forbade it. No one liked the dinner (Max couldn't fault them there), but they all cleaned their plates as if they wouldn't sit down to another meal for at least a month.

Sara said very little, but every time the door opened, she would turn her head to see who had entered. She must, thought Max, be waiting for her sister to put in an appearance, and it made him wonder what lay behind Anne's absence and Sara's anxiety.

He tried to spear one of the small roast potatoes, but it was as hard as a bullet, and he decided he'd rather keep his teeth intact. The roast beef had the chewing consistency of leather, but a starving man couldn't be too choosy. After a heroic battle with a mouthful of beefsteak, he changed his mind and set down his knife and fork. If this were his house, the first thing he would do was get rid of the cook.

"Our cook hasn't quite mastered the new stove yet," said Lucy.

"The new stove?"

Lucy nodded. "It's a marvel of modern engineering, or so Mama says, but that doesn't help Cook. She prefers the old way of doing things."

Martin spoke with his mouth full. "It doesn't matter which method Mrs. Hardwick uses, the food is still atrocious."

"Well, you cleaned your plate," Max pointed out.

"Sheer habit," replied Martin. "Since we were infants, our father wouldn't allow us to leave the table till we'd eaten everything that was put in front of us. 'Waste not, want not' was his golden rule. He was a skinflint, if you know what I mean."

Sara said dryly, "It's because of Father's golden rule that we live in this lovely house and you are enjoying the best education that money can buy."

Simon interjected, "What's the good of having money if you can't spend it?"

Goaded, Sara retorted, "If we spend every penny we have, we won't have any money left to enjoy."

"But Father left you millions," Martin said hotly.

"Hardly millions! And it's in trust. We're living off the interest. Can't you understand that?"

Constance said, "If we sold the house, we'd have plenty of money."

Sara looked at her stepmother as if she were a slow-witted child. "Constance," she said gently, "this is our home. We can't sell it."

Lucy said, "I like living here."

"If Sara would only give us our share of Father's money," Martin said, "we could all do what we like."

When Sara pressed her fingers to her temples, Max's temper ignited. She was beginning to look beleaguered, and that did not sit well with him. He reached for his wine-glass, took a long swallow—at least the wine was good—and cut across the babel of voices in the awful tone that invariably sent reporters and editors in the *Courier*'s offices scurrying for cover.

"I might have something to say about that."

Martin frowned at him. "What do you mean?"

Max smiled vaguely at no one in particular. "What I mean is that when Sara marries me, the trust is broken."

The sudden silence that followed was almost deafening, thought Max. He raised his glass and sipped slowly.

Simon got the message first. "Then you'll have control of our money."

"Your money?" said Max pleasantly. "Oh, no, you misunderstand. Your money belongs to you. I don't care what you do with it. But my wife's money—now, that's a different matter." He raised his glass in salute to Sara. "Did someone mention millions? Sara, I had no idea how much you were worth. You've been keeping secrets from me."

Martin turned his head away and muttered disgustedly, "Mama was right. He's nothing but a fortune hunter."

The look Sara blazed at Max was hot enough to boil water. Max remained as cool as ice. "Did you wish to say something, my love?"

"What I wish to say . . . my family . . . that is, I would never leave my family to fend for themselves."

"Of course not," agreed Max. "They'll always be welcome to make their home here with us."

A silence fell as the door opened. Footmen filed in and began to clear away the remains of the meal. The silence continued as the next course was served, but never was a silence more eloquent or more dangerously close to exploding into open warfare.

Max gazed at each person in turn. With the exception of Lucy, they were all complainers and wheedlers. He could see how they'd got that way, though. Sara allowed them to manipulate her with subtle and not-so-subtle appeals to her conscience. She felt guilty for having been her father's favorite, and tormented because the Carstairs fortune had come to her in its entirety. She wanted to do the right thing, and though her intentions were good, she was going about it the wrong way.

What this family needed, Max decided, was someone who would not be swayed by their temper tantrums and fits of pique, someone like him, someone who would whack them into shape so that they would take responsibility for their own lives.

He was well aware that his purpose in being here was a serious one, and went far beyond his relationship with Sara and her family. They would get to that later, after he'd discovered what had happened to William Neville.

The only thing he had to go on so far were the notes that had been sent from Winchester. He believed Sara on that point at least, because nothing else explained her anxiety to settle her affairs and escape to America. If William were dead, however, and he was convinced of it, the letters must have been sent by someone who was close to her, someone who knew where she was staying, someone, perhaps, in this very room.

THERE WAS NO OFFER OF AFTER-DINNER BRANDY for the gentlemen, not that Max wanted to encourage the Streatham boys to acquire any more vices than they already had, but he'd wanted some time alone with them, if only to prove that there was a new top dog in the pack, and they had better fall into line, or else.

They'd retired to the drawing room, sans Simon and Martin, who, without a word of explanation, had silently vanished into thin air, just like their sister, Anne. It seemed that good manners in this family were as rare as snow in the tropics. Yet no one saw anything wrong in it. To them, it was how they all normally behaved.

"Would you care for a sherry, Max?" asked Constance. She held a decanter in one hand and had set out two crystal sherry glasses.

They were sitting on chairs close to the grate. Now that Martin was no longer there to object, the fire had been lit. Sara and Lucy were at the piano, at the other end of the room, playing a duet.

"I'd prefer something stronger, if you have it," he said.

"Wouldn't we all?" Constance tossed her head and laughed, her green eyes flirting with him. "Not in this house, Max. You see, my husband was very abstemious in his habits. He didn't approve of strong drink. Sherry and wine were the only drinks we were allowed, and then only at Christmas."

"But he was a brewer."

"Yes. There's never any logic to how people behave, is there? He inherited the business from his father, but Samuel never really approved of it. Now that he's gone, we break out the sherry and wine on special occasions. It's not as I would have things, but Sara is mistress here, so sherry it is, like it or not."

"I see." He accepted the glass Constance offered him, took one sip, grimaced, and set the glass aside. He was thinking that, like it or not, he preferred brandy, and Sara would just have to get used to it.

He looked at Constance. Her delicate brows went up. "Yes?" she said.

"I was thinking," said Max, "that Sara has been away for three years, more than enough time for you to arrange things to suit yourself."

It looked at first as though she'd taken offence, then her generous mouth curved in a smile. "This will only take a moment," she said, then swiftly rising, she left the room. Not long after, she returned with a bottle and handed it to Max.

"We'll just have to use the sherry glasses," she said. "And just remember, if we're discovered, I know nothing about it."

This generous gesture went a long way to restoring Constance's credit in Max's eyes. He disposed of the sherry by pouring it back into the sherry decanter. He did it quite openly, but the pair at the piano were preoccupied, so his action went unobserved. After that, he poured out two glasses of brandy and set the brandy bottle out of harm's way on one side of his chair.

After one mouthful of brandy, Max began to feel a good deal more civilized, and he settled back in his chair to enjoy the duet. He didn't know much about music, but he knew that Sara and Lucy were good. Their nimble fingers flew over the keyboard in perfect harmony.

Their harmony showed in other things: how they sat on the bench, shoulders touching, smiles flashing; the odd chuckle from one or the other. Lucy, at least, was glad to have her sister home.

When the piece ended, it was the two at the piano who burst into applause. They were delighted with their performance, as their exuberance showed. As Max studied Sara, he felt like an artist whose model refused to sit still. Just when he thought he'd captured her, she moved, and he had to start over from scratch.

"I told you I'd been practicing," said Lucy in response to something Sara said.

They were smiling when they rose from the piano. Sara's gaze touched on Max, went beyond him and froze. Then all the life and laughter in her face suddenly vanished.

"Anne," she said hoarsely.

Max swivelled to face the door. A couple had entered, the woman standing motionless, a little ahead of the gentleman. Her garments were torn and sodden to the waist, her hair, as dark as Sara's, fell about her shoulders in wild disorder. No one would ever call this young woman pretty or beautiful. But her face was arresting—strong features, straight black brows, and eyes that looked huge against the pallor of her skin.

So this was Anne, he thought, and slowly got up, positioning himself so that he could observe both sisters easily.

Anne motioned with one hand. "Our gig overturned in the ford, on the other side of Stoneleigh. That's the reason I wasn't here to meet you. Can you *ever* forgive me?"

Sara blinked rapidly. "Your gig overturned?"

Anne nodded. "Mr. Thornley, the vicar, you know, suffered a concussion. So I couldn't leave him. If Drew hadn't come along, I don't know what I would have done."

This little speech brought a tremulous smile to Sara's lips. "You're here now," she said as she crossed to Anne, "and that's all that matters."

It seemed to Max that it was a restrained embrace, but it did not lack affection. Then Sara exclaimed over Anne's filthy garments, but Anne refused to be hurried away until Max had been introduced.

The eyes that searched his face were as deep a gray as Sara's. She looked shy and sweet and very uncertain. She stammered over her words. "I hope . . . I know you and Sara will be very happy. Welcome to Longfield." Then, with a little laugh, "And now, if you'll excuse me, I must change out of these wet garments. No, Sara, Lucy will help me. You must stay and talk to Drew. I won't be long." And with that, she slipped away, with Lucy following after her.

Sara gazed at the closed door for a moment, then, clearing her expression, turned to the young man beside her. "Drew, how are you?" she said.

"Happy, now that I've seen you with my own eyes. It's good to have you home, Sara."

He held out his arms, and Sara walked into them as if she belonged there. Max looked at Constance. She was sipping her "sherry," gazing at Drew Primrose over the rim of her glass. Max composed his features into a mask of amiability and waited, with diminishing patience, for the embrace to end.

The couple broke apart laughing. Sara made the introductions. "This is Drew Primrose," she said, "a good friend to our family, and a partner in our firm of attorneys. Drew, this is my betrothed, Lord Maxwell Worthe."

It was the reference to the attorneys that jogged Max's memory. He'd seen Drew Primrose before. He was the young attorney at Sara's trial who had assisted her defense counsel. Max remembered how Sara's eyes had fastened on this young man as though there were no one else in the courtroom.

He was powerfully built, considering his occupation, and Max judged him to be close to thirty. He had brown hair, blue eyes, and regular features that might have been considered pleasant but for the deeply etched lines on his forehead. It seemed to Max that, in spite of the present smile, Drew Primrose must frown a lot. His dark coat and beige breeches were well fitting and of superior quality, though not exactly fashionable. The eyes that looked into Max's were as clear as a mountain stream, and just as cool.

They made their bows; the usual pleasantries were exchanged. What was plain to Max was that the announcement of Sara's betrothal came as no surprise to Drew Primrose. What was equally clear was that the young attorney did not approve.

It seemed that no one approved of him, and this was a new experience for Max. Sara was an heiress, and any man who came near her was highly suspect. He didn't know whether to laugh or stand on his dignity. If they knew who he was, they'd be kissing his boots.

Sara linked her arm through Drew's and led him to the fire. "You'll have a sherry?"

"I'm afraid I can't," he replied. "I'm dining with the Heatheringtons, and I must go home and change. Good evening, Mrs. Carstairs." He nodded to Constance. "Please excuse my dirt. I wouldn't be here had Anne not insisted. She wouldn't allow me to leave without seeing Sara."

"I should hope not!" replied Sara. "A few minutes more won't make any difference to the Heatheringtons, will it?"

"Perhaps not. But I'm always punctual, and they're bound to worry about me."

"Max, do sit down. You're blocking the fire," said Sara.

Max sat, but Drew remained standing, unmoved by all Sara's entreaties. "I just wanted to make sure that Anne was all right," he said. "She was rather shaken by the accident."

Constance said, "What about poor Mr. Thornley? It seems to me that he was the one who suffered most."

"What is he like, our new vicar?" asked Sara casually.

"Pompous," replied Constance at once, and took a long swallow from her glass. "And I should know. He is chairman of the church committee that is planning our contribution to the fair."

The young attorney ignored this moot observation. "At any rate," he said, "no harm was done, and Anne is none the worse for her experience." He looked at Max. "I presume we shall meet again very soon, Lord Maxwell. You'll want me to give you an account of Sara's financial holdings and so on. You realize, I presume, that there's a great deal of money involved?"

Though he knew he was being irrational, because it served his purposes to be taken for a fortune hunter, Max was becoming thoroughly fed up with this low opinion of his character. And because he was annoyed, he behaved with less that his usual grace. "If you mean do I know that Sara is an heiress, the answer is yes. I'm one of those who believes that it's just as easy for a man to fall in love with a rich woman as a poor one. And I consider myself a fortunate man indeed to have captured Sara."

"Quite," was the frigid response.

"Would tomorrow be too soon? To go over Sara's financial affairs, I mean. It's not that I'm mercenary, it's just that my own finances are in such a muddle that I hoped I could borrow a small sum on account."

"Max, behave yourself," said Sara with a light laugh. "Sometimes you carry your jokes a little too far. Come along, Drew, and I'll see you out."

From beneath lowered brows, she nailed Max with a look that an exasperated mother might bestow on a delinquent child, then, all smiles again, she ushered Drew from the room.

Max wandered over to the window and looked out.

"You won't see them from there," Constance said, gazing at Max shrewdly. "The rooms across the hall look out on the courtyard, and that's where Drew's buggy is probably tied up."

"I assure you, ma'am . . ." began Max, then let his words hang on the air. He smiled sheepishly. "They seem very close," he said.

"Very. They grew up together, you see. Drew's father was the head gardener at Longfield. Drew was older than Sara, of course, and she hero-worshiped him. At one time, her father and I thought they might . . . well, that's old history. Nothing came of it."

"He's done well for himself," said Max. "There are not many gardeners' sons I know who have the education to become attorneys."

"That's because my husband paid for his education. It's what Sara wanted, and my husband could never refuse Sara anything. It wasn't charity, though. It was a loan, and I believe Drew paid back every penny."

Max assimilated this in silence and finally said, "He seems rather young to have so much responsibility. Isn't there a senior partner?"

"Yes, but Sara insisted that Drew, and only Drew, handle her affairs. She places a great deal of dependence on him, not only as an attorney, but also for managing Longfield."

"He's the steward here, do you mean?"

"I suppose that's one way of putting it. He looks after things, that's all I know. When he's not in Stoneleigh, he's usually to be found here. Not that we've seen much of him when Sara was away, but now that she's home, I expect we'll see a great deal more of him. Do you play cards, Max?"

He nodded absently. He couldn't make up his mind whether Constance was trying to make him jealous or whether she was one of those women who couldn't help letting her tongue run away with her.

He looked up to see that Constance had produced a pack of cards and was sitting at a green baize table skillfully shuffling them.

"Yes," she said, noting that Max was watching her dexterity with the cards. "I've had plenty of practice. Usually, I play solitaire. Well, you see how it is. Simon and Martin are away most of the time, and when they're here they find other things to do. Anne does church work; Lucy practices on the pianoforte. And Sara, well, to Sara, I was always the woman who tried to displace her in her father's affections. We're not very close. Shall we play piquet?"

Max took the chair opposite Constance's. "What about the others? Shouldn't we wait for them?"

"It may be some time before they appear. Drew and Sara haven't seen each other for three years. They'll have much to talk about, don't you think? Letters are a poor substitute for a good heart-to-heart conversation."

Max looked at the cards in his hand and rearranged them. His glass was empty. He reached for the bottle and filled his glass to the brim.

Thirteen

⚬

SARA WAVED TO DREW AS HIS BUGGY PULLED
out of the courtyard, the same shabby one-horse buggy
he'd acquired when he'd become a partner in the firm. Her
brothers could never see it without hooting with laughter.
One day, she promised herself, she was going to buy Drew,
if she could persuade him to accept it, a spanking new curricle that would wipe the mocking laughter right off her
brothers' faces.

Drew had meant a great deal to her over the years. He'd
been quiet and serious as a boy and was now a quiet and serious young man. But something was wrong; she knew
something was wrong. He'd been stiff and formal in the
drawing room. She'd expected him to be like that with
Max, but not with her, and not with Constance. Drew was
more like a member of the family.

She'd been away three years, and now everything was
different. What on earth was going on?

He'd mentioned the dower house, and that had really
shaken her. He wanted her to raze it to the ground because
vagrants had broken in, and the house was dangerous. The
roof, he said, could fall in at any time.

She'd fobbed him off with the excuse that she was thinking of having it rebuilt. But she couldn't put him off for long.

A horrible feeling of approaching doom settled over her. She had to leave this place as soon as possible, and she had to persuade Anne to go with her.

On that thought, she entered the house and made straight for Anne's room. Lucy was easily distracted and went off quite happily to look for sheet music that Sara had bought in Bath.

Anne was at her dressing table in a fresh gown of blue sarcenet, trying to do up her hair. It occurred to Sara, then, that Anne was painfully thin, and it took all her willpower to keep a smile on her face.

The eyes of the two sisters met in the mirror.

"Here, let me help you with that," said Sara, striving for a light tone. She crossed to Anne. "Even as a child, you were all thumbs when it came to doing up your hair."

"And you were always there to fix it for me, weren't you, Sara?"

There was an odd note in Anne's voice that Sara ignored. "Yes, well, that's what big sisters are for."

She gathered the fall of thick hair into a rope and twisted it into a plait to lie smoothly along Anne's neck. "Pins?" she said.

"I can only find one," said Anne. "I think I must have lost them all in the accident."

"It doesn't matter. I have enough pins in my hair to do both of us."

When the pins were in place, Anne got up and reached for her shawl.

"No. Wait," said Sara. "I want to talk to you. Just for a few minutes. It's been three years, and you were never much of a letter writer."

Anne sank back in her chair, and Sara sat on the edge of

the bed. Anne said, "Nothing much ever happened at Longfield, so there wasn't anything to tell you. But . . ."

"Yes?"

Tears filled Anne's eyes. "I've missed you, Sara. I've missed you so much. When I heard you were coming home, I could hardly believe it. You will stay for a little while, won't you?"

"Of course, darling."

Sara abruptly rose, went to kneel by Anne's chair and hugged her. It was something that she'd been doing all her life. She barely remembered their own mother, but she remembered comforting Anne after their father had gently told them that their mother was in heaven now and they had to be brave little girls.

She'd always been stronger than Anne, not emotionally, but physically. Anne had been susceptible to every childish ailment and had spent a good deal of time in the sickroom. And she'd spent time there too, not only to keep Anne company, but because she was so afraid the angels would take her sister to live in heaven with their mother. Childlike, she'd made up her mind that she wasn't going to let that happen, not even if she had to fight the angel Gabriel himself.

But Anne wasn't weak. It took a woman with stronger nerves than Sara's to live with William Neville as his dutiful wife.

Sara held Anne at arm's length. "You should have written more often."

"I know, but as you said yourself, I never was much of a letter writer."

Sara smiled. "You had plenty to say about Mr. Thornley. You like him, don't you?"

"He's been kind to me, if that's what you mean."

"I thought," Sara hesitated, then went on, "from the tone of your letters, that it might be more than that."

Anne looked down at her clasped hands. "How could that be? I'm still a married woman. We don't know what happened to William, and until we do, I'm not free to love anyone." She looked at Sara with an anguished expression. "Sara, if you only knew—"

A shiver of apprehension brushed over Sara's skin. "What?"

Anne's eyes fell away. "It doesn't matter."

"No, tell me."

"It's only that I wish I could remember what happened that night."

"Nothing happened. It was just as I told you. I put you to bed. I gave you laudanum. I stayed with you the whole night through. William did not come home that night." Sara got up. "Listen to me, darling," she said. "What if I told you that I . . . that Max and I are thinking of settling in America. Would you come with us?"

"You mean, leave Longfield forever?"

"We could come back for holidays."

Anne smiled sadly. "I'm happy for you, Sara. I like the look of your Max. Of course, you must go. But I can't leave Longfield."

"Can't or *won't*?" said Sara, suddenly turning fierce.

Anne touched Sara's hand. "Sara, please—"

But Sara wasn't ready to be placated. "Your devotion to a husband who abused you is pathetic! He doesn't deserve it. And what if he's not dead? What if he comes back? What kind of life will you have then? If you come with me to America, we'll both be free of William. Don't you understand that, Anne?"

Another sad smile briefly touched Anne's lips. "You're trying to fix things for me, Sara, just like you always did. But this is something you can't fix. No one can." Anne rose. "Let's join the others. I want to get to know your Max."

Despair welled up in Sara. "But . . ."

"You can't fix it, Sara," Anne said softly. "You can't change me or what I feel. So please, leave it alone."

ON THE SURFACE, THOUGHT SARA, IT WASN'T a bad evening as evenings went in Longfield. Max and Constance played cards; she and Lucy amused themselves at the piano; Simon and Martin eventually turned up, and Martin was persuaded to sing a duet with Anne.

Not a bad evening at all if she had not sensed the brooding tension in Max. Whenever she chanced to glance his way, she found his eyes on her, watching, assessing. It made her tense. She couldn't relax. The muscles in her neck seemed to freeze, and her stomach churned. She wasn't sorry when the tea tray arrived and shortly after everyone began to drift off to bed.

Max caught up with her on the stairs. "Anyone would think," he said pleasantly, "that you're trying to avoid me."

"Mmm?"

"Avoid me, you know, as in running away."

"No." She held the candle high to light their steps. "I'm just tired, Max, that's all."

When they came to her door, she turned to bid him good night, but he spoke first.

"Aren't you going to invite me in? We are engaged to be married, you know. That entitles me to a few privileges."

"Like what, for instance?"

He gave her a big, lazy smile. "You figure it out."

She already had, and if she hadn't been holding the candle, she would have slapped him. Then she smelled the brandy on his breath, and everything became clear. "You're drunk!" she said.

"Drunk!" He looked dumbfounded. "I'm a gentleman, and a gentleman knows how to hold his liquor."

"Where," she asked ominously, "did you get it?"

He rubbed the bridge of his nose. "A gentleman never carries tales out of school."

"What makes you think," she asked sweetly, "that you're a gentleman, Max?"

In a move that was too inept to worry her, he boxed her in with one hand on either side of the door. "Don't you remember the night we met? I wasn't a gentleman then, Sara. I was a bloody saint! And I've regretted it ever since."

"That night—" She heard the quaver in her voice and strove to even her tone. "That night is best forgotten."

"That's easy for you to say. You got your reward. But look at me." He held out his hands and made them tremble. "I'm reduced to a shivering jelly. Isn't it time I got my reward too?"

She showed him her teeth. "More than time, and if I had a whip in my hand, I would give it to you. *Good night, Max!*"

She turned the doorknob and whisked herself into her room, but tipsy or not, Max was too quick for her. His foot connected with the door, sending it back on its hinges, and he sauntered into her room. Sara put down the candle and hastened to shut the door, just in case anyone loitering in the corridor would get the wrong idea.

When she turned around, he was propping himself against one of the bedposts. "Do you mind if I smoke?" he asked.

"You mean . . . you smoke as well?"

"I smoke. I drink. I make love to beautiful women." Though his posture remained relaxed, there was a challenge in his eyes. "Do you have a problem with that, Sara?"

She was beginning to see the humor in the situation, and might have laughed if he hadn't mentioned making love to beautiful women. "Frankly, I don't care what you do."

"Thank you!"

With that, he strode to the fireplace and used the candle to light his cigar. As he exhaled the first puff of smoke, Sara coughed delicately. Max smiled.

"You don't approve of me, do you, Sara?"

"I don't approve of your methods, Max. I don't like to be coerced into doing what I don't want to do."

"And I'm here on sufferance."

"I didn't invite you here."

"But Drew Primrose, well, you welcome him with open arms."

Her brow puckered. "What?"

"Drew Primrose. He's the kind of man you really admire: prissy, straitlaced, a prude, in fact."

"You've been listening to my brothers."

"And your stepmother. You hero-worshiped him, she told me."

"That was when I was a child. But Drew is a worthy person. I respect him."

She was standing in the center of the floor, and he began to circle her, puffing away on his cigar, giving her the peculiar sensation that she was a statue in some musty museum and Max was studying her for flaws.

"Drew is a worthy person," he mimicked. "Now that puzzles me. What about William Neville? Was he a worthy person too?"

"You know the answer to that."

"Yet you had an affair with him."

Her eyes flashed then darkened. "Do you have a problem with that, Max?" she asked, throwing his own words back at him.

"As a matter of fact, I do." He threw his cigar in the grate, and crossed to her in two strides. "I'm a worthy person. Maybe not as worthy as your precious Drew, but a damn sight better than William Neville."

"So?"

"So, what about it?"

She went rigid. "So what about what?"

His hands grasped her shoulders and his mouth lowered to hers. He said huskily, "So why don't we finish what we started that night in Reading, when I climbed through your window? Sara, I know you want it as much as I do. So why are you holding me off? What have you got to lose?"

In the next instant, he went staggering back when she shoved him violently with the heels of her hands. Before he could recover his balance, she shoved him again.

"You crude, loathsome, drunken lecher." She fairly spat the words. By this time, she had him up against the door. Trembling with fury, she glared up at him. "Is this an example of how you make love to a woman? With insults? If that's the case, I'd be very surprised if you're not a . . . a . . ."

"A what?"

"A virgin, that's what! A callow youth could do better than you."

"Now, just a minute, Sara. I wasn't insulting you."

"No! You just a minute!" She was so furious, the words were practically choking her. "Don't you know it's bad form to cast a woman's past lovers in her face before you ask her to go to bed with you? It might have worked in the past for you, Max, but it does not work with me."

He said moodily, "You're a spitfire when you're angry, aren't you?"

Air swished from her lungs. "And you're a jackass when you're drunk."

"I am not drunk!"

"Then what are you?"

"Restless. Hot. Feverish. If I can't have you soon, I think I'll go insane."

She was speechless.

"Look," he said reasonably, draping his inebriated arms over her shoulders, "I don't see what the problem is. You rigged yourself out tonight in that beautiful gown just to seduce me, didn't you? Well, I'm seduced. So why don't you let me take you to bed, and I'll show you what worthy really means."

She choked over her words. "You . . . I . . . what?" Then,

on an earsplitting crescendo, "Out! Out! *Out!* If you don't leave me at once, I'll scream the house down."

She didn't give him time to obey her command, but hustling him aside, opened the door and propelled him into the corridor. Then she slammed the door on his bewildered face and quickly locked it.

After a moment, the doorknob rattled. "Sara!"

No response.

"I don't have a candle. It's as dark as pitch out here. How am I supposed to find my way to my room?"

"You can't miss it," she hissed through the door. "Your room is next to mine."

There was a moment of silence, then the doorknob rattled again. "Do I turn right or left, north or south, east or west? It's all so confusing. Why aren't there candles in the hall? I've heard of thrift, but this is ridiculous. Anyone would think you didn't have a penny to your name."

She ground her teeth together, but a few moments later, she opened the door and thrust a candle into his hand. "That way," she said, turning him around and pointing him in the right direction. "And," she added ungraciously, "mind you don't set the house on fire."

"Thank you." And with as much dignity as he could muster, he sauntered off.

Sara slammed her bedroom door and locked it. The room stank of Max's cigar, so she marched to her window and opened it wide. A light winked in the darkness, fluttered, then went out.

Drew must be working late, she thought, for the light had come from his office, the converted gardener's house where he'd been born and raised. He was conscientious to a fault. He often worked late into the night on estate business, and would occasionally sleep at the cottage, though he had a home to go to in Stoneleigh. And Max Worthe, *special correspondent,* had the gall to look down on Drew? Well, she knew who her friends were, and Drew was a true friend.

But if Drew was there, it would be safer not to go out tonight.

She raked her fingers through her hair, dislodging pins. Nothing was going as she hoped it would. She'd tried talking to Anne again. They didn't have to go to America, she'd said. They could find a nice little house in Ireland or Scotland. But Anne would not budge.

And if Anne would not leave Longfield, neither would she.

Then there was Max. He was turning out to be more of a complication than she had anticipated.

She looked down at the pretty gown she'd worn that evening, made a face, and began to wrestle her way out of it.

IN THE CONVERTED GARDENER'S COTTAGE, CONstance stretched, catlike in the confines of the small trundle bed, replete after their feverish lovemaking. She laid her hand on her lover's bare chest. "We're taking an awful risk meeting here, Beckett. Now that Sara is home, Drew won't be able to stay away."

Beckett rolled to the edge of the bed, rose, and lit a thin cigar from the candle on the mantelpiece. The cigars were a present from Constance. Not many footmen were treated so royally, he thought, and grinned. Courtesy of Constance, he had an endless supply of the finest cigars and brandy that money could buy, as well as personal trinkets that were easily turned into hard cash. She wasn't bad in bed either, though, like Sir Ivor, he preferred more tender flesh. He'd rather be banging the young daughter, Lucy, than the mother. But this wasn't only pleasure. This was a means to an end.

He, and no one else, was going to claim the reward for finding William Neville's remains.

When he turned back to the bed, she had covered herself

with the sheet. "You think he'll start staying over at the cottage now that Miss Carstairs is home?"

Constance watched him through half-lowered lashes. He was unashamedly naked, and muscles rippled in his arms and shoulders. He was young and strong and beautiful. She didn't care that he was Lady Neville's footman. He made life bearable in this godforsaken place.

Her voice thickened. "I don't know, but I don't want to take foolish risks."

"Are you still in love with him?" he asked whimsically.

She wished she'd never told him about Drew. But Beckett was so easy to talk to. He'd come into her life when she needed a friend, after Drew had rejected her. "I never loved him," she said. "We were both lonely, that's all."

"And what about me? What do you feel for me?"

"You know I'd do anything for you."

He threw his cigar in the empty grate and came to sit on the edge of the bed. Smiling, he pulled the sheet down till she was completely exposed to his view. "I want to make love to you in your own bed," he said huskily. "In Longfield."

Her eyes went wide and she shook her head. "Beckett, no. It's too dangerous. Someone could find us out."

"Not if we're careful. You could let me into the house and no one would be the wiser. You said you would do anything for me."

"No."

"I want to. It will be exciting."

He spread her legs wide and began to stroke into her with his fingers. When she moaned, he smiled. "Say yes to me, Constance."

She gave him the answer he wanted. He thought of Lucy, climbed on top of her and gave her what *she* wanted.

*A*FTER BECKETT HAD SEEN HER BACK TO THE main house, he took the path to the dower house. All his instincts told him that William was buried nearby. Sara Carstairs would not have had the time or opportunity to dispose of a body far from the house. But all his searching had come to nothing. He would never find William's body unless Sara Carstairs either led him to it or told him where he could find it.

He was well aware that Lord Maxwell Worthe was not interested in the reward. What he wanted was a story for his newspaper. No one at Longfield knew his true identity.

Beckett laughed. It seemed that both he and Lord Maxwell were cut from the same cloth. They were both ruthless in the pursuit of their aims. But he had the edge on Lord Maxwell. Five thousand pounds was a fortune to him. There was nothing he would not do, no risk he would not take to claim it.

Fourteen

THE FOLLOWING MORNING, SARA OVERSLEPT and awoke with a headache. She didn't feel like facing Max, not because she was angry with him, but because she was angry with herself. *Restless. Hot. Feverish.* That's how she'd felt last night after he left. The bedclothes were in such a jumble, it looked as though a hurricane had passed right through her chamber.

She wished there were someone older and wiser who could explain how this man could have such an effect on her. He was the *Courier's* special correspondent. All he wanted was a story for his newspaper. She didn't want to want him, but that night in Reading had opened a Pandora's box, and she was suffering the consequences.

She would fight it. She had no choice. Max Worthe was a dangerous man.

Her thoughts buzzed around her brain, aggravating her headache, and she decided that a ride around the park would do her good. She was descending the stairs when Max strode into the hall, and she pulled back so that he would not see her. It was obvious that he had been out riding. She was ready to turn and make for her room when he went through the door to the breakfast room. When the door closed, she quickly left the house.

It was a perfect day for riding. The ground was soft, though not sodden, from yesterday's downpour; the sun was out and the breeze from the west brought the warm air from the coast. A stableboy led out Sara's mount, an elegant mare with flashes of white on her nose and fetlocks. She nuzzled Sara's neck in a frenzied welcome.

"She looks like she 'as missed you, miss."

"No more than I've missed her," said Sara. "Where is Dobbs?"

"Rubbing down Arrogance, miss. Shall I get him for you?"

If Dobbs, the head groom, was rubbing down Arrogance, the only person who could have ridden him was Max. Sara was surprised. Arrogance had been William's horse, and William had ruined his temperament. No one could ride him now.

She shook her head. "No. I'm not going far, only to the downs. I'll speak to Dobbs later."

She went uphill, through a wide swath that had been cut in the dense grove of beeches and yews. There were no manmade lakes, none of the fountains or gazebos that were presently in vogue. Her father had restored the park as it was originally, a rich man's hunting chase. The only difference was, her father was so softhearted that he had never allowed anyone to hunt in it.

The thought made her smile.

For the first little while, Sara simply gave herself up to the pleasure of her surroundings. The sky was cloudless; the sun's rays filtered through the leafy canopy overhead, creating lace patterns on the turf; the smell of damp grass under her horse's hooves was sweet and heady.

Memories came to her, pleasant memories that were touched with nostalgia, happier days when she and Anne first learned to ride on Shetland ponies, with Dobbs, the same groom they had now, keeping a watchful eye on them. Life had been carefree and golden then, just like this golden day.

The trees began to thin out, and at the top of a rise, she halted. Ahead of her were the downs, treeless, but dotted with patches of gorse and broom, and grazing on the sweet grass, clusters of sheep that blinked up at her without much interest, then went back to cropping the turf.

The view from the downs was extensive. The village of Stoneleigh, on her far right, was a huddle of Bath stone dwellings on the banks of the river. Directly below her, Longfield and its stables and workers' cottages seemed like an oasis against the encroaching wilderness of trees. The dower house was shielded from view, but it was only a half mile below Longfield, and across the valley lay the rich pastureland and farms of Hampshire.

She touched her heels to her mare's flanks, and Bonnie broke into a canter. At this point, the downs were unsafe for riders. Primitive manmade earth dwellings had been cut into the chalky soil, and there was a ruined Saxon fortification that had crumbled into a warren of treacherous pits. When William disappeared, the place had swarmed with men searching for his body.

She didn't want to think about William or her problems. She just wanted to feel the wind on her face and the thrill of racing across the turf.

She touched her heels to Bonnie's sides again, and in a few leaping bounds, her mare broke into a gallop. They crested one rise, then another, and there was nothing to hinder their progress but the wide, wide skies. Sara felt the sun on her back, the wind fragrant with gorse and broom on her face and her spirits soared. She felt free, without a care in the world, and in that moment she was conscious only of the pleasure of her mare stretching out her long legs to eat up the turf at the speed of lightning.

At the summit of the downs, she slowed her mare to a

walk, then reined in. It was then that she saw him, a rider on a white horse coming toward her. She turned Bonnie in a half circle so that she could see him better. At first, she thought it might be Simon on Eclipse, but as the rider drew nearer, she recognized him as Sir Ivor Neville.

She was shocked. Sir Ivor never rode on this part of the downs, had never done so in her memory. To him, Samuel Carstairs and his family were only one step above the servant class and he would not demean himself by putting himself in their way.

As her shock wore off, a bubble of panic rose in her throat. Her first impulse was to take off. The last person she wanted to come face-to-face with was William's father. She quelled the impulse because she'd left it too late. Behind her was a wilderness of junipers and bramble bushes; on her right were the earth dwellings and the Saxon ruin. Sir Ivor had cut off her escape.

He stopped a good ten yards in front of her so that if she made a bolt for it, he could close in and cut her off. He was a ruggedly handsome man, but when he was angry, the veins in his nose and cheeks turned purple. He was angry now.

Her hand trembled as she stroked her mare's neck and she braced herself for what was to come.

He was breathing hard and his voice was harsh. "You proud bitch! Have you no shame? To come back here where you did my son to death? Is this where William's body is hidden? On the downs?"

Her voice shook as much as her hands. "I didn't hide your son's body. I was acquitted of his murder."

When he edged his horse a little closer, she tensed.

"Go back to where you came from!" he said furiously. "You're not wanted here."

"Longfield is my home. I'm here to stay."

She'd said the wrong thing. He had a crop in his hand

and he raised it threateningly as he slowly approached. Sara did not wait. She wheeled her mount and sent Bonnie racing across the turf.

There was nowhere to go but toward the treacherous Saxon ruins. It came to her as Bonnie's legs ate up the distance that this is what Sir Ivor wanted her to do. He was maddened by grief and rage. He truly believed she had got away with murder. If she had an accident on the downs, no one would be the wiser. And to Sir Ivor, she would be getting no less than she deserved.

She checked Bonnie's speed as they approached the ruined foundations of the fort. She heard Sir Ivor's mount thundering at her back, gaining on her, but she didn't allow it to panic her. This was her territory and she knew this part of the downs like the back of her hand. And so did Bonnie.

It took all of her concentration to send Bonnie soaring over the first open pit, check her, then send her over the next. A few short steps, then they jumped over another obstacle and the mare came down on a narrow track.

They were in the clear.

Sara did not look back. There was no sound of pursuit now but she couldn't bear to see the hatred on Sir Ivor's face. She had always despised him, but in that moment when she should hate him most, all she could feel was pity.

SHE WAS STILL THINKING OF SIR IVOR WHEN she left the stable block.

"If I'd known you were going out riding, I would have waited for you."

She whirled to see Max approaching her. He was coming from the workers' cottages.

He frowned when he saw her face. "Are you all right?"

She wasn't going to tell Max that she'd had a frightening

encounter with Sir Ivor. She said lightly, "I fell off my horse. I'm out of practice, I suppose." She looked back the way he had come. "You've been to see Drew?" she said.

"Yes, but he wasn't there."

"He'll be in Stoneleigh. He has other clients besides me, you know."

They walked side by side toward the house. "Constance tells me," said Max, "that he sometimes sleeps over at his office."

"Only when he is working late."

"Was he working late the night William disappeared?"

She suddenly halted and turned to face him. "You can't think Drew had anything to do with William's disappearance!"

"I'm asking a simple question."

"No," she said angrily. "He was not. He was in Bristol on business, if you must know. Besides, what motive could Drew have for doing away with William?"

"Sara, you're your own worst enemy. You won't allow that anyone had a motive but you. If William is dead, someone must have had a motive for killing him. And who knows what goes on inside another person's head?"

She wanted to weep. She was shaken from her confrontation with Sir Ivor, and now this. Max would never give up. He thought that she was innocent and he wanted to clear her name. But it wasn't that simple. It wasn't simple at all.

When he cupped her shoulders and kissed her, she made no move to evade him. It was a gentle kiss, nothing more than the brush of his lips on hers.

"What was that for?" asked breathlessly.

"That," he murmured, "was an apology for last night."

He kissed her again, but this time his hand cupped her neck and she couldn't draw away. After a moment, she didn't want to draw away. She felt safe in his arms, safe and cherished. Desire came quickly, then emotion. *If only, if only, if only* drummed inside her head.

Her hand fisted in his coat. Her mouth softened. She wanted that kiss to go on forever.

Max drew away first. He smiled down at her dazed expression. "It's the same for me," he said softly. "I've never felt like this before either."

Her heart slammed into her ribs. Her response was barely audible. "No."

"You'll come to it on your own sooner or later." He smiled wistfully. "I hope it's sooner. You've been too long alone, Sara, and I want to change that."

She wanted to believe him. She was in the act of putting her hand to his face before cold reason returned. Her hand went to her own temples instead. "I think I'm more shaken from that fall than I realized," she said. "A cup of sweet tea is what I need."

They walked back to the house in silence.

THEY WERE IN THE DRAWING ROOM DRINKING tea when Anne entered. Right behind her was, obviously, the vicar. He was older than Sara expected, fortyish, and dressed all in black. He had a square face, a strong mouth, and a long, aquiline nose.

Anne made the introductions, then immediately invited Mr. Thornley to sit down and have some tea.

He beamed at Sara. "Allow me to thank you, ma'am, for your generosity in supporting the work of our church. You may rest assured that every penny we raise will go to alleviating the misery of the destitute in our parish. I trust we can count on your help at the fair?"

She made some vague response, half expecting to detect revulsion or distaste in his manner. She'd been acquitted of murder, but that did not make her innocent in the eyes of the world. She need not have worried. The vicar exuded amiability. Her hands unfisted as she began to relax.

She let Max field the vicar's expressions of congratulations on their forthcoming marriage while she concentrated on Anne. Anne's face was composed and betrayed nothing that Sara could have taken for a particular affection for Mr. Thornley.

Max said, "Do you have many poor in the parish, Vicar?"

"Yes, Lord Maxwell. Even in a relatively prosperous parish such as ours, the poor are always with us." He added two more lumps of sugar to his tea. "But we must expect it, must we not? The world could not survive without the poor."

"I don't think I follow you," said Max.

"If the lower classes were not poor, they would never be industrious. They would spend their money on drinking and fall into worse temptations. Not," he hastened to add, "that that relieves us of our Christian duty to offer them our charity."

"You mean," said Max coldly, "the same temptations that the upper classes fall into?"

The vicar looked momentarily nonplussed. He studied Max as though he were an interesting specimen of moth he had pinned on a card beneath his microscope. "I mean," he said, "that the good Lord has ordained some to command and others to obey and serve. We each have our appointed place, Lord Maxwell."

Max raised his cup to his lips and took a long swallow. "Tell me, Vicar," he said, "has the good Lord ordained that infants as young as five years be taken from their parents to become climbing boys for sweeps? Do you know how many of those poor wretches are burned and suffocated each year, and that they are half starved to keep them thin so that they can continue to climb up narrow chimneys? And what about the children we send down mines to haul coal? Did God ordain that too?"

Mr. Thornley looked bewildered, but no more bewildered than Sara felt. She hadn't been paying too much attention to the conversation. She'd been thinking of Sir Ivor. Now that she was paying attention, she realized that Max was blazingly angry, but she didn't know why.

The vicar smiled. "You have a soft heart, I think, Lord Maxwell."

Max was unsmiling. "With all due respect, sir, you haven't answered my question."

There was a moment of total silence. The vicar went a fiery red. Max crumbled a piece of dry toast between his fingers, his stare never wavering from the vicar's face.

Anne said quietly, "It is not words that matter, but deeds, surely? And the money we raise at the fair will go to equipping the poorhouse infirmary. Isn't that what counts, and not words?"

The vicar nodded. "Your simple, childlike faith is a credit to you, Miss Carstairs."

Just as Max opened his mouth to respond, Sara said hastily, "The teapot is empty. Shall I ring for a fresh pot?"

*A*S SOON AS THE VICAR LEFT WITH ANNE TO pick up supplies for the Stoneleigh Fair, Sara said crossly, "Really, Max, you were very rude to Mr. Thornley."

Max's mouth twisted in distaste. "I've met Thornley's type before, though not too many of them are vicars, thank God."

"What type?"

"Ignorant, stupid men who don't know what they're talking about, and don't want to know, which is worse. If they knew, they might have to do something about it. Sara, do you know how they train climbing boys?"

"No."

"Their skin must be hardened so that they can climb the chimneys without tearing their flesh to pieces. They are forced to stand in front of a hot fire so that their knees and elbows . . ." He broke off, stared at her hard, then let out a long sigh. "No. Maybe it's best if you don't know."

His features were pinched and his eyes were brilliant with anger. She wanted to touch him, to say that she understood, but of course, she didn't understand anything.

"I'm sorry," she said. "I didn't know. And you're right. I never thought about it."

The pinched look gradually left his face and he smiled. "If you were a regular subscriber to the *Courier,* you would have known. We did a series of articles last year on the lives of the poor and it didn't make for pretty reading. In fact, it created a storm of protest from our readers."

"They sympathized?"

"The reverse. They thought we should be horsewhipped or locked up for our seditious views. Some prophesied that we would lead the country into anarchy. Most letters sounded just like Mr. Thornley."

"No one supported you?"

"A few." He sounded bitter. "But the poor don't read the papers, because most of them can't read. And even if they could, they haven't the money or time to waste on newspapers. They're too busy eking out a living in mills or hacking coal down the mines so that people like us can be comfortable. They're so poor, they sell their sons into slavery—apprentices, we call them. But their daughters, they have the worst life of all. They—"

He checked himself, drew in a long breath, and let it out slowly. "The point I'm trying to make is that the poor don't have a voice. Someone has to speak up for them. But you're right. I shouldn't have been rude to a guest in your house. I apologize for my conduct."

This was something she had never imagined, Max passionately involved in a cause. She knew the *Courier* only as a purveyor of sensational news, like her own trial. As she gazed at him now, her eyes wide and searching, she could not seem to get the real Max Worthe into focus.

Her throat hurt and her eyes burned. She spoke slowly. "You really are the strangest man, Max Worthe."

The smile began on his lips, spread over his face, and finally warmed his eyes. "That is the nicest thing you've ever said to me, Sara."

Their eyes held.

To cover her confusion, she spoke flippantly. "And you have my permission to be as rude to Mr. Thornley as often as you like. Constance was right. He *is* pompous."

Max took a long swallow of tea and regarded her thoughtfully. "You're worrying needlessly. Anne isn't in love with the vicar."

She hadn't realized she'd betrayed so much. "How can you be so sure?"

He made a face. "Because she strikes me as a sensitive person and the vicar is a clod!"

She laughed. "It doesn't take you long to make up your mind about people, does it, Max?"

The smile gradually left his face. "I made a mistake with you, Sara, which I bitterly regret. One way or another, I intend to make it up to you."

"Don't—" She shook her head, jumped to her feet and quickly left the room.

Max took another swallow of tea. It wasn't all bad, he told himself. He was bringing her round. Slowly but surely, he was bringing her round. At this rate, he would have her tamed to his hand before the next century rolled around.

S IR IVOR SLAMMED INTO HIS LIBRARY AND made straight for the sideboard with its tray of decanters. He poured himself a neat brandy, bolted it, then poured himself another. He wished the bitch had broken her neck when she'd taken those jumps. That she should have a charmed existence, a woman like that, who had cheated the hangman's noose by the skin of her teeth! She was a trollop. She'd started an affair with his son right under her sister's nose. He didn't blame William for taking her.

But he must keep away from her or, by God, he would find a hangman's noose around his own neck.

What he couldn't understand was where Lord Maxwell fitted into this. Was he the man she'd brought home as her betrothed? His wife said that he was. Well, Sara Carstairs would soon learn that she had overreached herself. Lord Lyndhurst's heir would not dream of marrying a brewer's daughter, let alone a woman who had been tried for murder. Lord Maxwell was an aristocrat. He would not compromise his family's great name by marrying a soiled dove.

All he had to do was wait and Lord Maxwell would come to him and explain himself. He wanted the story for his paper, of course. And maybe he had access to Sara Carstairs's bed as well. Sir Ivor smiled. That's all she was good for, some man's amusement.

The sound of girlish laughter came to him from the open window, and he wandered over to it and looked out. Lady Neville was in the rose garden with her footman. Another girlish giggle grated on Sir Ivor's ears. When they were first married, he'd told his wife that she had a laugh as crystal clear as a mountain stream, and he'd been made to listen to it for the last thirty years.

He sipped his brandy slowly. Jenny had a girlish laugh, but it was genuine. She was pure, and he liked them pure. He was in no hurry to deflower her. His body hardened; his breath thickened.

He put down his glass, shut the window and drew the curtains. Three pulls on the bell rope would bring Jenny to him. He went to the bell rope and pulled on it.

Fifteen

DINNER THAT EVENING STARTED OFF WELL enough. There was a saddle of mutton for the main course, and it was done to perfection. Everyone remarked on the improvement in Cook's culinary skills. Only Sara seemed to realize that they had Max to thank for it. She stared at him with raised brows.

He answered that look with a slight lift of his shoulders. The problem had been easily solved. No one had ever shown the cook how to use the new stove. She'd been given a sheet of instructions, which were useless because the poor woman couldn't read and was too ashamed to admit it. Not that she'd told Max she couldn't read, but he'd soon figured it out for himself.

It never occurred to him to enlighten the others. Whatever he did would be misconstrued, and since harmony reigned at the dinner table, he decided to let sleeping dogs lie. Besides, he'd got what he wanted—a dinner he could enjoy.

It was Anne, in all innocence, who stirred things up. "Dobbs tells me," she said, "that you had Arrogance out this morning and managed him very well."

"I think it's fair to say," said Max, "that Arrogance

managed me very well. He anticipates what I want to do, almost before I think of it myself."

"Max is very modest," said Sara, teeth gleaming, her tone of voice implying the opposite. She saw Simon's face and her next words withered, unsaid on her tongue.

Simon scraped back his chair and got up. "Who gave him permission to take Arrogance out?" he asked Sara. He was furious.

"Dobbs did, I suppose," said Sara. "What's wrong with that?"

"You let *him* take out Arrogance, but I can't?"

Anne said in a painfully husky voice, "Sara has nothing to do with it, Simon. She's been away for three years. You know that Dobbs decides who rides Arrogance now. He's a highly strung thoroughbred. He can be dangerous. He's thrown you more than once, hasn't he? Obviously Dobbs thought Max could handle him."

"How will I ever learn to handle him if I'm not given the chance?"

Anne's eyes dropped away. "I'll speak to Dobbs and see what he says. Maybe if Max went out with you—"

"Max!" Simon's mouth twisted in a sneer. "How very chummy! He may have won you over, but he hasn't won me."

"That's enough, Simon," Sara said quietly.

He gritted his teeth. "It's not enough, not nearly enough. Are you all blind? Can't you see what's going on? He's going to be master here! Nothing will be the same again. It would be different if he were fond of Sara, but he's not."

He turned to Sara. "Can't you see what he is? Oh, he's polished, I'll give you that. But he's a fortune hunter. *Lord Maxwell!* A courtesy title that was bought and paid for in trade, I don't doubt. He'll ruin you, Sara, ruin us all."

Sara rose slowly. She was clutching her napkin and her face was paper white. "You've said quite enough, Simon. Either apologize to Max or leave the room."

"I am not a small boy for you to lecture!"

"Then stop acting like one."

Simon uttered an oath and flung out of the room. Martin looked down at his plate, hesitated for a moment, then he, too, left the room.

One of those ghastly silences that Max was coming to think of as a "Longfield" silence blanketed the table. Sara sank back in her chair. One by one, they picked up their cutlery and began to eat.

Oddly enough, Max felt a certain sympathy for Simon. It had to be galling for a young man who fancied himself a Corinthian to be passed over for a stranger, especially a stranger he despised. If he'd known Arrogance was forbidden to Simon, he would have chosen another mount, if only to save the boy's pride. But Arrogance was only the tip of the iceberg. Something else would have come up to set Simon off.

It was more than time that he and Simon had a private, man-to-man talk.

Anne scraped back her chair. "I'd best go and calm him down," she said. And with that, she left the room.

ANNE WAS SURE SIMON AND MARTIN WOULD make for the stables, and she was hastening after them when she saw a horse and rider coming toward her. Drew Primrose reined in. The last person she wanted to meet was Drew Primrose. She'd found him once with her stepmother, and she couldn't look at him without letting her feelings show.

"Anne," he said.

She didn't care about finding Simon and Martin now. Turning on her heel, she quickly returned to the house. In the vestibule, she halted, taking a moment or two to compose herself. She didn't blame Drew for having affairs, because the woman he wanted was out of his reach. But she did blame him for starting an affair with Constance. It could so easily have been Lucy or Simon or Martin who entered his cottage that afternoon to find their mother in Drew's bed.

Constance hadn't seen her, but Drew had. She'd been standing transfixed in his office because she recognized the woman's voice coming from behind the closed bedroom door. She must have made some sound, because before she could slip away, Drew opened the door and stepped into the office. He was half-clothed, and his hair was disheveled. They'd stared at each other for a long, long moment, but neither of them had said a word. She knew she hadn't concealed her disgust. And from that day on, she could hardly bear to be in the same room with him.

Maybe she was making too much of it. Constance was lonely. Drew was lonely. She could accept that. What she could not accept was that they carried on their affair so close to home.

There was a mirror on the vestibule wall and she caught sight of herself pacing. She stopped and stared at the girl reflected in the mirror. She was no beauty. She'd known when William had married her that he'd married her for her money, and she'd been content. It was the most she could hope for, she'd thought then. Fate had played a cruel trick on her. Even the little she'd hoped for was swallowed up in a nightmare of brutality.

Sara didn't know the half of it. Sara thought she was a dutiful wife. But she hadn't been dutiful, and now she was paying for her sins.

She was frightened. Max Worthe was asking everybody a lot of questions. Sara had been acquitted. Why couldn't he leave well enough alone?

She breathed deeply and slowly, trying to calm herself. The vicar had told her that God was merciful. She wished she could believe it, because sometimes she thought she was living in hell.

Knowing that Max Worthe had the eyes of an eagle, she pinned a smile on her lips before she made her way upstairs.

*N*O ONE LINGERED IN THE DRAWING ROOM that evening. Everyone was preoccupied with his or her own thoughts. Constance pleaded a headache and excused herself; Max went for a walk; Lucy and Anne played a game of checkers, then drifted away; and Sara went in search of Simon and Martin.

They weren't in their rooms and none of the servants knew where they were. It was just as well, she told herself, as she dragged herself up the stairs to her own chamber. She would probably have lectured them again, especially Simon, and it never did any good.

She was sinking into self-pity when she entered her chamber. The same old thoughts crowded her mind. She'd tried to do the best for her family and they weren't even happy. With the exception of Lucy and Anne, they were quarrelsome, selfish, self-centered, and insufferably rude.

Had they always been like this?

Just once, she would like someone to ask her what would make *her* happy.

She wandered over to the window and looked out. Though it was almost ten o'clock, it was still light. It had started to rain again, but at least it was warm. There would be no need to light a fire tonight.

She breathed out slowly, and as she exhaled, she felt the self-pity wash out of her. Her family was abominable except in one respect: her trial for William's murder had made no difference to them. They didn't look at her askance or watch her speculatively, as others did, wondering whether she was innocent or guilty. They didn't fear she might turn on them. They treated her as they'd always done.

They thought she was innocent, of course.

If only she could leave things the way they were.

But she couldn't leave things as they were. She had to come to some decision about the dower house. She couldn't afford to rebuild it until she came into her money, and even then, she didn't want to rebuild it. Drew was right. It was better to raze it to the ground.

Her hand was being forced every way she turned. The time for prevarication was past. That's why she'd had a quiet word with Dobbs before dinner. She'd told him that every night from now on, he should take as many men as could be spared and make sure that there were no vagrants or gypsies or tinkers camping out in the dower house.

Tonight, somehow, she would find the courage to do what had to be done.

When she turned from the window, he eyes fell on her dressing table. Propped against her silver hairbrush was a folded piece of vellum. She knew what it was before she reached for it.

Her name was written on the outside in William's beautiful copperplate. Her fingers trembled as she tore open the wax wafer.

Welcome home, was all it said.

Sixteen

*I*T HAD STOPPED RAINING, BUT THE GRASS WAS drenched and the trees were shedding enough drops of water to make it necessary to raise the hood of her cloak. From time to time, Sara looked back at the house. There were no lights at any of the windows. All the same, she was careful to keep to the shelter of the trees and shield her lantern with her body. In her right hand, she grasped her father's pistol. It was heavy and clumsy, but it was also vastly comforting. She wouldn't have had the courage to leave the house in the dead of night without it, not after receiving that note.

Welcome home.

After all the agonizing she'd done tonight, she felt curiously detached, almost fatalistic. In the next few minutes, she'd learn the truth about William. She didn't know how it would help her. If William wasn't sending her these notes, someone else was, someone close to her. Someone who hated her.

The suspicion lay like a shadow on her heart. After the first wave of shock had receded, she'd stared at the note in black despair. Only someone in the house could have put the note on her dressing table for her to find, either a servant or one of her family.

She was glad Max had not been there when she received it. He wouldn't leave it alone. He'd probe and probe until he found the answer. And she was so terribly afraid of what the answer would be. It had been a mistake to allow him to come here. She should have defied him, told him to do his worst. What did it matter if he wrote about her in his newspaper? There were worse things than that. He wanted to clear her name, but if the truth ever came out, he would only destroy her.

A twig snapped close by and she froze. Every muscle in her body tensed, and she slowly raised the pistol in her right hand.

A badger shuffled out of the undergrowth. He wasn't afraid of her, but inquisitive. His bright beady eyes seemed to sum her up, then he sniffed and swaggered into the darkness.

Only then did she let out her breath. She wasn't a fool. She'd known she was taking a risk by exposing herself like this. But it had to be done. If not tonight, another night. This was why she'd come home.

She knew she was nearing the dower house when the familiar haze of summer scents wrapped around her, honeysuckle and jasmine and the heavier fragrance of roses. In her mind's eye, she could see the dower house as it used to be, before the fire, with a profusion of scented flowers carelessly draped over the garden walls.

Snatches of memories flitted through her mind. She was eight years old and standing on top of the wall. *I'm the king of the castle,* she'd cried out, and had promptly taken a fall. She'd been on the point of crying, she was so shaken, but Anne had started to bawl, and she'd had to comfort her sister instead.

Absurdly, tears filled her eyes now.

In those days, the house was rented out most of the time, but when there were no tenants to chase them away, the dower house had become their playground, hers and Anne's.

They'd learned all its secrets. And they'd kept those secrets to themselves.

Fear squeezed her heart, and she waited a moment until she had mastered herself. There could be no turning back now. On that thought, she made herself move, picking her way over tree roots and broken branches. At the big iron gate at the entrance to the garden, she halted. The padlock on the gate was broken.

The light from her lamp barely reached the house. Veiled as it was in semidarkness, it looked curiously untouched, and as quiet as a tomb.

She cursed herself for the stray thought, and before her courage completely deserted her, she quickly pushed through the iron gate and entered the garden. Little hills and depressions, now covered with weeds, pockmarked the flower beds. This was where the constable and his men had turned over the earth in their search for William's body. They'd also made a thorough search of the house and found nothing.

Other memories were beating at the edges of her mind, demanding to be let in, but she resolutely pushed them away. She made her mind blank as she crossed to the house, mounted the stairs, and entered the hall. Here, she halted, and raised her lantern high to view the wreck the fire had made of this once-lovely house.

And wreck it was. Blackened beams littered the floor like grotesque coffins. There was no gracious staircase now, only jagged remnants to mark its passing. She looked up at the roof. The light from her lantern did not reach that far, but she could see a patchwork of light and dark where the roof opened to the sky. Directly opposite her, facing the entrance, untouched by the fire, was the great stone fireplace with its inglenooks on either side.

The memory was as fresh as if it had happened yesterday. They'd been playing a game of hide-and-seek, she and Anne, when she'd stumbled upon it. She was hiding in one of the inglenooks, and Anne was coming closer and closer. She could never remember afterward what insanity had made her decide to try and climb the inglenook wall. She'd reached for one of the decorative bricks high above her head and had been left hanging when her feet lost their hold. As she'd tried to regain her balance, part of the chimney floor slid open.

They'd heard of priests' holes, of course, those hiding places for priests during England's bloody history, when Catholics were hunted down. There was one at Longfield, but it was no bigger than a closet. The one at the dower house was more like a small room.

She and Anne had told no one. For one thing, their father would have punished them if he'd known that they were playing in the dower house, and for another, they'd hugged the secret to themselves, as children do, feeling smug and superior because no one else knew about the room beneath the flagstone floor.

And it had remained their secret to this very day.

She swallowed hard and willed her pulse to slow down. Many moments passed before she steeled herself to go on. With head bent, she concentrated on navigating her way over debris and around obstacles to reach the fireplace wall. Six feet from the hearth she saw them, and all the air rushed out of her lungs.

By some trick of fate, two massive beams had fallen into the fireplace and barred her way. She might reach one corner of the chimney, but not the one she wanted.

She set down her lantern and pistol and tried to angle her body into the inglenook so that she could put her shoulder to one of the beams. It was impossible. A child might fit, but a child wouldn't have the strength to move the beams.

She wasn't ready to give up yet. She stood back for a moment, then came at it from a different angle, clasping the nearest beam with both arms and dragging on it with all her might. She gritted her teeth, feeling the strain across her shoulders and back, using muscles in her thighs and stomach she hadn't used in an age. She pushed, she pulled, she came at it from every direction. It would not budge.

Finally defeated, she sank down on a fallen beam. She could have wept. To have come so far only to meet with this brought her to the edge of despair. She didn't know what to do next. It would need a man or a team of oxen to move the beams. If she could find a lever of some sort, or a length of rope, she might stand a better chance.

She was reaching for the lantern when she heard a small, stealthy sound, like the crunching of gravel underfoot, coming from just outside the entrance. Her head whipped up and she listened intently. When it came again, she reached for her pistol and blew out the lantern.

*M*AX'S HEAD JERKED, DRAGGING HIM FROM sleep, and he stretched his cramped muscles. It took him a moment to come to himself. He was fully dressed and had fallen asleep in a stuffed armchair. Simon's chair. Simon's room.

He stretched again and got up. The candle was beginning to sputter, so he lit a fresh candle he found on the mantelpiece. It was three o'clock in the morning, and still no sign of Simon—or Martin, for that matter.

What in Hades did they get up to till this time of night?

Stupid question. When he was an eager eighteen-year-old, he'd got up to plenty, and his parents hadn't known a thing about it.

He might as well give up and go to bed. He wasn't going to have that man-to-man talk with Simon he'd been promising himself. But they'd have it soon, because he, Max Worthe, mild-mannered and easygoing though he might be, had had his fill of quarrelsome, bad-tempered infants. He didn't think this was a quarrel they would settle with words. Their fists, more like, but all done in a gentlemanly fashion, of course, one Corinthian to another.

In short, he was going to beat the living daylights out of that whelp. That was the only way to get Simon's respect. Martin, naturally, would follow Simon's lead. It was time Martin learned to live his own life instead of living in his brother's shadow.

Max felt in his jacket pocket and found a cheroot. He took the candle with him when he left the room.

RISING SOUNDLESSLY, SARA EDGED HER WAY to one side of the fireplace wall and flattened herself in the inglenook. Her pulse was racing again; her blood throbbed at every pulse point. Her breathing was becoming labored, so she pressed her lips together to stifle the sound of it. Slowly, slowly, she raised her pistol and cradled it in the crook of her left arm. She was sick with fear.

The minutes dragged by. From her position in the inglenook, she could see only one side of the hall. Because the upstairs windows were not boarded up and the roof was open to the sky, the darkness was not absolute, but marbled with paler shades of gray. One of those marbled shadows began to move. Then she knew it was a man.

He kept hard by the wall, moving cautiously as she had done when she'd entered the hall, to avoid fallen beams and masonry. His shadow merged with a darker shadow, and though she could no longer see him, she could trace his path by the tread of leather on debris on the floor. Occasionally he stopped, as though he, too, were listening for a sign of another presence.

He was level with her now. She could hear him breathing, smell him, feel his eyes searching the darkness for her. It wasn't her imagination. He knew she was here, and though she couldn't explain it to herself, she knew, sensed, that his purpose was sinister.

This was no vagrant looking for a place to bed down for the night. William's name drummed inside her head.

She longed to cock her pistol but was terrified that he would hear the sound of the hammer going back. Safer by far to stay where she was and wait it out, even if she had to stay here all night.

He passed by her, going to the back of the house where the family parlor used to be, and beyond that, the kitchen and pantry. She heard flint strike iron, once, twice, and panic rose in her throat. He'd found a candle or a lantern and was trying to light it.

A spate of thoughts tore through her brain. He'd been here before or he knew the house well; in another minute he would light the candle and discover her hiding place. He could be armed as well. She wouldn't stand a chance.

She had to get out of here before it was too late.

Though she was crippled by fear, she made herself move. Half crouched over, she began to grope her way to the entrance. She bumped into something and sucked in a breath. Then she heard him. He wasn't moving stealthily now. He knew where she was and he was making straight for her.

Blind instinct took over. She hurled herself over beams, gained the front steps, and threw herself down them. Her feet had never moved faster. A few bounding leaps took her to the gate, then she was through it, and running for her life.

She screamed when he grabbed her from behind. She would have screamed again, but those powerful masculine arms suddenly tightened around her rib cage till she thought her ribs would crack. She squirmed. She kicked out. His grip did not slacken. Almost as frightening as his sheer brute strength was the silence of his attack. Not a word passed his lips, not a threat or a warning. All she could hear was the harsh sound of his breathing.

When he lifted her off her feet, she flung back her head and connected with his face. He swore and relaxed his grip. Maddened by fear, Sara wrenched herself free, then in one lightning movement, lashed out with her pistol. The force of the blow made her cry out. Her assailant groaned and fell back. Sara whirled away and made a dash for the cover of the trees.

She was sobbing in sheer animal terror as she tore through a wilderness of briers and holly bushes. She wasn't looking for a place to hide. Like an animal of the wild, the quarry of a predator, she was panicked into a stampede.

It seemed like forever before she saw Longfield's porch light winking at her through the trees. She didn't slacken her pace. Though she had a stitch in her side, and her legs were cramping painfully, she made her feet move as if every moment would be her last.

As she hurtled out of the trees, a dark figure loomed up in front of her. She gasped and tried to check herself, but her momentum carried her forward. When strong arms closed around her, Sara went wild.

"Sara, will you stop struggling!"

Max's voice! It didn't calm her. In fact, it only enraged her, but she stopped struggling. "You!" she choked out. "It was *you* back there!" She sucked air into her lungs. "How dare you frighten me like that!"

Max looked over her shoulder. "Back where? What are you talking about? I've not long left the house. And what in hell's name are you doing out at this time of night?"

"As if you didn't know. You followed me! You deliberately tried to frighten me!"

"I did nothing of the sort. I've been waiting up for Martin and Simon. They're still not back. I came outside to smoke."

As she strove to regain her breath, she blinked up at him, and it came to her that Max was keeping his temper on a tight leash. He was angry because he thought she'd crept out of the house to meet someone.

She hadn't the stamina or enough breath to argue the point with him. More than anything, she wanted to be inside Longfield's stout walls, with every door and window locked against intruders.

Making an effort to pull herself together, she said in a shaken voice, "I didn't go out to meet anyone, if that's what you think. Can we talk later?" She pressed a hand to her eyes. "I've just had the fright of my life. Someone attacked me just now."

Tears welled up. She couldn't help it. Max looked so solid, so safe. Everything about him was reassuring, the faint smell of soap on his skin, the scowl on his face. She could tell that he'd been smoking, and though she hated the smell of tobacco, on this occasion, it pleased her more than the costliest French perfume. Even if she closed her eyes, she could still tell that she was with Max.

Max didn't pester her with questions. There was very little light to see by, but he could feel her whole body shaking. He put an arm around her shoulders and walked her to the back door.

"Where did it happen?" he asked quietly.

She shivered. She wasn't going to mention the dower house. "Not far from the house. Down there." She pointed vaguely behind her.

"You sound," he said, "as though you could use a large brandy, and it just so happens that I have a bottle in my chamber. Why don't you go there, lock yourself in, and I'll be up in a few minutes."

"Where are you going?" she asked quickly.

"I want to have a look around."

Her fear came back in a flood. "No! It could be dangerous."

"I know how to look after myself."

He released her, slid his hand into his coat pocket and produced a pistol. Only then did it come to her that her own pistol was missing. She couldn't remember where she'd dropped it.

Max said, "I won't go far. All I want is to make sure that no one is skulking around the house, all right?"

It wasn't all right, but before she could muster a protest,

he had pushed her into the back hall, snapped the door shut, and locked it from the outside.

There were several unlit candles on a table just inside the door. She lit one from the lamp that was burning and, shielding the flame with one hand, pushed through the door to the servants' staircase, and quickly mounted the stairs.

She went to her own chamber first, meaning only to tidy herself, but when she'd lit several candles, and had taken a good look at herself in the mirror, she was stricken. She looked like a witch. Her garments were mired in soot and there were smudges of soot on her face as well; her hair was a mess and there were thorns embedded in her hands.

She sank down on her dressing table chair as in a daze, and stared at her reflection. *How had it come to this?* Her eyes lost focus, and thoughts she'd tried to banish to the farthest corner of her mind flooded into awareness as though a dam had burst.

When she came to herself, she jumped up, went to the clothes press, and chose a fresh gown. Then she began to strip.

Seventeen

❦

THE BRANDY BURNED HER THROAT, BUT IT wasn't an unpleasant sensation. After two or three sips, she felt a little better, and after a few more, she was able to describe the attack on her in a fairly level tone. She told Max only as much as she deemed was prudent. She didn't mention the dower house, but she showed him the note in William's handwriting.

She was upset, she said, and couldn't sleep, so she'd decided to go for a walk. Once or twice, she looked longingly at the door. If only she could have a few hours' rest, she'd be better equipped to answer Max's questions. She wasn't sure how much to tell him or what she should leave out.

Max had lit the fire, and they were comfortably ensconced in stuffed armchairs on either side of it. He looked tired and pale, and there were dark circles under his eyes. He wore no neckcloth, and his clothes were rumpled.

"Could it have been a vagrant who attacked you?" he asked.

"No." She paused as the memory came back to her.

"Why not?" Max prompted.

"He didn't smell like a vagrant." She smiled faintly. "I

wasn't even aware of it at the time, but he smelled of cologne."

Max was staring at the fire. "Now let me see if I have this right." His voice was strangely uninflected. "This note was waiting for you when you went to bed." He held up the note that was written in William's hand. "You suspected that it came from William. And yet, you still went out, knowing that he might be waiting for you?"

She wasn't ready for this kind of cross-examination, not after what she'd been through. With each little lie, she was laying another trap for herself.

She said carefully, "I don't know what I thought, Max, but I certainly didn't expect William to be lying in wait for me. I couldn't sleep. I told you. I was upset. I went out for a walk. That's all there is to it."

He curbed his temper with an iron will. He knew she wasn't telling him the whole truth, but he didn't know how to force it out of her. It was obvious that she still didn't trust him, and that stung. But worse by far was his gnawing sense of helplessness. There was no question that she'd been attacked. If she'd come to him when she received the note, it would have never happened. He didn't know whether he wanted to gather her in his arms or shake the life out of her.

But he couldn't excuse himself either. He hadn't been convinced that she was in any real danger. He'd thought that the notes were malicious, the product of a warped mind. And that's all he'd thought.

He took a long swallow of brandy, then said, "I don't think it was William who attacked you."

"I might have said that yesterday, but not now. Surely this proves that William is alive?"

"Then why didn't he kill you?"

Her eyes went wide. "What?"

He said levelly, "If it were William, wouldn't he want to kill you? You've told me often enough that he wants you dead so that he can claim the Carstairs fortune through

Anne. So why didn't he come armed to do the job? He wasn't armed, was he?"

She shook her head slowly. "I don't know. But I fought him tooth and nail. Maybe he wanted to make it look like an accident."

He thought for a moment, then finally said, "We can't overlook the possibility that it was someone else."

She shrank back in her chair. "No," she said. "I won't believe that."

"Sara, you must face facts. Who had access to your bed-chamber? Who could have left you that note?"

She said quickly, "William could. He knows the house well. He could have slipped in when we were at the dining table and no one would have known."

He went on regardless. "It could be Simon. Or Martin. They left the dining room first and they still haven't come home."

"That's absurd." Her throat worked convulsively. "They wouldn't hurt me. They've probably stolen away to go to a cockfight or something. It wouldn't be the first time they've stayed out all night."

She was shaken, but so was he, and he was determined to drive home his point. "Or Anne could be behind it. She left the dining room, and she has the most to gain if something were to happen to you. Oh, I know she didn't attack you personally, but she might have had an accomplice."

"No," she said. "No! I won't listen to this."

His voice turned savage. "And let's not forget the inestimable Mr. Primrose. Maybe he'd rather you were dead than see you go to another man. With Constance, of course, it could be jealousy or some other motive we have yet to discover. It could be anyone, Sara, *anyone*. Do you understand?"

She put her glass down and slowly got up. Her eyes were naked with pain. Her voice shook so hard, he had to strain to hear her words. "Why are you torturing me like this?

Can't you see it isn't necessary? I'm not stupid. I know well enough that if it wasn't William who left me that note, it must be someone close to me. And do you know something?" Her voice rose shrilly. "I don't want to know who it is. I don't want you to investigate. I don't want you to entrap anyone. I want you to leave it alone, Max. Just leave it alone."

He'd miscalculated. She was more shaken than he'd realized. He put out his hand in a placating gesture. "Sara, I'm sorry. You're right. It's probably William, or someone we haven't thought about yet. Look, I was only trying to convince you that you mustn't take foolish risks. It's too dangerous."

"Dangerous!" She plowed her hands into her hair. She said bitterly, "There wouldn't be any danger if I hadn't listened to you. I should have followed my original plan. I should have married Mr. Townsend. Then this nightmare would be over. Everyone would be happy. Then we could go back to being a family again without all this suspicion poisoning our minds."

She swung away from him and began to pace. Her hands were still caught in her hair, clasping her head as if she were nursing a monumental headache.

He said quietly, "Sara, we're not going to leave things as they are. We've got to find out who attacked you, no matter who it is. You must see that."

She whirled on him then, a wild-eyed fury and she quickly crossed to his chair. "Don't tell me what I have to do! What do you know about it?" Her voice was cracking with emotion. "What good will it do if I find out that Simon or anyone else in my family attacked me tonight? It would destroy us as a family. We'd all have to take sides. Do you think I'm going to let that happen? Besides, you said it yourself. Whoever it was didn't try to murder me. Maybe all he wanted was to frighten me. I'm not judging him. Oh God, I'd be the last person to judge anyone. My father should have treated us all equally. He shouldn't have left everything to me. How can I blame my family for turning against me? No one knows what anyone will do when they're desperate or put to the test. But it's not too late. I'm going to put things right. I swear to God, I'm going to put things right."

She began to pace again. "If I raised my offer, maybe Mr. Townsend would still marry me." She spoke her thoughts aloud as they occurred to her, either oblivious or uncaring of his presence. "Yes, that's what I'll do. I'll make him an offer he can't refuse."

He came out of his chair.

"Should I write to him? No. It would be better to talk to him in person, don't you think? Tomorrow. I'll return to Bath tomorrow, then, I'll . . . I'll . . ."

Suddenly, she covered her face with her hands and her shoulders began to heave. "I can't breathe," she choked out.

Max reached her in two strides. He put his glass to her lips and forced her to swallow. She choked, sputtered and pushed his hand away. He tried again, and this time she swallowed, then she let out a long shuddering breath.

"Thank you."

"Now sit down in that chair and drink every drop of that brandy."

She obeyed. After a while, she looked up at him. "It's hopeless, isn't it? I don't know what to do, which way to turn."

He knew that it wasn't only the attack on her that was tearing her to pieces, but suspicions too painful to admit to anyone. Money was a powerful motive for murder. That's why she wanted to marry and break the trust. It wasn't only because she feared William was alive.

He went down on his haunches so that their eyes were level. "Feeling better?"

She nodded. "You've seen us at our worst—my family, I mean. Things were different when my father was alive."

He thought he was on safe ground when he said, "He

was a hard man to live with, wasn't he?" But again, she surprised him.

"Well, maybe we needed it. The discipline, I mean. You can't know how much I miss him."

"You sound as though you loved him."

"Actually, I *adored* him. We didn't always see eye-to-eye . . . but . . . Oh, Max, what am I going to *do*?"

The words jumped out of his mouth before he had a chance to think about them. "You're going to marry me, of course."

She was astonished. So was he. Slowly, his lips curled in a bemused smile. *Why, in heaven's name,* he asked himself, *does she have to be the one?*

She blinked slowly. "What did you say?"

"I said that you should marry me."

"You'd marry me, just like that?" She snapped her fingers.

"No. Not just like that. I've given this a great deal of thought, and I think it would be the best solution for both of us."

She said scathingly, "You'd go that far, just to get a story for your newspaper?"

He almost lost his temper before he remembered that she was still shaken from the attack, still confused and in need of comforting. He took the glass from her and set it down, then clasped both her hands. "Listen to me, Sara," he said. "I don't have to marry you to get my story. Even if you were to marry Townsend, I'd still hang around. And where would Townsend be? He'd take his money and leave. Someone has to stay here to take care of you.

"I know you think that once the trust fund is broken, the danger will be over. But are you sure? I'm not convinced that this has anything to do with money. If I'm right, it wouldn't matter if you went into hiding again and waited to come into your fortune when you turn twenty-five. Someone wants to hurt you. They found you before, and they will find you again."

"Don't you think I know that?" she said miserably.

His voice dropped and he stared at the scratches on her hands. "If you marry me," he said, "we'll both get what we want. If you're right, the danger will be over because the trust fund will be broken. But if I'm right, whoever wants to harm you will have to deal with me first."

Her eyes searched his face. "You'd go that far, just to protect me? But why?"

He gave her reasons that he knew she could accept. "Because I feel responsible. Because my newspaper stirred up public opinion against you. Because I was wrong about you and I want to make amends."

She tried to withdraw her hands. "I don't know, Max. I just don't know."

He felt as if his fate were hanging in the balance. In a voice that was strangely unlike his own, he went on, "And because, if you marry someone else, I'd just have to kill him." He flashed her a crooked smile. "Tell me I'm wrong about us. Tell me you don't want me as much as I want you, and maybe, just maybe, I'll find the strength to let you go."

He pulled on her hands and raised her to her feet. He could see that his little speech had made quite an impression on her. Her eyes were wide, dazed, disbelieving.

He'd never considered himself an unscrupulous man, but he was well aware that he was taking advantage of the situation. She was still suffering from shock. She was lost and confused. As she said herself, she didn't know which way to turn. He justified what he was doing by telling himself that it was only a matter of time before she came to him of her own free will. But events were moving too fast. Time was something he couldn't afford to give her.

He wrapped his arms around her. "Say you'll marry me, Sara."

Her eyes teared. "It wouldn't be fair to you, Max."

"I'll be the judge of what's fair."

His lips settled on hers. "Max," she breathed out, half protest, half plea.

She stopped thinking when he crushed her against his hard length and took her mouth with a passion that sent her senses reeling. She clung to him for support, her head pressed into the crook of his arm as the kiss went on and on.

His hands moved over her, pressing her closer. She felt his arousal, and her own body clenched in response. The part of her mind that could still think told her that she wasn't being prudent. She didn't care. She was alive. She'd never felt more alive in her life. No one knew what would happen on the morrow.

When she started struggling, Max released her, but it was only to free her arms so that she could twine them around his neck. Then she dragged his head down to renew the kiss.

Surrender. She was giving into him. And his bed was only a step away. His body was urging him to take her, and so was his common sense. If he took her now, there would be no going back. On the other hand . . .

He was debating with himself, and that was a fatal mistake. The scrupulous part of his nature won the battle. He'd never taken advantage of any woman, and he certainly wasn't going to start with the only woman he'd ever wanted to be his wife.

With the greatest reluctance, he raised his lips an inch from hers. "Does this mean you'll marry me?"

There was a heartbeat of silence as she tried to make sense of his words. "Yes," she whispered, "yes," and she gave him her lips again.

He kissed her softly. "You're sure?"

"I'm sure."

That was all he wanted to hear.

She cried out when he suddenly stooped down, swept her into his arms, and held her high against his chest. "What—?"

"I'm taking you to your room. No. No arguments. You've been through a lot tonight. I said that I would protect you and I meant it, even if it means protecting you from myself. What you need is a good night's sleep, and that's what you're going to get."

For a moment or two, she was totally humiliated, until she saw something in his eyes, banked fires tinged with humor, and she contented herself with burying her head against his chest. Max was right. She was exhausted, too exhausted to put her thoughts in order. All she knew was that Max was here, and just for a little while, she needn't worry about anything.

He took her to her room, deposited her on her bed and warned her that he'd give her five minutes, ten at the most, to get ready for bed, then he'd return to watch over her. He waited until she'd locked the door, then made for the servants' quarters upstairs and roused one of the footmen. He had plans to make, things to do, and he needed someone he trusted to watch over Sara. After he'd given the footman his instructions, Max returned to her room.

She was drifting into sleep when the memory of the attack flashed into her mind. "Max?" She hauled herself up and looked wildly around her chamber. He was sitting in the chair beside the fire, reading a book.

He rose at her cry of alarm and quickly crossed to her. "What is it, Sara?"

She shook her head. "Nothing. Just . . . Max." Then she snuggled down in the bed and closed her eyes again.

When her breathing was slow and even, Max brushed her hair back from her face and discovered a long deep scratch from her ear to the base of her neck. He traced it with his fingertips, and rage ignited in the pit of his belly.

He wasn't as forgiving as Sara, not nearly as forgiving. When he found the person who had attacked her, he would exact a fitting revenge.

He was still staring at that scratch when there was a knock on the door. He went to answer it.

Eighteen

$\smile$

SARA WAS SITTING UP IN BED DRINKING A glass of hot chocolate that her maid had brought only a few minutes before. Though Martha had greeted her with the cheery news that it was a beautiful, warm summer day, Sara felt cold and shivery. It was late, almost noon, but she couldn't summon the will to get up. All she wanted was to pull the blankets over her head and forget that anything existed outside the safety of her own chamber.

No one looking at her would have known that she'd been attacked last night. The only obvious injuries were the long scratch on her throat and the scratches on her hands. If she had to, she could explain them away by saying that she'd been playing with one of the stable cats. There were also grazes on her knees, but no one was likely to see them.

She didn't want anyone to know about the attack, because she didn't want to answer awkward questions. But most of all, she didn't want to raise the kind of suspicions that were going through her own mind.

Much as she wanted to, she couldn't stop reliving every moment of the terror she'd been through: those powerful masculine hands, grabbing her from behind, imprisoning her arms to her sides. The fear, the panic, when his arms had tightened around her, cutting off her breath. The mingled smells of sweat and cologne—or was it only the fragrance from the climbing roses and honeysuckle?

The details were becoming blurred, but she would never forget her terror.

She was shaking again.

There was so much to think about, so much to worry about. She didn't know which way to turn, what to do next. She hated this feeling of helplessness. Max was offering her a way out, but she was reluctant to take it. She didn't know what to do for the best.

Her eyes strayed to the chair Max had occupied last night. If he hadn't been there, she wouldn't have had the courage to close her eyes.

And last night she had promised to marry him.

She touched her fingers to her lips, remembering how he had kissed her. When she felt her body quicken in arousal, she gasped, threw back the covers and slid from the bed.

WHEN SHE CAME DOWNSTAIRS, A FOOTMAN told her that there was a gentleman waiting for her in the morning room. His name was Mr. Fallon, but beyond that, the footman knew nothing, except that he'd been waiting for some time.

The young man who rose at her entrance was of medium height and had a pleasant, open expression on his face. His hair was receding at the temples. She approved of his garments, dark blue coat and beige breeches. There were no tassels on his boots.

"How can I help you, Mr. Fallon?" she said, and indicated that he should take a chair. She sat on the sofa.

He came to the point at once. "Lord Maxwell asked me to give you this letter before he left for Winchester. It will answer all your questions."

She took the letter from him without being aware of it. She felt numb. The first thing that occurred to her was that Max had changed his mind about marrying her and didn't know how to tell her. But the thought was short-lived. Whatever Max was, he was no coward.

Mr. Fallon went on, "He didn't want to waken you. He left very early, you see. That's why he left that letter with me."

Baffled, she opened the letter and began to read. She could trust Peter Fallon, Max said, because he and Peter were friends as well as colleagues. Until he returned from Winchester—and he should be in Longfield later that evening, all going well—Peter would look after her. Meantime, he would procure a special license from the bishop, and when he returned, they would be married at once in Longfield's chapel. He would brook no delay, for reasons that must be obvious. All that she had to do was stay close to Peter and make sure the vicar was there.

There was no going back now. Dear Lord, what had she done?

"Are you all right, Miss Carstairs?"

She looked up to see Peter Fallon studying her. "You don't look like a bodyguard," she said.

He gazed at her levelly. "Brawn isn't necessary in this case. You must never be left alone. That's what Lord Maxwell told me. Wherever you go, I'll be close by."

"And how are you going to manage that? I'm not going to tell my family that you're here to protect me. It would only upset them. I'd have to tell them about . . ." She hesitated, unsure of how much Max had confided in this man.

He finished the sentence for her. "About the attack on you last night? I understand. You may count on me to be the soul of discretion."

She stared at him for a long moment, then said coldly, "Who are you, Mr. Fallon?"

He answered her easily. "I work for Lord Maxwell. If

you want to know more, you'll have to ask him. But for our purposes, we'll simply say that I've been commissioned by Lord Maxwell to write about the architecture of Longfield. That should explain my presence here. But I'll be wandering around, keeping an eye on you. If you leave the house, I want to know about it."

"Indeed!" She rose abruptly. "Max has taken too much upon himself this time."

He got up as well. "Yes, he's good at doing that. Miss Carstairs, please be reasonable. You won't even notice that I'm here. And when Max gets back, you can have it out with him."

She wanted to be angry, but his crooked, rueful half smile was hard to resist. She found herself softening, and in spite of herself, the corners of her mouth turned up. "You sound," she said, "as though you've been the object of Max's methods as well."

"Frequently," he assured her, and suppressed a theatrical shudder.

She laughed. "Wait here," she said. "First, I want to warn—that is, *tell* my family that Max and I will be married tonight, then I'll come for you and introduce you to them."

Peter Fallon remained standing until Sara had left the room, then he sat down again and poured himself a fresh cup of coffee from the silver pot the maid had newly delivered. He'd already consumed one plateful of currant scones with lashings of melting butter and he wondered if he should ask for another. That was one thing about Max. He always thought of a fellow's comfort, especially if that friend—employee?—was doing him a favor. He had only to pull the bell-cord and a servant would come running and give him whatever he wanted.

That's where he would begin, he decided, with the servants. If one of them had delivered that note to Miss Carstairs last night, he would soon discover who it was, not by putting questions to them directly, but by coming at it obliquely. His methods were different from Max's and, in his own modest opinion, far more effective. Servants knew more than their masters and mistresses gave them credit for. There was no saying what else he might find out.

He drank his coffee absently, his broad brow pleated in a frown. So that was Sara Carstairs. He'd seen her at the trial, but not clearly, not full face and without her bonnet. Now that he had seen her, he wasn't surprised that Max was smitten. It wasn't her beauty, though she was pretty enough with her dark glossy hair swept off her face and her expressive gray eyes. It was something else, a curious blend of pride and fragility. But was she a murderess? Max had either changed his mind or the question had become irrelevant.

He yawned and yawned again. He wasn't surprised that he was tired. He'd been up half the night. One moment he'd been snug in his bed in his lodgings at the Cat and Fiddle, the next moment he'd been shaken awake by one of the Longfield footmen and dragged out to the house to confer with Max. He'd heard the rumors that were circulating in Stoneleigh, that Miss Carstairs was betrothed to some fortune hunter or other, and he'd wondered what the devil was going on.

Well, now he knew, and it rocked him back on his heels.

Max had been very terse before he left. There had been no talking things over as they usually did, only a curt recitation of events to bring him up-to-date and a series of orders. First and foremost, Max wanted to keep Miss Carstairs safe until he returned. She wasn't to go anywhere alone. Then Peter could begin digging for answers. Max wanted to know who had put the note on her dressing table, who was in a position to know and forge William Neville's handwriting, and where everyone was last night when the attack took place. The obvious answer, that Miss Carstairs was responsible and that there had been no attack, either had not occurred to Max, or he refused to consider it.

He was turning that thought over in his mind when she

returned. The color was high on her cheeks and there was a martial light in her eyes.

"If you'll come this way, Mr. Fallon," she said, "I'll make the introductions."

THERE HAD NEVER BEEN A MORE DISMAL WED-ding than this. It might as well have been a funeral, except that it wasn't sorrow that permeated the atmosphere so much as disappointed hopes. Well, Max was in no mood to charm Sara's family out of their sullenness. He'd had a grueling ride to Winchester and back in one day, and he was tired and irritable.

What on earth was keeping Sara and Simon? If this interminable Longfield silence went on much longer, he would drop off to sleep.

He glanced around the chapel. It was in one of the round towers and couldn't have held more than twenty people. On this occasion there were six of them, including the vicar. Martin was reading a book; Constance was staring straight ahead of her; Anne was praying; and Lucy was petting a kitten.

Only one thing mitigated Max's ill humor. Neither Simon nor Martin had a scratch on them. It didn't seem likely that either of them had attacked Sara last night. For her sake, he hoped he was right.

But where the devil was she?

If she'd had a change of heart, that was too damn bad. He wasn't giving her a choice. He'd tried chivalry, and if that didn't work, he would fall back on more primitive methods. He would carry her off to his hunting lodge in Cornwall and keep her there until she came to her senses. A blind man could see what was between them. How could one woman be so dense?

Five minutes, that's all he would give her, then he was going after her.

The vicar was fussing again. Max got up from his pew and went over to him. "What is it now?" he asked testily.

In a tight undertone, the vicar said, "This is all highly irregular. You should be married in church, not in a private house. And in the morning, as is the law of the land."

"The bishop has cleared everything, hasn't he? Perhaps you'd like to take your quarrel up with him?"

That silenced the vicar.

As it should, thought Max, because he *had* cleared everything with the bishop. Of course, it helped that his father and Bishop Hyde had been friends since schooldays. He'd explained that he was afraid that his bride would be mobbed if she were married in the local church, and that there was a chapel at Longfield. He'd also stressed the necessity for haste. The bishop had given him an oddly sorrowful look, but he'd signed all the necessary papers.

It was only on the ride back to Longfield that it occurred to Max he might have inadvertently misled the old cleric into believing that his bride was on the point of giving birth to their first child—out of wedlock. That would explain the sorrowful look.

He didn't know why he was grinning, because if it got back to his parents, there would be hell to pay.

Max turned as the door opened. Sara, leaning on Simon's arm, entered. The chapel was small, with only a center aisle. A few steps took her to Max's side. She'd taken a great deal of trouble with her appearance, Max noted with approval. Her hair was dressed in tiny ringlets that were held in place by a white ribbon. Her gown was of ivory satin, and over it she wore a long-sleeved matching spencer that buttoned all the way to her throat. She carried a spray of white flowers in one hand.

His tiredness and irritability dropped away. He took her hand. Her fingers were trembling. She looked as though she would bolt at the least provocation. He lowered his head to catch her softly spoken words.

"You haven't signed the marriage contract," she said.

These were not the words he'd hoped to hear. It was on the tip of his tongue to tell her that he could buy and sell her ten times over. Well, twice anyway. What stopped him was mere whimsy. He wanted Sara to trust him without reservation. He wanted her to have the same faith in him as she had in her miserable family. He wanted—

She squeezed his hand.

"What?" he asked, none too gently.

"Max, there's still time to change your mind."

His gaze narrowed on her face. Her eyes were fragile, uncertain, worried. Good. He'd give her something else to worry about.

"Not a chance," he said, "because you, my love, are going to make it worth my while."

The vicar cleared his throat, and the service began.

CONSTANCE HELPED HER UNDRESS FOR BED. She didn't want Constance's help, but didn't feel that she could refuse when it was her stepmother's gown she had borrowed for the occasion. There was little chance of Max's interrupting them. He'd fallen sound asleep at the dinner table and had to be helped to his bed.

Not that she blamed him. Her family had sat grim and silent throughout the meal, although they'd had plenty to say for themselves when Max was gone. It was Anne who had silenced them.

"Are you all blind?" she'd cried out. "Can't you see that Sara is in love with Max and he with her? He doesn't care about her fortune. This is a love match."

They'd all been stunned, herself included.

She thrust the memory from her, slipped into her dressing robe, and turned to face Constance. "Thank you for lending me your gown. If I'd had a gown especially made up, I'd have wanted something like this. It's truly beautiful."

"I had hoped to wear it to your wedding myself." Constance sighed and shook her head. "But I never thought it would be a wedding like this. I don't know what your father would say if he were here. You were always so level-headed. But you're no better than any other silly young girl, I suppose. You've allowed yourself to be taken in by a handsome face and a set of broad shoulders."

Sara touched her fingers to her brow and smoothed her frown away. "There's more to Max than that."

"Is there? How do you know? Who are his parents? Where does his money come from? Does he have any money? I very much doubt it. Oh, no, my girl, he has rushed you into marriage before we've had a chance to find out anything about him. He's a fortune hunter, that's what he is, and he'll be the ruin of us all." The flashing green eyes suddenly softened, and she said in a coaxing tone, "It's not too late. You can have the marriage annulled. Put him off for a night or two, until Drew comes home and you have a chance to consult with him."

"I don't want to consult with Drew. I know my own mind."

When Constance opened her mouth to speak, Sara silenced her with a curt motion of one hand. She didn't want to quarrel with Constance or anyone on her wedding night, but she'd had enough of these unprovoked attacks on Max.

"From now on," she said, "you will speak of Max with respect, and that goes for Simon and Martin, too. If the task is too much for you, then I suggest you leave Longfield at once. I mean it, Constance. I was never more serious about anything in my life."

Constance's jaw went slack, then she sucked in a long audible breath and glared at Sara. "The trouble with you," she said, "is you don't know who your friends are. I never thought to hear such words from you."

"You wouldn't hear them if you'd only behave."

With the gown over one arm, Constance marched to the

door. But she wasn't finished yet. She swung to face Sara. "You have grossly misjudged your brothers. Why do you think they were sent down from Oxford?"

"Because they got in a fight over some trollop."

"Oh no. Because they got in a fight over you. They were defending your good name. And that's not the first or the last time they've rushed to your defense. Don't tell them I mentioned it. They would be angry with me if they knew."

"What? Constance . . ."

With a triumphant smile, Constance sailed out of the room.

Sara felt sick inside. She remembered how she'd lectured her brothers when they'd told her they were being rusticated for the rest of the term. The fight was over a lady's honor, Simon had told her, and when Martin would have said more, Simon had cut him off.

She took a few paces around the room as thoughts chased themselves inside her head. At the window, she halted and looked out. There was no light winking at her from Drew's cottage. He was so nearly a member of the family that she'd wanted him at her wedding, but Simon told her that Drew had gone to Winchester on business.

If only Bea were here, she could advise her. But Bea had refused to come to Longfield because she knew how much she, Sara, had come to depend on her, and she didn't want to come between husband and wife.

Dear Lord, what had she done?

She sat on the edge of her bed thinking, thinking, thinking.

Nineteen

❧

S HE WAS ABOUT TO SNUFF OUT THE CANDLES
on the mantelpiece when Max entered. Startled, she
blurted out, "What are you doing here?"

He had removed his jacket and was wearing only his
white shirt and black trousers. Amused and relaxed, he said,
"Where else would I be on my wedding night? I apologize
for falling asleep at the dinner table. The ride to Winchester
took its toll, but I'm perfectly rested now."

It wasn't easy, but she managed a smile. "I understand."
She clasped her hands to conceal their trembling. "Max,
about last night . . ."

"What about last night?"

"I think I may have given you the wrong impression."

"What impression is that, Sara?"

She couldn't hold that probing stare, so she turned away
and fingered the spray of white roses Anne had given her to
carry at her wedding. They were in a vase on a chest of
drawers, and as her restless fingers plucked a bud, their
sweet scent drenched the air.

"I don't want this to be a real marriage, Max," she said.

When she turned from the dresser, he was right in front
of her. Her heart was thudding so hard, she wondered if he

could hear it. "I don't want this to be a real marriage," she repeated, this time looking directly into his eyes.

He heard the words, but her eyes were telling him a different story. He should be used to it by now. Every time he got close to her, she raised the drawbridge. She didn't know how to give in gracefully.

She expected masculine umbrage, temper, but he smiled at her with a curious gravity. "You'll have to do better than that, Sara, or I'll be forced to call you a liar and a coward."

Her voice was cool. "The trouble with you, Max, is you're used to women falling into your arms."

His brows rose. "You have an exaggerated idea of my conquests. I admit I've had passing interests, but I've never asked any woman to be my wife."

Shame suddenly engulfed her. "Oh, Max, I'm sorry. I didn't mean it. It's just that . . ." She shrugged helplessly.

"Is it because you think I'm a fortune hunter?"

"Of course not. And I apologize for my family. They've been beastly to you."

"Is it because you think I'll publish the story in my newspaper?"

"Not if you say you won't."

"Would I be likely to, now that you're my wife? Don't you trust me? What is it, Sara? Tell me."

He was so close, she could feel the warmth of his body, smell the soap on his skin. Her senses were coming alive. She made a half move to turn away and found that she couldn't because he had boxed her in.

She inhaled sharply. "Max, you know who I am. I'm Sara Carstairs. I was acquitted of murder, but that means nothing to most people. They still think I'm guilty, and maybe I am. How could you ever be sure?"

"So that's it." He smiled fleetingly. "I know you're innocent, because I know you and they don't."

His words were both sweet and chastening, painfully chastening. She had to swallow before going on. "I never wanted a real marriage. If we were to have children, how could I live with that? The stigma? The shame?"

He ached to gather her in his arms and kiss her fears away. He resisted the impulse because he wanted her to let down the drawbridge of her own free will, without any tricks from him.

He said, "Simon and Martin are coping, aren't they? I don't hear them complaining."

"No, they don't complain, but they don't have an easy time of it either." Her lashes swept down, concealing her expression. "Constance told me that the reason Simon and Martin have been expelled for a term is because they got into a fight defending my good name." She raised her eyes to his. "Now do you see how it will be?"

He gave her one of those smiles that started on his lips, creased his cheeks, and slowly filled his eyes. "Remind me to shake their hands at breakfast tomorrow."

Temper heated her eyes. "Max, this is serious."

"As I am well aware. When did Constance tell you this, by the way?"

"Not long ago, when she helped me undress."

Now all was becoming clear. "And you had a sudden attack of conscience?"

"I realized how selfish I was, if that's what you mean. I wasn't thinking about what was best for you. I was thinking about what was best for me. But it's not too late. I'm sure we can have the marriage annulled or something."

There they were again, those silent messages in her eyes that made lies of all her words. She was trying to be noble and she was botching the job. He could no more leave her now than cut out his own heart.

Unsmiling, he said softly, "I know what's best for me, Sara. What I want to know is what's best for you."

"What?"

"What do you want, Sara, really want?"

What she wanted was standing right in front of her, his

vivid blue eyes holding hers in a look that stripped away every defense. The candlelight glinted in his fair hair like strands of pure gold. She thought he was the most beautiful man she had ever known.

His hands were by his sides and he made no attempt to touch her. It wasn't necessary to touch her. He wasn't trying to hide what he was feeling. He wanted her, and her little speech might as well have remained unsaid.

Her voice was husky. "I don't want to hurt you, Max."

"No, but you will. Just as I'll hurt you. It's inevitable, Sara, because we're human. I'm willing to take my chances; how about you?"

He held out his hand, but he didn't touch her, and she understood that he was giving her a choice. It was a choice no one should have to make. She was shaking her head, but she couldn't fight her own heart, and her heart made the choice for her.

His hand closed around hers and he pulled her slowly into his arms. On a stifled breath, he said, "There's no going back now, do you understand? Not tonight. Not ever."

He said something else, something about a drawbridge that she didn't understand, then she went on tiptoe and, on a soft sigh of surrender, twined her arms around his neck. She felt the sudden jump of his heartbeat against her ribs, then his mouth was on hers, his lips filling her with his scent and flavor. The pleasure was so intense, she could have wept.

When the kiss ended, they were both trembling. Max didn't know whether he was awed or appalled. It had never been like this before. His body was starved for her and was clamoring for him to take her. He'd wanted her for so long. He'd thought endlessly about the night they'd met and his damnable imagination had given that night a different ending.

He breathed in her fragrance and a jolt of desire whipped through him. His hands brushed over her shoulders and his fingers fisted helplessly in the soft mane of hair. He'd dreamed of those dark tresses draped over him like a curtain as her lips skimmed over every inch of his bare skin.

On a shaken laugh, he got out, "One of us has to slow down. Help me, Sara."

Her voice was sleepy, dazed. "Don't stop now." She rubbed her body against his. "I'll die if you stop."

"Damnit, I'm trying to be considerate."

"I don't want you to be considerate."

And it was true. William had taught her to fear the brute strength of men, but not for one moment did she confuse Max with the kind of man William was. She reveled in the feel of hard masculine muscles that tensed beneath her fingertips; reveled in the solid shield of his powerful chest. She wanted to press herself close to him. She wanted to possess him; she wanted to be possessed.

His mouth took her again, ravenous, demanding. She answered that demand with a passion that made his head spin. A torrent of heat swept them to the brink. His hands raced over her, freeing her of her robe. He dispensed with the tiny buttons on her nightgown, then pulled back the edges of her bodice and feasted on her warm flesh.

When she moaned, he laughed softly, pulled her to the bed and tumbled with her on the mattress. It took only a moment to free her of her nightgown, then he stripped out of his own clothes and stretched out beside her.

His hands brushed over her, molding her soft flesh, teasing, caressing every curve and valley. When she put her hands on him, and began her own shy exploration of his body, his breath began to rasp in and out of his lungs. His body shuddered with excitement at the soft mewling sounds she made.

"Sara, I don't think I can wait," he said hoarsely.

"I don't want you to wait."

She was frantic with need. She wasn't a complete innocent; she knew what came next, and already her body was vibrating like a finely tuned violin. Someone else had taken over, some glorious, primitive creature that refused to be limited by Sara Carstairs's fears and inhibitions.

When he knelt above her, her throat tightened unbearably. She had never known a man like this—friend, lover, protector, champion. If only she was worthy of him.

"Tears?" His fingers touched her lashes and came away wet.

"You are so beautiful, Max," she whispered, and meant it. "I'm afraid I'll disappoint you." And she meant that too.

A smile flickered on his lips, but it was fleeting. "Idiot," he murmured. Chest heaving, he parted her legs and mounted her. She wrapped herself around him and held on tight.

His first thrust drove the breath from her body. The pain was searing. She dug her nails into his back and tried to arch away.

Max froze as though he'd turned to stone. *She was a virgin.* That was something he had never considered. *She was a virgin.* It couldn't be true. But it was true. She was so tight, his body was ready to explode. A finer man would let her go. He could no more let her go than he could fly to the moon.

He clamped his teeth together as she began to squirm. Beads of sweat broke out on his brow. Her movements to evade him were only driving him deeper into her body. Every muscle quivered as he fought desperately to hold onto his control.

When the pain subsided to an uncomfortable tightness, she let out a pent-up breath, then her whole body went lax.

Max raised his head and looked down at her. He kissed the pout from her mouth. "If only I'd known, I could have made this easier for you."

"If only I'd known, I wouldn't be here! I liked it better the last time. In fact—"

He stopped her words with a kiss, a slow, sensuous possession that made her forget all about the tightness in her loins. When he thrust again, she sucked in a breath, bracing for pain. It was incomprehensible, but there was no pain, only a pleasure that made her catch her breath.

Carefully, slowly, he brought her up again, lavishing her with kisses and softly spoken words of praise. His words became more ardent, more sexually explicit. Her breath caught on a flood of pleasure. Her body tightened.

Max felt her body climax beneath his, heard her wild cry of rapture, and he buried his face in her hair and let the wildness take him, too.

The minutes slipped by. Their breathing evened. Max shifted to his side, and raised on one elbow to see her better. Her lips were red from his kisses; her hair was in wild disorder. He reached for a strand and rubbed it against his cheek. "Are you all right?" he asked softly.

Love-sleepy and love-dazed, she looked up at him. She touched a hand to his bare chest. She felt both awed and humbled. How could something so earthy and carnal rock her soul to its very foundation? "I feel fine."

He combed back her hair and found what he was looking for—the scratch on her neck. He traced it reverently with the tips of his fingers. There was a bruise on her hip and grazes on her knees. He traced them too, then kissed them.

Startled, she blinked up at him.

She lay there in wanton abandon, more desirable than any woman he had ever known. But beyond the desire, he felt a fierce determination to protect her. She took appalling risks. Someone had succeeded in hurting her. If that didn't frighten her, it sure as hell frightened him.

And now tonight, she'd brought a lie to their marriage bed. There was only so much a man could tolerate.

He bent over her and kissed her on the lips. "You're sure you're all right?"

There was something in his look that made her cautious. "I'm sure."

"Good." His features hardened, and he said in a different voice entirely, "Now would you mind explaining what in blazes is going on? You've never had a lover. So why did you lie to me, Sara? Why did you lie about William Neville?"

A shaft of fear went straight through her. "What do you mean?"

"At the trial, your letters to William were read out. You were lovers." He shook his head, baffled. "But you were never lovers."

"Oh, that." She was suddenly cold, and reaching for her nightgown, she slipped into it. "Those letters," she said, "were doctored."

"They were counterfeit?"

"No, I wrote them all right, but that was long before William married Anne. I was eighteen, and I thought I was in love with him. I didn't date the letters. William did that after my father died, then he tried to blackmail me."

Her voice was husky, and she stopped from time to time to catch her breath. "He was always short of money. It didn't matter how much I gave him, it was never enough to pay off his gambling debts. Thankfully, he preferred London to Hampshire. When he was away, we were all happy. But when the money ran out, he always came back for more."

She swung her legs over the edge of the bed and sat with her shoulders hunched over. Max waited a moment, and when she remained silent, he said gently, "He put dates on the letters to prove that you and he were having an affair behind your sister's back?"

"It didn't work. I told Anne the truth, that I'd written the letters when I was a young girl and thought I was in love with him. She didn't know that William and I had ever been more than acquaintances. No one did. We kept it a secret because William feared his father would disown him if he knew about me, and when we couldn't meet, we exchanged letters. What a romantic fool I was in those days."

Again, she fell silent, and Max said, "Don't stop there, Sara. Tell me everything you remember about William."

She turned her head and looked up at him. "Why?"

"Because he's had such a profound effect on your life, and I want to understand."

"He destroys everything he touches."

He was aware that she'd used the present tense. "I can see that. What happened, Sara? What made you fall out of love?"

"His violent temper; his jealous rages." She gave a tiny shrug. "He frightened me. I taxed him about a rumor I'd heard. There was a local girl who was supposed to be pregnant with his child." She looked into Max's eyes. "They said that William forced her to get rid of the child she was carrying, and she died. I didn't believe any of it. But when I asked William about it—he looked frightened. He went crazy. He said it was all lies. And he hit me."

Max's breath hissed through his teeth.

"I don't think he meant to. He was as shocked as I. He couldn't apologize enough. I told my father I'd walked into a door. After that, I wanted nothing to do with William. He wouldn't accept that. It got so I became a prisoner in my own house. I was ashamed to tell my father about my romance with William, if one can call it that. Had I done so, things might have turned out differently for Anne. Eventually, he gave up and went back to London, and I thought that was the end of it."

She rose from the bed, scooped her dressing robe off the floor, and shrugged into it. Max reached for his trousers and pulled them on. He couldn't take his eyes off her. She was small-boned and delicate. He could span her waist with his hands. A man would have to be an animal to raise his hand to her. He hoped fervently that Neville was still alive, that one day they'd come face-to-face, because he'd tear him limb from limb.

"Then one year," she said, "Miss Beattie and I went on a

touring holiday to Scotland. We were gone almost three months. When I returned, I found that William had married Anne."

"How could your father have permitted it? I mean, William Neville! I knew him slightly in London, and he was a known wastrel and gamester."

"My father knew nothing of his life in London. And William could be charming when he wanted to be. There were rumors, but that's all they were. And don't forget, William was Sir Ivor Neville's heir. The Nevilles are the oldest family in his part of Hampshire. Everyone respects them because of their name.

"And my father was jubilant. One day, a title would come into the family, when William inherited. What could I say? It was too late. Anne was already married. I hoped for the best. But I feared the worst. And I was right. When my father had a stroke, William showed his true colors."

She wasn't aware that she had plucked a rose from the vase and was shredding its petals. "When William began to take his temper out on Anne, my father wasn't in a position to protect her. I went to Sir Ivor and begged him to intervene, but he refused. He'd disowned William even before he'd married Anne, because of his wildness. And after he married Anne, he wanted nothing to do with any of us."

She whirled to face him. "I wasn't ready to give up yet. I thought the law would protect Anne. I thought I could order William off our property. I wanted Anne to leave him. I wanted her to live with me." There was a catch in her voice, and she paused to clear her throat.

"Do you know what I learned, Max? I learned that a wife is a husband's property. She can do nothing without his permission. He owns her, he literally owns her. If she has powerful male relatives, she stands a better chance, but a woman on her own is helpless.

"Well, my father found a way to keep William in check.

He changed his will and left everything to me. Anne had some money when he died, but she was no longer a great heiress. I was, and I learned to control William with money. When he was a good boy, I rewarded him, and when he was bad, I punished him. The trouble was . . . the trouble was . . ." Tears clogged her throat and she trailed to a halt.

Max said softly, "The trouble was, William had a powerful weapon as well. Anne."

She nodded. "I was afraid to leave her alone with him. I spent most of my time at the dower house, and if I couldn't be there, Drew took over. That's why he practically lived on the estate. The only time we got any relief was when William went off to London. But he always came back."

He waited until she'd gained control of her emotions. "You became engaged," he said softly.

She nodded. "I didn't love Francis, but I liked him well enough. I thought if I had a husband, he could control William better than I could. If William went crazy when his friends told him about it, it wasn't because he loved me but because he thought Anne wouldn't get her share of my father's money."

She didn't see his hands fisting at his sides. "Sara—" He hesitated, but he had to know. "What happened the night William disappeared?"

Her voice was anguished. "I don't know, Max, and that's the truth. I honestly don't know."

"Sara." He stretched out his hand. She came to him at once. He tilted her face to his and pressed a kiss to her lips. Then he dug in the pocket of his trousers, produced a handkerchief and made her blow her nose.

When she drew in a long breath and smiled up at him, he said, "Why did none of this come out at the trial?"

She shrugged. "Because it would have been too damaging, that's what Mr. Cole, my barrister, said. Don't you know that a trial is like a game of chess? Your counsel will only present evidence that helps win your case. No one cares about the truth."

"But the letters—"

She shook her head. "I was told that the jury wouldn't believe that William had added the dates later, because no one knew he and I had known each other before his marriage to Anne. It was the same with the passages in the letters that Mr. Cole said were 'warm.' I was quoting William's words back to him. I was too innocent to understand that simple words can be double-edged. It was just too complicated to explain the letters, too incredible, so Mr. Cole didn't even try. To tell you the truth, I don't think he believed in my innocence."

He said savagely, "Cole should be shot!"

"Why? He got me off, didn't he? That's all that matters in a trial, winning and losing. You can hardly expect me to find fault with him for that."

"I'm not thinking about that! Of course I'm grateful that Cole got you off. But the letters! It was because of the letters that I couldn't get around the fact that William was your lover."

She made a small sound, a teary sigh with a hint of pique. "What about my other lovers?"

"What lovers?"

"My *legion* of lovers."

He grinned. "Oh, I discounted those months ago."

"Max, we've only known each other a few weeks."

"Really?" He smiled down at her and smoothed unruly strands of hair back from her face. "I feel as though we've known each other forever. Now what did I say?"

Her hands fastened around his arms. "That's exactly how I felt in Reading, the night you climbed in my window."

"I wish," he said seriously, "that I'd climbed in your window years ago." He kissed her eyes. "I wish I'd been there for you when your father died." He kissed her chin. "I wish I'd been there when William hit you." His voice was razor-edged. "I would have killed the bastard before I'd have let him harm a hair of your head. Sara—"

Her fingers covered his mouth. Her eyes were misted with tears. If he said any more, all her defenses would crumble, and she'd start bawling like a baby. She'd been in control for so many years. She'd had to be strong to protect the people she loved. But she glimpsed how it could be with a man like this. To have no secrets, to share her worst fears. She hovered, uncertain, but years of self-discipline held sway, and she took a step back from the brink.

"I don't want to think about William," she said. "Just for a little while, I want to forget. Help me forget, Max."

His hand slowly lifted, and he traced the bones of her face. "Something is troubling you."

"No. It's just that—"

"What?"

"I wish I knew how to seduce my husband."

He gave her the smile she loved. "I'll show you."

It turned out to be sheer torture for Max. Her mind wasn't bent on pleasure, as was his, but on the pursuit of knowledge. Like a scholar researching her subject, she tested every part of his anatomy and stored her findings in her mind for future reference. It was hard to believe that he was her first lover. She had no modesty, only an inquiring mind. While he was ready to explode, she sat back on her heels, brows knit in concentration as she put him through hell.

The end came for him when she replaced her fingers with her lips. He suddenly pounced and rolled with her on the bed.

"But, Max, darling," she cried out, her shoulders shaking with laughter, "I haven't finished yet."

He was captivated by the transformation in her. This is what he wanted for her, he thought fiercely—eyes sparkling, skin flushed, white teeth flashing as she let the laughter take her. She looked young, and mischievous, without a care in the world. He had a flash of recall: Sara at her trial like a block of ice, not a trace of emotion showing on her finely sculpted face.

She caught the odd look in his eyes, as though he were displeased about something, and her smile faded. She said tremulously, "Did I shock you? Was I too bold?"

He framed her face with both hands. "What you are is perfect," he said.

"Oh, Max, don't put me on a pedestal. I'll only disappoint you."

"I have no intention of putting you on a pedestal. What I'd like to do is chain you to my bed and pounce on you every chance I get."

"Pounce on me?"

"Like this."

They were both smiling when their mouths met. And he didn't pounce on her. He gave her all the patience and finesse he would have given her before, if he'd known he was her first lover. Smiles disintegrated; their breathing grew thicker; their bodies flowed together. Passion was there, but banked. He was in no hurry. With every kiss and caress, he tried to show her what he did not think she was ready to accept with words. So he told her she was beautiful; he told her that she pleased him; he told her that he'd been waiting for her to appear all his adult life.

She felt as though a vise were squeezing her heart. He was making love to a woman he didn't know. There was no escape now, not from him.

It was better not to think at all.

She held him close, her hands running ceaselessly over his warm flesh, and showed him with the gift of her surrender what she could not admit in words, not even to herself.

Twenty

~~~

ONE MINUTE SARA WAS TALKING TO SIMON over the breakfast table, and the next minute Max came striding in, swept her up in his arms, and carried her out to a waiting carriage.

Simon threw down his napkin and went after them. "What in blazes do you think you're doing with my sister? Answer me, damn you! Put her down!"

Sara was alarmed as well. "Max, what's going on?"

His darkly lashed eyes glinted down at her. "You could say I'm abducting you."

When Simon swore, Sara said crossly, "Don't be an idiot, Simon. Max wouldn't abduct me."

"Then what is he doing?"

They had reached the carriage and Max, with Sara held high against his chest, turned to face Simon. The glint in his eyes had turned into a steely-eyed glitter. "What I am doing," he said, "is taking my wife on our honeymoon. Do you have any objections?"

"A honeymoon!" said Sara. It was the last thing she expected.

"Do you have any objections?" Max asked her in a different tone.

She looked up at his smiling blue eyes and forgot that she'd been on the point of saying that it would be nice to be consulted. "No," she said. "None at all."

"Open the door, Simon," said Max.

Simon opened the door. "What about the Stoneleigh Fair?" he demanded.

Max deposited Sara inside the carriage and followed her in. "What about it?"

"I've entered you in the boxing contest. You told me I could."

"That's not till Saturday. We'll be back by then."

Simon shut the door. "See that you are!"

It was only as the carriage moved away that he thought to ask Max where he was taking Sara, but either Max did not hear or he didn't want to answer.

Martin strolled up just then. "What was that all about?" he asked.

Simon kicked a pebble and sent it flying into the shrubbery. He was still scowling. "They're going on a honeymoon," he said.

"Oh." Martin looked quickly at Simon's thunderous expression then looked away. "Do you know what I think, Simon? I think Anne is right. I think Max is in love with Sara."

"In love?" Simon forced a laugh. "You gullible fool! Does a man who loves a woman rush her into marriage before the lawyers have had a chance to draw up marriage contracts?"

Martin had started to bristle. "How do you know they haven't done that already, before they came here?"

"Sara would never do anything behind Drew Primrose's back. She'd want his advice, wouldn't she? And he's not here."

"I never thought of that."

They turned and began to walk back to the house.

"Look," said Simon, "I know perfectly well that whoever Sara married wasn't likely to give us a share of Father's fortune. After all, we're only the stepsons. But what galls me is that this courtesy-title upstart will bilk Sara of every penny she has."

Martin shrugged. "There's nothing we can do about it."

"Perhaps not. But I'd like to see him take a fall." Suddenly, Simon threw back his head and roared with laughter.

Martin eyed him uneasily. "Simon, what have you done?"

Simon put one arm around his brother's shoulders and grinned. "You'll just have to wait till Saturday to find out."

*H*E WAS TAKING HER TO THE COAST, TO A small village on the estuary of the river Test. It was only a three-hour drive away, and as the miles slipped by, Sara found herself relaxing. Max was impossible; his laughter was contagious. They were taking time out for themselves, he said. This was the only honeymoon he'd ever had or was likely to have, and he refused to have it ruined by meddlesome relatives who begrudged them their happiness. For three days and three nights they were going to enjoy themselves. They were going to forget about their troubles and think only of the present moment. He was going to love her as she'd never been loved before.

The vise that was never far from Sara's heart tightened fractionally, and blinding tears stung her eyes. If only it could be this easy. She kept her head averted, because she didn't want to spoil Max's pleasure. She was becoming such a watering-pot, she who never cried, that she couldn't stand herself anymore.

Max's lips brushed her nape. "Three days, Sara. Can't you empty your mind of everything but us for the next three days?"

Three days. It sounded ominous. She wanted this to last forever.

"Well?"

She turned to look at him. The blinding tears turned into a blinding smile. "Empty my mind? Max, don't you know that you're all I think about now, you and what we do in our bed? Is that what you want me to forget?"

When he bent to kiss her, she pushed at the hard wall of his chest with her splayed hands.

"What?" he asked.

"If you ever bestow that special smile of yours on another woman, I'll . . ."

He grinned. "Yes?"

I'll kill you. She suppressed a shudder. "I'll make you sorry you were ever born. That smile belongs to me. Do you understand?"

His grin faded. "What were you going to say? Sara, tell me."

She was able to give him a sultry smile. Her hand dropped to his thigh and brushed higher. "What do you think?" she murmured.

He kissed her then, as she meant him to, and when the kiss was over, she asked him to tell her how he came to be the publisher of the *Courier*.

He gave a long sigh, but he followed her lead all the same.

THE ROOM THEY WERE SHOWN INTO OVER-looked the estuary and beyond that the gleaming city of Southampton. The window was, in fact, a French door and opened onto a tiny wrought iron balcony. Sara was captivated.

"How did you find this place?" she asked.

Max was directing the inn's footman who had brought up their boxes. It registered on Sara's mind, but only vaguely, that this adventure wasn't as spontaneous as she had thought. The carriage, the boxes containing their clothes and toiletries, must have required some forethought on Max's part.

Max waited until the footman retired before he answered her. "I spent many summers here when I was a boy, recuperating from an inflamation of the lungs. That's why my father insisted I take up sports, and boxing in particular. To make me stronger. And it worked."

She couldn't imagine Max as anything but strong and vital, and it gave her quite a pang to think of him as mortal, just like anyone else.

"Anne wasn't very strong when she was a child," she said. "She spent much of her time in the sickroom too, reading, writing poetry, that sort of thing."

He shrugged out of his coat and threw it over a chair, then he undid her spencer and sent it the same way. His hands ran over her arms and fisted in her hair. He loved the way her lids grew heavy and her breasts rose and fell.

"I used to write poetry," he said, "when I was a boy."

Her arms went round his waist. "You did? I can't imagine you as a poet."

"Would you like to hear a sample?"

"Mmm." She was breathing in the scent of him.

"Now let me see. Oh yes—

> *There was a young lady of Farnham*
> *Whose . . . uhm . . . baubles were larger than cannons*
> *But when she disrobed, they were found to be frauds*
> *And her husband . . ."*

"Stop! You call that poetry? That's nothing but a crude limerick. Even Simon and Martin can do better than that."

"I didn't say I had any talent."

Laughter bubbled up, slowly at first, then gathering momentum until her shoulders shook with the force of it. Her lips were twitching, her eyes had turned several shades lighter. It was what he wanted for her, what he wanted from her. He was going to show her that life was meant to be enjoyed.

One step took him to the bed, but he had to drag her that one step. His eyes crinkled at the corners. "What's the matter, Sara?"

She gestured to the open window. "Do you know what time it is? It's still daylight."

He tugged on her hand. "I said I would pounce on you every chance I got, and that's what I'm going to do. Give me some credit. I spared you in the carriage."

Her jaw went slack. "In the carriage! You mean . . ."

He nodded. "Not that I've ever tried it, you understand. But with you, I could be tempted."

She rarely blushed, but she could feel a tide of color rising in her throat. He was going to have her now, she could see it in his eyes, and the familiar weakness began to invade her bones.

When he suddenly pounced on her, she shrieked, and went rolling with him on the bed. They were both laughing when he kissed her. He raised her head, and his smile gradually faded. She shifted restlessly.

"Why do you always study me, Max? Why do you stare at me like that?"

"Because I want to know what's going on inside your head. I want to know what you're thinking and feeling."

"You already know."

"Do I? I wish I could believe that."

She didn't know how to answer him, but no answer was required. He sighed into her mouth and kissed her with an urgency that made her forget everything but him. He took her quickly, without removing their clothes, and she found the desire beating through her blood to meet whatever he demanded of her. There was no one like him. There was nothing else in the world like the feel of his lean muscular body moving on hers. She should be happy, but when the climax came, she felt as though her heart had shattered as well.

· · ·

IT WAS IMPOSSIBLE TO BE UNHAPPY FOR LONG around Max. He set out to charm her, and she was in the mood to be charmed. He made her laugh; he taught her how to play again. Much of the time she was in a sensual daze. Max saw no reason to confine their lovemaking to their bed. If they went walking on the beach or in the woods, he could always find a secluded corner where he could make love to his beautiful wife. What shocked Sara wasn't the knowledge that Max was a lusty, demanding lover. It was her own capacity for love, her own sexual appetite that stunned her. All it would take was a sideways glance from Max, and the blood would start to pound at every pulse point in her body. Until she met Max, she hadn't known such feelings existed.

When they weren't making love, they talked, but they tried to avoid anything that might cast a shadow on their happiness. She learned a little more about his family. He was an only child, he said, and one day he would inherit his father's title.

They were eating dinner on the little balcony outside their room, and Max studied her as he took a sip of wine. "Don't let it alarm you," he said. "My parents live very quietly at Castle Lyndhurst. My father spends his time managing the estate and my mother is a great help to him." He saw the leap of fear in her eyes, and he went on casually, "We don't mix with royalty or the Prince of Wales's set. You'll fit in very nicely with my family, Sara."

"I don't fancy living in a castle, Max."

"You won't have to. I'm a newspaperman. We'll live in London."

"Do your parents know about me?"

"I sent a letter to them by express when I saw the bishop about a special license."

She leaned forward slightly. "Do they know my name? Do they know who I am?"

"Sara, I dashed off a note. And there's only so much one can put down on paper. They'll know soon enough when I take you to meet them. They're in Derbyshire, right now, and won't be back in Hampshire for several weeks. Then you'll meet them."

Meet them. She hadn't thought that far ahead. Where were her wits? What was she thinking?

His strong fingers tipped up her chin, bringing her eyes up to meet his. "I know they're going to love you," he said, "but whether they do or not doesn't matter a damn. Look at your family. If I listened to them, I would tie a millstone around my neck and throw myself into the sea."

She couldn't help smiling. "They are atrocious, aren't they?"

He patted her cheek. "That's better. Just remember, we made our vows to each other, not to our families. Now, if you're finished eating, I thought we could hire a couple of horses and ride along the seafront before it gets dark."

She looked at that irresistible smile and surrendered. "I would like that," she said.

THE THREE DAYS SLIPPED BY TOO QUICKLY, then there were no more days left to share, and they were on the road again, making for home. The nearer their carriage came to Longfield, the more quiet Sara became. Her thoughts began to circle: William; the dower house; the notes that could have come from anyone.

She heard Max sigh. He reached for her and drew her across his lap. His irresistible smile was nowhere in evidence. He looked serious.

"I wouldn't take you back to Longfield," he said, "if I thought I couldn't protect you. I'll be there. Peter Fallon will be there. No harm will come to you."

"I've been thinking about that," she said. "Max, what's to stop us from going on a proper honeymoon? I've never been to Ireland, and I hear it's beautiful. Maybe Anne would like to come with us."

Just as she loved his special smile, she loathed his special stare. It was probing, searching, and the only way to evade it was not to be caught in it at all.

"Sara," he said quietly, "you're not keeping something to yourself, are you? Something I should know?"

She made her eyes go blank and she told him the truth, but it wasn't the whole truth. "You want to find out who has been sending me those notes, and who attacked me when I was out walking. But I'm not sure that I want to find out. And now that I'm married, I think all that will stop. Can't we leave it at that? At least for a little while?"

"Maybe. Let me think about it."

She made to move off his lap, but he drew her back. "Let me love you," he murmured.

She looked around the coach's interior. "Max, it isn't possible. There isn't enough room."

"I can manage, if you help me."

This was another look she was coming to know: his eyes were heavy-lidded; his nostrils were slightly flared; his lips were parted and his breathing was becoming audible.

It started the slow beat of blood in her own body. "Max," she shook her head, but she allowed him to position her so that she kneeled over him with her thighs straddling his lap. He kissed her slowly, wetly, and his hands cupped her bottom, his fingers flexing in her soft flesh. He rained kisses down the long line of her throat and his mouth fastened around one distended nipple through the fabric of her gown.

"Max," she said weakly, and her hands curled around his shoulders to steady herself.

He adjusted their clothes, and she mewled like an animal in pain as he filled her body. He smiled briefly, a lover recognizing the sounds of his mate's arousal. "You're so . . .

giving," he said through clenched teeth, "so perfect for me. I'll never let you go."

The coach's swaying, the slow rhythm Max imposed on her, his boldness—the pleasure was too intense, and her body began to shudder in reaction. She called his name in a keening cry of distress, then she buried her face in the crook of his shoulder as the pleasure overwhelmed them both.

THEY WERE LAUGHING TOGETHER WHEN THEY entered Longfield's Great Hall. As Sara ran up the stairs with a spring in her step, Max turned away and made for the small anteroom that he had arranged to be turned over to Peter Fallon for his own personal use.

Peter looked up at his entrance. "Well," he said, "you're looking relaxed and well."

With arms above his head, Max stretched his cramped muscles and grinned up at the ceiling. "Never felt better, Peter. I think marriage must agree with me. So, has anything interesting happened while we were away?"

"That's it?" Peter sat back in his chair. "That's all you're going to tell me, and now it's back to business?"

Max grinned. "As you said, I'm looking relaxed and well. That ought to tell you everything you're too shy to ask and I'm too chivalrous to tell."

Peter stared, blushed, and after a moment grinned hugely. "I was talking about . . . I was thinking of the sights, you know, places of interest. Oh, never mind. The most interesting thing that's happened is that Sir Ivor was here earlier this morning, and he was fit to be tied."

"Ah. He heard about my marriage. I thought I would go over later and break the news to him. Maybe I'll go anyway."

"You won't find him at home. He's under the impression that you've taken your bride to Castle Lyndhurst and he said he would go there and confront you in person. You should have heard his language. You were a disgrace to your name and class. You were a viper. You were a liar and a cheat. He would ruin you. He went on and on. I had no idea he had such a temper."

Max let out a sigh. "I suppose I should pity him. William was his only son. And he truly believes that Sara is guilty. At any rate, he won't find anyone at Lyndhurst. My parents are visiting my uncle's family in Derbyshire."

He edged one hip onto the desk and helped himself to the last scone on a blue-edged plate. "What did the others say when Sir Ivor was here?"

"Nothing. No one was here but the servants and myself. The whole family is involved in preparations for tomorrow's fair. And Sir Ivor refused to come into the house. He did all his ranting and raving in the courtyard."

"He recognized you?"

Peter made a small sound of derision. "Hardly. I'm only the hired help, a servant. To people like Sir Ivor, I might as well be invisible. I told him I was your private secretary."

Max bit into the scone and stared into space.

Peter watched him for a moment, then said, "Your true identity is bound to come out sooner or later, and when it does, no one is going to tell us anything. Your wife's family, the servants, the locals—they'll all be mad as fire when they find out you publish the *Courier*."

Max wasn't thinking about the *Courier*, but about Sara. She hadn't wanted a real marriage because of the stigma attached to her name. The thought of meeting his parents had really shaken her. Until the whole business of William Neville was cleared up, she would always be afraid that people would reject her.

He looked at Peter. "All the more reason for us to redouble our efforts and find out what happened to William Neville. Are you any nearer to knowing who left the note on Sara's dressing table?"

"Oh yes, and several interesting things besides."

Max listened intently as Peter went through a complex account of where all the servants were at the critical time. It had something to do with the fires not being lit that night, but what it came down to was that only three people had been in the bedroom wing between the time Sara left her room to go to dinner and when she returned to go to bed. They were the maid, Constance, and Anne.

"Can't you narrow it down?" asked Max.

"I don't think it's the maid. Martha is a little chatterbox. She can't keep secrets. And besides, she has no motive, or none that I've discovered. But Constance . . ." Peter smiled complacently, "well, Constance is proving to be quite a surprise."

Max frowned. "In what way?"

"She's having an affair with Drew Primrose, and if what I've learned from backstairs gossip is true, she's had many lovers since her husband died. That's why she's not invited anywhere, not because of your wife, but because the good ladies of Stoneleigh are afraid Constance will try and seduce their husbands."

"Oh, God!" Max glowered down at Peter's smiling face. "What you don't seem to understand," he said, "is that Constance is now a member of my family and I'm responsible for her."

Peter's smile turned into a huge grin. "And I'm sure it couldn't happen to a nicer fellow, but before you go calling anyone out, just remember, she's the predator. Poor Drew Primrose didn't stand a chance. Everyone knows he's eating out his heart for your Sara. He's human, that's all."

Max's mouth tightened. "Maybe he's sending those notes. Maybe he sent them to bring Sara back into his orbit."

"I don't think—"

"It makes perfect sense to me. Maybe he got Constance to put the note there for him. And that's another thing.

Drew Primrose was supposed to be in Bristol on business when William disappeared. I doubt if anyone checked on his alibi. From the very beginning, the magistrates and constables decided that Sara was guilty and they looked no farther. I want you to check out Primrose's alibi."

"Fine," said Peter, sighing.

"What about those notes?" Max asked. "Who was in a position to copy William's handwriting?"

"Just about everybody and his dog. I've narrowed it down to about twenty people. We're not going to get anywhere with that line of questioning."

"It was worth a try. Anything else?"

Peter grinned. "For what it's worth, I'm becoming quite an expert on architecture in West Hampshire."

Max frowned. "Architecture?"

"Isn't that the cover you invented for me? And I tell you, Max, it's fascinating. There was this builder, Congreve, who went around West Hampshire during the Civil War making secret rooms for cavaliers who were on the run from Cromwell's men."

"What has this to do—? Oh, I see. You mean William's body could be hidden anywhere."

"Afraid so."

Max swallowed the last bite of scone. "What," he said carefully, "are the servants saying about Sara?"

"Now, this *is* surprising." Peter leaned back in his chair, balancing it on two legs. "They don't care whether she's innocent or guilty. They think that sooner or later someone would have done away with William. They despised him. I think they would lie in their teeth to protect Sara. They wouldn't make good witnesses for the prosecution or the defense. They're not impartial and it's obvious."

Max walked to the door. "Remind me," he said, "to increase the servants' wages after this is all over." He turned to look at Peter. "And remind me to give you a substantial bonus. You've done well, Peter."

"A substantial bonus? How much are we talking about?"

"A thousand pounds."

Peter got up. "I'll leave for Bristol first thing tomorrow."

"It's not that urgent. Stay for the fair. I'm entered for the boxing match. That's when I aim to teach Sara's brother his manners."

O N THINKING IT OVER, MAX DECIDED TO RIDE over to Sir Ivor's place just in case the old boy had changed his mind about haring off to Castle Lyndhurst. It was a wasted journey. Sir Ivor, the butler said, was away from home and was not expected back for a few days. Lady Neville was resting and not receiving visitors.

When he got home, he was crossing the hall when he heard voices, raised in anger, coming from the library. One of those voices belonged to Drew Primrose. The other was Sara's, but her voice was less angry, more placating.

He crossed to the library, knocked once on the door and entered. Sara whirled to face him.

"Oh, Max," she said running to meet him, relief making her voice crack, "I wish you would talk some sense into Drew." She linked her arm through Max's and led him into the room. "I suppose I was very bad not consulting him about our marriage contract. But I was living in London at the time, and it seemed so much easier to go to a firm of London attorneys."

Drew Primrose was bristling like a dog about to go on the attack. His eyes were fixed on Max. He spoke through his teeth. "You waited until I was out of the way before you rushed Sara into marriage."

"Why," said Max pleasantly, "should I do that?"

"So that there would be no time to draw up a marriage settlement. So that you could have everything your own way! Isn't that how fortune hunters work?"

Sara gasped. "Drew, you have no right to say that."

Max's first impulse was to plant his fist in the attorney's face. It was his sense of fair play that stopped him. Any attorney worth his salt would have been angry. Sara was a substantial heiress. He, Max Worthe, was unknown. And now, with no contracts signed, he could do whatever he liked with his wife's money. He could even leave her destitute.

He patted Sara's hand and said mildly, "My attorneys would be very angry with me, too, Sara. If anything happens to me, most of what I own will pass to you."

No one took him seriously. Drew's lip curled and Sara clicked her tongue. "Will you be serious, Max? We *have* a marriage contract. I showed it to you. You read it. That it's not signed is only an oversight that we can correct right this minute."

She gestured with one hand, and Max saw that the document that was so important to his wife was lying on a long library table.

Drew Primrose was not placated. "Are you mad, Sara? You can't break up the estate like that. Anne should be provided for, yes, but your father already made provisions for your stepbrothers and stepsister. They are not your blood. They have no claim on the estate."

"Ah, so you've read Sara's marriage contract, have you?" said Max. "Well, at least we agree on something." He looked at Sara. "I don't think settling all that money on your younger siblings is good for them. Let them wait. If we think they deserve it, we'll give it to them, but not until they're older and wiser."

Drew said coldly, "Do you expect me to believe that you'll provide for Sara's family?"

"I don't care what you believe. But you're right about marriage settlements. I'll tell you what I'll do. I'll write to my attorneys in London and ask them to come here to discuss terms with you. How does that sound?"

"No," said Sara. "No."

Neither man looked at Sara.

"Why should I believe you?" demanded Drew hotly.

Eyes clashed and held. "Because I'm not giving you a choice."

For a moment or two, there was a silence, broken only by the sound of a dog barking somewhere in the distance. It looked as though Drew Primrose would say more, but his face suddenly flushed, and snatching up his hat, he strode from the room.

"I cannot like that man," said Max, staring at the open door, "not even when he has your best interests at heart."

"Max."

He looked at Sara.

"Are you going to sign the marriage contract or aren't you?"

"We don't have to go into that right now," he said. "Sara, there's no need to look at me like that. Your own attorney doesn't want me to sign. It's not well thought out. Let's leave it for a little while, until my attorneys get here. Let them agree on settlements, then we'll both sign."

Her face was parchment white and her voice trembled. "You knew, you *knew* why I had to marry. I never made any secret of it. I don't want the kind of marriage settlement lawyers draw up. I want to protect my family. That's all that ever mattered to me. I would never have married you, *never,* if I thought you wouldn't sign that contract."

A muscle tensed in his cheek. "You're angry and don't know what you're saying."

"Oh, don't I!" she cried passionately. "Townsend isn't in your class. No wonder you got rid of him." She was trembling with fury and hurt pride. "So what's your price, Max? Just tell me your price and I promise I'll meet it."

His eyes narrowed, their expression so threatening that she flinched when he stepped toward her. But he went by her and went out the open door. She heard him calling for one of the servants and moments later, Max came back into the room accompanied by Peter Fallon and a footman.

"We'll need witnesses," he said without looking at her.

He made her sign first, then he signed and finally the two witnesses. It was over in seconds. No one spoke. Everyone could tell that Max was in the grip of some violent emotion. He left with Peter Fallon, without looking at her or saying another word.

"You can go, Arthur," she told the footman.

Her marriage contract was still on the table, the ink still wet. She sat down and stared at it. She'd got what she wanted, but she was just beginning to realize that the price was far more than she wanted to pay.

Twenty-one

SATURDAY MORNING DAWNED WITH SPOTTY showers, but by the time the advance party arrived on Stoneleigh's common to set up the marquee and booths for the fair, the wind had chased the offending rain clouds away, and everyone agreed it was an ideal day to hold the fair.

This was to be Sara's first public appearance since returning home, and she was torn between a desire to show the world how little she cared for its good opinion and an equally strong desire to lock herself in a cupboard until the fair was over. She got little sympathy from Max. Whatever she wanted to do, he said, was fine by him. Peter Fallon would stay with her if she wanted to remain at Longfield. But he had been roped in to selling tickets at the fortune-teller's tent and he wasn't going to back out now.

He had come to her bed last night and made love to her. Though the rapture was still there, there was something missing. They weren't together. After they'd made love, she'd tried to explain why the marriage contract was so important to her. Max had heard her out in silence, sighed, then turned on his side and gone to sleep. She had fretted half the night away.

If it hadn't been for Anne, she didn't know how she would have got through the last few hours. Anne understood her terrors only too well. She'd found Sara a job that would, for the most part, keep her out of the public eye. They were behind a canvas partition in the marquee where the ladies of the church were serving teas to a never-ending stream of customers. Their job was to fill the empty plates that came back and send them out again with fresh sandwiches and sliced cake. The only people Sara had to talk to were the ladies who were working with her and those who brought back their plates to be refilled.

At first, they'd worked in silence, but it wasn't a hostile silence. It seemed to Sara as if everyone was afraid they would say the wrong thing. She'd known these ladies before her trial and had liked and respected them. They were the wives of local farmers and business or professional men. She'd visited them in their homes and entertained them at Longfield. But now her tongue seemed to be tied in knots and she couldn't find a thing to say.

It was Anne, painfully shy Anne, who heroically broke the silence time after time, referring to husbands and children and drawing Sara into the conversation, until they were all chattering away as though Sara had never been tried for murder.

She wasn't exactly enjoying herself, but it wasn't as bad as she'd thought it would be, not nearly as bad.

Anne wiped her sweaty brow with the back of her hand. "It must be time for us to have our break," she said.

"Break?" Sara didn't want a break. She wanted to stay right where she was.

She wasn't given a choice. Two other ladies came to relieve them, and Anne was helping her out of her apron before she could think of an excuse to stay behind.

"You can't hide in here for the duration of the fair," Anne said in an undertone. "Constance and Lucy will be out there keeping places for us at their table. It will be all right, you'll see."

It couldn't be worse, Sara told herself, than facing all the curious spectators at her trial. She took a moment to compose herself, then, with a nod to Anne, and lifting her chin, she entered the main marquee.

The noise was deafening. Ladies were scurrying from table to table, whisking away dirty dishes and setting out fresh crockery and cutlery. There was no standing on ceremony here. The only object was to raise money, and mistresses in aprons thought nothing of waiting on their own servants. No one noticed Sara.

They saw Constance and Lucy. Sara would have gone to join them, but Anne put a restraining hand on her arm. "William's mother is with them," she said.

Sara's eyes flew to Constance's table and she saw what she hadn't noticed before. Lady Neville was in an invalid chair and she was gesturing with her hands, smiling first at Constance, then at Lucy.

Anne said, "William's mother has joined the ladies' guild at the church, and though I wouldn't say we are friends, we are on speaking terms. Now that William is gone, I think she regrets having disowned us both."

Sara said nothing, but she hadn't forgotten or forgiven the cruel way the Nevilles had treated her whole family. They were neighbors, but they might as well have lived at opposite ends of England.

Anne flashed Sara a quick look. "Shall we go over? Are you up to meeting her?"

She would never be up to meeting William's mother again. She shook her head.

"Who," she said, a moment later, "is that striking-looking gentleman standing beside her?"

"That," said Anne, "is Beckett. He's Lady Neville's footman. She never goes anywhere without him."

No man could have looked less like a footman. He was too good-looking, too dramatic, dressed as he was in black, and far too bold with his eyes. But if he was bold, so was Constance. As Sara watched, her stepmother dropped her napkin. Both she and the footman bent to pick it up and their hands touched beneath the tablecloth, then they smiled into each other's eyes.

Sara was coldly furious. Lucy was sitting right beside her mother, but fortunately, she was listening to Lady Neville and had missed this brazen act.

"They're lovers," said Sara. She looked at Anne. "They're lovers, aren't they?"

Anne shrugged. "Sara, don't interfere."

"Of course I'm going to put a stop to it. Constance is Lucy's mother. She should know better."

"Don't blame Constance." Anne's lips trembled. "She's lonely. And it's not her fault that she's beautiful and men find her desirable. Leave her alone, Sara. People must be allowed to live their own lives."

A horrible suspicion flashed into Sara's mind, and she gave Anne a sideways glance. She knew that her sister was deeply unhappy, and she prayed that this footman had nothing to do with it. She wished she could say something, but this was the second time that Anne had warned her to keep her distance.

Lady Neville's footman had caught sight of them. His bold eyes roamed over Sara and he smiled. Her look was frigid. Laughing now, he bent his dark head and whispered something in her ladyship's ear. A moment later, he wheeled the chair toward the exit.

"It seems," said Sara, "that Lady Neville isn't up to meeting me either."

Lucy smiled as Sara took the chair next to hers. "We were just talking to Lady Neville," she said. "Did you know her daughter, Sara?"

"Caroline," said Sara and nodded. "But not very well. She was a year or two younger than Anne, and the Nevilles did not mix with Stoneleigh society."

"She died very young," said Anne. "I remember her father took her to the best physicians in London and they could do nothing for her."

"Speaking of Sir Ivor," said Sara, "is he here? Because if he is, I think I'll make myself scarce."

"Me too," said Lucy. "I don't like him at all. In fact, he makes my skin crawl."

"Lucy!" Constance fingered the pearl pendant at her throat. "You are chattering. Pour the tea for your sisters."

Sara half turned in her chair and gazed at the exit. It was the first time in her memory that Lady Neville had attended the local fair. If she'd known the Nevilles would be here, she wouldn't have had the courage to come.

She looked at Constance and Anne and Lucy. Everything seemed normal enough, but there were undercurrents here that she didn't understand. And there wouldn't have been undercurrents if Lady Neville and her footman hadn't stirred them up.

What in heaven's name was going on?

Peter Fallon came up and joined their table.

"Where is Max?" Sara asked.

"Telling fortunes," he said, chuckling, "and do you know what? He's really good at it."

"Max is telling fortunes?" Sara was astounded. "I thought he was only going to sell tickets."

Peter pushed his cup and saucer toward Lucy and watched as she poured out his tea. "The local doctor, I forget his name, was supposed to be the fortune-teller, but he was called away, so Max took his place. They've rigged him out as a gypsy with golden earrings, no less. You wouldn't recognize him if you saw him."

There was a moment of silence, then everyone began to laugh.

. . .

$\mathcal{M}$AX LOOKED UP FROM HIS CRYSTAL BALL AND saw Simon, a big smirk on his face, standing just inside the tent flap. "Your fortune is easy to tell," said Max. "I see a tall, fair-haired stranger in your life who is going to have a profound influence on your future." He stared down at his crystal ball. "You can make this easy on yourself or hard; the choice is yours." He looked up and grinned. "But one way or another, things are going to be different for you, Simon."

Simon's smirk had been replaced by a vicious scowl. "You look ridiculous with that scarf around your head and those dangling earrings!"

"Do I? I don't feel ridiculous. In fact, it wouldn't surprise me if, in a former life, I *had* been a fortune-teller. I have a talent for it. As you'll soon find out. That will be threepence, please."

"What?"

"I don't tell fortunes for nothing. Threepence, if you please. Don't be such a bad sport. It's all in a good cause."

Simon fished in his pocket and counted out three pennies, which Max deposited in a jar that was filled to the brim with coins.

"Talking of sports," said Simon, "it's time for the boxing contest."

Max rose. "Who is going to take my place here?"

"How should I know?"

"I can't just leave my post! This is a little gold mine we've got going here. Look, take this jar to the vicar and tell him the problem. If he can't find someone to replace me, he'll have to do it himself. Go on. I'll be all changed and ready when you get back."

"Give it to me!" Simon reached for the jar of coins, hoisted it in his arms, and quickly left the tent.

After pulling the red kerchief from his head, Max carefully

removed his brass hooped earrings. He was really sorry to give up the earrings.

LOOK AT THAT," SAID MAX AS HE AND SI-mon left the fortune-teller's tent. He was pointing to the long queue of people who had lined up to see the fortune-teller. "My fame has spread. There was only a trickle of people when I took over from Doctor Laurie. I don't know what they'll do when they hear the vicar has taken over from me. They may even riot."

"Don't let it go to your head," said Simon. "It's not your talent as a fortune-teller that has drawn that crowd. What they want to see is the fortune hunter who has snagged my sister."

Max shook his head. "Do you know, I've never met a family like yours? It's not only Sara. You're all the same. Money is all you ever think about. Don't you know how to have fun? Enjoy yourselves? That doesn't take money."

Simon flashed Max a look of pure dislike. "That's easy for you to say, now that you've got control of my father's fortune."

Max studied Simon for a moment or two. "Sara didn't mention—"

"What?"

"Sara didn't mention our marriage contract?"

"Not to me. Why?"

A slow smile tugged at the corners of Max's lips. "I thought—"

"What did you think?"

"I think," said Max with a broad smile, "that your sister is beginning to see the light. Where is she, by the way?"

"She's washing up dishes, now that the teas are over."

"Alone?" asked Max sharply.

Simon misunderstood the edge in Max's voice, and be-cause he was thoroughly annoyed with Max's good humor, he said spitefully, "Of course she's not alone. Drew Primrose is with her. You'd think he'd know better, now that Sara is a married woman." He had his reward when Max's lips thinned.

Max saw Simon's smirk and said tightly, "I was going to go easy with you, but that last remark has made me change my mind."

Simon gave an exaggerated shiver. "What, no holds barred?"

"No holds barred," agreed Max grimly.

They walked on in silence, past booths that were mostly deserted now that all their wares had been sold. The crowds were thinning out, though the flame-thrower and sword-swallower were still doing a brisk trade. In another hour, the fair would be over, and the monumental task of clearing up would begin. But there was one attraction that kept most of the men hanging around—the boxing contest.

It was as far from the ladies' booths on that small common as it could possibly be, and if the vicar had had his way, it wouldn't have been there at all. But the fair was not under the jurisdiction of the church. It was run by the mayor and aldermen, and they were astute businessmen who knew how to part a man from his money.

The area was roped off, and Simon gave a shilling to the ticket collector to pay admittance for himself and Max.

"Sam," said Simon to the ticket collector, "this is my brother-in-law, Max Worthe." Then to Max, "Sam is our local butcher."

Max saw a small, monkey-faced man dressed in a dirty apron, who was eyeing him as though he were a side of beef.

"Well, what do you think?" asked Simon.

Sam Weaver shook his head. "I'll give 'im one round, if 'e gets that far."

Max took umbrage. "My dear man—"

He got no farther. Simon took hold of his arm and dragged him away. "If we don't get there soon, we'll be disqualified. We're last on. Can't you hear them? The crowd is getting restless."

When he came out of the crush of men, Max saw that a platform had been built so that the spectators could have a good view of the ring.

"This is my brother-in-law," said Simon to the man who was evidently in charge.

Max's name was duly marked off, and after shaking hands with Simon, and wishing him luck (a convention of the sport), Max disrobed till he was down to trousers and boots. He'd hoped for a chance to limber up, but there was no time, he was told, and he was hustled into the ring.

Then all became clear to him.

"Lord Maxwell, sir," said his opponent with an evil grin. "Wot is you doin' here? I thought you'd learned your lesson in Reading."

Mighty Jack Cleaver, all seven feet of him, stared down, a long way down, into Max's stricken face. Max thought of Simon, and rage rolled through him like a torrential river. He knew he could outbox Jack Cleaver with one had tied behind his back. What he could not do was make an impression on the man. Those muscles were made of iron. But all Jack had to do was bide his time and get in one iron-fisted punch, and it was match over.

Simon had set him up.

If he had any sense, Max told himself, he would say it was all a ghastly mistake and beat a hasty retreat. It was probably what Simon expected him to do. But Simon had vastly mistaken his character. It was now a matter of honor.

He searched the crowd for Simon and found him with Martin, in the front row, right next to the ring. Martin was clutching a towel, and Simon held up a bottle of water and jiggled it.

The scoundrels were his seconds.

Martin looked worried, as well he might, but Simon was laughing his head off. Max ground his teeth together.

The referee entered the ring at that moment. Cheers all round from the crowd. Max and Mighty Jack shook hands, then took up their positions. At a word from the referee, the fight began.

Martin closed his eyes. "Tell me when it's all over," he told Simon.

"Good God!" said Simon. "Max just hit the champion right in the solar plexus and he didn't even flinch."

"Who, Max?"

"No. Mighty Jack. You have to give it to Max, he—! *Martin, did you see that? Did you see that?* Max landed a punch . . . oh no."

Martin opened his eyes. Max was flat on his face. He shook his head once, twice, then dragged himself to his knees and finally tottered to his feet. The crowd went wild.

They went at it again. Mighty Jack moved around the ring like a great oak that had uprooted itself. Max was obviously the better boxer, but compared to the champion, he was a mere sapling.

"What a sport!" said Simon, whistling in admiration at one point.

Then Mighty Jack landed a punch, and Max spun like a top and his momentum carried him into his own corner. He got to his feet, but it was the end of round one.

Martin and Simon scrambled into the ring. Max's nose was bleeding, and he was breathing hard and fast. Simon poured water down his throat while Martin used the towel to stop the bleeding.

Simon said, "All right, Max, you've proved your point. No one is going to think the less of you if you concede defeat now."

"Concede defeat? *Concede defeat? Never!*" said Max through gritted teeth. "I'll go till I drop."

Now Simon was beginning to look worried, and that pleased Max. He closed his eyes and prayed for a miracle.

Martin said, "You have a powerful right hook, Max. Why don't you hit Mighty Jack on the jaw?"

Max opened one eye and glared up at Martin. "Because," he said, "my arm doesn't reach that far."

The second round was no better than the first. Simon and Martin were no longer worried; they were scared to death. Max was puffing like a broken-down bellows. He was staggering, and blood was running from his nose and mouth. But he adamantly refused to give up.

When he came out for the third round, the crowd fell silent. His knees were buckling, but he kept his fists up. Everyone knew Mighty Jack had only to deliver the coup de grâce and it would be all over for Max.

Max knew it too. He dodged and weaved to evade those iron fists, but he was winded and couldn't get a punch in. But Mighty Jack did, and down Max went again. It looked as though the referee would stop the fight, and the crowd began to boo. Max pulled himself to his feet.

Someone in the crowd shouted, "We're with you, yer lordship! We're with you!" and the crowd yelled its support.

Mighty Jack was momentarily distracted. Max lashed out and caught the champion a blow to the throat. The champion stepped back, shook his head, and swatted Max as though he were a pesky fly. And Max went down again.

Simon clutched Martin's arm. "It's all over. It's got to be all over this time. Why doesn't the referee stop it? Stay down, Max. *Stay down!*"

Before his horrified eyes, Max got up on one knee, then the other, and pulled himself to his feet.

"End of round three," cried the timekeeper, and the crowd cheered, and cheered and cheered.

"He's won!" screamed Simon. "Max has won!"

Both brothers embraced violently, then, with a roar, they jumped up on the platform and ran to Max.

Max stood there in a daze. He didn't know what was going on. He'd only gone three rounds, and he knew this was the end for him. He couldn't hold up his head, never mind his fists.

Mighty Jack was pumping his hand and telling him what a fine fellow he was. Simon and Martin were bellowing in his ear that he was the only man in Stoneleigh who had managed to go the three rounds with Mighty Jack. He'd won a sovereign, it seemed. Someone was holding his arm up, and the spectators were cheering madly. None of it made sense to Max.

"This calls for a celebration," cried Simon.

He stripped off his coat and threw it over Max's shoulders.

Max, the victor, had to be carried from the ring by his seconds. Mighty Jack strolled after them.

The fight had lasted all of five minutes.

SARA WAS WAITING FOR THEM AT THE TOP OF the stairs. Her arms were folded across her breasts and her brows were down. Everyone was in bed, and she was in her nightclothes. Max had an arm looped around each of her brothers' necks, and he was definitely the worse for wear. His cheek was swollen and there was a cut on his lip. They were carrying on like mischievous schoolboys.

And she could smell the drink on them.

Their snickering stopped when they caught sight of her. She didn't say a word, not one word, but marched to her bedroom and held it open for them. They had to edge their way sideways to get Max through the door.

"I won a sovereign, Sara," he said. "Don't ask me why. It's for you. Simon, give her the sovereign."

Simon gave Sara the sovereign, which she deposited on the table without a thank-you, and without even looking at it.

"I suppose," said Max, "it's like bringing coals to Newcastle. I mean, what can a rich wife do with a sovereign?"

Simon snickered.

Martin said, "Now, Sara, there's no need to look like that. We were celebrating. In the King's Head. All of Stoneleigh was there. And we hardly had anything to drink. Tell her, Max."

"We hardly had anything to drink," said Max.

Martin grinned from ear to ear. "Max is a hero in Stoneleigh, Sara. Max, tell her."

"I'm a hero," said Max. "Ouch! Careful, Martin. That hurt!"

Sara pointed to the bed, and her brothers reverently eased Max down on it, but he wouldn't lie down.

"Is she often like this?" Max asked. "You know, silent and pouting?"

Simon laughed. "No. She usually lectures. But we're only her brothers. I suppose she has to watch her step with you."

"I am not pouting," said Sara, stung into replying. "What I am is . . . what I am is . . ."

"Yes?" said Max, squinting up at her.

Lips pressed together, she reached for him to help him disrobe, but her touch was not gentle, and Max groaned.

Simon pulled her away. "Careful, Sara. Max has taken a beating that would kill most men." He couldn't keep is excitement down as the memory came back to him. "You should have seen him! Against Mighty Jack Cleaver, no less! What a pounding he took. Martin and I were scared to death because Max wouldn't stay down. Don't you understand, Sara? Max won the contest! He was the only man in Stoneleigh who managed to go three rounds with the champion."

Sara looked as though she would burst into tears. "Oh, Max," she said. "What have these wicked boys done to you? Is this Simon's doing?" She went down on her knees beside Max and looked into his battered face. "I know you thought you were going to box with Simon."

At these words, Simon went scarlet.

Max said, "It wasn't Simon's fault. Can we talk about this later? I need help getting undressed. I want to soak in a warm bath, then I want a large glass of brandy to take my mind off my aches and pains." He looked at Sara. "Sara, help me."

"Oh, Max." She sniffed and reached for one booted foot, but when she saw his knuckles, she gasped. They were scraped raw. "Max, Max," she said softly. Eyes brimming, she brought his hands to her cheeks and looked up at him.

He gave her the smile that always made her melt with yearning.

Simon nudged Martin with his elbow. "Let's get out of here," he whispered.

Martin nodded. "Too much sugar for my taste."

They tiptoed to the door. Martin slipped away, but Simon turned back. "Max—" He paused and cleared his throat. "I was wondering if you would . . . that is . . . when you're on your feet again, of course, well, I'd consider it a great favor if you would take me out on Arrogance."

"I'd like nothing better," said Max quietly.

When the door closed, Sara said, "What was that all about?"

"I think your brother just apologized to me."

Sara started on his boots. "I didn't hear him say 'I'm sorry'!"

"Oh, well, men have a different way of apologizing from females." He saw that she'd removed one boot. "You did that as though you were born in a stable."

"I have two younger brothers," she said, as though that explained everything.

It did to Max. "Whom you love very much."

"Well, of course. I adore them. But that doesn't mean I'm blind to their faults."

Max's laugh turned into a moan, and Sara was instantly contrite. "Was I too rough?"

"No, no. I'll be all right, but a glass of brandy would help."

She removed his other boot and left him to go to his room for the brandy. When she returned, he was propped up in bed with his back against the pillows. His face was several shades whiter than when she'd left.

"I'm going to send for the doctor," she said quickly.

"No." He took the glass from her and sipped carefully, then said, "He won't thank you for calling him out when there's nothing wrong with me, nothing that a good night's sleep won't cure. Trust me, Sara. I've been in enough fights to know that I'm not hurt in any way that counts." He gave her a huge grin. "Last time, I only went two rounds with Mighty Jack. I must be getting better."

His little speech made her both cross and teary. She didn't like to see him like this, all battered and cut up. But it was his own fault. No one could force him to fight against his will. And he was practically telling her that he would do it again.

Not if she had anything to do with it. But now was not the time to argue the point with him, not when he looked so weak and helpless. All she said was, "I'll ring for Arthur to draw you a bath."

"Good idea."

When she came back to the bed, he held out his glass. He'd hardly touched the brandy. She took it from him and set it on the table.

He closed his eyes. "Drew Primrose was at the King's Head," he said. "He told me that you hadn't given him the marriage contract you made me sign. Does this mean you're having second thoughts?"

She took a moment to think about it. "Perhaps," she hedged.

"I'm glad, because that contract would only be the ruin of your family. I've been giving this a great deal of thought, and I have my own ideas about what's best for them. Would you like to hear what I think?"

She sat on the edge of the bed. "You've only known them for a few weeks, Max."

"And that means I can see them more clearly than you."

She doubted it, but she was interested in what he had to say. "All right. Go on."

He needed no further encouragement. "Let's start with your brothers," he said. "They're just like all young men their age. They'll give us many sleepless nights before they settle down. But let's wait until they know what they want to do with their lives before we decide how to help them." He yawned. "And while we're at it, let's enrol Martin in a different college at Oxford. Right now, he's too much in Simon's shadow. They'll still see each other, but Martin will make his own circle of friends. He needs to learn to stand on his own two feet. We'll consult him, of course, but I think he'll listen to me now." Another grin. "That's my reward for being pounded by Mighty Jack."

He touched her cheek with his fingers and they came away wet. "Now, what have I said?" he asked, bewildered.

"I don't know." She wiped her eyes with the sleeve of her robe. "I don't know why I'm turning into a watering pot."

"If I'd had to look after this family for as many years as you, all on my own, I wouldn't be a watering pot, I'd be a raving lunatic."

He was rewarded with a watery chuckle.

His hand tangled in her hair. "You're not alone now," he said seriously. "I'm here. I'm your husband. Don't shut me out. Don't ever shut me out."

The cold hand of reality touched her heart, and she bent her head so that he couldn't read her expression. His fingers moved gently from her hair to her cheek, then he tipped up her chin so that she couldn't evade his eyes.

"What is it?" he asked softly.

"I was thinking of Constance," she said.

"Ah, Constance. She has the right idea, you know. A Season in London would be just the thing, not for Lucy, but for her. She's lonely, Sara, and she's a menace, not only to herself but to every man in Stoneleigh."

"Don't I know it," said Sara with feeling.

"She's lonely," Max repeated softly. "A woman like that needs a husband. And once she's married, she'll be much happier, and so will we."

Sara sighed. "It's not as easy as that. We don't have friends and acquaintances in London, and even if we did, who would want to marry someone whose name is Carstairs?"

"I did."

She chuckled. "Yes, but—"

He silenced her with a wave of his hand. "I have friends and acquaintances in London. But let's not get caught up in mere details. Once we know what the problem is, we can think of ways to solve it. And it seems to me that money won't solve this family's problems."

"I never said or believed that money would solve all our problems. Yes, I wanted to protect Anne, but I also wanted to fulfill my father's dying wishes, that's all."

He linked his fingers through hers. "And you did, by marrying me. He trusted your judgment. That's why, in his will, he allowed the trust to be dissolved on your marriage. Now there are two of us to decide how best to take care of your family."

She smiled at Max. "I remember thinking," she said, "that night in Reading, that you were a good, kind man. I think I must have had a guardian angel who sent you to the wrong room that night."

"And I remember thinking," he said, "that fate had touched me on the shoulder, and that if I didn't accept it, I would always wonder what I'd missed."

She bent over him, and their lips met, but the pressure of her hand on his chest made him wince, and she pulled away.

"Admit it, Sara," he said, "I'm the best thing that ever happened to you."

"I'm not denying it, but—"

"But what?"

She wasn't sure that she was the best thing that had ever happened to him. "I wish Anne could be as happy as I am."

"If we could solve the riddle of William, I think she would be happy, or at least she would be at peace."

"I thought we were going to forget about William. I thought you said you were no longer interested in getting the story for your newspaper."

His lashes were drooping, and he missed the flash of fear in her eyes. "I'm thinking of us," he said, yawning. "I don't want William casting a shadow over our lives. We'll find him, Sara, or at least we'll give it a good try."

He gave a slow, sleepy smile and edged onto his side. "When are you going to admit it, Sara?"

Fear shivered through her. "Admit what?"

"That you love me? Then I'll admit . . ." He sighed.

She stood there, staring down at him, her heart beating frantically against her ribs.

There was a knock at the door, and she went to answer it. It was Arthur, the footman. She sent him away. Max was sleeping and she didn't want to waken him. She didn't want him to say the words, because she didn't know how she would answer him.

She covered him with the eiderdown, and made herself comfortable on one of the chairs. But no matter how hard she tried, sleep would not come.

Twenty-two

*I*N THE FOLLOWING DAYS, NO HINT OF THE TUR-
moil that raged inside Sara showed on the surface, and the
fiercer the turmoil, the quieter she became. She'd been living in a dream world, allowing herself to drift with the current, and that current had dashed her up on a rocky shore.

The problem with William wasn't going to go away.
Max wouldn't allow it. He was determined to clear her
name. She had no choice, now, but to face whatever
awaited her in the dower house. But she would do it without Max, because she had more to worry about than
herself.

There was more to it than that. She'd fallen in love with
him. Love, she discovered, was painful. She'd made mistakes, serious mistakes, but she wouldn't allow anyone to
pay for them but herself. If her worst fears were realized,
she would pay the penalty, even if it meant losing Max. The
last thing she wanted was for him to be tainted with her
guilt.

She made her plans with care. The first thing she did was
find another pistol to replace the one she'd lost, and this
time, she promised herself, if someone attacked her, she
would not run away. Then she checked on the supply of

laudanum in the medicine box and found it more than adequate for her needs. Finally, she gave the order to have the dower house cleared of all rubble and fallen beams. She told Drew that she had engaged a builder to look over the empty shell and assess whether it was worth the money to rebuild it, and she didn't want any accidents to happen while workmen were poking around.

The work began at once. Sara went through the motions of taking up her life again. She went to church services; she visited the local shops; she spent time in the sickroom with Max; but she was only biding her time until the dower house was ready.

From the very first, the day after the fair, Max knew something was wrong. He was confined to bed, and though Sara was pleasant when she read to him or shared his dinner tray, he recognized the look on her face. She was too calm and too pleasant by half. She'd withdrawn into her shell, shutting him out. He thought he understood why. She was afraid of her feelings, afraid to admit that she loved him because it would make her vulnerable. Well, that was too damn bad. He hadn't been looking for love either, but now that it had found him, he didn't go around whining about it. It was done. There was no changing it. She might think that she could keep him at arm's length, but as soon as he was on his feet again, he was going to prove how wrong she was.

It came to him gradually that there was more to it than that. One of the workmen had found a pistol beside the path that led to the dower house, and he sent it up to the "master." The footman delivered it to Max. It belonged, he said, to Samuel Carstairs. No one knew how it had come to be near the dower house, but Max thought long and hard about the night Sara was attacked and he began to add things up.

His suspicions intensified when Sara suggested he might like to move back into his own room, just for convenience, and those suspicions solidified into convictions when he learned workmen had begun to clear out the dower house.

℘ETER FALLON WAS AWAY FOR FOUR DAYS, and on his return, as he approached the front steps, Max, with a glass of brandy in one hand and a thin cigar in the other, came forward to meet him. It was late, and the candles had been lit. As a footman carried his box upstairs, Peter picked up a candle and led the way to his office. From the drawing room upstairs came the sound of someone playing the piano, a violent piece. *Scarlatti*, thought Peter, and the music suddenly stopped.

After the usual casual conversation between friends, he got down to business. "Drew Primrose," he said, "as far as I can determine, was not in Bristol the night William Neville disappeared. I checked the hotel where he was supposed to be staying; I checked with the clients he was supposed to have seen. Oh yes, he was there and he did see them, but one day later than he would have us all believe."

"And it's only a day's drive from Stoneleigh to Bristol," said Max. He was doodling with a pencil on a piece of paper.

Peter stared at him for a moment. "That's it?" he said. "You send me to Bristol to find out if Drew Primrose has an alibi, and when I tell you he hasn't, you're not even interested?"

Max looked up. "I'm interested. Very interested."

"Or maybe you're still feeling under the weather?"

"I'm perfectly recovered from the fight, if that's what you mean."

"All right. But something has happened to take the stuffing out of you. What is it, Max?"

Max smiled, but there was no smile in his voice. "Small things that add up. You see, Peter, I think that tonight we've reached the crisis point. And now that you're back, you can be of great help to me."

"How?"

Max told him in a few clipped sentences, then rose to leave. Peter was still trying to recover from the shock of what Max had asked him to do when Max shocked him even more.

"Oh, by the way," said Max, "don't drink that brandy." He gestured to the untouched glass of brandy he'd left on Peter's desk. "My wife gave it to me and it's laced with laudanum."

HE WAS SEETHING WITH A RESENTMENT HE could hardly master. They were husband and wife; they were lovers. She had no hesitation in giving him her beautiful body. But her heart wasn't his. He didn't think she had a heart to give.

He'd tried making excuses for her, and he knew that some of them were valid. Her caution had been learned in the harsh school of life. She hadn't survived by being free with her trust, and maybe she'd had good cause to distrust him in the past. But once they became lovers, none of that should have mattered. And it hadn't mattered until he'd practically asked her to give him the words. And from that moment on, a veil had come down. She'd cheapened something precious that had flowered between them and turned it into dross.

She must think him a simpleton not to have put two and two together. She couldn't seem to understand that he didn't give a damn about William Neville. What he cared about was protecting her, but she still saw him as a threat to her precious family.

And, fool that he was, he might have forgiven her everything if she had not offered him, with her own hands and a sweet smile on her face, a glass of brandy that a schoolboy would have known was doctored.

He'd taken one sip and left the drawing room at once,

because if he'd stayed, he would have been tempted to throttle her.

She would go to the dower house, of course, after she'd made sure that he was practically insensate with her laudanum. He would catch her in the act, and this time, by God, there would be no half-truths and evasions.

He went to his own room first, a room that he used only to store his belongings. If he'd agreed to his wife's oh-so-casual suggestion that he sleep in his own room, where he could smoke whenever he pleased, he might have been spared the laudanum. Damn her cheating soul to all eternity!

He found a glass just like the one Sara had given him and poured enough brandy into it to convince her that he had swallowed some of her witch's brew. His temper was on a short leash when he made his way to her bedchamber.

S HE WAS SITTING AT HER DRESSING TABLE IN her nightclothes, brushing out her long dark hair. She looked as fragile as a fine porcelain figurine. But Max no longer believed what his eyes told him. He knew she was as hard as nails.

He closed the door softly and crossed to her. She watched him in the mirror as he took a long swallow of brandy from the glass in his hand.

"You left the drawing room very suddenly," she said.

"I went outside to smoke a cigar. You have beautiful hair. May I?"

He put his glass down and took the brush from her. There was something different about him. With his tawny hair, he looked like a slow, sleepy lion and just as unpredictable. She glanced at the brandy glass and wondered if the laudanum had something to do with it.

Their eyes met in the mirror. He wasn't brushing her hair. He was running his fingers through it, fluffing it out in voluptuous disorder.

"We haven't made love for several days," he said.

"No." She inhaled deeply. "Did you mind?"

He began to brush her hair. "Of course I minded. You're incomparable, my love. In fact, I'd say you're the most responsive, passionate woman I've ever had in my bed, and that's saying something." He put the brush down and reached for his glass.

"Max, I don't think you should drink any more of that brandy. You don't sound like yourself."

He lifted the glass to his mouth and tipped it back. He smiled at her, not the smile she loved, but a twisted smile with a hint of cruelty in it.

"You know what they say," he said. *"In vino veritas."*

He put the glass down, drew her back against his thighs, and framed her face with both hands. Her heart was pounding; her fingers curled into fists.

"Do you know what I think, Sara?"

She shook her head. She was beginning to be frightened.

"I think . . ." His words were becoming slurred. "I think love is highly overrated, don't you?"

She swallowed hard. "I haven't thought about it."

"Take us, for example. Take that first night in Reading. We didn't know each other. It wasn't love. What we felt was purely physical. I remember thinking that I wanted to make you my mistress. How in hell's name did we ever get to be married?"

"You said," her mouth was completely dry, "you said that you felt as though fate had touched you on the shoulder."

"Did I? Perhaps I was being gallant." He chuckled. "I can be charming when I want to be. Then, so can you, my love."

She felt as though a shard of glass had pierced her heart. He wasn't himself. It was the laudanum that had loosened his tongue. But he couldn't say these hateful things if he hadn't been thinking them.

She shrugged out of his grasp, rose to her feet and turned to face him. In a few minutes, he would fall asleep. All she had to do was get him into bed, and he would fall asleep. She couldn't let herself be ruled by hurt pride at this stage of the game.

She took a step toward him and looped her arms around his neck. "Make love to me, Max," she whispered huskily. "Take me to bed and make love to me."

Something inside Max quietly died. She should have slapped him for his taunts and insults; she should have ordered him from her room. Instead, she had lowered herself to the level of a prostitute.

He had no intention of taking it further. He was going to yawn, stagger to the bed, and let events overtake them. But the need to hurt her as much as she had hurt him was driving him hard, and when her lips touched his, his arms came around her in a crushing embrace.

His mouth was hot and hard and cruelly demanding. This wasn't what she expected. She hadn't drugged him. All she'd done was unleash something wild in his nature that she hadn't known existed.

She went limp in his arms, hoping that would placate him, but his mouth roamed down her throat to the soft swell of her breasts. He dispensed with her dressing robe and tore open the front of her nightgown, then slipped it from her shoulders so that it slithered to the floor.

"Look at you," he said, "ripe for me."

He filled his hands with her breasts, then laved her nipples with tongue and lips and teeth till she was shivering with need.

His mouth was on hers again, his tongue thrusting and withdrawing in a way she had never imagined a man could kiss a woman. His hands moved over her, touching, taking, and she was moaning her pleasure into his mouth.

With his mouth still consuming hers, he lifted her in his arms and carried her to the bed. There was no tenderness in him, no gentleness, no giving. He was so aggressive in his masculinity that she should have been afraid. She was anything but afraid. He had stirred something in her as well, something she hadn't known existed until now.

He loved her as he'd never loved her before, demanding total control of her body. And all that was feminine in her nature beat through her blood in answering fire. He allowed her no modesty, and she felt no shame. With his hands and mouth he learned every inch of her intimately, and she abandoned herself to pleasure. To want like this drove everything from her mind but him.

He stripped out of his clothes and kneeled above her. She looked up at him, helplessly lost in sensation. As their eyes locked, she sensed his hesitation.

"Max?"

He spoke harshly. "Let's not spoil things with words."

For a moment, a look of pain softened the harsh tension in his face. "My God," he muttered, "what am I doing?"

He suddenly wrenched himself away from her and flung himself to the other side of the bed. With his back to her, shoulders hunched, he tried to even his harsh breathing.

He did not look at her. "I apologize," he said. "No man should treat his wife in that shameless way. I don't know what came over me."

The hurt spread through her in waves. His words turned what to her had been a beautiful experience into something sordid, and she was ashamed.

"It was the . . . the brandy," she said.

He sighed and drew the coverlet over them. "Was it the brandy? I wonder."

She turned on her side, away from him. *It was the laudanum,* she thought, but she hadn't ingested any laudanum or brandy. So what was her excuse?

She lay there quietly, listening. The laudanum had started to take effect. Max's chest was rising and falling; his breathing was soft and even. She waited until she had command of her emotions, then she slipped from the bed and began to dress.

. . . .

WHEN THE DOOR CLOSED SOFTLY AFTER HER,
Max was up like a shot. He dragged on his shirt and
trousers, then his coat, and picked up his boots. Once he
reached the landing, he listened. As he'd hoped, she'd taken
the servants' staircase. She'd have to retrace her steps because he'd had the foresight to lock the door into the back
hall. It would slow her down and give him time to get there
first.

When he got outside, he put on his boots. Peter Fallon
came out of the shadows to meet him. "All set?" asked Max.

"I'm not much good with a gun." Peter held up the pistol Max had given him.

"Then you'd better take care," said Max, "because Sara
will be armed and I bet she knows how to use a pistol."

Peter said incredulously, "She'd shoot me?"

"Not if she knew it was you, but how could she tell in
the dark? Remember, your job is to follow her and see that
no harm comes to her. Don't enter the dower house. Wait
outside until I call you."

"You're sure she'll go to the dower house?"

"I'm sure," said Max savagely.

SHE ENTERED THE DOWER HOUSE SO STEALTHILY
and soundlessly that he was almost caught in the light of her
lantern. He was positioned just inside the doorway behind a
massive beam that still supported part of a ceiling. He'd
been right about the pistol. He caught the gleam of it as she
passed him.

He quickly pulled back when she turned her head. She
was careful, looking every way to make sure she wasn't being followed. Most women would have been terrified to
come out alone at night after someone had already attacked
them. But Sara must think the risks were worth it.

He knew why she was here. There would be a small cell, a hiding place for a priest, or a body, but he hadn't a clue where to look. He'd already gone over the house and tried every nook and cranny. He'd pulled on decorative bricks and metal rods and handles; he'd examined the floor for a trapdoor. Anything. There was nothing.

Without Sara, he would never find it.

He had a few bad moments when he lost sight of her. She'd moved past the great stone fireplace to the back of the house. He would give her a minute or two, he decided, then he'd go after her. But she wasn't gone for more than a few seconds. Careful Sara. Once again, she'd been checking to make sure that she was alone.

Her steps took her to the stone hearth, to the fireplace with the inglenook on either side, and here, she put down her lantern and pistol. Max's heart picked up speed. In his own search, he'd come back to the fireplace time and again. It seemed like the logical place. But he hadn't had any luck. He hadn't found a door or anything out of the ordinary except the decorative bricks high on the walls of the inglenooks. He'd tried to twist or turn and pull every one, and he'd been stymied.

Sara had moved into the inglenook on the left of the fireplace. He didn't know what the hell she was doing. She seemed to be climbing the wall. She must be out of her mind. She was going to overbalance. Her arm reached up for a handhold. There was a sound of metal sliding on metal, then a dull thud, and Sara jumped down.

So that's it, thought Max. There was a sequence to the mechanism for opening the door. Sara had used her foot, waited a second or two, then pulled on one of the decorative bricks. Ingenious. No wonder neither he nor the officers of the law who had searched the house had found it.

It was time to make his move, before she got to her pistol.

"Sara," he said, and stepped into the light.

He gave her credit for cool nerves. Or maybe she was just frozen like a terrified rabbit.

"It's Max," he said, and slowly, slowly, began to cross the distance between them.

She stood her ground. The nearer he got, however, the more he could see the emotions flash in her eyes—shock, fear, and finally, the ironclad control that never failed to rattle him.

Her chin went up. "You didn't drink the brandy I gave you."

"You mean the laudanum." He couldn't keep the bitterness from his voice. "No, I didn't drink it."

Her eyes faltered. "Then what . . . ? You wanted to humiliate me. The laudanum had nothing to do with it."

He might have felt ashamed if he weren't still burning from the knowledge that she'd tried to drug him. If her pride was bruised, his was crushed. "I wondered how far you would go to keep me in that room." He made a bow that was so exaggerated it was insulting. "Even I didn't expect you to go that far, Sara. What can I say except that your eagerness made me forget the respect I owe my wife?"

Her brow lifted. "Then my sacrifice was in vain, was it not?"

Her contempt stung, but this had gone on long enough. He picked up her pistol and pocketed it. He looked at the fireplace, from inglenook to inglenook. There was no entrance to a secret chamber.

"Where is it, Sara?" he asked.

Her head drooped. "On the other side of the fireplace. But before you go in there, I want to confess that I and no one else murdered William Neville. Do you understand? I murdered William."

No shock registered on Max's face. He said casually, "Oh, I understand more than you think." He picked up the lantern. "Don't even think of running away."

She let out a choked laugh. "Where would I go that the *Courier* would not follow? You should be proud of yourself, Max. You vowed to find the final resting place of William Neville, and you've succeeded."

"Sara—"

She turned her back on him. He stared at that rigid spine for a long moment, then uttering a soft oath, he walked around the fireplace. The opening was on the floor hard by the wall. It wasn't necessary to enter it. He went on his knees and lowered the lantern through the opening. The room was about six feet square. Several people could have hidden in it, but it wasn't high enough for an adult to stand upright. There were cobwebs in plenty. But there was nothing else.

This was not William Neville's final resting place.

He went back to Sara. She was sitting on the floor with her knees drawn up to her chin. Her head was resting on her knees. She looked up at him.

"So you found him," she said tonelessly.

"No, Sara. The room is empty. No William Neville. Nothing."

For a moment it seemed that she didn't understand. Her face was frozen. She didn't breathe. Suddenly she came to life. With a little cry, she scrambled to her feet and ran to the opening in the wall. Max followed her.

"Take the lantern and have a look," he said.

She took the lantern from him, went down on her knees, and lowered it through the gap in the floor. When she pulled back and set the lantern down, her shoulders were heaving.

She sat down, knees drawn up, with her back against the stone wall. Her face was showing her fatigue. "What does it mean?" she whispered. *"What does it mean?"*

Max longed to pull her into his arms and tell her that everything would be all right. But it wasn't all right. Until she told him the whole truth, until they knew what had happened to William, she would never be free.

He said quietly, "William came to the dower house that night."

She nodded, and used the sleeve of her coat to wipe the tears that had begun to leak from her eyes.

"Tell me what happened."

"I've told you most of it already. I was upstairs nursing Anne. William had sent for me that morning. Anne was miscarrying. He'd beaten her, you see. She needed someone to nurse her. I think William felt guilty. He always felt guilty when he was sober. That's why he didn't stay. He couldn't face me. He went to get the doctor, then he went to the local tavern to fortify himself with drink. I made up my mind, then, that I would kill him before I'd let him lay a hand on Anne again.

"He arrived home drunk and in a furious temper. He'd heard I was going to marry Francis. He knew what that meant. The marriage contracts were being drawn up. I'd instructed my lawyers to provide for Anne so that William could never touch the capital. He'd heard about it and was crazy with rage. He had gambling debts, he said. He had to have the money right away. But this time, I couldn't help him. He wouldn't believe me and threatened to hurt Anne.

"I barred him from going up the stairs. If I'd been thinking straight, I would have had a pistol and put a bullet in his brain. But all I had was my own strength. And, my God, I used it."

When she put her face on her knees and began to weep in great wrenching sobs, he put a hand on her shoulder to draw her into his arms, but she violently shied away.

Max let his hand drop. His face was starkly white.

She scrubbed her face with her hands. "I was no match for him, of course. He felled me with one blow and threw me against the fireplace wall." Her voice tightened, but she did not waver. "I picked up the poker and went after him as he climbed the stairs."

Max felt his world tilt on its axis. He looked at what was left of the staircase, a few stumps that had once supported, he imagined, a solid, intricately carved oak staircase. He could see William climbing the stairs. What better way to hurt Sara than to take his vile temper out on the sister she loved. The fury pumped through his blood and lodged in his throat.

She stared down at her hands. "I hit him," she said, "on the back. Then he turned and came after me. I remember hearing Anne crying out and something fell and shattered on the floor upstairs." She wouldn't look at Max, couldn't look at him, so she closed her eyes. "I hit him again and again. Suddenly, I realized he wasn't going to get up and come after me, so I threw the poker away."

She took a long, steadying breath and cleared her throat. "I don't know how long I stood there petrified, staring down at him. Finally, I went down on my knees to check his injuries. There was a deep gash on his forehead, and the blood was soaking into his neckcloth. I think he must have fallen against the fender. I don't know. I felt his pulse. Nothing. I couldn't hear him breathing. My one thought, then, believe it or not, was to save him.

"I was panic-stricken." She scrubbed her face again, and waited a moment before going on. "I ran to the kitchen, to the pantry where Anne kept the medicine box. I was looking for smelling salts. I gathered towels and a basin of cold water and a bottle of brandy. I couldn't have been gone for more than a few minutes. When I ran into the hall, there was no sign of William."

When it looked as though she wouldn't say more, he said quietly, "Then what made you think William's body was in the priest's hole?" Still no response, so he went on, "Did Anne kill him?"

"No!" The word echoed off the walls. She shook her head and said in a broken whisper, "No."

"What then, Sara? *Tell me!*"

"She was there, sitting on the bottom step. But she was in a daze. I'd given her laudanum, no more than the doctor prescribed, and she didn't know where she was. I suppose she heard William and me fighting and had come downstairs to investigate. I asked her where William was. She didn't answer. She didn't understand. I was only too glad to think that I hadn't killed him, and that he'd left the house. I took Anne back to bed, but the bleeding had started again, and I couldn't leave her. It was the worst night of my life. I thought William might return with his friends or the constable. I don't know what I thought. I wanted to get help for Anne, but I couldn't leave her." Her voice caught on a sob. "I couldn't leave her, and she was in no condition to walk to the main house."

She looked at him now, and for an instant, all the anguish and fear from the memory of that night was plain to see. Her breathing was harsh and her voice thick with emotion. "In the morning, the constables came. It was obvious they suspected Anne or me of murdering William. So I told them that William had not come home that night. It was only later that I began to believe that I really had killed him and that in the few minutes I was in the kitchen, Anne had dragged his body to the priest's hole and had hidden it there. Later, when she was better, I asked her if she'd seen William that night, but she can't remember. All she remembers is William beating her and losing a baby that she really wanted. I would have looked in the priest's hole, but it was too late. The authorities had sealed off the house. Then I was arrested. And after the trial, I waited too long. The house burned down. I had to leave Stoneleigh. You know the rest."

There was a long silence after that. Sara put her head on her knees, and Max pulled a thin cigar from his pocket and lit it from the lantern. He stood beside Sara, his back propped against the stone wall and inhaled slowly. He watched the smoke he exhaled float for a moment in front of his face then quietly dissipate. Above his head, he could see the stars.

"Why didn't you tell me all this before?" he said at last.

She looked at him with tired, dull eyes. "Because you *are* the *Courier*, Max. I wasn't afraid for myself. After all, I was acquitted and can't be tried again. But Anne is different. I was afraid of what your paper would do to her. I was afraid the authorities would believe that Anne and I had been in it together. They can't charge me, but they can still charge Anne. But they can't charge her now, can they?"

"No." He sighed. "And you thought I couldn't be trusted?"

"I trusted you with myself, but not with Anne." She paused. "Or at least, I wasn't willing to take that chance."

He inhaled again. "So what do you think happened to William?"

"I think," she shivered, "that he's alive. Who else could have written those notes? What would be the point?"

Max might have argued with her, but he saw her shiver again, and he decided that this was not the time to go into it. They had a lot to talk about, a lot to straighten out between them.

He felt as weary as she looked. "I want you to go back to the house," he said, "and stay there. Peter Fallon will go with you. Try to get a good night's rest. We'll talk in the morning."

He would have helped her to her feet but he didn't want to see her flinch from his touch again.

"Peter is here?" There was no real interest in her voice.

"He's standing guard outside the house."

He walked her to the front steps. When he whistled, Peter appeared at the garden gate. "Go with him," said Max.

She blinked up at him. "What are you going to do?"

"I'm going to find out what happened to William," he said.

"Are you going to publish the story in your newspaper, I mean, about Anne and me?"

He walked off without answering her.

Twenty-three

～

*M*AX HAD NO DIFFICULTY FINDING DREW
Primrose's cottage. Though there were no lights shining
from its windows, there were lanterns hanging on posts,
spaced out at intervals, to light the way to a row of workmen's cottages farther up the hill. It was long after midnight, but he didn't give a damn about the time. He was in a
filthy temper, and it showed in the way his fist hammered
on the door.

His fist was only an indistinct shape, but he stopped
hammering, unfisted his hand and turned it over. He would
never have put himself in the same class as William Neville.
He would never dream of lifting his hand in anger against a
woman. But there were other ways of making a woman
submit. He'd been angry when he'd made love to Sara
tonight. He'd imposed himself on her. Would she forgive
him? And how could he make her understand something
he didn't understand himself?

He thrust the thought from him and began to hammer
on the door again. When no one called out or came to answer, he used his booted foot to force the lock. He walked
into a velvety darkness and promptly fell against an obstacle
in his path. Cursing softly and fluently, he groped his way to

the wall where he expected to find the fireplace. He was in luck. On the mantelpiece, he found the ubiquitous tinder-box. It took several tries, but eventually he got the tinder going, and he put the flame to the candle he found on the mantel. That done, he turned to survey the room.

It wasn't as small as he'd expected. Then he remembered that Drew Primrose's father had been the head gardener at Longfield. His cottage would be bigger than those of the ordinary laborers. This room would have been the front parlor, but it was now converted into an office. A flat-topped desk was positioned in front of the window. It was a chair he'd bumped into when he'd entered. Books and ledgers lined the walls.

He went through a door and found the kitchen. The only furniture was a table and chairs. There were pots and kitchen utensils, and everything was as neat and clean as a doctor's surgery. There were two bedrooms, one starkly empty, the other containing only a bed and a chair.

Drew Primrose had done well for himself, considering his humble beginnings. But he wouldn't have got so far if it hadn't been for Sara. It didn't seem likely that if he loved Sara, he had sent her those notes, but he'd been caught out in a lie, and that made him suspect in Max's eyes.

He returned to the office and placed both his candle and pistol on the flat of the desk. The curtains were already drawn. Whether or not he found what he was looking for here, he would go to Stoneleigh and roust Drew Primrose out of his bed. There were questions he wanted answered right now, not tomorrow or the day after that. And there was every chance that after he'd questioned Sara's attorney, the mystery of William Neville would begin to unravel. He'd learned a lot tonight, not enough to unmask a mur-derer—and he was still sure that William was dead—but enough to narrow the field. Odd bits of information were beginning to click in his mind. A few more pieces of the puzzle were all he needed, then he would have the whole picture.

All the desk drawers were locked. He returned to the kitchen, found a sharp knife and set to work. In the top drawer, there were papers and letters, in fact, just what Max was looking for. From his coat pocket, he removed the last note in William's handwriting that Sara had received, and began to compare it with the writing on the letters he'd removed from the drawer. Nothing matched.

He started on the next drawer and the next, with the same result. When he forced open the bottom drawer, the deepest drawer, he found a bottle of brandy and an assortment of odds and ends. One by one, he removed each article from its hiding place and set it on the desk. There was a muslin kerchief, a pearl earring, one white kid glove and a monogrammed lace handkerchief. Max shook his head. These were the kind of mementoes a man with a romantic frame of mind would keep as souvenirs of love affairs. There were no such mementoes in his desk drawers.

They belonged to Sara, he thought, and temper sizzled through him. He picked up the lace handkerchief, unfolded it and examined the monogram. His brow pleated in a frown. He was tracing the initials with his finger when he heard footsteps approaching the front door. Dropping the handkerchief, he reached for his pistol, took two paces back, out of arm's reach, and waited.

The door opened and Drew Primrose entered. "I thought we agreed—" He stopped short when he saw Max, and a look of utter surprise spread over his face. "You?" His glance flicked to his desk, then to the gun in Max's hand. "What," he said in an awful voice, "do you think you're doing?"

Max cocked the pistol and gestured to a chair beside the empty grate. "I thought it was time," he said, "that you and I had a private conversation without Sara there to protect you."

Neither his words nor the gun cowed Drew Primrose but just the opposite. He looked as though he might spring at Max.

"Try it," said Max, "and I'll put a bullet in your kneecap, then I'll have you up on a charge of attempted murder."

"This is my home! You're a trespasser!"

"On the contrary. This is my property, by right of my marriage to Sara. Sit down, Mr. Primrose, and I'll put my pistol away."

Though he still bristled with hostility, Drew Primrose walked to the wooden chair by the fireplace and sat down. Max put his pistol on the desk, within easy reach, then propped himself against the chair. He'd smelled strong spirits on the other man as he'd passed him, and a whiff of cologne, cheap, flowery cologne.

Max said easily, "I didn't know there were any fleshpots in Stoneleigh, but by the smell of you, I'd say you'd just come from a brothel." When there was no reply, he went on, "Now that really surprises me. From everything I've heard and learned about you, I would have said you were the straitlaced type, you know, nose always to the grindstone, conscientious, a little holier than the next man."

The younger man's face flushed scarlet, and he said furiously, "I don't have to account for my movements to you, or my character. So tell me what you want and get out."

"Fine. Let's not mince words. You can begin by telling me where you were the night William Neville disappeared."

"The night—" Drew Primrose stared and went on staring.

"Where were you, Mr. Primrose?" asked Max quietly.

"I was in Bristol."

"Not so. I had someone check on you and you didn't arrive until the following night."

"And you think—what? That I killed William Neville and disposed of his body?"

"That's exactly what I think. You were in love with

Anne Neville, were you not? Her husband brutalized her. So you got rid of him."

Drew Primrose sat motionless, appalled. "How did you know about Anne?" he asked hoarsely.

Max picked up the lace handkerchief, and looked down at it. "This is Anne's handkerchief. It has her initials on it." He looked at Drew Primrose. "Everyone thought it was Sara you loved, and why shouldn't they? Anne was married. You were always hanging around Longfield. You became the steward here and spent most of your nights in this cottage. But that wasn't so that you could be near Sara. It was always Anne with you."

"What if it was? That doesn't mean I killed William." He stared at his hand and made it into a fist. "I wish I had killed the bastard," he said fiercely.

"Was Anne carrying your child? Is that why you killed William? Because he found out about you and Anne?"

Drew Primrose's head snapped back. "No! You've got it all wrong. Anne and I have never been lovers."

"You sent those notes to Sara, didn't you? You wanted to bring her back to Stoneleigh then get rid of her so that you and Anne could inherit the Carstairs fortune."

"What notes? I don't know what you're talking about."

Max gave the other man no time to think before he flung each question at him. "It was you who attacked Sara when she went to the dower house. You would have murdered her, wouldn't you?"

"No! I didn't know Sara was attacked!"

"Were you and Anne in this together?"

"No!"

"Where is William Neville's body?"

"I don't know."

"Then tell me what you do know, Mr. Primrose, because as far as I can see you and Anne have the most to gain by doing away with William Neville and Sara."

Drew Primrose was white to the very roots of his hair.

His mouth was slack; his eyes unblinking. A shudder passed over him. "You couldn't be more wrong," he said.

Max let out a long breath. "Then tell me the truth. Tell me where you were the night William disappeared."

Drew swallowed. "I was in Bath—no, listen to me—I was on my way to Bristol, but I stayed over in Bath that first night, with a woman I'd met at the White Hart. I was in despair, I suppose, and saw no reason I should not console myself with a pretty woman. Yes, I loved Anne and she loved me. I'd finally persuaded her to leave William and come away with me. Then she learned she was with child, William's child, and she said that changed everything. I was hurt, furious, I don't know what. So I found a woman to make me forget."

He got up abruptly and stood with shoulders stooped, his back to Max, one hand supporting himself on the mantelpiece. "I didn't kill William, but I wished for his death many times." He turned to look at Max. "I hope he is dead."

Max looked into that ravaged face and felt pity rise in him. He said quietly, "You must have suspected that Sara or Anne had murdered William?"

"I never suspected Anne. She doesn't know how to hate."

"But you suspected Sara?"

"Yes. At first. I knew there was only one place she could have hidden the body, and I waited till the constables were no longer swarming over the place before I checked on it. It was empty."

Max said incredulously, "You knew about the secret chamber in the dower house?"

For the first time since he entered his house, Drew smiled. "Anne told me about it a long time ago, when we were children."

"And," said Max, eyes narrowing, "if you had found William's body, what would you have done then?"

Drew's smile vanished and he stiffened. "I wouldn't have gone to the authorities, if that's what you think. I would have got rid of it somehow. I would have taken it miles away from Stoneleigh and dropped it down one of those chalky holes in the downs. But I would have chosen a place where it could be found."

Max had never liked Drew Primrose, but he suddenly found himself warming to the man. Anyone who helped Sara could always count on his goodwill.

"You wanted the body found," said Max, "so that Anne would know she was a widow and was free to marry you."

A bitter smile twisted Drew's lips. "I wanted the body found to clear Sara's name. If William's remains were discovered miles away, it would have been impossible for her to get there and back. That's all I was thinking about, clearing Sara's name. Anne was already lost to me. She suspected me of murdering William, you see. She doesn't believe I spent the whole time in Bristol, and, of course, she's right. And I told her often enough that I would kill William if he ever hit her again. He beat her. She lost the baby. What else could she think?"

He sat down again and put his head in his hands. "I've never given up my search for William, just to prove to Anne that I didn't murder him." He looked up at Max. "I went to London and visited all the places he used to frequent. I kept up with his friends. William simply vanished into thin air."

"Sara thinks he's still alive."

"I doubt it. A man like that needs a constant supply of money to feed his gambling habit. Sara was like a bottomless pit. William was bitter after her father changed his will. He felt that the money should have been his." He shook his head. "Without Sara, where would he get money? His own father had disowned him. William had nowhere to go. He must be dead."

Max's shoulders slumped. When he'd arrived at Drew's

house, he thought he had just about worked everything out. Now he was back at the beginning.

Drew said, "So what's all this about notes and someone attacking Sara? Did you make that up to try and entrap me?"

Max showed him the note that had been left on Sara's dressing table; he told him about the attack. When Drew got over his shock, he began to ask questions and speculate, and finally, he shook his head.

"If I had murdered William," he said, "the last thing I'd want is to stir things up by sending Sara notes or jumping out at her in the dark. I'd let sleeping dogs lie. But I don't like the sound of this. Get her out of here. Take her away from Stoneleigh. William is still casting a shadow on all our lives."

Soon after this, Max left. Drew's parting words were turning over in his mind, and he quickened his steps. Things were beginning to click again, only in a new pattern, but there were still odd things that did not make sense.

Before he reached the house, he knew something was wrong. There was no light shining from Sara's bedroom window and no light in Peter Fallon's office. He broke into a run.

With candle in hand, he made for Peter's office first. It was empty. Blood began to beat through his veins in slow, thick strokes. He took the stairs two at a time. Sara's room was empty as well.

He went to Simon's room next. Simon roused from sleep when he heard Max bellowing his name. "Good God, Max, do you know what time it is?"

"Where's Sara?"

"Sara? I don't know."

"Get dressed. I want the whole house roused. I'll get the servants. You get everyone on this floor. We'll meet in the drawing room. And be quick about it."

The tension in Max's voice had communicated itself to

Simon. He was already reaching for his clothes. "What's happened to Sara?"

"She's missing."

*L*IGHTS SHONE FROM ALL THE WINDOWS IN THE house as Max and every footman at Longfield spread out, each with a lantern in his hand. At Max's order, they began a slow descent toward the dower house, like beaters going before the hunters to flush out game. Max had sent Simon to Stoneleigh to rouse the constable and Martin to get Drew Primrose and then the workers in the cottages.

He had a terrible feeling in the pit of his stomach. Instinct told him that time was running out and if he didn't find Sara soon, it would be too late. He was wound up so tight he wasn't sure he was breathing.

They found Peter Fallon on the path, halfway between the dower house and the main house. There was a nasty gash on his head, but his injuries were not mortal. He was unconscious, but a mouthful of brandy from Max's flask brought him round.

"Who did this?" asked Max.

"I didn't see him. It was Sara he wanted. He took her, Max. I don't know where."

Drew Primrose came up at this point, asking questions that Max didn't have time to answer. Max started barking out orders. Drew was to take over the search for Sara; two of the men were to carry Peter back to the house, then one of them could go and fetch the doctor.

He didn't wait for the men who were bringing Peter back to the house. He hoped, prayed that Sara had been abducted and was not lying dead or dying under some bush. He had something to do, something he would have done long ago if Sara had not warned him to leave her family alone.

Constance and Anne were in the drawing room, both of

them staring out the window, following the progress of the searchers by their lanterns. They both turned at Max's entrance. Anne had put on a dark, long-sleeved dress that buttoned to her throat. Constance was still in her nightclothes.

Anne's hand curled around the back of a chair, and she seemed to stagger against it. "Tell me at once, Max. Is it bad news?"

"No. It's no news."

"Thank God!"

Constance put her hands over her face and began to weep.

Max said, "Where's Lucy?" He was trying to keep his voice calm and steady so that he wouldn't panic Anne and Constance as he was panicked.

Anne said, "I put her back to bed. She doesn't know Sara is missing and I didn't tell her. What is it, Max? Why are you here and not looking for Sara?"

"I think one of you knows where Sara is," he said baldly.

"*What?*" Constance's hands dropped from her face and she stared at Max in mute astonishment.

Anne's face had turned a paler shade of white, but her voice was strong. "How could we know, Max?"

"Think back," said Max, "to the night I quarreled with Simon at the dinner table. He was angry because I'd taken Arrogance out. I believe that sometime after dinner, one of you slipped into Sara's room and left a note that was meant to frighten her."

"What was in the note?" asked Constance unsteadily.

Max's impatience was beginning to show. "It doesn't matter!" He tried to gentle his tone. "All that matters is that one of you left a note, and I want to know which one of you it was. Listen to me. This isn't a game. I'm not saying you meant any harm to come to Sara. Maybe you didn't know what was in the note. But one of you left it there, and if I don't find Sara soon, it may be too late. So answer me! Now!"

Constance's face twisted with fury. "How dare you suggest such a thing!"

Anne held up her hand, silencing Constance. "I didn't leave a note, Max, I swear it."

Constance shook her head. "No! I didn't! I swear it!" She was beginning to look frightened, and Max knew he had found the weak link in the chain.

"But you know who may have left that note, don't you, Constance?"

"No." Her voice was quavering.

Max suddenly lashed out with his hand, bringing it down hard on a small table, and Constance retreated a step, then another. Max went after her. "Tell me, damn you, or if anything happens to Sara, I swear I'll see you hang for murder."

"I didn't think . . ." Constance gulped back tears of sheer terror. "He wasn't gone for more than a minute. He said he'd dropped a glove . . ."

"Who, damn you? Who?"

"Max, stop this." Anne's hand was at her throat. "Can't you see you're only frightening her? It must have been Beckett. He's Lady Neville's footman. You must have seen him at the fair. He goes everywhere with her." She looked at Constance. "Are you going to tell him or shall I?"

Constance slumped against a chair. Her eyes were bulging and her mouth was working. "My God, what have I done?" she whispered.

Anne heaved a sigh. "Constance and Beckett are lovers," she said. "I saw him in the corridor that night, and told Constance that if she ever again slept with one of her lovers under this roof, I'd tell Simon and let him deal with it."

"It was only once," Constance wailed, "only once."

"Thank you," said Max. "Now go downstairs and make yourselves useful. There's an injured man coming in and I want him to have the best of care." He turned to go. "And when the constable gets here, tell him I've gone to Sir Ivor

Neville's place and he'd better get there soon or I'll have his head."

When he was gone, Constance sank down on a chair. Her face was lined with misery. "He said he loved me. He said he wanted to see where I slept. He said he wanted to make love to me in my own bed so that next time I slept in it, I would remember him."

There was an uncharacteristic edge to Anne's voice. "Will you stop thinking about yourself? You heard Max. We are to make ourselves useful. There are men out there looking for Sara. When they come in, they'll want something to eat and drink. So get dressed and meet me downstairs."

Constance nodded, rose and used the hem of her negligee to wipe away her tears. "You must hate me," she said.

"No, Constance. I don't hate you. Don't you know that people who live in glass houses don't throw stones?"

Anne put her arm around Constance, and they left the room together.

Twenty-four

◦───∾───◦

SARA HEARD THEIR VOICES AS IN A DREAM, but she was too weak to call out for help. There was a blazing pain in her head, and her jaw felt as though it had been hit by a flatiron. Someone was holding her down and she didn't have the strength to fight him off. She moaned and tried to open her eyes, but her lids were too heavy.

To keep the nausea at bay, she breathed slowly and deeply, and as her wits came back to her, so did her memory. She'd been knocked senseless as she tried to help Peter Fallon when someone jumped out at them as they walked back to the main house. It was the same man who had attacked her before. She'd smelled the cologne on him; she'd felt the same powerful arms lift her off her feet as she'd sunk into oblivion.

With a gasping cry, she opened her eyes and tried to rise, then moaned as needles of pain shot through her head. Panic rose up in her when she realized she was bound at the wrists and ankles to a wooden chair. She pulled, she strained, she gritted her teeth and flexed her fingers in an effort to free herself. All she achieved was to drive the leather bonds deeper into her flesh.

She heard the voices again and moved her head cautiously to determine where they were coming from. There was a door to her right that was slightly ajar, and the voices, a man's and a woman's, were coming from the other side of that door.

Blind instinct took over and she froze like an ice sculpture. She didn't want the people on the other side of that door to know she was awake, because she was terrified of what they would do to her next.

Calm, stay calm! she told herself fiercely as she gulped air into her lungs.

She blinked to clear her vision and tried to make out where they were keeping her. There were candles at intervals on the walls, dappling the room in a ghostly light, and for one wild moment, she thought she was in the chapel at Longfield. The stone walls were circular and mellowed to gold with age; the small windows were set close to the ceiling; and at the far end of the room there was an altar with candles on it. But there were no pews in this chapel. There was only the altar, the chair she was strapped into, and one other chair with wheels. An invalid chair. And the moment she saw that chair, Sara knew where she was.

It made perfect sense to her now. The people who hated her most in the world were Sir Ivor and Lady Neville.

She choked back her fear. They wouldn't go to these extraordinary lengths unless they were maddened by hate. They couldn't afford to let her go. Abduction was a capital offense.

To take her mind off that horrible thought, she concentrated on her surroundings, and her eyes narrowed against the light of the two flickering candles that were set at either end of the altar. Between the candles, there were two miniature portraits on stands, and though she was too far away to make them out clearly, she knew well enough whose portraits they were. The room smelled of incense and roses.

This wasn't a chapel; it was a shrine.

There was a step at the door and quelling every emotion but her will to survive, Sara lowered her chin to her chest and deliberately relaxed her cramping muscles in an effort to appear completely inert.

There were two of them. One voice, she expected to hear, Lady Neville's. But the man was not Sir Ivor. Then he could only be Lady Neville's footman, Beckett.

"How hard did you hit her?" asked Lady Neville.

"Harder than I wanted to. I had to. She fought like a tigress."

"Did she see you?"

"Does it matter? Her companion didn't see me, so you need not be afraid that we've been discovered. Anyway, it will be all over soon. All I need is five minutes alone with her and she'll tell me what we want to know. Afterwards you can do with her as you like, just as long as I get my money."

"Five minutes alone with her?" Lady Neville giggled. "Beckett, you must think I'm a fool. If I give you five minutes alone with her, you'll ravish her. Only it's impossible to ravish Sara Carstairs. She's a whore. She took her first lover when she was twelve years old. She's insatiable."

Beckett laughed. "I think I may be next on her list. The looks she gave me at the fair! If Constance hadn't been there, I'm sure I would be sharing Sara Carstairs's bed by now."

"Lord Maxwell," said Lady Neville tartly, "might have something to say about that."

"You think he loves her?"

"Hardly. Mark my words, this is a trumped-up marriage. Once Lord Maxwell gets his story, he'll have no use for Sara Carstairs, and he'll soon get out of this make-believe marriage. All I meant was that he won't let anyone else get too close to her."

"So we're all after the same thing!"

"Of course. But if you want your reward, we'll have to find William's remains first." She sighed. "I always thought we'd find him in the dower house."

"So did I, especially after she had workmen take out those huge beams. Lord Maxwell must have had the same idea. He arrived first, and I had to clear out in a hurry."

"And you're sure William's remains aren't there?"

"I already told you, I heard her talking to Lord Maxwell's man before I grabbed her. She didn't lead them to William's remains. There's only one way to find out where William's body is, and that's to make her talk. As I said, give me five minutes alone with her, and she'll be only too happy to tell me."

Lady Neville's voice was alight with amusement. "You'll have your time alone with her *after* she tells us what we want to know. Do you understand?"

"I can wait."

"See that you do."

Sara felt as though she'd swallowed a huge ball of chicken fat. She could feel the oiliness in her throat as it went down, and her stomach began to heave. She couldn't stop herself from moaning.

"Well, at least we know she's alive," said Lady Neville in the same amused tone. She twitched her skirts as she approached Sara. "You should have been more patient, Beckett. You were supposed to wait till Sir Ivor was away from home before you brought her here."

"That was your idea, not mine. It's hard to get near her now, she's so well guarded. I saw my chance and took it. Besides, Sir Ivor won't disturb us. Little Jenny will keep him occupied."

"That's enough, Beckett! You will always speak of Sir Ivor with respect. Do you understand?"

The footman turned sullen. "Well, what are you waiting for? Bring her round."

Sara caught the fragrance of roses on Lady Neville's

clothes and braced for what she guessed was coming. The next instant, she was coughing and sputtering as she inhaled from an opened bottle of larkshorn. Tears started in her eyes and she strained away from the violently acrid odor. Lady Neville said nothing but she kept the bottle close to Sara's nose till she was satisfied that Sara was fully conscious. Only then did she take a step back.

Tears streamed down Sara's face and she sucked great drafts of air into her lungs. Her whole body was trembling uncontrollably, and she tried to master her fear. No one was coming to help her; no one knew where she was. She was at the mercy of a woman who truly believed she'd murdered her son, and a man who had the morals of a tomcat. She did not know which one she feared more.

Stay calm! Stay calm!

She looked at her abductors. The footman was in black livery; Lady Neville was in her nightclothes. Her negligee was a girlish pink confection that made her look clownish, not younger.

"Lady Neville!" The tremor in Sara's voice wasn't all play-acting. She looked down at her bonds, gasped, and began to struggle. "Why am I here? What is the meaning of this?"

She didn't see it coming, but she should have been prepared. Lady Neville suddenly lashed out with her hand and struck Sara full across the face. She would have struck Sara again if the footman hadn't intervened. He grasped Lady Neville's wrist and dragged her away.

Sara was rigid with shock and pain. But the slap had done more than make her sick with pain. It doused her panic. If she was ever to get out of her alive, she would have to keep her wits about her.

"Get hold of yourself," gritted Beckett. He stood between Lady Neville and Sara. "If she faints on us again, how will that help us?"

"She killed my son!" Lady Neville dashed a hand across her eyes. "She killed my son!"

"I was acquitted of his murder," Sara cried out.

Lady Neville let out a hissing sound. "Only because William's body was never found." She dragged herself from her footman's grasp, walked to the altar and returned with one of the miniature portraits. "Look at him!" she commanded, her voice cracking.

Sara looked into the face of William Neville, a younger William than she had known. His thin face was framed with dark curls. His lips were full and turned up in a smile. No one would have known, looking at that charming expression, of the cruelty that lurked beneath the surface.

She swallowed hard. "I'm sorry," she said, "but—"

Lady Neville stamped her foot. "Don't lie! It had to be you! I waited up for him that night, but he did not come home." Her face was sharp with malice. "You didn't know that, did you, that William still came to see his mother? He was everything to me, and I to him. He told me all about you and how mean you were with money. But I was never mean to him. I always gave him whatever I could spare. And it was so unjust. The money belonged to him. He would never have married beneath him if you hadn't turned his father against him."

This portrait of domestic bliss explained a great deal about William's character, but Sara did not dwell on that. "*I* turned Sir Ivor against William? How could I do that?"

Lady Neville's voice lashed out like a whip. "By telling lies about him. You spread rumors about him. You said he raped his own sister. And when Sir Ivor heard about it, he disowned William. But it was all your doing."

"Caroline?" Sara felt as though she'd stepped off the earth and was being sucked into a void. Her eyes darted to the altar, to the portrait of Caroline. Was Caroline the local girl William had deserted? As from a great distance, she heard her own voice say, "Did Caroline say that William had raped her?"

"She was dead, wasn't she? Oh, you were clever. You

waited until she was in her grave before you started spreading those vile rumors."

Sara looked into those pale, venomous eyes and knew that no explanation of hers would be accepted. Lady Neville's hatred was so intense it was palpable.

The footman was becoming restive. "This is getting us nowhere. I haven't planned and schemed just to listen to family history. I want that reward, and the sooner we learn where William's body is, the sooner I can claim it."

Lady Neville did not answer. She replaced William's portrait on the altar, kissed it, and the other one, then came to stand directly in front of Sara. "I have prayed for this day for so long," she said. "When you went away, I was distraught. I thought I would never see you again. But I found a way to bring you home, didn't I, Sara?"

The words came automatically. "You sent me those notes in William's hand."

A brilliant smile. "But of course. Then Beckett and I waited patiently for your return so that you could lead us to William. Beckett said that you would want to make sure that William was dead. But you didn't lead us to my son's grave, so we decided something more drastic was required. And here we are."

Panic began to soar in Sara again. With her hands and legs bound, she was helpless to defend herself. She wondered wildly if she should scream. She'd learned from their conversation that Sir Ivor was home and there were bound to be servants. But this manor was as big as a small castle. She doubted if anyone was still awake, and even if she screamed and someone heard her, how would they find her?

She looked at Lady Neville. Even if she knew where William's body was, she did not think that would save her. She was looking into a child's face, a cruel child who cared nothing for justice except as it applied to herself.

"Oh, Max," she sobbed, so softly, it was almost inaudible.

But Lady Neville heard and pounced. "Oh yes, let's not forget your dear husband. You thought you were so clever, snaring Lord Maxwell. Did you really think that the Worthes of Lyndhurst would accept you as their daughter-in-law? Lord Maxwell was using you. He is the owner and publisher of the *Courier*. All he wants is a story for his newspaper. That's what he told Sir Ivor. Lord Maxwell wouldn't marry you, a brewer's daughter! Time will prove me right."

Sara discarded most of this little speech as the ravings of a deranged woman. The pain of losing a son had festered inside Lady Neville and affected her mind. She was unpredictable and out of control.

She looked at the footman. He was staring at her with an enigmatic smile on his face. Her fingers curled around the arms of the chair. "Think before you do anything stupid," she said to him. There was a plea in her voice. "Lord Maxwell isn't a fool. He'll figure out that you had something to do with my abduction. And if it's money you want, I have money in plenty. I'll give you the reward if you let me go."

"No!" The cry came from Lady Neville.

Beckett's smile showed a flash of white teeth. "Don't worry! I'm not such a fool. I know all about ladies and how they keep their promises."

Sara cried, "Is money so important to you?"

The smile instantly turned into a sneer. "Spoken like at true lady," he said. "What do you and your kind know about a life in service? You've never done a day's work in your life."

His head descended, and Sara could see the fury burning in his eyes. She tried to strain away, and her spine flattened against the back of the chair.

"I make thirty pounds a year," he said. "Thirty! And most footmen make only half that amount. We're as good as the people we serve, but they treat their dogs better than they treat us. Well, I'm ambitious. I have plans for my life, and the reward will set me up very nicely."

Sara gasped when he framed her face with his hands.

"That's right," he said, "you would do well to fear me. I shall be very upset, you see, if I don't claim that reward. In fact, I've set my heart on it. And I've got a terrible temper. There's no saying what I'll do if you don't tell me what I want to know."

"What Beckett means," said Lady Neville, "is that he'll kill you if you don't tell us where William is, but if you do tell us, we'll let you go. Oh, I know you can't be tried for murder again, but the world will know that you killed my son. So you see, Miss Carstairs, you're going to pay for your crime, one way or another."

"I can't tell you where William's body is," Sara cried out, "because—" She looked first at one hard face, then the other, and knew the truth would not save her. "Because . . ." she faltered, then went on, "you'll never find it. I'll have to take you there."

"She's lying," hissed Lady Neville. "She's playing for time."

"Let her finish. Go on. Tell me where it is, and I'll decide whether you're lying or not. And if you are, God help you."

The words came more easily now, because Peter Fallon had been speculating on where William's body might be hidden when they were attacked by Beckett. "It's on the downs, in one of those old Saxon fortifications that looks down on Longfield. But you'll never find it. It's covered over with brambles and briers. The constables didn't find it, because no one knows about it but me. I found it when I was a child and made it my secret hiding place."

Lady Neville's face twisted with grief and fury. "And that's where you met William that night! You lured him there, then you killed him."

She took a quick step toward Sara, but once again, Beckett intervened. "If you hurt her," he bit out, "we'll never find your son's body." He looked at Sara. "I don't believe you. You've been twice to the dower house in the middle of the night. The first time, I followed you. After that, I knew you'd go back there. I've been waiting night after night for you to try again. If William's body isn't in the dower house, it's somewhere close by. And the dower house is nowhere near the downs. It's in the opposite direction."

Sara's brain had never worked faster. "It was a ploy. To make sure that I wasn't followed. Do you think I'm such a fool that I wouldn't test the waters first? But both times, I was foiled. And wasn't William's horse found on the downs? That's where he is, I tell you."

A look passed between mistress and servant, and after a moment, Lady Neville nodded. She let out a pent-up breath. "I'll wait here for you. But just remember who is paying you the reward. If you don't find William's remains, you'll get nothing out of Sir Ivor."

"I'm not likely to forget."

Sara flinched when he suddenly turned on her with a knife in his hand, then she let out a choked sob. He only wanted to cut her bonds, first those on her wrists, then those at her ankles. He'd seen the terror on her face and he was smiling.

"Stand up," he said.

Sara obeyed, but she was swaying like a woman who'd had too much to drink. Her head was buzzing with thoughts, her blood was pounding in her ears. Lady Neville had said she would stay behind, and though having only one to contend with improved her chances of escape, she didn't want to be left alone with the footman.

You'll have your time alone with her after she tells us what we want to know.

The words spun around in her head. She didn't think this

particular footman would follow anyone's inclinations but his own.

"Now let's see you walk," he said.

Sara took one step and staggered, but she made herself go on. If she was ever to get out of this alive, she'd have to do a lot more than walk. She'd have to run like a deer.

"Let's go," said Beckett. He put his knife to her throat. "But remember, if you try anything, I'll slice off your fingers one by one. And they're such pretty fingers."

He grasped Sara's elbow and propelled her toward the door. Lady Neville held it open for them. "I shall be here, Beckett, waiting for your return. Then we'll go to Sir Ivor together and tell him the good news."

She shut the door on them and turned back to the shrine she'd made to her children. She felt curiously serene. She'd made a promise to her son that no matter how long it took, she would bring his murderer to justice. At long last, that day had arrived.

THE HOUSE WAS A MAZE OF LONG, NARROW corridors and staircases that came out on landings that led to other long, narrow corridors. Sara thought she understood why Beckett had chosen this roundabout way of leaving the house. He must know where all the servants were quartered, and wanted to avoid meeting anyone she could appeal to for help. Even if she screamed, she didn't think anyone would hear her.

She didn't have a plan except to get away from him and hide herself until morning, when the house would begin to stir. She knew she would never outrun him on the downs. She didn't have the stamina. She felt groggy and weak. She had to make her move while they were still in the house.

But to get away from him, she needed darkness, and her hopes faded when she saw that there were candles burning in wall sconces in every corridor. There should have been a footman on duty to douse those candles hours ago, and she wondered if it was Beckett's job. From what she'd learned of him, he wouldn't give a straw for what was expected of him. He deeply resented his position as a footman and would do as little as he could get away with.

"This is Lady Neville's wing of the house," he said, the first words he'd spoken to her since they'd left Lady Neville's apartments. "She and I have it to ourselves, except for her maid, and she's not on this floor. If you were to scream no one would hear you."

She felt the slow throb of blood at her throat.

He stopped beside one of the wall sconces and plucked a candle from it. "There are no candles where we are going," he said.

He made no move to walk on, and she edged away from him, trying to make her movement as natural as possible. But try as she might, she couldn't think of a thing to say.

He crowded her into a doorway. "You fancy me, don't you?" he said.

Her skin began to crawl. She badly wanted to smack the leering smile from his face, but she knew better than to antagonize him. In fact, she should be doing the opposite. Would he believe her? "Yes," she said tremulously.

He smiled into her eyes.

After pocketing his knife, he reached for the doorknob right by her hip, and pushed the door inward. Sara quickly stepped back, away from him. He followed her in, shut the door and locked it. As he deposited the candle on the mantelpiece, Sara took a quick look round. She didn't waste time examining the big four-poster bed with its elaborate drapes. She was looking for a weapon and she found it on the hearth, beside the brass fender.

He slipped off his coat and folded it neatly over a chair. Sara tried to be as casual as he, but her fingers were trembling so hard, she couldn't undo the buttons on her coat.

She jumped when she looked up and saw that he was standing right over her. His hand cupped her shoulders and she fought the urge to strain away.

Dark eyes glittered down at her. "You stupid bitch. Did you really think you could fool me? You're playing for time, hoping someone will rescue you. Well, there's no rescue from this."

He grabbed her hand and thrust it against his body. When she felt his arousal, terror ripped through her and she acted instinctively. She struck him across the face. He moved like lightning and sent her spinning to the edge of the bed. When he sprang at her, she twisted away and stumbled toward the fireplace. Swiftly stooping, she picked up the poker and whirled to face him.

He put his hands on his hips and chuckled. "I'm going to make you pay for that slap," he said. "But you want me to, don't you? Some women like it rough."

Before he had stopped speaking, he leaped for her. But she was ready. She swung the poker in an arc and caught him across one shoulder. It wasn't enough to fell him. With a roar of rage, he wrestled her to the floor. She fought him like a madwoman. They rolled together and sent a chair toppling. Kicking, bucking, she freed one hand and poked a finger in his eye. On a howl of pain, he pulled off her. She raised to her knees and began to crawl toward the poker. On the way, she encountered his coat and felt the sharp edge of his knife.

It was in her hand before he realized his danger. He lunged for her and she drove the knife into his thigh. There was a moment of astonished silence, then he doubled over in pain.

"Bitch!" he panted. "Fucking bitch! I think you severed an artery."

"I hope I have."

"Bitch! Help me. I need a doctor."

Sara did not bother to answer. She picked up his coat,

found the key to the door, and quickly opened it. She threw away the knife, then she began to scream. She ran the length of the corridor and screamed and screamed and screamed.

As if in answer to those screams, she heard a thundering from below, and a moment later, Max's voice roaring her name. All her aches and pains were forgotten as she went hurtling down that last flight of stairs.

"My God! Sara!"

Max leaped for the bottom of the stairs as she went catapulting into his arms.

Twenty-five

S ARA DID NOT ALLOW HERSELF MORE THAN A few seconds' comfort in those strong arms before she pushed out of them. First, she wanted to hear about Peter Fallon, and after Max had assured her that Peter was on the mend, she told him in a few sentences how she came to be there.

She rushed her last words. "And I stabbed him, Lady Neville's footman. I think he may be bleeding to death. In one of the bedchambers." She looked back at the stairs. "I don't know which one."

"I don't give a damn if he *is* bleeding to death. It will save me the bother of killing him!"

Sara tugged on Max's sleeve. "If you won't think of him, think of me. I don't want to be tried for murder again."

"Where," said Max, "is Sir Ivor?"

He was looking over her head, and when Sara turned, she saw a footman in black livery standing in the shadows. For a moment, her heart stopped, then she saw that it wasn't Beckett, but an older man. The night porter, she thought, and sniffed back tears of relief.

"There's no one up but me," said the footman. He

pointed to an ornate clock on the vestibule table. "Everyone's asleep."

"We'll soon change that," snapped Max.

He thrust Sara from him, produced his pistol, and fired a shot into the plaster ceiling. The report of the shot echoed like a cannon going off.

It was too much for Sara. She put her hands over her ears. Reaction set in, and she began to tremble uncontrollably.

"Brandy," said Max. "What you need is a large glass of brandy." Then to the footman, "Take us to Sir Ivor's library."

"No one is allowed—"

"Now!" roared Max.

Doors were opening and slamming, and people were calling out in alarm. Nothing, it seemed, put this footman off his stride. He picked up a candle and said stiffly, "Come this way."

Once they were in the library, Max pushed Sara into a chair. "Please, Max," she said, her lips trembling, "you must find Beckett and stop the bleeding."

"Don't worry, I'll find him." His voice rose dramatically when he addressed the footman. "Get my wife a brandy. And lock the door when I'm gone. On no account are you to leave my wife alone."

"Max, please, *go*!" Sara cried out.

He nodded and left.

After the footman had locked the door, he brought Sara a glass of brandy. She was shivering so hard that when she tried to drink it, she spilled drops down the front of her coat. She must be getting hysterical, she thought, because when the footman took up his position by the door, just as though everything were normal and she was paying an afternoon call, she began to giggle.

Now that she was out of danger, she couldn't seem to get a grip on herself. When her spasmodic giggles turned into hiccups, she put the glass to her mouth and took a long, hard swallow. Then she coughed and sputtered, and tears started to her eyes, but those tears weren't all caused by the brandy she had swallowed.

She was cold, so terribly cold.

She turned to the footman and adopted Max's imperious tone. "I want the fire lit," she said.

This was soon done, and she changed chairs to get closer to the warmth. It was a big fireplace, twice as big as any at Longfield, and in no time at all, she felt toasty warm. She took another swallow of brandy, sank back in her chair, and watched the flames lick around the kindling and logs. Footsteps and voices sounded in the corridor, but she paid no attention. She was staring at the fireplace, but she was seeing the fireplace in the dower house.

For three years, she'd suffered torments not knowing whether she or Anne had murdered William. And when the notes had started to come, she'd begun to believe that William was still alive. But if Lady Neville had written the notes, then William must surely be dead.

Then where had he gone that night, after he left the dower house?

He would go to someone who had the means to pay off his gambling debts. That's why he'd come to her. Gambling debts had to be paid at once. It was deplorable, but there was some sort of unwritten code amongst gentlemen that damned a man if he reneged on gaming vowels but forgave him if he neglected to pay his bills to his tailor or bootmaker or even to his servants and dependents.

Lady Neville said that William had had an appointment with her that night, but he hadn't turned up. She always gave him whatever she could spare. But that wouldn't have been enough for William, not nearly enough. And Sir Ivor wouldn't help his son. They hadn't spoken to each other in years.

She sipped her brandy absently and came at the problem from a different angle. Who had the motive and opportunity to kill William? That was the question that had led to her own arrest and trial. Her thoughts drifted and she began to recall tonight's events, especially the last hour in Lady Neville's private apartments. Something struck an odd note. Little Jenny. Something about little Jenny. She dwelled on that thought, and before she had time to weigh anything, her mind began to make fantastic connections.

It couldn't be true.

She started over and slowly, piece by piece, put the puzzle together until a picture began to emerge.

It was too fanciful. And even if it were true, she could never prove it. She didn't know how she'd got started on this bizarre train of thought. One minute, she'd been sipping brandy, staring at the fireplace, and the next she'd been transported to the dower house and the last time she'd seen William.

She put down her glass and got up. She felt as though a charge of electricity had just passed through her. It was only a theory, but it made sense. And there was one sure way of proving it.

Just as she began to move, someone knocked on the door. Sir Ivor's voice barked out an order, and when the footman unlocked the door, Sir Ivor strode in. Right behind him was Max.

It didn't surprise Sara to see that Sir Ivor was fully dressed. He wouldn't lower himself by appearing in public in a nightshirt and a dressing gown. He was as immaculately turned out as always—beige breeches, dark blue coat, pristine white shirt. Max looked as though he had thrown on his clothes when his house caught fire.

The first thing Sir Ivor did was to send his footman to the front door to await the arrival of the constable. Max crossed to Sara.

"The footman? Beckett?" he said. "He was trying to make a run for it. He didn't get very far. He left a trail of blood. But he's all right. He's locked up and guarded and once the constable arrives, he'll be questioned. Meanwhile, he's not saying anything."

"And Lady Neville?" she asked.

Sir Ivor's voice lashed out. "She will be joining us presently, once her maid dresses her." He was very angry and red veins stood out on his nose and cheeks. He approached Sara. "I'm sure she knows nothing, and, I might add, I don't for one minute believe this trumped-up story of abduction. If anything, I think you and Beckett are in this together, but what you hope to gain is beyond me."

Max spoke through his teeth. "My man was struck down tonight as he escorted my wife home. He might have been killed. Let Lady Neville and her footman try to explain their way out of that."

Sara said quickly, "You said Mr. Fallon was all right."

Max did not break eye contact with Sir Ivor. "He suffered a concussion, that's all. But it could have been worse."

Sir Ivor swore violently, turned away and stalked to the sideboard with its tray of decanters. He spoke over his shoulder as he poured himself a drink. "I'm warning you, I'm pressing charges. This is nothing less than break and enter. And if Beckett maintains his innocence, then the charge will be attempted murder."

"Don't worry." Max patted Sara's hand. "They won't get away with it. We know you were abducted. Peter was able to tell us that much. And we have witnesses who will testify that Beckett was in the house the night you received that note."

"Hah!" Sir Ivor turned, a hard, scornful smile on his face. "If Beckett was in your house, who let him in? My God, Lord Maxwell, you, of all people, should know that this woman has no morals. She was carrying on an affair with Beckett under your very nose."

"Why you—"

Sara's hand on Max's arm prevented him from springing at the older man. "No, Max! No more violence! Please!"

Max's eyes searched her face, and his expression soft-ened. "You look," he said, "as though you're ready to col-lapse. I should take you home, and I will as soon as we talk to the constable. Can you wait that long?"

"If I have anything to do with it," said Sir Ivor, bolting his drink, "she'll be accompanying the constable to the toll-booth. She hasn't changed. This is just like the last time."

Max said something soothing to Sara, but she didn't hear him. She was thinking that Sir Ivor was right. It was so simi-lar to the last time that chills were running up and down her spine. She would be arrested and imprisoned in Winchester until her trial. The gossip would start up again and everyone would have a salacious story to tell about Sara Carstairs.

It was similar, but it wasn't the same, because this time she could speak up. She didn't have a sister to worry about. She didn't have to fear that if she told the truth she'd be sending Anne to the gallows.

"You hypocrite!" Her eyes were like ice and fixed on Sir Ivor's face. She took a step toward him, then another. "You liar! You coward! You saved your own skin last time by making me your scapegoat. And maybe I helped you be-cause I kept my silence. But it isn't going to happen this time around."

Both men were looking at her as though she'd gone mad.

"Sara—" said Max, frowning.

"No, listen to me! He murdered William. He murdered his own son. I know how it happened and I know why."

"I think," said Sir Ivor, "your wife has lost her senses. But do go on. This is highly entertaining. At least it will pass the time until the constable arrives."

Max looked worried. "I'll get you a glass of brandy," he said.

Sir Ivor sauntered over to his desk and took the chair be-hind it. He looked amused, and that put a dent in Sara's confidence. She automatically accepted the glass Max gave her and put it to her lips. Then she saw that one of Sir Ivor's hands was balled into a tight fist. It was a trick she had used at her trial. Her face would be serene, but all her fears and tension would be focused on the tight fist she concealed in the folds of her gown.

"William," she said, looking at Max, "wanted money that night. He was in desperate straits and he came to me first. I couldn't help him even if I wanted to. The lawyers had drawn up my marriage settlements. You know we fought, and you know that afterwards, William left the dower house. Where would he go, Max? Who would have the kind of money to cover his gaming debts? Think about it. There were only two people in Stoneleigh with that kind of money, myself and his father."

"He wouldn't come to me," Sir Ivor burst out. "I had disowned him when he married your sister."

"No," said Sara. "Your quarrel with William took place long before he married Anne. And you didn't disown him. He disowned you."

"You're mad!"

Sara turned to Max. "I told you that William got very angry with me once when I taxed him about a rumor I'd heard."

Max nodded. "He'd fathered a child on a local girl, then deserted her."

Sir Ivor sighed. "If you must know, that's why I disowned him, that and his wildness and gaming."

Sara's voice was shaking. "But it wasn't a local girl. It was your own daughter. I don't believe she died of a lung fever. I don't believe you took her to London to see the best physicians. You took her there to get an abortion. She was sixteen years old and she died! How could you do it?"

Sir Ivor's face was starkly white. "Who told you these lies?"

"Beckett," said Sara, shamelessly lying. "He knows all about you, Sir Ivor. He told me."

He stared at her without blinking, then turning to Max,

he said hoarsely, "It was necessary to protect our family name. William and his own sister! How could I let that get out? You're a man of the world. You would do as much to protect your own family's name."

"You're mistaken," Max said, his lips stiff, his nostrils flaring. "My only concern would be for the girl."

Sir Ivor gave Max back stare for stare. "I'm not apologizing for anything." He looked at Sara. "If I'd wanted to kill William for what he'd done to my daughter, why would I wait so long? Why not kill him at once? She died the year before he married your sister."

"That's what puzzled me," she said, "until I realized William had nothing to do with it. You were the father of your daughter's child. I think Caroline told William and you paid him off to keep his mouth shut. But when he'd spent the money you'd given him, he came back for more." She appealed to Max. "That's how William worked. He blackmailed me, and when the money ran out, he always came back for more. He did the same with his father. And that night, I think Sir Ivor came to the end of his tether and killed William. Isn't that what happened to me? I wanted to kill William, too, but I would never have let someone else take the blame for it."

Sir Ivor was breathing hard. "I refuse to listen to any more of these disgusting lies."

Even Max was shaking his head. "Sara, these are serious accusations."

She ignored this interruption. Eyes on Sir Ivor, she asked harshly, "How old is Jenny? You know Jenny, don't you, Sir Ivor? Little Jenny? She works for you. She's a maid. Beckett said that you would be with her tonight. Is she twelve? Thirteen?" Then on a broken whisper, "My own sister, Lucy, said that you made her skin crawl. I should have questioned her, but it never occurred to me that you would molest her. Even your own wife knows that you like little girls. Is that why she has never grown up? How many little girls have you molested, Sir Ivor? Do you think you can keep it a secret? I'll find out. I promise you. I'll find out."

"Lies!" roared Sir Ivor. "The ravings of a lunatic! You can prove nothing!"

Sara breathed out slowly. "Oh, but I can. You killed William that night, in this very room, then you hid his body in the secret chamber beneath the fireplace. Max, look at the fireplace. I know it doesn't have inglenooks, but it's almost a replica of the fireplace in the dower house. Look at the decorative bricks. This fireplace was built by the same builder who built the fireplace in the dower house."

"Congreve." said Max. "Peter told me about him." He moved to the fireplace wall and examined it carefully. "My God, Sara, you're right."

"There will be a sequence—"

She broke off when Sir Ivor suddenly grabbed her from behind, with one arm across her chest, locking her in a vise-like grip. He had moved with the speed and silence of a panther. There was a pistol in his hand and when he cocked it, Max spun round.

"Don't make any sudden moves," said Sir Ivor, "or the girl dies." He put the pistol to Sara's head.

"I didn't believe half of what Sara said," said Max.

"Neither did I," said Sara. "And to tell the truth, most of it was guessing. Max, I love you."

"I'm taking her with me." Sir Ivor began to drag Sara toward the door. "If you try to interfere, I swear I won't think twice about putting a bullet in her head."

Max spread his arms wide. "You'd best put the bullet in me." He advanced slowly, cautiously. "Because, if you harm a hair of her head, I swear I'll track you down and kill you with my bare hands." He looked over Sir Ivor's shoulder. "Ah, Constable. You've arrived just in the nick of time."

"What the hell!" exclaimed Constable Evans, a big beefy man who stood framed in the doorway.

When Sir Ivor took his eyes off Max, Max leaped for him.

He lashed out with his booted foot, like an athlete executing a high jump, and Sir Ivor's pistol went spinning out of his hand. Sara dragged herself free and Max landed a wicked right hook on Sir Ivor's jaw. With a gasp of pain, Sir Ivor sank down on his knees. Defeated, head bowed, he made no protest as the constable manacled his hands behind his back, then dragged him to his feet.

"And now," said the constable, "would you mind telling me what in Hades in going on here?"

THE CONSTABLE WAS IN NO HURRY TO LOOK for secret rooms where bodies might be hidden. After it had dawned on him that he had just arrested the most powerful man in West Hampshire, he had become much more cautious. He was wishing now that young Streatham had gone to Magistrate Orr's house instead of to his own. There would be hell to pay if he overstepped himself in this affair. He had six children to feed, and if he were dismissed from his position, he didn't know how he would put bread on the table. That's why he had sent Streatham back to Stoneleigh to get the magistrate. Orr was gentry himself. He would know how to handle this little lot.

He really hated it when he was called out to deal with the upper classes. They were all the same. They thought they had only to tell you something and there could be no questioning it. That was the problem. They were all telling him different stories.

And his position was made more awkward because one of Sir Ivor's accusers was Sara Carstairs, the woman he'd arrested three years before for young Neville's murder. She was married now to a man of some importance, and he didn't know whether to call her Lady Worthe or Lady Maxwell, so he wasn't calling her anything. He wished Orr would get here and take charge.

There were four of them now, because shortly after he

arrived, Lady Neville had been wheeled in in her invalid chair. Of them all, she was giving him the most trouble. She kept squawking about dire consequences for him because he'd arrested the wrong person. The others were quieter as they waited for Magistrate Orr to arrive. In fact, Sir Ivor sat there like a block of stone and had hardly opened his mouth. Sara Carstairs's eyes were closed, and her husband kept urging her to take another sip from the glass of brandy he was holding to her lips.

The constable looked at Max. "What was that, sir?"

Max's patience was just about at an end. He'd soon come to see that the constable was slow and plodding, but this was the limit. The man must be a dolt if he couldn't tell that Sir Ivor was guilty of something.

"Look," he said, trying to be patient, "you caught Sir Ivor with a pistol to my wife's head. He knew we'd discovered where his son's body is hidden, and if you would only give me a few minutes to find the mechanism to open the trapdoor, I'll prove it to you."

"Not," said Constable Evans, "before Magistrate Orr gets here, sir. He's the only one with the authority to search Sir Ivor's house." He wasn't sure if that was the truth, but he was taking no chances.

Lady Neville's childish face showed both fear and anger. "This is an outrage! Of course William isn't here. Only Sara Carstairs knows where he is. Don't you understand anything, Constable? I brought her home for that very purpose, to lead me to William's body. And if you hadn't interfered, that's exactly what she would have done."

For the first time in a long while, Sir Ivor stirred. "What are you saying, Jessica? How could you have brought that woman home?"

"I sent her letters in William's handwriting. Oh, Ivor, why do you think I joined the ladies' guild at the church? Why do you think I made friends with that impossible woman, Constance Carstairs, yes, and promised to help launch her daughter in society? It was only to discover Sara Carstairs's address so that I could send notes to her in William's hand. To bring her home, you see. To make her wonder whether William still lived."

She looked around and saw that everyone was watching her, and like a precocious child, she played up to them. "No one knows what Sir Ivor and I have suffered not knowing what happened to our son. Just to give him a Christian burial would give us so much comfort. How can you doubt that Sir Ivor loved William? He offered a reward to anyone who could discover William's whereabouts. You shouldn't be badgering my husband with questions. You won't find William here." She pointed a trembling finger at Sara. "His body is hidden on the downs. She was taking Beckett there when Lord Maxwell arrived. Ask her." Her voice cracked. "Make her show you where she has hidden my son's body."

Sir Ivor was sitting on the edge of his chair, his hands still manacled behind his back. "You brought that woman home to Stoneleigh? Without a word to me?"

Lady Neville blinked at her husband's harsh tone. Her thin eyebrows rose. "Beckett wanted the reward, Ivor. He said you might not give it to him if you knew. It was the only way I could get him to help me. And he thought you might not approve of our methods." She clenched and unclenched her hands as it came to her that Sir Ivor was livid. "I did it for you, Ivor. When you kept increasing the reward, I knew how much finding William's remains meant to you. I knew, then, that you loved William, and I wanted to help you find him."

With a savage oath, Sir Ivor jumped to his feet. "You stupid cow!" he roared. "You have sent me to the gallows!"

When Sir Ivor started toward Lady Neville, Max quickly intervened and dragged him back. "Stupid cow!" Sir Ivor yelled, struggling against Max's hold. "Can't you see what you've done? She was the one person I feared. I didn't want her to come back here, asking questions, stirring things up. I was safe just as long as she stayed away."

There was an appalled silence.

Sir Ivor came to himself with a start. He was appalled, too. He was frozen, his face haggard. After a moment, he shook his head and let out a long breath.

Lady Neville's voice verged on the hysterical. "Why are you saying these things, Ivor? That woman killed William. Sara Carstairs. Everyone knows it. No one will ever make me believe that she didn't do it."

Sir Ivor looked at the constable. "My son's body is exactly where Lord Maxwell says it is, right under our feet. If you depress the first brick on the left, then the fourth brick from it, a trapdoor will open behind that basket of logs. I confess to the murder of my son. He was a wastrel and a ne'er-do-well. We quarreled. I hit him. And that's all I'm going to say. Now get me out of here before I'm forced to listen to another word from that stupid cow."

"You're giving me permission to search your house?" asked the constable.

"Yes! Get on with it! Just get me out of here!"

Constable Evens called in two men whom he'd brought with him and told them to take Sir Ivor outside and wait.

Lady Neville had covered her face with her hands and was weeping copiously. "It's not true," she sobbed. "Sir Ivor loved William. It's that woman's fault. She must have bewitched him. He's taking the blame for her, don't you see?"

She was still rambling in this vein when the constable emerged from the priest's hole under the hearth. "He's there," he said, "or what's left of him. I found this watch. It's engraved on the back with the name 'William Neville.' "

"Let's go home," said Max, and he held out his hand to Sara.

Twenty-six

LONGFIELD WAS ABLAZE WITH LIGHTS WHEN Sara and Max arrived home. She was riding pillion on Arrogance, and the moment her feet touched the ground, she picked up her skirts and began to run. The Great Hall was bustling with people, and when she entered, a hush gradually descended. Then suddenly, everyone began to cheer.

Sara searched the sea of faces until she found the person she wanted. Anne had a platter of sandwiches in her hands. She put the platter down and, with a little cry began to push her way through the crush of servants and searchers toward Sara. Laughing and crying together, they fell into each other's arms.

Finally, Sara held Anne away from her. "Listen to me, darling," she said. "William's body has been found. His father has been arrested for his murder. Do you understand? William's body has been found. It was under the fireplace in Sir Ivor's library. All these years, William's body has been in Sir Ivor's house."

Anne looked stunned. As Sara's words finally registered, however, she put her hands over her face and began to weep. Constance came up to them at that moment, with

Martin only a pace behind her. They both looked ravaged with grief.

"Oh, Sara, can you ever forgive me?" Constance whispered brokenly.

Sara knew, then, exactly how Beckett had got into the house and left the note on her dressing table. She held out her arms. Constance walked into them and held on tight. "Thank God you're safe," Constance sobbed out. "Thank God!"

They clung together, Sara, Anne, Constance, and Martin, then they broke apart with teary smiles. Sara looked around and saw Max watching her. She put out her hand, and he came to her at once.

During the next hour, Sara had to repeat her story over and over again, first to her family, then to Peter Fallon, who had heard the commotion in the Great Hall and refused to go back to bed until he'd heard how it had all turned out. Finally, she had to go through her story again when Simon arrived home with Magistrate Orr and the constable.

They met in Peter Fallon's office, with Drew Primrose present as her attorney. Max handed round brandy before they began. The magistrate, who was new to the area, had a sad face and a sad smile, which, oddly, had a soothing effect on all present. Most of the time he listened.

When Sara had told him all that she knew, he said, "What puzzles me is how you came to believe that Sir Ivor was the murderer."

"I didn't see it at first," Sara said, "because I couldn't think of a motive. It was something Beckett said that made me sick to my stomach, but I was too panic-stricken to think about it until later. Beckett said that Sir Ivor wouldn't interrupt us because little Jenny would keep him occupied. My imagination took over and I thought to myself that if William had known about little Jenny, or others like her, he would have blackmailed his father, and he'd keep on blackmailing him until he tried it once too often." She took a sip of brandy as her fingers began to tremble. "Then I thought about William's sister. It was all guesswork on my part. I don't even know whether it's true or not."

A look passed between Constable Evans and Magistrate Orr. Finally, the magistrate said, "We found Jenny. She's only twelve years old. Your conjecture in this instance was right."

"Not only in this instance, sir," said Constable Evans. "We've had complaints about Sir Ivor these many years, but there was nothing we could do about them because we had no proof."

Sara said, "I bet William had proof. Maybe not about the others, but about his own sister. That's something that Sir Ivor wouldn't want to come to light—that he'd raped his own daughter!"

A look of pain crossed Sara's face and Max said roughly, "Can't this wait till tomorrow, gentlemen? My wife is on the point of collapse."

"No, wait," said Sara. "I want to hear what Lady Neville and Beckett are saying."

"Lady Neville," said Magistrate Orr, "is still insisting that you murdered her son. Even her husband's confession has no effect on her. As for Beckett, now that he knows he has no powerful friends to help him, he's singing like a bird. He insists he was just following Lady Neville's orders. He's been looking for William's remains ever since she took him on as a footman. And when he did not find them, they decided to lure you back to Longfield. They were hoping you would lead them to William."

The magistrate looked at Max. "Your arrival on the scene upset their plans. Beckett was afraid you'd find William's remains before he did, so he decided to hasten things along by abducting your wife."

Drew said, "I wonder if Beckett was the trespasser who broke into the dower house."

"He admits," said the magistrate, "that he'd gone over it a score of times, trying to find a secret chamber, and had found nothing. He became even more convinced that William's body was there when Lady Maxwell went there shortly after she came home."

"He tried to abduct me then," said Sara, shivering.

"As I said, he feared Lord Maxwell would find William's remains first and deprive him of the reward, so he tried to hasten things along. You might say that after that, he took up residence in the dower house, at least when it was dark, because he was sure you would return."

When Magistrate Orr stood up, so did the constable.

Sara was still thinking about the young girls Sir Ivor had molested. "How much of the truth will come out at Sir Ivor's trial? I mean about his motive for killing William."

"Very little," said the magistrate. "Sir Ivor has freely confessed to the murder of his son, but the only motive that he will allow is that he lost his temper and struck William when they quarreled about William's gaming debts."

"Maybe it's better that way," said Sara, her bitterness and disgust plain to see. "Oh, not for Sir Ivor's sake, but for the sake of his young victims."

"Whatever his motive," said Drew, "he'll hang for his crime. And no one in Stoneleigh will shed a tear for him."

And on that bitter note, he quit the room.

*A*NNE WAS WATCHING FOR DREW, AND WHEN HE came out of the anteroom, she dropped everything.

"Drew!" she called out.

He looked at her blankly, said something inaudible under his breath, then turning on his heel, strode for the door.

It took Anne a moment or two to get over the shock of what was virtually a slap in the face. She called his name again, and when he ignored her, she raced after him.

She caught up with him in the courtyard. She grasped his arm and dragged him round. "Drew," she said, "please listen to me."

She had to stop for a moment to even her breathing, and in that pause, he said coldly, "We have nothing to say to each other, Anne, not now."

She held on to his arm when he would have turned away. "Drew, *please* listen to me. I've suffered just as much as you, more, in fact, because I've been alone and you've found solace with others."

His lip curled. "Don't pretend you cared. You found solace in your religion. Do you think we can go back as though nothing happened? For three years you wouldn't speak to me; you wouldn't look at me. Now you know that I didn't murder William and you think that makes it all right? If our positions had been reversed, if I'd believed you had murdered William, I would never have abandoned you."

There was a frightening finality in his expression, but it did not deter her. She owed him this much. "Listen to me, Drew," she said. "If I hurt you, I hurt myself more. Yes, I thought you had killed William, but I never held you responsible for his death. I blamed myself. And I was desperate with fear because I thought you would be found out. So, I made a pact with God. If he would spare you, I would give you up. I thought that was the penalty I had to pay for the sin of loving you."

Tears were streaming down her face. "It doesn't matter if you've stopped loving me. It's such a relief to say it at last. I love you, Drew. I never stopped loving you. That's what I want you to know."

When he didn't reply, she turned back to the house.

"Wait!"

She turned to face him.

"Why did you stay on at Longfield? If you promised to give me up, why not leave here and start a new life somewhere else?"

"I think you know why. Just to see you, just to be near you, was all I had. I couldn't give that up, too."

With a strangled cry, he reached for her and crushed her in his arms.

BY THE TIME SARA AND MAX CLIMBED THE stairs to their chamber, Sara was practically sleeping on her feet. But there was something she had to do before she went to bed or she knew she would fret all night. "I must see Lucy," she told Max.

He understood. He'd heard her refer to Lucy when she'd confronted Sir Ivor. While she went into Lucy's room, he waited outside. She was only there for a few minutes and she was smiling when she came out.

"What did she say?" asked Max.

"She said that once, when she was waiting outside the church for her mother after a guild meeting, she saw Sir Ivor trying to entice Ellie, one of the blacksmith's daughters, into his coach. I'll say this for Constance. She raised us girls to be wise in the ways of men. So, nothing daunted, our Lucy marched right up to them, grasped Ellie's hand, and told her that her mother was looking for her. After that, Lucy kept a careful eye on Sir Ivor. But I wish she'd told me. Or Constance. That's the trouble, isn't it? We know, but we never do anything. Lady Neville knew about Jenny. How could she have let it happen?"

They walked to their room in silence. Max was thoughtful. Somehow, he felt tainted by just being a man, and it wasn't a feeling he was used to.

"What will happen to Lady Neville and her footman?" she asked.

"With a good lawyer, they may escape hanging and spend the rest of their lives in prison."

She slipped out of her coat and threw it over a chair. "You don't think that's too harsh?"

"For what they did to you? Hardly. I wouldn't care if they hanged."

She turned her head to look at him. "Peter Fallon told me that you were against capital punishment."

He took her in his arms. "Seeing a loaded gun at your wife's head can make a man change his mind about a lot of things."

"Hah! At least I didn't invite Sir Ivor to shoot me. I don't think that I shall ever forget you, arms spread, telling him to put a bullet in you. I wanted to kill you myself for putting me through that."

He grinned. "The lengths I had to go to, to force those three little words out of you. Say them again, Sara. I promise, it won't hurt."

"I love you, Max."

"And I love you."

He was just about to kiss her when she yawned. "Ouch." She put a hand to her jaw. "It's still sore."

"Let's get you to bed."

When she was sitting on the bed, he knelt beside her and slipped off her shoes. "Did you really believe that the *Courier* would come first with me? Is that why you wouldn't confide in me, Sara?"

"Don't make too much of it, Max. If I'd had only myself to think about, I wouldn't have hesitated. But there was Anne, you see." She fell back on her elbows and smiled dreamily up at the ceiling. "But that was yesterday. A lot can happen in a few hours. A man who is willing to lay down his life for his wife can't be all bad."

"Sara!"

She giggled. "I feel light-headed. I suppose it's the result of finally clearing my name. Anne is safe. And all those suspicions about my family that tore my peace to shreds have finally been laid to rest." She sniffed back tears. "I'm ashamed of myself now for ever having doubted them. They're dears, aren't they, Max?"

"I wouldn't go that far."

When she giggled again, he frowned. "How much brandy did you drink tonight?"

"Let me see. Two or three glasses, but that's only because you kept forcing them on me."

She held up her arms as he dragged her gown over her head, then she flung herself back on the mattress. "I want the story printed in the *Courier* as soon as possible."

"Do you indeed?" He drew back the covers and settled her between the sheets.

Her head lifted. "You can't fool me, Max. I know you can hardly wait for me to fall asleep so that you can creep along to Peter Fallon's room and write up your story."

"And you don't mind?"

"Not this time around, because I know you're on my side." She rolled away from him and let out a soft sigh. "I feel sorry for anybody who has you for an enemy." She growled like a jungle cat.

"Sara?"

"Mmm?"

"There's something that's puzzling me."

"What?"

"If you'd found William's body beneath the fireplace in the dower house, what would you have done next?"

She rolled back to him. "I don't know, Max. I didn't want you involved, but . . . I suppose I would have come to you eventually, and asked you to help me dispose of his remains, you know, put him in a box and bury it in the downs. But I was hoping that it would not come to that."

He stared at her hard, then let out a disbelieving laugh.

"Well, what else could I do?"

"Nothing. I'm touched. No really, I mean it."

When she snuggled beneath the covers, and her eyes closed, Max knelt with one knee on the bed. "Sara," he said, then cleared his throat. "I must say something about my shameful conduct last night."

"Mmm?" She didn't open her eyes.

Max combed his fingers through his hair. "I was maddened because you'd given me laudanum. When I came in here? I was mad with hurt pride. I lost my head. That wasn't me, at least not the man I recognize. I'm sorry if I frightened you, or if I disgusted you."

He put out a hand to brush stray tendrils of hair from her face, thought better of it, and let his hand drop away. "What I'm trying to say—" he said desperately, "Oh hell. Not all men are like Sir Ivor. Damn it, Sara, I love you. You must know I would never hurt you."

Her eyes flew open and with a gasp of outrage, she hauled herself up. "Sir Ivor!" she cried. "Don't you dare mention yourself in the same breath as that monster. You didn't frighten me. You didn't disgust me, or hurt me. I thought it was beautiful. Wondrous, if you must know."

She nestled in his arms. "What was shameful was that you didn't finish what you started. I may never forgive you for that. Are you still dressed? Come to bed, Max. Hold me, just hold me. I need to feel the arms of a good man around me so that I can forget that men like Sir Ivor exist."

"Sara!"

Max felt his heart swell with love and gratitude. He quickly disrobed, blew out the candles, and climbed into bed. Sara curled into him trustingly, her head nestled in the crook of his shoulder, her arm around his waist. He couldn't stop touching her, his hands running up and down her spine, pressing her closer to the shelter of his body.

A long while later, he grinned and said, "It was wondrous, wasn't it?"

He looked down at his wife's face. Sara was sound asleep.

Twenty-seven

A FEW DAYS LATER FOUND MAX AND SARA in Longfield's drawing room catching up on their correspondence. They were waiting for their lawyers to arrive so that the marriage settlements could be signed and sealed. Sara was looking over Max's shoulder, reading what he had written.

"You don't have gout!" she said.

"It's a code," he replied. "My friends will know what to make of it."

"And what does it mean?"

"It means," he looked up at her and smiled, "that my footloose days are over. I'm well and truly shackled."

"That's odd," she said, "I feel just the opposite. Marriage to you has freed me of all my chains. I'm the happiest woman in the world."

"Go back to reading your letter, Sara, or I won't be responsible for what happens next."

She laughed and went to the window seat, where she curled up and spread open her letter. "It's from Bea," she said. "I wrote to her right away and told her about Sir Ivor. This is her reply."

Max turned in his chair to get a better look at Sara. To say that he'd come down with a bad case of gout was the only way to explain to his friends how the love of his life affected him. He was no poet, and if he told them how he really felt, they'd think he was a sap.

"Well?" he said. "What does Miss Beattie say?"

"Mmm?" Sara looked up. "Oh, you know Bea. She thinks you're Prince Charming. She always knew that you were right for me, that sort of thing. She's not even shocked to learn that you're the *Courier's* owner. She says that God works in mysterious ways. Well, we can vouch for that. I told her we'd be making our home in London, and she says that as soon as we're settled, she'll come for a visit."

He said softly, "You don't mind making your home in London? I know your heart is here."

"Now, that's a silly thing to say. My heart isn't here."

"Where is it, then?"

She folded Miss Beattie's letter and slipped it into her pocket, then came to him. Taking his hands in hers, she placed them on her heart. "Wherever you are, that's where my heart is."

He brought her hands to his lips and turning them over, kissed her palms tenderly. "Oh, my dearest love——"

He broke off when the door opened. Anne slipped into the room. "Max," she said, "Drew would like a word with you. He's in the library."

Sara looked at the clock. "Have the lawyers arrived?"

"No," said Anne. "Drew wanted to talk to Max first. And I want to talk to you, Sara."

Max rose. "I was expecting this." Then to Sara, "Prepare yourself for a shock, Sara. You're not the happiest woman in the world."

"What?"

Max left, and Sara studied her sister. Anne's color was high; her eyes were sparkling. She approached Sara with slow, halting steps.

"Oh Sara, I'm going to marry Drew," she said. "He still loves me. After all these years, he still loves me. I'm so happy, I can hardly bear it. Say you're happy for me, too."

Sara stared at Anne without blinking. At last, she let out the breath she was holding. "Of course I'm happy for you, but don't you think that this is rather sudden? How long have you loved him?"

"Oh, since I was about three years old. Is that long enough for you?" Anne smiled into Sara's bewildered eyes. "Love isn't always easy, Sara, as it is for you and Max. Nothing went right for Drew and me, but at last we can be together. Don't begrudge us our happiness."

Sara said reverently, "Oh, my love, I never would, I never could. You deserve to be the happiest woman in the world. It's what I've always wanted."

"Sara, it's not tragic! Don't cry!"

"I *never* cry," said Sara, and wept in her sister's arms as though her heart would break.

THE LATEST EDITION OF THE *COURIER* ARrived that evening by special messenger, straight from the presses in London, and set the whole house in a buzz. There were enough copies for every member of the family, and Peter Fallon took it upon himself to deliver them.

Simon was the first to read it and he went tearing along to his brother's room. A few minutes later they dashed to their mother's room to find Constance dressing for dinner.

She took the paper that was thrust under her nose and read the headline. "Sir Ivor Neville Arrested for Son's Murder."

"Not that," said Simon excitedly. "Read on. The third paragraph."

Constance complied. "Sara Carstairs, who was acquitted of William Neville's murder three years ago, found the secret chamber in Sir Ivor's house. With her was her husband,

Lord Maxwell Worthe, the *Courier*'s publisher and heir to the Marquess . . ." her jaw dropped, ". . . of Lyndhurst."

She looked at her sons. "What does this mean?"

"It means," said Martin, "that it really was a love match and Max is not a fortune hunter."

Simon made a face and clapped his brother on the shoulder. "What this means, Martin," he said, "is that we won't have to go to hard-hearted Sara when we're under the hatches. We'll go to Max. He's a soft touch. And he has more money than Sara."

Constance was unconvinced. "I've heard of the Lyndhursts. Don't they live in that broken-down castle between Winchester and Aylesford? They may have a title, but I never heard that they had any money."

"That's how old money likes it," said Simon, adopting his man-of-the-world pose. "Trust me, Mother. At Oxford, we all know about Lord Lyndhurst. If it weren't for him, half the colleges would shut down for lack of funds."

Martin let out a low whistle. "You mean, Max's father is *that* Lyndhurst?"

"Of course! From what I've heard, he and Lady Lyndhurst are both slightly dotty." Simon touched his index finger to his head. "You know, eccentric, but they're old blood and old money just the same."

Constance reached for her handkerchief and blew her nose. "Max was here earlier, and said that we should all have a Season in London, but I refused. Without Lady Neville to sponsor us, I didn't see the point."

"Lady Neville!" Simon looked astonished. "She's not in the same league as Lady Lyndhurst. If I were you, I'd tell Max you've changed your mind."

Martin said, "Weren't the lawyers going to meet this afternoon to draw up marriage settlements?"

"So?"

"I was just wondering what Sara has decided about our future. Maybe she'll tell us at dinner."

There was a knock on the door and the maid entered. "Lord Maxwell," she said, "would like to see you all in the library."

Constance looked around for her stole, and when she looked up, she found that she was alone.

Simon entered the library brandishing the *Courier* above his head. "Sara," he called out, "you're a heroine. Have you read this piece in the *Courier*?"

"I didn't know it was here."

"And shame on you, Max," Simon went on, "for letting us all make fools of ourselves."

"Simon," said Constance, "sit down and hold your tongue."

Max waited until the whole family had assembled. Peter Fallon would be joining them for dinner, but this was family business, and only family members were invited, and that included Drew Primrose.

Max stood with his back to the fireplace. When everyone was seated, he nodded to the footman on duty who handed round a silver tray with long-stemmed glasses of iced champagne.

"Champagne?" Lucy's eyes were as big as saucers.

"This is a special occasion," said Max. "I have an announcement to make. Anne and Drew are going to be married just as soon as it can be arranged."

There was a stunned silence, then everyone began to speak at once and to offer their congratulations. Max glanced at Constance. He'd had a word with her earlier to prepare her for the announcement, but Drew had got there before him. She didn't disappoint him. Her smile was serene; her congratulations seemed sincere. Anne and Drew looked relaxed and happy. So far, so good.

Max raised his glass. "To Drew and Anne," he said. "Long life and happiness."

"To Drew and Anne," everyone chorused. "Long life and happiness."

Max nodded to the footman, who then left the room. "There's another reason for celebration," said Max. "Today my wife feels that she has fulfilled a sacred obligation, but I'll let Sara explain it in her own words."

Sara looked at each of her siblings in turn. Her face glowed with happiness. "Before he died," she said, "Father asked me to take care of you all. Today, when Max and I signed our marriage settlements, I felt a great happiness, knowing that I'd carried out Father's last wishes." She smiled at Max. "Perhaps what I did wasn't wise, but it was right. Thank you, Max, for allowing me to do it."

All eyes expectantly turned to Max. "What it amounts to," he said, "is that your father's fortune will be divided equally amongst his children and stepchildren. And I'd just like to add that Anne is in favor of this arrangement." He paused then went on, "But before you all get carried away with grand schemes on how you will spend your share, let me warn you that I and my father, Lord Lyndhurst, will be your trustees until you each reach your twenty-fifth birthday. That's when you'll get your capital and it will be intact. Do I make myself clear?"

They looked as though he'd just announced a death in the family, so he took the opportunity of saying more. "I'll tell you what my father told me when I came into some money. The money you are getting represents someone else's hard work and sacrifice. If you use it frivolously, you dishonor your benefactor."

"Good Lord!" Martin exclaimed. "You sound just like Sara."

Max gave them his shark's smile. "As long as you've got that right, Martin, we should deal well together."

Simon winked broadly at his brother before turning back to Max. "So far," he said, "all we've heard is how our father's estate is going to be settled. As head of the family, I have the right to know what provision you've made for my sister."

"Quite right," said Max, drowning out Sara's sharp rebuke. "Perhaps Drew, as Sara's attorney, wouldn't mind answering that."

"I have no hesitation in saying," said Drew, "that Sara is well provided for. Her jointure comprises all the income from the *Courier* and Lord Maxwell's other business interests. And, of course, the usual widow's dower, you know, one-third of the income from any lands and properties Lord Maxwell may hold."

Simon was trying to do sums inside his head, but gave up when he came to infinity. He nodded mutely.

"You don't seem very impressed, Sara," said Martin, looking at her curiously.

Sara was savoring her champagne, thinking that she had a lot of living to catch up on, and Max was just the man to help her do it. "I am impressed," she said. "I'm rich in the things that really matter." She gave Max a sideways glance. "Money is such a burden. I'm happier now without it. Max taught me that. Besides, it's not as though I'll have to take in washing to make ends meet. I'm content."

Everyone thought this was a huge joke, and their laughter reverberated off the walls. Max was watching Sara with a veiled expression.

She said brightly, "Shall we go into dinner?"

SARA ENTERED HER CHAMBER TO LOOK FOR A shawl, and noticed a copy of the *Courier* on her bedside table. She picked it up and had read only the first paragraph when Max entered. He came to stand behind her and cradled her in his arms.

"I haven't been alone with my beautiful wife since the lawyers got here," he said.

She turned in his arms and kissed him. "I know. There will be time later when we go to bed."

His arms tightened when she tried to slip away. "Sara—"

"Yes, Max?"

"Would you still love me if I were a rich man?"

She gave a low throaty chuckle. "Now what has brought this on?"

"Just answer the question."

She considered for a moment. "As you said yourself, Max, we're rich in everything that counts. We have our health. We have each other. We have enough to live on comfortably from the *Courier* and my inheritance. And you're the one who keeps telling me that money doesn't matter. No. I like you just the way you are."

He frowned when she pushed out of his arms and began to wander aimlessly around the room, touching first one object then another. She suddenly looked up and smiled. "At least no one can call you a fortune hunter now, Max. I'm worth only a fraction of what I was worth when I got up this morning. Do you know what I think? I think your family is going take *me* for the fortune hunter. Isn't it ironic?"

He took a step toward her. "My family?" he asked carefully.

"You know, Lord and Lady Lyndhurst, who live in a broken-down castle on the other side of Winchester, and who just happen to be one step away from royalty."

He gave her a crooked smile. "Actually, they're two steps away from royalty, and they're exactly as I described them to you. My father runs the estate and my mother is a great help to him. And I never said Castle Lyndhurst was broken down. In fact, it's in perfect condition. My mother wouldn't have it any other way."

Hands on hips, she said indignantly, "I distinctly remember you saying at the dinner table that your parents lived in a decrepit ruin of a place."

"And so it is, on the outside. But once you get past the ruined walls, it's in perfect condition."

"And you didn't tell me my fortune wasn't a patch on yours."

"Oho! So you've finally figured it out. In my circles, my dearest love, it's not considered polite to boast about one's wealth. Honestly, Sara, I never gave it a thought. Right from the start, you marked me down as a penniless adventurer, a no-account Corinthian, and that impression was branded on your mind."

"What's wrong with being an adventurer? In fact, I was hoping you would teach me to be an adventuress."

He caught the glint of amusement in her eyes. "And so I shall, my love, so I shall. Beginning right now."

She shrieked when he made a dive for her. With a great whoop of laughter, he tossed her on the bed. She struggled madly but he soon subdued her.

"How did you figure it out?" he asked.

"Lady Neville taunted me with your great station in life. 'The Worthes of Lyndhurst,' she called your family. As though the Carstairs were nothing! Then Bea's letter today. She said that Lord Lyndhurst's heir was the most eligible bachelor in England, and I should kiss your boots for taking me on. Hah! Don't you dare laugh at me, Max Worthe! I come from the Carstairs of Longfield, and I'm every bit as good as you. My great-great grandfather, let me tell you—"

He kissed her into silence. Laughing down at her, he said, "My parents are going to love you. You're not really upset, are you, Sara?"

She fingered his neckcloth. "Well, at first, I was disappointed. I never wanted to marry into the aristocracy. I thought, if Max's parents are anything like Sir Ivor and Lady Neville, I'll divorce him."

"They're not!" he said, suppressing a shudder.

"Well, of course, they're not, or you wouldn't be you."

That piece of flattery deserved another kiss and he gave it to her.

She smiled up at him, her heart in her eyes, and she murmured, "And because you're you, you could never disappoint me. Rich or poor, whoever you may be, you're the man for me. I love you, Max Worthe, with my whole heart. In fact—"

"You *adore* me," said Max, and kissed her again.

Sounds of laughter drifted up the stairwell. A door slammed along the corridor. Someone began to play the piano. Max and Sara did not hear. The world outside themselves had slipped into oblivion.

About the Author

Best-selling, award winning author, Elizabeth Thornton, was born and educated in Scotland, and has lived in Canada with her husband for the last thirty years. In her time, she has been a teacher, a lay minister in the Presbyterian Church, and is now a full-time writer, a part-time baby-sitter to her five grandchildren, and dog walker to her two spaniels.

Elizabeth enjoys hearing from her readers.
If you wish to receive her newsletter, e-mail her at:
thornton@pangea.ca

or visit her web page at:
<http://www.pangea.ca/thornton/>

or write to her at:
Elizabeth Thornton
PO Box 69001 RPO Tuxedo Park
Winnipeg, MB R3P 2G9
Canada

Watch for Elizabeth Thornton's
next suspenseful, unforgettably passionate
historical romance in fall 2000.
Read on for a preview. . . .

SHE WAS AFRAID TO OPEN HER EYES, AFRAID that he would be there, watching her. She had no illusions about his capacity for violence. She'd become a threat to him. He had to get rid of her.

How much had she told him?

The words echoed inside her head like a silent scream. It took a long time for the sound to fade. She mustn't panic. She had to think things through. How much had she told him? She couldn't remember.

When she tried to swallow, a blurred memory crystallized and slowly came into focus. He'd locked her in her room and subdued her by forcing her to drink from the goblet in his hand. Laudanum. She'd ingested laudanum. That explained why her head ached and her throat was dry.

She breathed slowly, deeply, willing herself to come fully awake. Her eyelashes fluttered, but they were like lead weights and she couldn't lift them. But her senses were taking other impressions: the soft feather mattress beneath her; candlelight flickering on her eyelids; the windowpanes rattling; the hiss of the rain.

The rain. She remembered the rain. It was raining when she and Gracie crept out of the house under cover of darkness. They had a boat waiting on the river. That's how they were going to escape. But he'd unleashed the dogs, and she knew she would never make it.

"Go!" she'd screamed at her terrified maid. "He mustn't find you with me!" But the wind whipped the words from her mouth. She tried again. "I can't make it! Tell Lady Octavia I can't make it." She'd pointed to the river and given Gracie a shove, then she'd veered toward the gazebo. And in the dark, the dogs had followed *her* scent, and her husband had followed the dogs.

He didn't know yet that Gracie was missing. When he found out, the questions would begin all over again.

She'd planned it so carefully: the boat, the hiding place; money to live on until her attorneys had settled everything. She still didn't know how he'd found out.

But he didn't know everything. He didn't know why, after almost thirty years of suffering in silence, she had chosen this moment to break free of her intolerable marriage.

"It's this stupid women's league you belong to that's put these insane ideas in your head, isn't it?"

She was practiced in hiding her feelings and looked at him blankly. "What league? I don't understand."

"Don't lie to me!"

His lips were pulled back in an expression that was reserved for her only. In government circles and in his clubs, her husband was known for his affability and charm.

He'd grabbed her arm, then, and dragged her to the mirror. "Look at yourself," he sneered. "You're an old woman. You're pathetic. You'd never survive without someone to look after you. You have no money. How did you think you would manage? Who was going to help you? *Who? Who? Who?*"

His words registered, but barely. She was looking at her reflection as if she were seeing a stranger. The hollow-eyed woman who stared back at her was old, with stooped shoulders and a frail, defeated expression on a face that had once been considered beautiful.

This pathetic old woman had not fulfilled the promise of the young girl whose portrait hung above the white marble mantel in Rosehill House. At eighteen, she'd had a sparkle in her eyes, and looked out at the world with all the confidence of youth. She hadn't known then that she was cursed. She was an heiress, and in the games men played, that made her a pawn.

He hadn't finished berating her, and as the ugly words spilled over, something inside her snapped. There was more to her than this cowering creature in the mirror, and if there wasn't, she might as well be dead.

So she'd told him, not everything, but enough to wipe the sneer from his face. Then she'd tried to make a bargain with him: If he would let her go and give her enough money to live on, she would take her secret to the grave.

What a fool she'd been to try and make a bargain with the devil. She was going to take her secret to the grave anyway. He was too close to achieving all he'd worked for to let a mere woman stand in his way.

She'd been afraid so many times that she thought she knew everything there was to know about fear. But this was different. She'd involved others, and if he discovered their names, they, too, would pay the penalty for her sins.

Footsteps sounded in the corridor, *his* footsteps, and at last her eyes opened. He would know, now, that Gracie was missing. Her throat tightened; her chest heaved. *She mustn't give in to panic.* He didn't know everything, and there was no way he could find out unless she told him.

A name was humming inside her head, and with the name came a face. Gwyneth. Her eyes burned.

When the key turned in the lock, she pulled herself up. A strange calm possessed her. She'd been a sniveling coward all her married life. This was one fight she wasn't going to lose.

London, March 1816

When Gwyn turned the corner into Sutton Row and saw the curricle stationed right outside her front door, there was no sense of foreboding, no premonition that Jason Radley was about to enter her life again. This was just another ordinary day. She'd spent the morning at the Ladies' Library in Soho Square, where she worked three mornings a week, and she'd stopped off on the way home to buy a loaf of bread. She was late and was hurrying home so that she could share the midday meal with her young son before her first piano student of the day arrived.

Then she saw the curricle.

There was no alarm on Gwyn's part, only the fervent hope that the father of one of her pupils had come to settle his account. Then, she'd be able to pay something toward the arrears on her rent, and on Saturday, she and Mark would treat themselves to an ice at Gunther's in Berkeley Square.

When she approached the curricle and observed the groom standing by the horses' heads, she frowned. He was dressed in a maroon frock coat with silver frogging on the epaulettes and turned back cuffs.

The Radley livery. She'd know it anywhere.

As her heart picked up speed, her steps slowed. She wasn't ready for this; she would never be ready for this. As soon as the thought occurred to her, she became impatient with herself. She and Jason were different people now. If they put their minds to it, they could speak civilly to each other. But the question that sprang to her mind was why had he tracked her down.

Her heart was beating fast when she entered the house. Gwyn took a few paces into the parlor and halted.

Tall, dark, and handsome didn't do him justice. He was remarkably good looking in a rugged sort of way, with vivid green eyes and a physique that an athlete might have envied. He was her cousin, twice removed, and the last time she'd spoken to him was eight years ago.

He looked leaner and harder, the result, she supposed, of the burdens he'd assumed when he'd become master of Haddo Hall. She'd heard that in those first years he'd staved off bankruptcy by sheer determination and hard work, and now he was one of the richest men in London. It was not what she had expected. She'd thought he'd take the easy way out and marry for money. There had been no shortage of applicants for the position of Mrs. Jason Radley, as she remembered.

Damn him! Why had he never married?

He was regarding her gravely, completely at his ease, waiting for her to speak first. She moved past him to sit on the sofa, close to the fire. "How are you, Jason?"